COYOTE'S WIFE

Also by Aimée & David Thurlo

Ella Clah Novels

Blackening Song
Death Walker
Bad Medicine
Enemy Way
Shooting Chant
Red Mesa
Changing Woman
Tracking Bear
Wind Spirit
White Thunder
Mourning Dove
Turquoise Girl

Plant Them Deep

Lee Nez Novels

Second Sunrise
Blood Retribution
Pale Death
Surrogate Evil

Sister Agatha Novels

Bad Faith
Thief in Retreat
Prey for a Miracle
False Witness
Prodigal Nun

COYOTE'S WIFE

✖ ✖ ✖ ✖ ✖

AN ELLA CLAH NOVEL

AIMÉE & DAVID THURLO

A Tom Doherty Associates Book
New York

M THURLO

This is a work of fiction. All of the characters, organizations, and events
portrayed in this novel are either products of the author's imagination
or are used fictitiously.

COYOTE'S WIFE

Copyright © 2008 by Aimée and David Thurlo

A Forge Book
Published by Tom Doherty Associates, LLC
175 Fifth Avenue
New York, NY 10010

www.tor-forge.com

Forge® is a registered trademark of Tom Doherty Associates, LLC.

ISBN-13: 978-0-7653-1716-2
ISBN-10: 0-7653-1716-8

First Edition: October 2008

Printed in the United States of America

0 9 8 7 6 5 4 3 2 1

To Fred and Betty Hill,
just 'cause they know so much

ACKNOWLEDGMENTS

To MK, for her continued help with the Navajo language.

COYOTE'S WIFE

ONE

—— ✖ ✖ ✖ ——

High up in the Chuska Mountains on a winding forest road, Special Investigator Ella Clah of the Navajo Tribal Police took time to enjoy herself. While her second cousin Justine drove the pickup, she gazed down at the New Mexico side of the Navajo Indian Nation. It felt good to be up here today, on the hunt for piñon and cedar logs instead of fugitives or suspects.

She'd always loved this particular section of the forest road. In places the trees were so close on both sides it was like driving down a blue-green tunnel lined with the rich scent of pines. Ella breathed in the humidity, a sensation usually missing down on the desert floor or atop the mesas of the Colorado Plateau, where she'd lived most of her life.

This had been a perfect morning. The golden leaves on the scrub oaks all around them intermingled with the pine-covered slopes and brought back a kaleidoscope of pleasant memories. After hiking for over two hours, searching for just the right pieces, they'd found four lengths of beautifully twisted cedar and piñon—thick cuttings that would be perfect for what Herman, her mother's husband, had in mind.

"Thanks for the help in tracking down the right pieces,

partner. Once Herman peels off the bark, then sands and stains each piece of trunk, these will make gorgeous one-of-a-kind table lamps. You should see his work. I'm buying two from him—one for me, and one for Dawn."

Justine smiled slowly. "Okay, before you award me a merit badge for forest skills or woodcrafts, I have to 'fess up. I had a personal stake in this. One of the lamps he's making is for me. I saw his work in your mother's sitting room and placed an order with him. The lamp will look great on the table by my living room sofa."

Ella laughed. "*That's* why you were being so incredibly helpful on your day off!"

"Well, that, and the promise of lunch at your mom's," Justine answered, laughing.

Ella joined her.

Before long they passed a small meadow, and Ella grew wistful. "I miss trips like these up into the mountains, cuz. My family used to come up for firewood every fall about this time. When Clifford and I were younger, Mom and Dad used to rely mostly on the heat from an old wood and coal stove they'd bought and hauled all the way from Colorado. We already had propane by then, but Dad's ministry was just getting started and they were trying to save money any way they could. Clifford and I would come up here with Dad and compete to see who could gather the most wood. Dad was the judge, and whoever brought in the most didn't do chores for a week. The loser would have to do them all."

"I missed out on that kind of thing growing up in town with no fireplace or stove. We always had natural gas. So who'd win the contest, Clifford?"

Ella smiled slowly. "Naw, it was me, at least until Clifford finally wised up. He loved chopping wood, and spent most of his time with the axe. I'd get whatever was on the ground first, then saw up the dead stuff that was too heavy to carry. When Dad measured our piles, mine was usually bigger. It used to irk Clifford to no end," she said laughing. "I think it was a testosterone thing with him. He loved that axe!"

"You've always played to your own strengths. That's why you close more cases than anyone else in the department," Justine said.

"That and a lot of stubbornness. I won't give up." Ella leaned back in her seat, basking in the radiant glow of the sun coming though the windshield.

She'd just closed her eyes when a warm spot near her neck suddenly began to burn like a hot coal. Realizing with a start that it was the badger fetish she wore—Ella jerked upright, as if stung by a bee. She'd never figured out just how it worked, but the fetish would always get hot when danger was near.

Ella reached over automatically for the handgun at her waist, and although she didn't draw her weapon, she kept her hand right next to it. On call twenty-four–seven, she was required to remain armed even on her days off.

Aware of Ella's reaction, Justine jumped. "What?"

"Something's not right. Keep your eyes open." Ella searched among the trees to her right, then glanced in the side mirror. There was nothing back there but the dirt road and a trail of dust rising up into the air.

She'd just turned back to her left when a bloody figure staggered out from behind a tree, directly into the path of the pickup. "Look out!" Ella yelled.

Justine swerved to the right, then touched the brakes, going into a barely controlled skid.

The man in front of them turned at the sound of the sliding tires, his face contorted in fear. His red-gloved hand went up in a vague attempt at protection. Then he pitched forward onto the road.

Still sliding, Justine uttered a curse, and whipped the pickup to the right again. The tires came dangerously close to the edge of a steep drop-off and Justine whipped the wheel back to the left and stood on the brakes. They slid a dozen feet, then came to a stop, raising a cloud of dust.

"You missed him! Good job," Ella yelled, throwing open her door and jumping out of the cab. "Call 911," she added, coughing from all the dust.

The figure, dressed in work clothes, was lying on the road behind them, facedown. The dust the pickup had raised was settling on the fabric of his heavy denim shirt, darkening what appeared to be a sleeve completely soaked in blood.

As Ella ran up, the man turned his face toward her. His hollow wheeze was followed by a strangled cry of despair. The next instant he went limp. His head dropped to the ground, his mouth open, his eyes staring at nothing.

The coppery scent of blood was strong and Ella's heart was hammering. Her thoughts racing, she searched for the source of his bleeding. Aware of the dank, earthy smell that clung to him, she kept her breathing shallow.

Ella had been at her job for too long not to know death when she saw it, but she still checked. Reaching down, she touched the pulse point at his neck. His body twitched, and she flinched. Then all movement stopped. The man was beyond their help.

Crouching down, Ella studied the body before her. His left arm was completely drenched with blood. Through a tear in his left sleeve she could see a five-inch diagonal cut on the inside of his arm, about halfway between his elbow and his wrist. The cut went into the bone. It could have been the result of his having thrown his arm up to ward off the slash of a big knife, or maybe a machete.

Justine came running up, carrying the first aid kit she'd

left behind the seat. "How is—oh," she added, seeing Ella shaking her head.

Ella focused back on the body of the Navajo man. The sticky sweet smell of blood on his shirt and jeans was so thick in the still air it nearly made her gag. Although she'd seen more than her share of dead people, she normally arrived on the scene well after the fact. This . . . made it more personal somehow.

"I guess it's time for these," Justine said, opening the first aid kit and bringing out some latex gloves. "Sorry, I only have one pair for each of us."

"It'll do until Tache arrives with the crime scene van." As a Navajo, touching anything that had been in direct contact with the dead was repulsive to her. Unfortunately, that would invariably happen when she stripped off the latex gloves, unless she'd worn two pairs. It wasn't that she was afraid of the *chindi*, the evil in a man that remained earthbound after death. It was more of an ingrained reaction. Illogical, but as natural to her as avoiding the number thirteen or walking under a ladder was to an Anglo.

"Suspicious death, right?" Justine said, reaching for her cell phone.

"Yes, until we know otherwise, so get Carolyn, too. We're going to need the tribal ME's expertise on this."

Justine turned away, preferring not to look at the body while making the calls.

Ella, wearing her latex gloves, pulled out the victim's wallet and examined it. The victim was George Charley, a forty-five-year-old Navajo man who worked in Shiprock.

Ella returned to Justine's truck and emptied the paper bags they'd used for snacks. With the victim's wallet in hand, and the bags in the other, Ella walked back to where the body lay.

Justine, who'd completed the calls by then, took the

paper bags from Ella. After taking a close look at the wallet, she placed it into the cleanest-looking bag and labeled it with the time and her signature.

"If the address is current and my memory is correct, the victim lives—lived—near Long Lake." As a sign of respect, Ella avoided mentioning Mr. Charley by name. "There's not much of anything out that way until you reach Naschitti, and no phone service. At best, he's several hours' walk from there, so unless he was drunk and wandered off, he must have gotten here either by horse or vehicle. The employee ID says he worked for that new high-tech company, StarTalk, in their Shiprock warehouse. Check at the station and see if we can get a location on his next of kin."

Justine called in and, after a few minutes, hung up and looked at Ella, who'd finished searching his pockets. "He's got a wife. She's apparently not employed and lives at the address on his operator's license. Also, as you suspected, there's no phone service at his home."

"We'll process the scene first. Once we're done, we'll go by the residence and notify his wife."

"What do you think, was it an accident of some sort? Or do you think someone cut him and hijacked his vehicle?" Justine asked. "I didn't see you pull out any car keys from his pockets."

Justine, petite and young-looking, but with a seasoned hardness in her eyes, stepped closer and looked down at the body again. "I don't see any obvious wounds on his torso. There's that gash on his forehead. But his arm . . . that much blood means a severed artery." Justine pointed to the deep, jagged cut that Ella had noted earlier.

"More than a knife did that," Ella said after further visual examination. "His skin was ripped apart, not sliced. Either he cut himself on a saw blade in a freak accident, or someone came at him with a chain saw and that's a defensive wound. There's also that cut on his head, but that looks more like he bumped himself, judging from the swelling."

"This reminds me of what happened to a friend of mine who worked at a lumberyard," Justine said. "One day he caught his sleeve on the blade while trying to brush away some sawdust. He'd turned off the saw, but the blade was still spinning. It pulled his arm right into the jagged teeth. Poor guy nearly died, even with the hospital just five minutes away. This might have been a similar type of accident, except this guy was alone and too far from help. He couldn't stop the flow on his own, and just ran out of time—and blood. That would be my guess for the cause of death."

"Carolyn will have to make that determination," Ella said. "But I think you've probably nailed it. Notice the sawdust all over his shirt and glued to his hands? He may have been out gathering firewood, cut himself with his saw, then panicked and ran. But you'd think he would have run to his truck," Ella added. "You don't hand carry wood this far from home. You haul it. And losing that much blood, I doubt he could have walked too far from the accident site. Check the area, but stay close enough not to let the body out of your sight. I'm going to backtrack using the blood trail. His vehicle has got to be out here someplace."

"And the chain saw or whatever he cut himself on," Justine said, then added, "I've cancelled the EMTs, by the way."

"Good. Keep an eye out for anything that might be evidence, just in case this wasn't an accident."

Ella followed the trail of blood and mostly dragging boot prints up a steep hillside, finding a place where he'd obviously fallen before leaving the road. George Charley must have either become disoriented, or decided to take a shortcut.

Back on the dirt road, the victim's trail, lined with drops and puddles of blood, made a path that wound back and forth, much like that of a drunken man. She was amazed that the victim had been able to walk as far as he had. He must have been in shock as he headed off in search of help.

Then she found deep tire tracks in the road, angling off to the side, downslope. The blood trail continued, so she followed. A late-model pickup had crashed through a sapling, dropped down into a stand of low junipers, running them over, then struck a sturdy piñon head on. From the damage to the front she guessed the victim had probably been alert enough to brake somewhat, but not enough, obviously. It was the tree itself that had finally stopped the forward motion of the vehicle.

The scenario appeared obvious at first glance. For some reason Mr. Charley had swerved sharply and ran over whatever vegetation had been in his path. After coming to a stop, the rear tires had dug holes in the soft ground, explaining why George Charley had taken off on foot. The big Dodge Ram, with its powerful Hemi engine that could outrun most sedans, had become stuck.

The blue paint on the side of the late-model Dodge was scratched and the door was dented, evidence of his collisions after leaving the road. It seemed pretty clear that George had lost control, dizzy from the blood loss. The windshield wasn't broken, but the rearview mirror was askew, and there was a small amount of blood on it.

The door was open and, as she approached, Ella could see a blood trail that extended into the cab on the driver's side. She looked inside, careful not to smudge the single set of boot prints. Nothing in there could account for what had caused the wound on his arm. The keys were still in the ignition, and the red light on the instrument panel showed that the engine had died, the gears still in reverse. To her, it appeared that George had been racing to find help, had passed out, and run off the road. The crash had probably caused the bump and cut on his head, the result of being thrown forward and striking the rearview mirror. Stuck and unable to back out, he'd left the vehicle and set out on foot. That had only hastened his fate.

Ella stepped back and examined the bed of the truck. There was no sign of a chain saw or any woodcutting tool inside, or anywhere around on the ground. The tailgate was down, and the bed was a third full of firewood, many of the pieces showing evidence of having been freshly cut. Firewood farther up toward the road showed that some of the load had shifted and bounced out.

Ella reached into the cab and pulled out the keys, careful not to make contact with the blood, which was evidence. She then wrote down the vehicle tag letters and numbers for the New Mexico plates, and walked back up to the road. Following the tire tracks and trail of firewood that had bounced out of the truck, she hoped to find the place where George Charley had met with his fatal injury.

After walking for about a quarter of a mile, Ella found the spot where the truck had originally been parked just off the road. Up slope, about fifty feet, was a chain saw on the ground beside two halves of a freshly cut pine log. Dirt had been kicked up, as if the chain had still been running when it hit the ground. As she got closer, Ella saw the dried blood on the bar, pieces of flannel cloth and bloody dirt, plus chunks of something she didn't want to even think about on the chain.

Ella methodically took in the rest of the scene. Several pine branches, freshly sawn, were resting on the ground beside a red plastic gasoline container. A double-bladed axe was leaning against one of the bigger logs, and beside it, a bow saw. Right next to that were six beer cans, three of them unopened, three apparently empty.

"What an idiot!" Ella muttered. The man had been drinking while cutting wood.

Ella reached for her cell phone as she studied the ground where the truck had been parked. From the dug-out exit marks, she could see that George had driven off in a hurry. Blood had also collected on the ground on the driver's side where he'd paused to open the door.

Unable to get a cell phone signal from her current location, Ella walked back to the road. There, she discovered a second set of footprints that, judging from the pattern, had come from Nike athletic shoes and didn't match George's boots. Someone had come up to within fifty feet of where the victim had been working, but no closer.

Noting that one of the shoe prints was on top of an arrival tire track, but partially erased by George's hurried departure, she walked back down toward where the truck was parked. Though she searched carefully, she was unable to find any more of the athletic shoe prints. Either the person hadn't gone that far, or maybe the trail had been permanently obscured when George had driven away. Of course there was also a third possibility—maybe the tracks had been deliberately erased. Yet the more likely explanation was that someone had walked over out of curiosity, seen George cutting wood, maybe even had a conversation, then left. She'd have the beer cans checked for prints in case the visitor had been offered a drink.

Ella returned to the road, then followed the athletic shoe prints, which went in the opposite direction. They disappeared next to a set of fresh tire tracks which were clearly not from the big Dodge. From the signs, the person in the athletic shoes had climbed into a vehicle at this location.

After sketching the shoe and tire pattern onto a page of the small notebook she always carried with her, Ella jogged back down the road to join Justine. Thoughts of the second person somehow causing the accident from a distance seemed pretty unlikely, but she still wanted to follow up on the identity of whoever had come by.

She'd been away for nearly forty minutes by the time she joined her partner again. Minutes after Justine had moved her pickup off the road, they heard the sound of vehicles coming up the mountain. Ella watched the crime scene van and the ME's unit come into view.

TWO

✖ ✖ ✖

While Officer Ralph Tache climbed out of the van, Justine waved Carolyn to a spot beside her, then went to help Tache. Carolyn, wearing a long, white lab coat, climbed slowly out of her vehicle, then grabbed her medical bag from where it had been resting on the passenger's seat.

Dr. Carolyn Roanhorse, a Navajo, was an exception to normal procedures in New Mexico, where nearly all suspicious deaths were the responsibility of the state Office of the Medical Investigator. The Navajo Nation had been granted special status because they'd been able to provide their own highly qualified medical examiner.

Carolyn had been a full-sized woman for as long as Ella had known her, and she made no apologies or excuses for it. As a doctor, she knew the dangers of being overweight, but she liked herself exactly as she was.

Unfortunately, a few months ago her knee had begun bothering her. Ella had heard a rumor that Carolyn had finally decided to go on a diet but, from where she stood, Ella could see no traces of its effectiveness.

Carolyn gave Ella a nod, motioned for her to stand back,

and approached the victim, her entire focus on the body. As she crouched, Carolyn gave out an agonized yelp. Ella took a step forward, but Carolyn shook her head and gestured for her to stay back.

"I'm fine," she snapped. "It's just this idiot knee of mine." Concentrating on her work, she brought out the small audio recorder she carried in her black bag and began recording her initial impressions.

Ella instructed Ralph Tache, the third member of their Special Investigations Unit, to work here with the ME. Then she and Justine loaded some evidence containers and equipment into her pickup and drove up the road to process the other two relevant scenes. A few minutes later they approached the spot where George's truck had gone off the road. Ella gave Justine a few minutes to observe and take photographs before they moved in closer.

"Maybe he saw an animal and swerved trying to avoid it, or he could have just passed out for a second. He was probably feeling really light-headed," Justine suggested.

"Add to that the three beers he'd already powered down," Ella said.

"You're kidding."

"Nope. The empties are right next to his tools, which suggests he was the only one imbibing. Could you check out the cans for prints, though, just in case George shared? Let's check out the truck, get photos, collect anything relevant, then go on farther to where the incident occurred."

Nearly an hour later Ella returned to the site of George Charley's death. Carolyn had finished her work, and was zipping up the body bag with Ralph's help.

"I'm done here. Have you got anything else for me?" Carolyn asked, seeing Ella.

"No, that's it. We found a bloody chain saw at the scene where I believe the deceased's wounds were inflicted. I'll have that delivered to the morgue, along with copies of all the photos."

"A chain saw seems a likely instrument of death, but it would have had to have been an extremely sharp one, because there's almost no bruising along the edges."

"The saw looked brand new, and we'll be collecting plenty of tissue samples from the blades."

"Good. Except for the bump on his head, which was probably from a fall or the equivalent, there's only that one jagged, diagonal laceration beneath his left forearm. The injury resulted in severed muscles and blood vessels, including the artery."

"There was so much blood. Did he bleed out?" Ella asked.

"Exsanguination would have eventually occurred, but some victims have been known to do incredible things before losing consciousness. Cutting himself, then driving to find help, and walking a few hundred yards or so before passing out, it's all within the realm of possibility."

"So, at this point, does it look more like an accidental death than a homicide?" Ella asked. "I found half a six-pack at the scene. The man had been drinking."

Carolyn rolled her eyes. "That increases the odds of an accident, obviously, but I can't be one hundred percent certain yet. The angle of that laceration on his arm makes it a little tricky. He could have been holding the chain saw with only his right hand, then reached across with his left. Or it *could* have been a defensive wound. If an attacker came at him with the chain saw, he could have put up his arm to protect himself." Carolyn demonstrated by holding her arm in front of her face, as she shied back. "That would account for the wound being on the lower part of his forearm, and at an angle."

"But why would an attacker take only one swipe at the

man? I saw the victim of a chain saw attack once, and I've also read about others. In almost every single case, the victim was cut to pieces. A perp has to really be amped up to use a chain saw."

"Agreed. So, in this case, the odds are the man inflicted the wound on himself. I'll run all the usual toxicology tests. We'll see if he had drugs in his system and how much alcohol."

"We'll process the saw for prints and reconstruct the blood spray pattern. That'll narrow things down, too." Although it appeared to be an accidental death, Ella would need to go through all the steps before a final pronouncement was made.

Carolyn stood up slowly, unaided, and looked around. Ella smiled, knowing who she was searching for. "He's not here," she said. Sergeant Joseph Neskahi, an officer who joined their Special Investigations Unit during times of crisis, had once made an unkind comment about Carolyn's weight. Since that fateful day, he'd become her number one choice whenever a body had to be bagged or moved.

Ella motioned for Ralph. "We'll load the body. Don't worry about it," she added, noting how Carolyn was favoring her left leg. She wondered if Carolyn would be upset if she bought her a cane. It was something to consider—for a friend.

Once the body had been secured into the back of the van, Tache joined Justine farther up the road and Carolyn and Ella were left alone.

"Thanks for the help," Carolyn said softly.

"No problem. You should consider hiring an assistant. You're one of a kind for the tribe and you certainly deserve full-time help, particularly now that your leg's bothering you."

"I had much the same thought, and the budget will allow

it," she admitted. "But, as you can imagine, it's not an easy thing to do. Navajos trained in medicine want to help the living. They don't want anything to do with postmortem. And I'd hate to hire someone from outside the tribe."

"There's got to be someone out there who's right for the job," Ella said, searching her own mind for a possibility she might suggest, but coming up empty.

"Before I go, let me take a look at the place where you found the saw," Carolyn said, after a beat. "It'll help me complete the picture in my mind as I work on the body, and maybe I'll be able to help you reconstruct the incident."

"It's a fifteen-minute walk. You want me to drive you over?"

Carolyn shook her head. "I'll drive. Get in."

Brushing aside her reluctance, Ella climbed into the van. She'd only ridden in the vehicle one time before. It had given her the creeps then and it was no different now. "How's the diet coming?" she asked, trying to get her mind off it.

"Slow. Fast food's always a temptation. I used to love fixing meals in my beautiful kitchen but I hate to go in there now that Michael's gone."

Ella knew she was referring to Dr. Michael Lavery, her ex-husband. Michael, a retired medical examiner, had wanted Carolyn to travel with him, but Carolyn's ties to the tribe that had paid for her education were strong. Carolyn took pride in her work and had never let the tribe down. In the end, their conflicting goals had pulled them apart.

"Is the divorce final?" Ella asked.

Carolyn nodded. "It has been for about six months." Seeing the surprised look on Ella's face, she added, "I haven't wanted to talk about it. Michael and I were wrong for each other, that's all. But some dreams die hard, you know?"

Ella nodded, thinking of her own life. "The work we

do . . . it interferes with everything. But it's a vital part of who we are. We need it, as much as the job needs us."

When they reached the scene Carolyn walked over to the crime scene van. Justine had placed the chain saw in a big, labeled cardboard box to protect it during transport.

Carolyn lifted the lid and examined the blood-splattered machine. "No doubt this was the cause of death."

Almost as an afterthought, Carolyn pulled out her cell phone, then after checking for a signal, shook her head. "A cell phone out here wouldn't have done him much good either."

"We really could use reliable phone service in areas like these," Ella said.

"Speaking of that, what do you think of the new satellite phone service Abigail Yellowhair's son-in-law, Ervin Benally's, proposing?" Carolyn said as they headed back to her van.

"I'm trying to find out more about it, but there's no doubt in my mind that reliable phone service could end up saving lives."

"That's my stand, too," she said, then approaching her van, added, "it was good to see you, even under these circumstances."

"Yeah, it's been too long. We should try to get together soon," Ella said, stepping back as Carolyn opened the driver's side door.

"I'd love to have you over for dinner, but unless you're into quick salads, there's not much I can offer you."

"Salad's fine. I'll bring some diet drinks. We'll settle on a date once our calendars are clear."

As Carolyn drove off, Ella's next task weighed heavily on her—calling on the next-of-kin. It would fall to her since Justine would be busy wrapping things up here on-site.

"Ella, while you were gone, I got a call from Dispatch,"

Tache said, coming up behind her. "The pickup's registered under Ervin Benally's name, not the victim's. Justine said that the vic works at StarTalk, Benally's company, so there's a connection. I've already instructed Dispatch to have someone contact Mr. Benally and find out what's going on."

"Chances are he borrowed the truck, right?" Justine said, coming over.

"Probably. But it's certainly an interesting coincidence. Did you get good photos of the tracks left by our unidentified bystander, the one with a weakness for Nikes?"

"Yeah, and the vehicle tracks, too. Wide, like a pickup's, but not much tread. Not like the new Goodyear tires on the Dodge. We'll have to canvass the area and find out who else might have been up here today," Justine said.

"First things first. I'd like to borrow your truck, partner, so I can go notify the man's next-of-kin. Can you two ride out together?"

"Sure, but if you give me a few more minutes, I'll be able to go with you. We're almost through here," Justine said.

Ella helped them finish processing the scene, then Tache headed back to the station. Circling back, Ella and Justine took the quickest route to the vic's home, munching on apples and some granola bars Justine had thoughtfully brought along for midmorning snacks. On the way there, Ella called her mom and told her they wouldn't make lunch, then she contacted the station and verified that George Charley had borrowed Ervin Benally's Dodge Ram pickup.

"No one was able to question Ervin Benally directly, but his wife told the officer making the call that both men started out together. Then George dropped Ervin off at Sheep Springs for some unknown reason and went on by himself to gather wood," the woman dispatcher reported.

Ella signed off, then filled her partner in. "We'll check this out ourselves later," Ella added.

Following the directions Justine received from Dispatch, they followed a set of winding roads past Chuska Peak. Then, at long last, now in the foothills west of the range, they approached a small wood frame home nestled between two hills. Beyond, they could see the main highway running north/south, and a few houses that were nothing more than dots in the distance.

"That must be the place, directly ahead, just past that small herd of sheep," Justine said. "I don't see a vehicle."

They drove past a low creekbed lined with brush and filled with grazing sheep, then parked a hundred feet from the house. Not knowing just how traditional Mrs. Charley was, they decided to wait for an invitation before approaching. The simple courtesy was the only good thing they had to offer the woman inside, who was about to receive some very bad news.

Soon a woman in her late forties came out to the makeshift porch—a painted warehouse pallet that served the purpose. She gestured an invitation and waited for them to come up. Ella noted how her hands were wound tightly around the bottom of the barn coat she was wearing. It was as if she'd been expecting bad news.

"I hate this," Justine murmured, climbing out of the vehicle and fastening her shield to her belt beside her weapon. "She must have recognized us. Her husband's probably late coming home, so what else could we be bringing except bad news?

"Once she sees our badges and sidearms, it'll confirm the worst, even before we say a word." She walked toward the woman. "We're police officers. Are you Mrs. Charley?"

"I'm Marilyn," she answered nodding, her voice shaky.

Ella broke the news as kindly as possible, giving the general details, and though the woman made no sound, a flood of tears ran down her face.

Stepping away from them, she dropped into a chair on

the porch, shaking. "This can't be happening." She looked at Ella, not making eye contact—a Navajo taboo—but her expression held such defeat that it tugged at Ella's heart.

"This doesn't seem possible. How could it end this way? And what do I do now?" Marilyn added softly, desperation tainting her words. "When we moved here, we left my family and friends in Arizona. I'm all alone."

Ella looked at her in disbelief. Respect for clans and extended family ties practically guaranteed a Navajo could find relatives almost anywhere. "What about your husband's relatives?" Ella asked softly, reminding her.

"We don't get along." She took a long, shuddering breath and looked up quickly. Although Ella had expected to see sorrow on her face, she hadn't been prepared for the look of fear and dread mirrored there. "They don't know . . . and they'll have to be told. But I have no transportation. If my husband borrowed his boss's truck as you said, then our pickup must still be in Shiprock somewhere, maybe at the StarTalk warehouse."

"It's still there. I'll want an officer to check it over first, but we'll be releasing it soon, maybe tomorrow," Ella said.

"My husband's relatives will have to be told before then. You have to help me," she pleaded. "Can you take me over to see them now? I don't want to do that alone."

Ella looked at Justine. This really wasn't part of their job. Yet, whether real or imagined, the woman's sense of alienation had touched her. Years ago, after she'd joined the FBI, she'd lived in many different cities far from the Rez. She'd learned then how someone could feel lonely even in the midst of a crowd.

Ella nodded to Justine, and soon Marilyn Charley was on the rear bench of Justine's truck.

"My husband's family doesn't like me. They may make us wait a long time."

"Probably not when they see you pulling up with two police officers," Justine said. "We'll make sure they see our badges when we step out of the truck."

Marilyn almost smiled. "You're right. They'll probably come out quickly, hoping you've arrested me."

Justine glanced at Marilyn in the rearview mirror. "Don't anticipate so much. Take things moment by moment. Sometimes I think that's the only way to get through life."

Ella glanced at her partner. It was sound advice. She'd followed that philosophy herself once. Then she'd become a mother and her outlook had changed dramatically. Now she lived with one eye on today and another on tomorrow.

THREE

—— ✖ ✖ ✖ ——

Following Marilyn's directions, it didn't take long for them to arrive at another, larger wood frame house just off the main highway about a mile south of the community of Naschitti. Justine parked about halfway down the driveway, then got out and stood by the pickup, badge in plain sight. Ella joined her, making sure her shield was also visible beside the holster of her sidearm.

"Someone just looked out the front room curtain," Ella said to Marilyn. "They know we're here."

"My husband's uncle, Hoskie Charley, will come out— eventually," Marilyn said, getting out to join them. "He never does anything quickly."

After ten minutes, a man in his seventies, wearing dark blue jeans and a red plaid flannel shirt, walked out onto the concrete step. He took a long look in their direction, then came toward them slowly. His hair was silver and tied at the nape of his neck. As he got closer, he looked at Ella and Justine, then finally at Marilyn.

"You've come with the police. What do you want with us?" he asked Marilyn. His gaze was cold, almost accusing.

"I have bad news, uncle of my husband," she said.

"Your nephew passed away in an accident while cutting firewood."

His expression softened for a moment, and he looked at Ella, who nodded in confirmation.

Hoskie stood rock still, staring at his boots. A thick and heavy silence stretched out between them. Then, after a long pause, he raised his head again and looked at Marilyn. "Then you're finally free to do whatever you want," he said in a strangled voice.

He nodded to Ella and Justine, then turned his back on them and returned to the house.

Ella and Justine exchanged surprised glances, but neither commented.

Marilyn stood by the pickup, tears streaming down her face. "My duty here is done."

"Come on, we'll take you home," Ella said softly. "Then once we take a look at your husband's truck, we'll see if someone at StarTalk can return it to you. Do you have a set of keys we could borrow?" Ella added as an afterthought, recalling they'd only found keys to the Dodge.

"The keys will still be in the truck—in the ashtray. My husband never locked the doors. If you *could* have someone drive it over to me, I'd sure appreciate it."

As they rode back in silence, Ella mentally replayed the scene she'd just witnessed. There was more going on here than met the eye.

When they arrived at Marilyn's house, Ella noticed an old, faded navy blue pickup that hadn't been there before parked by the side of the house. No driver was visible.

"Looks like you've got company," Ella said. Perhaps Marilyn's claims of being completely friendless hadn't been exactly accurate—unless George's pickup had been returned, somehow.

"It's my neighbor," she said. "Thanks for the ride."

As Marilyn hurried inside, Ella glanced over at Justine. "Whoever that is apparently feels it's okay to go inside the house even if no one's home. Can you get a clear look at that tag?"

Justine pulled forward a bit, and read off the vehicle's license plate information to Ella, who wrote it down. As they headed back to the road, Ella called it in.

"The pickup belongs to Wallace Curtis. From the address on the driver's license, he lives just a few miles from the victim's home," Dispatch answered.

Ella lapsed into a long silence and Justine didn't interrupt her thoughts. "We're missing something, partner," Ella said slowly.

"Yeah. I get that feeling, too. Maybe we should go back and talk to Hoskie Charley."

"I want to find out more about Wallace Curtis first. And let's try to keep this low-key for now," Ella said.

"Are you thinking we're dealing with a love triangle? If so, maybe George Charley's wound was a defensive one after all. And there were those other shoe tracks where the accident or murder went down. Do you suppose Wallace wears Nikes?"

"The ground *was* packed hard in places, and the perp might have smoothed his own tracks closer to the body. But there are other ways to commit a murder, too. Maybe Marilyn slipped George something in his food, or he might have been darted with a drug from a distance. Animal control certainly uses them a lot around here to deal with vicious dogs and the occasional bear in the backyard, so it's not totally impossible. I'll call Carolyn and see if she can expedite the toxicology report. I'll also have her check the body for any other marks."

"That dart theory—not bad—but if that's the case we should have found the dart," Justine said.

Ella thought about it a moment. "Not if it was knocked out of him later when he went crashing through the woods. If that's the case, it could be almost anywhere. Mind you, it's pretty unlikely, but if that's what happened, it would have left a puncture mark on the body and chemical traces in his blood. Carolyn will be able to prove or disprove this theory for us," Ella said. "But we need to keep in mind that our victim wasn't supposed to be alone today. Ervin Benally may know something we can use."

"Want me to give him a call when we get back to the station? Find out who knew where they were going, and like that?" Justine asked.

"Yeah. We need to cover every base."

They returned to the station, and by the time Ella filed her report, it was already 5 P.M.

Just then, Justine poked her head inside Ella's office. "I spoke to Mr. Benally briefly. He was shocked to hear about the incident, but wasn't much help. He told me he had a meeting tonight, but suggested I come by StarTalk tomorrow if I had any more questions," Justine said.

"I dusted everything for prints, even the beer cans," she added. "They all came from the same person, presumably the victim. Ralph has all the other evidence we collected, and is going to deliver a copy of the fingerprints, the chain saw, and a set of photos to the ME. He doesn't need me for that, so if you don't either, I'm heading home."

"I'm leaving too. Big Ed's asked me to attend a tribal chapter house meeting later tonight, so I want to catch something to eat and see my kid before I go. Benally is supposed to be there to talk about his project. If I get a chance, I'll speak to him concerning the incident. See you early tomorrow, partner."

As Ella drove home, the reception Marilyn Charley had received at the home of her in-laws still bothered her. What wasn't she seeing? In-law problems were common, but families stuck together, particularly in hard times.

Realizing she was trying to force answers when she didn't have enough facts to go on, Ella decided to give it a rest. She'd tackle all that again in the morning. Depending on how closely management associated with labor at StarTalk, maybe Ervin Benally could shed some light on the Charleys' relationship.

As she drove up the road leading home, Ella's thoughts turned to Dawn. She was looking forward to seeing her nine-year-old daughter tonight. They'd never been closer. Maybe it was because everything around them was changing.

Rose was more involved with her new husband Herman these days. Kevin, Dawn's father, was gone, too, pursuing the next step in his career, according to him. Yet the biggest change in her and her daughter's lives these days was the presence of Reverend Bilford Tome, or Ford, as he preferred to be called by those close to him.

Ella and Ford's relationship had started as a mutual help society. She'd needed a way to get Rose and her friends to stop fixing her up with just about anyone they could think of. Ford, charismatic, good-looking, and single, had faced similar problems with his congregation. In fact, he'd been the first to suggest that they be seen in public together as often as possible. Yet in their attempt to pass muster as a couple, something unexpected had happened. They had become one.

Dawn had accepted Ford's presence in their lives, but she was also reluctant to share Ella's free time with anyone else. Though it was a constant balancing act, Ella had managed things so far.

A short time later, Ella walked into her home through the old front entrance. Herman was in the living room playing a video game with Dawn, and Ella could hear Rose in the kitchen. Dawn called out a quick hello, but never took her eyes off the screen and her animated race car.

Ella greeted Herman, gave Dawn a quick kiss, then left the room to go shower and change. By the time she came back into the living room, Dawn met her holding a plate filled with a huge Navajo taco. The fry bread and spicy meat mixture was heavy with cheese and smelled delicious.

"*Shimasání* said that you can sit down at the coffee table or in the kitchen, but you're not allowed to leave this house before you eat," Dawn said, "not after missing lunch."

Smiling, Ella sat down on the couch, plate in hand, and motioned for Dawn to join her. "Get another fork and help me with some of this. If I ate all the food your *shimasání* puts onto my plates, I'd never fit into my jeans."

Dawn laughed. "You're thin, *Shimá.*" She ducked into the kitchen and came back moments later. "Will you be back late?" she asked, taking a mouthful.

"I don't know. You've been to some of our chapter house meetings. They can last an hour, or go on all night," Ella said, then switched the conversation. "What did you do today?"

"Reverend Ford came by," she said as they continued eating. "We played video games for a while, and he helped me with a math problem. He's nice, but he's as busy as you are sometimes. Anyway, that's what he told me. We waited for you until about four, but then he had to leave."

Ella nodded, finishing her food. "He and I both have demanding jobs, you know that. But our work makes everyone's lives safer and better." She set aside the plate they'd both emptied in record time, and reached out and tickled her daughter. "But nothing is as important to me as you are."

Dawn squealed, and laughed, moving away.

"I love you, Pumpkin," Ella said seriously.

"Mom, you *can't* call me that anymore," she said, horrified. "You promised! It's embarrassing."

Ella sighed and gave her daughter a quirky half-smile. "It *was* your nickname for a very long time."

"Yeah, but I'm in fourth grade now. I'm not a baby anymore."

"No, you're not." Ella stood up. "Which is why I know you'll understand that, as much as I want to stay home and spend the evening with you, I've got to get going."

Dawn nodded, looking very much like an adult for just a few seconds. "The tribe needs you, so we've got to share."

Ella could hear Rose's words echoing through her daughter. "You're a terrific kid," she said, giving Dawn a quick hug and kiss.

Later, as she drove north toward Shiprock and that community's chapter's house, Ella phoned Carolyn. There was no answer, so she left a message. She'd need that toxicology report as soon as possible.

Ella put the case out of her mind for now. It was time to focus on the chapter house meeting—the traditional equivalent of town meetings on the Navajo Nation, which were divided into geographical "chapters." Tonight's presenter was Ervin Benally. He was the head of StarTalk, the Navajo telecommunications company. This evening's meeting was supposed to be informal and would include a question and answer portion that everyone was hoping would remain focused and peaceful.

At Big Ed's request, Ella would attend, and then submit a report tomorrow on the potential applications of that technology to the department. The uncertainty of radio and cell phone communications on the Rez had made for some tough times for the department. Although many memos and official handouts on the situation had been distributed, her boss wanted to hear from someone who didn't sit behind a desk.

As Ella approached the chapter house, located southeast of the main highway junction in "downtown" Shiprock, she noted that every parking place around the small stucco building seemed to be taken already.

Ella ended up parking down the street and walking about a hundred yards. She approached the side door of the building where several men were gathered, talking, while kids played under the outside lights.

A quick look around assured Ella that their guest presenter had arrived. A new-looking white SUV—the indigo blue and silver StarTalk company logo on the door—was parked right by the sidewalk. Seeing Sergeant Joseph Neskahi, in uniform, standing just inside the door, Ella nodded in greeting.

"I didn't expect to see you here tonight, Ella," Joe said, joining her. "I heard that you ended up with a suspicious death and three scenes to process today. It gets really busy when you're shorthanded."

It didn't surprise her that Joe knew about the death of George Charley. Joe had wanted to become a permanent part of her Special Investigations Unit for almost a year now, and always kept well informed. He'd taken all the required courses, and had proven his value on many investigations in the past. Since the department's budget hadn't allowed her to hire another full-time team member, Joe kept getting shifted back and forth between her unit and patrol duties.

"There are still a few unanswered questions about this incident. If we need a lot more legwork before we can close the case, I'll ask that you be transferred over to us."

"Off the record, how soon do you think you'll be making that decision?" he asked.

His tone had been casual, but she knew Joe too well not to be able to detect the eagerness behind the remark. "I have no idea," she answered honestly.

"Should I stay in touch?"

"Not necessary. I know how to find you," Ella answered.

Looking past Joe, she saw the huge crowd gathered inside. All the folding chairs were filled, and at least a dozen men and women were lined up along the walls. "Standing room only?"

"Yeah. Lucky somebody is saving me a seat up front. Everyone wants to hear about this new phone thing. The idea of being able to reach anyone, anytime, on the Rez appeals to a lot of folks. But there's opposition here, too. Some feel our people are facing more pressing problems—not being able to heat their homes in winter, getting electricity, and still having to haul in drinking water. They want issues like that addressed and resolved before considering luxuries like telephones."

Only on the Rez could a telephone be considered a luxury. Then again, when there wasn't enough food to feed a family, or ways to keep warm in winter, priorities shifted.

Ella stepped into the room and saw another familiar face—Abigail Yellowhair. The late State Senator James Yellowhair's wife had become quite a power by her own right. Abigail had a real Midas touch when it came to business. Once the scandals surrounding her husband had died down, she'd turned most of her husband's marginal business ventures into profitable ones.

From what she'd heard, Abigail was one of StarTalk's major investors. That had earned her the title of vice president, which she shared with her daughter, Barbara—Ervin's wife. Abigail was careful, conservative, and as smart as they came. Although she'd helped the PD out on a few occasions before, Ella's own experiences with Abigail Yellowhair weren't all positive. There was an almost instinctive distrust between them that had been there for as far back as Ella could remember.

Calvin Bidtah, wearing a large silver concha belt and his best turquoise and silver bolo tie over his western-style shirt and jeans, rose from his chair and walked to the podium. He cleared his throat, then led the group in the pledge of allegiance and then a Navajo prayer.

After that, the meeting began. Two pending issues involving disputes between neighbors about grazing rights were addressed first. The discussion, which turned into arguments, went back and forth. Finally, the matter was settled.

At long last it was time for the item on the main agenda. Ervin Benally rose from his seat in the front row and walked to the podium. He hooked a portable microphone to his shirt, then stepped away, no notes in hand. Ella knew right then that either the man was thoroughly prepared, or destined for deep water.

"Most of you know me and my family," he said, waving his arm back toward the chairs behind him where Abigail Yellowhair sat beside Barbara. "We've been working hard for over a year to bring you a service that will make things better for everyone on the Navajo Nation. As it is right now, only forty percent of The People have telephones. We can change that. Through our inexpensive satellite phone system, which will be subsidized by the tribe to make certain every household can afford to participate, we can finally stay in direct contact with our families, neighbors, and emergency services."

Though Ervin was small in stature, he was a dynamic, charismatic man who commanded everyone's attention with just one look. Slender and boyish in the face, he was like a hummingbird in a flower garden, all energy and movement.

Everyone focused on him as he walked back and forth, full of gestures and animated expressions.

Ella was reminded of the old school evangelists—much like her father—who took instant control of a crowd and held them spellbound with just the force of their personalities. Though as a speaker Ervin would have still come in a distant second to her father, he was a beacon of confidence—a leader who could make things happen. Barely thirty years old, he was *The* visible force behind StarTalk. Ella hoped that the product would match the presentation, because Ervin was certainly coming across well.

Ella listened to Ervin explain the technical details behind StarTalk. The satellite phones would be able to interface with any other phone—cell or landline—and were licensed to communicate through Low Earth Orbit satellites already in place. It sounded like a very practical solution. At long last, they'd have an effective phone system that would require very little infrastructure.

"Almost sounds too good to be true, doesn't it?" she heard someone whisper in her ear.

As she turned her head, she bumped her nose against a chest of gargantuan proportions. Teeny, as Bruce Little was known to his closest friends, stood a step behind her. Teeny resembled a ceiling-high rain barrel with arms. At close to seven feet tall, he commanded respect simply by entering a room.

"What do you think of all this?" Ella whispered, knowing his expertise in electronics was second to none.

"I've looked into the details. If he can pull it off, it's going to work to everyone's advantage."

If it hadn't been for budget cuts and management decisions made at Tribal Council levels, Teeny would have never left the police department a few years ago. Yet, in retrospect, leaving the P.D. had been a very lucrative step in Bruce Little's career. These days, as a security and IT consultant, Teeny earned far more than he ever would have on the force.

"Service crews will take care of any equipment problems. These people are being trained as we speak. All are Navajo," he continued in a whisper. "StarTalk doesn't require cell towers or transmission lines that'll interfere with our holy sites either, so that's a big plus. Their biggest problem will be educating the users and distributing the units."

Ella listened as Ervin went into details about a portable, solar-powered charging system for those many Navajo homes without electricity. "Is it workable for the department?" she whispered to Teeny. "I know he's making it sound good, but I have to report to Big Ed. He's going to want more than the PR slant we're getting here tonight."

"You'll have to go outside to use it—a direct line between antenna and satellite is needed—but it'll be as reliable as you can get," Teeny answered.

By then, Ervin had finished his presentation and people began asking questions. Not everyone present welcomed StarTalk, and the murmurs and anger from some of those attending made that very clear. Yet Ervin seemed to take the opposition in stride, countering their arguments smoothly and persuasively.

At long last, with no more questions, Ervin thanked everyone at the gathering, but before he could finish, a loud shout came from just outside the door.

"Hey, I said stop that!" a man yelled again.

Ella heard a curse and then the sound of breaking glass. Police instincts rising to the surface, she raced out the side door, Teeny at her heels.

Outside, Ella caught the fumes of fresh paint about the same time she realized some of the windows on the white StarTalk vehicle were smashed out. Two figures were crouched by the side of Ervin's SUV, wearing ski masks over their faces. One, holding a wrecking bar, was warding off elderly Mr. Nez, or *Hosteen* Nez.

"Police! Don't move!" Ella shouted, knowing that the chances of that happening were slim to none.

The men broke into a run instantly, scattering in two directions as they sprinted across the parking lot.

"I got the one on the right," Ella said, seeing Sergeant Neskahi right behind her. Without looking, she knew Teeny was either helping Neskahi, or had gone to his truck to give chase.

Ella passed *Hosteen* Nez, who was cursing angrily at the fleeing figures, shaking a clenched fist. She moved effortlessly in the limestone gravel, trying to keep the fleeing suspect in sight as he passed between an old pickup and a sedan two rows farther ahead.

Running was one of the things Ella did best. She wasn't really a sprinter, but no one could touch her when it came to endurance. Unless the guy got to his vehicle in a hurry, she'd catch up to him. It was inevitable.

The man left the parking lot, racing across the main highway at the intersection without a glance for traffic. Running out of steam, he continued at a fast jog up the side street, which was lined with parked cars and trucks, an overflow from the chapter house meeting.

Ella increased her pace, closing in on him. Though focused mostly on the running target, Ella caught a glimpse of someone inside an SUV parked just ahead. She slowed, not knowing if the driver had seen her coming. Suddenly the vehicle roared to life and pulled out in her path, headlights on bright, blinding her.

"Look out!" Ella yelled, moving to the right, but the SUV turned, too, still heading straight at her.

"Crap!" Feinting right, Ella leaped to the left instead, sliding across the hood of a parked sedan. There was a thud as she careened off the vehicle, falling to the sidewalk hands first. She scraped both her palms, rolled, then slid into some old goathead vines in the dirt beyond. She ended up on her belly, like a baseball player trying to avoid the tag. The closest base, however, was the post of a mailbox three feet away.

Trying to ignore the stickers she felt in her thighs and arms, Ella brushed herself off as she scrambled to her feet, looking around for the SUV and suspect. Her pistol was still in its holster, but the grip was probably badly scuffed. Hopefully, the cell phone in her pocket wasn't crushed.

Hearing a car door, she saw the man she'd been chasing dive into the SUV. The driver sped down the highway, slid to a stop long enough to pick up the second vandal, then raced off again. Neskahi, chasing them down the highway on foot, wasn't close enough to intervene. The vehicle quickly disappeared, the taillights fading as they headed east out of town.

With squealing tires, Teeny suddenly appeared at the intersection in his pickup, racing out from the chapter house lot. Neskahi pointed east, and Teeny took off, leaving tread marks as he hit the gas, his powerful truck fishtailing slightly on the asphalt.

Ella smiled. They'd never get away.

Her momentary satisfaction vanished in an instant as an old pickup suddenly pulled out from the diner just a hundred yards farther down the road. Teeny had to stand on the brakes, his truck sliding to within inches of the other pickup before coming to a stop.

Ella's heart jumped to her throat as she saw that the driver of the old pickup was Mrs. Yazzie, one of her mother's Plant Watcher friends. The woman made Rose look young by comparison.

As Ella hurried toward them, she could hear Mrs. Yazzie shouting Navajo obscenities at Teeny through her open driver's side window.

Neskahi joined Ella, handheld radio in hand, and fell into step beside her as they jogged forward. "I called Dispatch, hoping an officer between here and the Rez line could intercept the SUV, but no such luck. They've notified the sheriff's department, asking them to keep an eye out."

"That's a long shot, but it's worth a try. At least Bruce got lucky. I thought he was going to t-bone that pickup for sure," Ella said.

"Me, too," Neskahi said. "The old lady pulled right out into traffic—never even looked!"

Ella had intended to try and calm Mrs. Yazzie, but before she could get there, Teeny was already out of his truck, talking to her. Teeny could intimidate almost anyone but, amazingly enough, he could also charm people when he so chose, much like an oversized teddy bear. By the time Ella reached them, Teeny had put a smile on Mrs. Yazzie's face.

Teeny stepped out into the highway, held up his hand to stop a car coming from the east, then motioned the elderly woman to proceed. Mrs. Yazzie drove past Ella and Neskahi, waved, then made a sharp left and entered the chapter house lot.

"I know her. She cleans up after chapter house meetings, can you believe it?" Joe said. "She can barely see—and heaven knows she can't drive—but she keeps the place spotless."

Ella and Neskahi joined Teeny, who'd pulled his truck off onto the shoulder. "Did either of you get a good enough look at the driver to be able to identify him?" Ella asked.

"All I saw was the back of his mask. And there were no plates on the SUV," Teeny said.

Ella looked at Joe, who shook his head. "I can describe their clothing and size. My guy looked a little thinner than the other runner. That's it, except for the color of their ski masks."

"Then let's go see what kind of evidence we can find back at the scene. Maybe we can get some prints or some other trace evidence."

As Ella reached the parking lot adjacent to the chapter house, she saw people milling around Ervin's white vehicle. Getting closer, she noticed that the vandals had crossed out the sign painted on the driver's side door with a big, sprayed on red x. Above it was a crudely sprayed word—StarCrock. In addition to that damage, the windshield had been shattered, probably with a jab from the wrecking bar. Unfortunately for forensics, that tool was now in the hands of *Hosteen* Nez.

Dozens of people, among them the StarTalk guests, were outside watching as she and Neskahi came up. Turning to Neskahi, Ella said, "Joe, you've got charge of the scene if you want it. I can give you my statement in the morning before you file a report."

"No problem," Neskahi replied.

As Ella approached, Ervin was examining the damage and his wife was on her cell phone. Abigail Yellowhair stepped forward to meet her and Neskahi and, from the expression on her face, Ella knew to expect a challenge.

"They got away, right? As usual, the police department's response is too little, too late," Abigail said.

Ella could see that Abigail was furious and wanted a public confrontation. Determined not to give it to her, Ella stepped over and smiled at *Hosteen* Nez. "Uncle, would you set that down, please? The sergeant might want to check it for fingerprints."

Nez smiled apologetically, then set the wrecking bar on the curb and stepped back.

"At least tell us what you intend to do about this," Abigail demanded.

"It'll go down as an expensive act of vandalism, plus a

few other charges," Ella said. "Right now, we're going to try to get a complete description of the suspects and gather evidence. We'd appreciate *everyone's* cooperation and understanding, so will everyone who's not a police officer stand back for a moment?" she added, addressing the crowd.

"You were chasing them. Don't tell me that you didn't get close enough to take a look at them," Abigail demanded, her voice rising another octave.

"Two officers and a former officer gave chase, but all we have are general descriptions of size and type of clothing— plus a vehicle make and color. Perhaps you've heard *Hosteen* Nez mention that they *were* wearing masks?" Ella said in a voice completely devoid of emotion. She would *not* allow Abigail to get to her.

Nez nodded. "They certainly were, the cowards!"

Ervin took his eyes off his damaged vehicle for a moment, and Abigail immediately stepped up beside him. "Just a minor irritation, son-in-law," she said. "The good people of this tribe know what you're bringing to them will benefit everyone. Don't let cowards like these vandals slow down your mission for StarTalk, not even for a moment."

Ella had to give it to her. Abigail could grandstand to an audience better than anyone else she'd ever met. She had everyone's attention now. Ervin nodded almost imperceptively, then taking his cue from her, faced the crowd.

"Some people are afraid of anything that means change, even if it's for the good of the *Diné*, The People," he said loudly. "But we have a right—and, in fact, it's our duty—to stand up to those who take the law into their own hands and try to take away our choices through their acts of violence."

People smiled and nodded though, to Ella, Benally's words were reminiscent of a political speech—covering everything, touching nothing.

She turned away, hoping to leave once Neskahi, who had

disappeared for a few minutes, reappeared. Then she saw him, now equipped with a camera, approach *Hosteen* Nez, probably their best witness, and begin questioning him.

Knowing Joe would take care of things here, Ella headed out. She was done for tonight.

FOUR
✖ ✖ ✖

Ella was in her office at eight o'clock the following morning when Joe Neskahi came in. "I found your statement in my basket this morning, and your note asking me to drop by your office."

"Sit, Joe," she said, waving him to a chair. "I wanted to ask you how the investigation went at the chapter house last night."

"It turns out that wasn't the first time Ervin Benally's been targeted. He's been getting some threatening e-mails, and someone scratched up the plate glass doors at his company's headquarters," he said. "I know Benally's pickup played a role in that suspicious death you're investigating. That made me wonder if there could be a tie-in between the incidents."

"There might be," Ella said. "Did you get anything else?"

"After you left last night, I took a closer look at Benally's SUV and found a dead rat on the driver's seat. When I spoke to Benally, he wasn't surprised. He told me that he's been having trouble with vandals. He's reported all the incidents that required his insurance company's involvement, but basically ignored the rest. Things are getting expensive for him. He knows his personal pickup will be pretty much unusable on the Rez anymore, with the dead man's blood all over the interior. Now his company's wheels are damaged, too."

"Did you advise Benally to keep us up to speed on the situation? Ignoring harassment isn't always a good idea. If we could lift some fingerprints off his door or get a computer expert to look into those e-mails, we may end up with a lead."

"Benally will cooperate from now on. He just assumed he'd be wasting our time. I told him that we can't act if we're kept in the dark. I also explained that the vandals and their partner in the SUV will be facing a variety of charges, including assault on an officer and reckless endangerment."

"Good. He needed to understand how things work."

Joe nodded in agreement. "After most of the people left, I waited with the family for the tow truck from the garage to arrive. Benally had his guard down by then and I could tell how worried he was about the situation. He has no idea who the vandals are, but he believes they're probably Navajo."

"Does he think they're targeting his company, or him personally?" Ella asked. "These weren't just taggers."

"I asked him that myself, but he got really defensive. Then his wife, Barbara, and Abigail Yellowhair came over. They'd heard him raise his voice and I think they wanted to make sure Ervin didn't blow his cool. Abigail insisted that she was going to repair his damaged company vehicle, and replace the new Dodge pickup George Charley had used," Neskahi added.

"I'm planning on following up on that investigation later today. Did you get any additional details, like why George dropped Ervin off and went up into the mountains alone?"

"Abigail confirmed that Ervin and George had planned

to go gather firewood together. Ervin likes to get away from time to time, and he had a new chain saw he wanted to try out. George needed the wood. So Ervin met George at the StarTalk warehouse and they took off in Ervin's truck. Just before they reached Sheep Springs Ervin got a call on his cell phone about some problem back at the business. Ervin told George to drop him off at the gas station at Sheep Springs where he'd be getting a ride back to Shiprock. George continued on into the Chuskas to gather firewood. You know the rest."

"Any fingerprints from last night?" Ella asked.

"Just odd smudges. I think the perps had something on their fingertips, like superglue, or else they burned their fingerprints off. There were no footprints. Nothing but gravel in the lot, remember?"

"Good work, Joe. Thanks."

Joe stared at the floor, letting the silence stretch out between them, but didn't leave. Realizing he had more to say, Ella waited and didn't interrupt his thoughts.

At long last Joe cleared his throat. "Abigail Yellowhair's not a suspect or anything, right?"

"Why do you ask?" Ella answered, curious.

He cleared his throat again. "Abigail wanted me to go to dinner with her. She said she wanted to discuss a few things with me." He paused awkwardly, shifted in his seat, then continued. "It may sound nuts, but I think she's into me. Her late husband was big and beefy, too, so maybe that's part of it. Thing is, I really don't want to go out with someone close to my mother's age, even if she's still hot and rich to boot," he said. Then after a brief pause, he added, "But if there's a reason for me to do so—if she's implicated in what's happening with her son-in-law, or if you think she's holding back—I'd go, but keep it professional."

"Abigail's not a suspect at the moment. Nobody is yet.

But here's a bit of advice. However you choose to handle this, be aware that Abigail's a very powerful woman and she *does* hold grudges. If you slight her in any way, or even if she thinks you have, she'll remember for as long as she lives. Abigail's made her fortune in business by remembering who owes her favors and playing to that," Ella said.

Joe nodded slowly. "Thanks." He stood up. "Will you need me here today?"

"No, but I want you to know that I'm going to push hard to get you permanently assigned to my team. I don't know if I'll get anywhere, but I'll do everything I can to make it happen."

"I appreciate that," he said, his glum expression brightening immediately.

Making a call to StarTalk, Ella learned that there'd been a problem with a shipment the day before that had required Ervin's return. Satisfied for now, Ella began working on her report about the StarTalk presentation. She'd only been at it for a few minutes when her buzzer sounded. Big Ed wanted her in his office. She'd been expecting him to call her in, but she'd hoped for more time to work on the report.

Gathering her notes, Ella went down the hall to his office. She sat down on the chair directly across his desk, sorting through her papers, and Justine, who'd come in behind her, took the other.

Big Ed's office, befitting the police chief in the Rez's largest community, was the largest in the building. A few months ago, Clair, the chief's wife, had insisting on redecorating. The massive oak desk and the matching bookshelves, even the oak file cabinets, all held her stamp. Only the chief's old fabric chair remained. Parting Big Ed from that chair would have taken a team of horses.

Hearing the creak of the chief's chair as he leaned way back—a feature not found in most current office furniture—

Ella glanced up. "I've got my notes on last night's StarTalk meeting," she said, "but I haven't written a formal report yet."

"We'll get to that," he said, setting down the PDA he'd been using. "Right now I've got other concerns. I understand one of StarTalk's employees turned up dead yesterday." He tapped his finger on the report Ella and Justine had handed his secretary earlier.

Justine cleared her throat and looked at Ella, who nodded. "I've been working on the deceased's background. George Charley was a warehouseman. In the beginning, we didn't have any evidence to suggest his death was connected to his place of employment."

"Subsequent information has now been obtained that puts some doubt on that conclusion," Ella added, recounting what they'd learned. "But I should point out that the facts and physical evidence at this stage *do* support accidental death. Of course, if toxicology results indicate the man was drugged, then we'll be dealing with other possibilities."

"There's another, albeit circumstantial, connection," Big Ed said, his voice low and thoughtful. "The fact that Ervin was unexpectedly called back to the warehouse . . . have you verified the reasons for that?"

"It was legit," Ella said, noting that Big Ed still looked unconvinced.

"Considering all the problems Ervin Benally has been having, I'd like you two to dig a little deeper."

"We're planning on it. Our case is far from closed. Even before the trouble at the chapter house, new questions were already popping up." She filled the chief in on the strange behavior and comments made by the deceased's uncle.

"Then as we dropped Mrs. Charley back at her home, we spotted a pickup parked there," Ella continued. "What made us curious was that the person was already inside the house. We checked things out and found out that it was registered to Wallace Curtis, who lives about a mile away."

"Interesting," Big Ed agreed with a nod.

"It's possible we're dealing with a love triangle," Ella said. "If so, the wife might have slipped the husband something in his food or drink before he left. Or the chain saw could have been turned against him by someone else. We found another set of footprints in the area, but don't know how close that person ever got to the victim. Some of those tracks were obliterated by the Dodge when George left the scene."

"Let me know what you turn up."

"We're waiting for Dr. Roanhorse's toxicology report," Ella said. "But I should also mention that it appeared the deceased consumed three beers at the site. The alcohol could have made him more susceptible to an accident."

"Did the victim have life insurance?" Big Ed asked.

Justine glanced down at her notes. "No life insurance. He was new with StarTalk, so not even his medical insurance had taken effect yet. He wouldn't have been eligible for benefits for another five months."

"I'll need to know as soon as possible if there's any connection between this death and StarTalk, other than bad timing. I've been getting calls all morning from our elected officials. Most of them have gone on the record backing the StarTalk satellite phone venture, and they're worried that bad publicity now could hurt the tribe's plans to go forward with it," Big Ed said. "Of course they're politicians, so what most of them are really worried about is getting reelected. If there's even a hint of corruption at StarTalk, the opposition will have a field day."

"If I've got Benally pegged right, he'll turn this incident around and use it to StarTalk's advantage," Ella said. "He'll claim fewer accident victims like George Charley will die if they have reliable and affordable phone service."

"It's the vandalism Benally and StarTalk have been experiencing that worries me, Shorty," Big Ed said. "Things like that have a tendency to escalate, bringing on copycat attacks on other targets, private and public. Mrs. Yellowhair called me the moment I arrived at the station this morning. She reminded me that the new power plant under construction met with the same type of opposition at the beginning."

Big Ed paused, but they could see he had more on his mind. "Benally . . . how's he taking this personally? Is he coping, or getting rattled? Some of these technical geniuses have difficulty dealing with real-life problems."

Ella paused before answering. "I don't know him well enough to say. He can handle a crowd—at least when it's business-related and nobody actually gets physical."

"According to Mrs. Yellowhair, the incidents of harassment her son-in-law has been subjected to have increased this past week. She told me that the attacks haven't included her daughter so far, but she made it clear that if that happens, she'll expect police protection for her. The next call I received came from the tribal president."

Ella wasn't at all surprised. Abigail believed in taking action . . . even when she shouldn't. "Do you think Mrs. Yellowhair will become a problem for us as we investigate?"

"If we don't get answers fast enough for her, she might. That's why I'm ordering you to make this case your priority. Use whatever resources you need. These perps attempted to run you down, and I want to make sure that endangering the life of one of my officers costs them big-time."

Once the meeting ended, Justine left to see if the ME's report had come in yet, but Ella remained seated.

Noting she was still in the room, Big Ed's gaze focused on her. "Okay, Shorty, what else is on your mind?"

"I know all about the budget constraints, chief, but I'd really like Joe to be permanently assigned to my team. He's shown persistence, initiative, and all the necessary skills. He belongs with us."

"You've been shorthanded for a long time now," he admitted. "Neskahi can work with you now, at least, and I'll see what I can do about getting him a long-term assignment."

"Thanks," she said, standing. Big Ed's word was his bond. If he said he'd try, he'd give it his best shot.

Ella returned to her office, lost in thought. Too many questions continued to circle in her mind about George Charley. The man's connection to StarTalk didn't make things easier, especially after what had been happening to Ervin Benally.

She'd just sat down behind her desk when the phone rang. Ella picked it up immediately and heard Carolyn's voice on the other end.

"I need to talk over a few things with you, Ella. Can you come over? I've been trying to reconstruct the incident."

"No problem, but while I've got you on the phone, can you tell me if the vic's blood contained any traces of drugs, and also how much alcohol was in his system?" Ella asked.

"Can't say. I don't have the tox screens yet, but I put a rush on the results, so I *may* have that information for you by the time you get here. We're now using the Albuquerque Metro Police Crime Lab for these reports. The state crime lab is much too slow, what with their staffing and funding issues."

Ella didn't press her. Carolyn rarely speculated before getting all the data collected. She dealt with facts.

Ella drove directly to the hospital, parked near the rear doors, and went downstairs. The tribe's morgue was in the basement of the tribal public health hospital in Shiprock. The glass-encased autopsy room was just beyond the unmanned outer office. Carolyn had been searching for an office clerk for years but no one had ever applied for the job.

Seeing Carolyn working, Ella tapped on the glass, but made no further attempt to get her friend's attention. Carolyn knew she was here and that was enough.

Alone, Ella took a seat by Carolyn's desk and proceeded to wait. As she looked around she saw ample evidence of Carolyn's major weakness—chocolate-covered peanuts. Empty bags of the candy had been rolled up into balls and were scattered all over the desk.

"Don't say it," Carolyn snapped as she came into the room. "Stupid vending machine. I blew my diet, big-time. But life's short. I'm reminded of that every day."

Ella didn't comment. Dieting never put her friend in a good mood, but breaking it didn't seem to improve her attitude either.

"Come in with me while I try and fit the events to the physical evidence. We talked about this in general terms already, but I've now had a good chance to examine the wound. The fingerprints Justine sent over match those of the victim, by the way, though that was pretty much a slam dunk already."

Carolyn led the way to the autopsy room. The minute Ella stepped inside the glass partition, the smell of meat—more precisely, gamy meat—hit her. Her experiences had taught her to try and breathe slowly through her mouth, not nose, and she managed to keep from gagging.

Although she would have rather been almost anywhere else in the known universe, she'd learned a long time ago to stomach whatever was part of her job. She swallowed again as she saw the corpse on the stainless-steel table. Pale brown, almost amber eyes stared sightlessly at the ceiling, and she tried not to look at the chest cavity, spread open like the flaps on a cardboard box.

"You want to hold the saw, or his arm?" Carolyn asked, a gleam in her eye.

Ella stepped over and picked the saw off the counter. "Stupid question, Doc."

Carolyn motioned her over, then held out her own left arm. "Easier than standing him up, huh? Just don't start that thing for real."

They experimented with various angles, maneuvering the heavy saw and Carolyn's arm, finding ways to match the wound and the chain bar.

"The simplest answer is that he reached for something with his left arm and got too close to the chain. He was holding the saw with just his right hand," Carolyn concluded. "Blood from the artery would have gushed forward, which accounts for the splatter pattern we found on the ground and its relative absence on the bar of the saw. Blood and tissue would have been thrown forward, away from the user because of the rotation of the chain. If the bottom or lower tip of the saw had caused the wound, the splatter would have been thrown back toward the handle—and the user's feet. Earlier I'd wondered if the wound might have been a defensive one, but the splatter is all wrong for that unless the attacker managed some kind of backhand. And taking into account the angle of the wound, that's almost impossible."

Carolyn had Ella choreograph the motion that would have been needed. It was awkward and unlikely, and it put Ella so out of balance she nearly dropped the saw.

"Okay, so it certainly looks like an accident as a result of carelessness. But could it have been helped along?" Ella suggested, setting the saw back down on the counter. "The toxicology report?"

"It came in while you were driving over. There was alcohol in his system, .04 to be exact, so he wasn't legally drunk. His judgement would have been somewhat compromised, but at that level, there shouldn't have been any physical impairment, in my opinion. And no drugs showed up," she added.

Ella took a deep breath. "On the face of it, it appears to be an accident, but the link to Ervin Benally and StarTalk still bothers me. To me, this fatality was just too coincidental."

"How's StarTalk figure into this?" Carolyn asked as they went back into the office.

Ella briefly explained about the vandalism the night before and described what she knew about the earlier incidents. "I can't link what's happening to Benally with this man's death," she said, cocking her head toward the morgue, "but it just doesn't feel right."

"Coincidences happen sometimes," Carolyn said slowly. "You may be looking too hard for something that's just not there." Carolyn walked to the coffeepot by the wall. "Want some?"

Ella looked at her watch, noting it was ten-thirty. "Half a cup," she answered. "I'm meeting my daughter for lunch at school in a little bit. Today's their science fair. She's worked really hard on her project. You wouldn't believe how competitive she is."

Carolyn smiled. "Wonder where she gets that? How's she doing these days, with Kevin not around?"

"She's fine, but she really misses her dad. She and Kevin did a lot of things together. When he took that post in Washington, I think Dawn felt abandoned. Kevin does call her every week, sometimes twice, and he sends her some pretty spectacular presents. He still hasn't figured out that Dawn wants *him*—not what he can give her."

Carolyn nodded. "So what's new with you?"

"Not much," she said with a trace of a smile, aware that Carolyn was fishing for information about her and Ford.

"Come on, spill it. Those of us who make our jobs our life depend on gossip to fill in the gaps."

Ella burst out laughing. "Oh, please. Like my life is that different from yours? Add the fact that I have a kid, and that means Ford has to take third place. But the reason things work out so well between us is because he feels like we do about our jobs. He's on call all the time, or pretty much so. When we get together, we're so relieved to have time off we enjoy every second."

"Joke around all you want, but you're comfortable with that separateness. You've been keeping him at arm's length for over a year now," Carolyn said in a thoughtful voice. "It's the religion thing, isn't it? You're not used to all the rules he's chosen to follow."

It had been nothing more than a shot in the dark, but Carolyn had hit close to the mark. "The real problem is that I *am* used to those rules. My dad was a preacher, and when I was at home, I followed them too. But I'm an adult now and I can't pretend to be something I'm not. I want more . . . or maybe less."

Carolyn laughed. "Sounds like you're describing my diet." She rubbed her knee absently. "I've got to lose some weight, but I *hate* dieting. The first three letters of that word say it all. The thing is, I enjoy everything about food—the selection, the preparation, the eating—and particularly the flavor you can only get from fats. To me, dieting is a bit like giving up a very comfortable friendship."

"You need to find lower-calorie things to prepare," Ella said. "And stick to portion control."

"Portion control I can handle, but using low-cal substitutes means settling for odd tastes or completely flavorless food. But I guess I better get used to it."

"Your knee must really be bothering you," Ella commented, knowing her friend.

Carolyn nodded. "Since I'm not going to have surgery, that leaves dieting. So here's a heads-up. Don't bring anything fattening to this office, and don't expect my attitude to improve these next few months."

"Warning taken."

Ella left a short time later. Sometimes she wasn't sure how Carolyn made it. Ella had her family to keep her sane. Carolyn didn't have anyone else in her life—and the nature of her work caused most Navajos to want to keep her at a distance.

Knowing Carolyn needed a distraction and some company, Ella made up her mind right then to set a date soon for their low-fat dinner.

FIVE
✖ ✖ ✖

As she drove to her daughter's school down in Shiprock's east valley, Ella called the station. With luck, there'd be no crisis for the next hour or so and she'd be able to give Dawn her undivided attention.

To her great relief, except for the ongoing investigations, nothing new had come up. Ella parked in the crowded school parking lot and saw her daughter waiting in the lobby beside the old gym—now a multipurpose room. Today was a special day. Classes had been abbreviated and parents had been invited to come to the science fair.

Seeing her, Dawn jumped up and down, waving from behind the glass. Had it been anyone else, Ella would have seen that as a kid happy to see one of her parents. But with Dawn, she recognized it for what it was—a frustrated kid waiting for her mom to finally show up. She checked her watch. She was about twenty minutes late.

"Hey, Pumpkin," Ella said, coming in the main entrance.

Dawn's eyes grew wide. "Mom, sh-h-h! Don't call me that here, okay? They'll think you're calling me a fatty."

Ella stared at her kid, blinked, then seeing how serious

Dawn was, fought hard not to burst out laughing. Dawn was rail thin and growing like a weed these days. "Or that you're orange. Okay. Got it."

Dawn tugged at her sleeve, pulling her into the multipurpose room. The cafeteria line was just ahead; on the left, and to the right, rows of the folding cafeteria tables, the same kind Ella had grown up with. Beyond, toward the stage at the far end, were rows of smaller tables covered with science project displays.

"We're having spaghetti and meatballs," Dawn said, going up to join the line. "The garlic bread is pretty good, too."

Ella stepped up to the serving area and looked at the food in the serving trays behind the glass. Her mind instantly went back to the corpse at the morgue—the elastic bands of muscle, the reddish interior of the man's chest cavity. Even the big meatballs looked like . . . She swallowed hard.

"Hey, Mom, you okay? You look . . . funny," Dawn said, looking up at her with a furrowed brow. "You've eaten here before, you know."

"I'm fine. Just not very hungry. I'll have something to drink, though. Milk, or juice. And maybe a roll."

"Are you sure? They make the best spaghetti, really!"

Ella nodded. "I'm sure they do, but I think I'll stick to a buttered roll and a carton of milk. Okay with you?"

Dawn shrugged. "Whatever. But the only thing better is on pizza day."

Ella sat down across from Dawn at one of the long cafeteria tables with the fold-down benches and listened as her daughter chattered away. The lunch crowd had thinned because they'd come in at the tail end, but two other children and their equally late parents came to join them a short time later. After introductions, and as the children chattered, Ella's mind drifted. As she was usually working this time of day, her thoughts never strayed away from business for long.

Glancing around, sipping from the carton of milk, she looked out the twin doors leading back into the lobby. A tall woman was standing there looking in their direction. Then Dawn made a comment, and by the time Ella turned back to look, the woman was gone. Though Ella hadn't been able to place her, there had been something familiar about the figure.

Ella's gaze strayed back to the doors a few more times as the parents and children around her discussed the event. That's when she caught another glimpse of her. The woman's back was to them now, and she was looking at the big glass display case that held the school's awards and trophies from years past.

"Mo-o-o-m!" Dawn said, poking her in the ribs. "Mrs. Lee asked you a question."

Ella looked at the young Navajo mother sitting across from her at the table and smiled. "I'm sorry. My mind drifted. Ask again?"

"I was just saying that it must be difficult to be a mom and have a demanding career like yours."

"It is," Ella said. "But I've got a great kid," she added, looking down at Dawn, who stared at the plate, embarrassed.

As Ella leaned back on the bench, she saw the woman again. This time she was at the outside exit doors looking in at the displays, and Ella was able to get a clearer look. She was around Ella's weight and height, which was unusually tall for a Navajo woman, and had shoulder-length black hair with reddish highlights.

Ella was still trying to remember where she'd seen the woman before when Dawn tugged at her sleeve. "Come on, Mom. It's time to go over to the displays. Wait until you see how cool everything looks!"

As they bussed their trays, Ella reasoned that the woman

was undoubtedly a parent—maybe someone pressed for time who'd skipped lunch to peek in at her kid's project. Why else would anyone hang around?

"Where's the school's security guard? I haven't seen him today," Ella asked Dawn.

"Mr. Vigil? He's usually in the parking lots during lunch, watching cars, or looking for kids who've sneaked out from the playground. Did you want to see him right *now*? It's eleven-thirty and you still haven't looked at the projects yet."

Hearing the exasperation in her daughter's voice, Ella smiled. "It'll wait. I hadn't seen him, so I wondered."

They crossed the former gym to the side where the science projects had been set up, and Dawn proudly walked to her own, just below the stage. Three foam-backed poster-board sections stood in a self-supporting U shape. All were filled with photos of Dawn's pony and hand-lettered charts with data. The header, on a piece that connected the two side pieces in slots, read ANIMAL BEHAVIOR—TEACHING A HORSE A TRICK.

The display included photos of Dawn with Wind and the different types of treats she'd used. Each was listed under REWARD VARIABLES. Ella noted with a chuckle that at one time Wind had turned down marshmallows, Dawn's favorite treat.

"This came out fabulous, daughter! You kept great records—even recording the time of day and the weather, knowing that those factors affect horses and they can behave differently then. I'm so proud of you!" Ella said, beaming at her. "I especially like your attention to detail."

"Details are important. You told me that, remember? I want to be a police detective, too, when I grow up," she said, smiling happily.

Ella felt a bittersweet tug hearing Dawn say that. It was

flattering to know that her daughter admired her. On the other hand, she'd hoped to see Dawn in a career that would give her a greater measure of safety and a more secure future. But she was worrying needlessly. Dawn was very young, and she'd change her mind a zillion times between now and then.

"Your hard work really shows," Ella said.

"Thanks for taking the photos and checking my spelling and sentences, Mom. My teacher complimented me on my English and grammar, too."

Just then one of the teacher/parent judging teams approached, congratulated Dawn, and handed her a red ribbon for second place. Dawn smiled, held it up so Ella could see it, then put it up on the display with a tack.

As the judges continued down the line, Dawn looked at Ella. "Maybe I would have come in first if I'd done my project on native plants, like Mrs. Mendoza suggested, but you've always said I should do what's right for me. *Shimasání* loves plants and would have helped me out, I know, but I love horses more!" she said with a happy shrug.

Ella chuckled softly. She had no reason to worry. Dawn would eventually choose the career that was right for her. Her kid was an individualist, and chances were that wouldn't change. Although that thought gave her some measure of comfort, a part of her continued to worry. Dawn, a police officer . . . No, on second thought, she couldn't see Dawn in any job where she had to take orders. Hopefully, becoming a rap star would never be on the list.

"Congratulations again, daughter! I'm very proud of you! We'll celebrate soon, I promise, but now I've got to get back to work." Looking toward the twin outside doors and seeing the same woman she'd seen before still hanging around, Ella gave Dawn a quick kiss and hurried out.

"Bye, Mom," Dawn called out, then turned to talk about her project to some parents who'd come up to admire her photos.

Once outside, Ella discovered the woman was nowhere in sight. Taking it as a good sign, Ella walked toward the tribal SUV, halfway across the lot. As she reached the row where she was parked, Ella saw the shadow of someone standing around the other side of her unit, beside the door.

Ella's muscles tensed and her senses went on full alert. Automatically she reached up and felt the badger fetish. It was cool to the touch—a good sign.

Standing still for a second, she studied the woman's reflection in the passenger's side mirror and concluded that she wasn't armed. In that tight sweater and close-fitting jeans, anything larger than a set of keys would have been obvious. Ella breathed easier, but remained on her guard as she walked around the front of the vehicle and met with her.

"I've been wanting to speak with you," the woman announced.

"Well, now's your chance. Do I know you from someplace? You look a little familiar." Ella responded casually.

"I was a patrol officer in the tribal department and we used to pass each other every once in a while when my shift began. We were never introduced, as I recall."

Ella remained on her guard, trusting the instinct that told her to expect trouble. "I guess not. Is there something I can do for you? . . ."

"Roxanne. I'm Roxanne Dixon," she answered.

"So how can I help you, Roxanne?"

Roxanne smiled, but the expression never reached her eyes. The only thing shining there was a cold, almost lethal intent. "I'm dating Kevin."

Ella stared at her for a moment, but when Roxanne didn't say anything else, answered, "Well, congratulations.

That means you probably know that Kevin and I have separate lives and we haven't been a couple for years. We're dating whom we choose now. So what do you want with me?"

"I know that you two stay in contact because of Dawn, so I thought you could help me out. I accidentally misplaced Kevin's new home number after he moved, and I need to get in touch with him." She brought out a small pad and a pen from her jacket pocket, then looked at Ella expectantly.

Ella was still getting bad vibes about the woman, and Kevin was a lawyer. Maybe this was some kind of scam, or an attempt to track down and harass Kevin on some legal issue. Whatever the reason, Roxanne had used Dawn to track her down, and that didn't sit well with Ella.

"I'll be glad to pass your message on next time I talk to him, but neither of us gives out personal information without the other's permission," Ella said, opening the driver's door.

"So you're refusing to give me his number?" Roxanne said, her voice a rough whisper.

"It's not personal, so please don't take it that way. I never give out anyone's private phone number. But if you really need to speak with Kevin, just call the tribal offices in D.C. I'd bet he's there until late every night."

"I need to discuss something personal with him and I'd rather not interfere with his work at the office. Just give me a break, okay? His home number?"

"I'll tell you what. He'll be calling tonight to ask my daughter about the science fair. I'll tell him we spoke and ask him to contact you right away," Ella said, then added, "Does your child have an exhibit at the gym?"

"No. I don't have any kids. I just came to look at your daughter's project. Kevin will want to know all about it, and that she was awarded a red ribbon."

"I prefer that my daughter be the one who gives him the

news, actually," Ella said coldly. "Our meeting here is now over. If you have no business being on school grounds, I suggest you leave."

Roxanne's eyes grew hard. "I'm here as a *friend*—not an enemy. Get over yourself." Without another word, she turned and strode to a large, green four-door pickup parked two rows over.

Ella remained where she was until the truck left the school grounds, then went back inside to find Dawn. She saw her daughter still beside her project, talking to some of the parents.

Dawn spotted Ella the second she entered the big room, and waved. Ella went to join her daughter and listened as she explained her project to the visitors.

While Ella waited, she watched the doors, making sure that Roxanne hadn't come back. When the parents moved on, Ella stepped close to Dawn. "I spoke to a lady outside by the name of Roxanne Dixon," Ella said, giving Dawn a description. "If she ever approaches you, I want you to call one of the teachers *immediately*. Then ask the teacher to call me, okay? I don't want that woman around you."

"Sure, but I don't remember anyone with that name," Dawn said. "Should I?"

"No. But remember what I've told you, okay? It's important."

"Okay."

As another group of parents approached Dawn's table, Ella went back outside. She strolled around the parking lot for a few minutes, but the four-door green pickup was nowhere to be seen.

Ella found Mr. Vigil, the school guard, alerted him, and then the office staff. At long last she returned to her SUV and began the drive back to the station. On the way, Ella dialed Justine.

"Have you ever heard of Roxanne Dixon? She's supposed to have been one of ours," Ella said.

"Yeah, I remember Roxanne. If I recall right, she left the department about a year ago, something about anger management issues. I might be able to get you more information off the record, but it would mostly be gossip," Justine said. "Personnel files are sealed unless a tribal employee is under formal investigation."

"I know. Ask around and see what you get, but make sure you keep it under the radar for now."

Ella hung up, lost in thought. Things weren't adding up right. If Roxanne and Kevin were dating, or had dated in the recent past, how come Kevin hadn't mentioned her before when they were together with Dawn? And why hadn't he stayed in touch with her after he moved to Washington? Had Kevin experienced her "anger management issues" firsthand?

Knowing how Big Ed felt about guarding the privacy of his officers, her chances of taking a look at Dixon's file without a legal reason were almost zero. The fact that Roxanne had been at Dawn's science fair to try and push for Kevin's personal number wouldn't be enough.

Better to go through Justine and talk to Kevin later on as well, or send him an e-mail once she got home. And later, if she got any indication that Roxanne could pose a danger to Dawn, Ella knew Big Ed wouldn't hesitate to help. He might not actually let her look at Roxanne's file, but she was sure he'd at least brief her on Dixon's history with the department.

As she arrived at the station, Ella met Justine in the hall.

"Good timing," Justine said. "Big Ed has called the Special Investigations Unit to his office."

"Any idea what this is about?" Ella asked, falling into step beside her.

"Not a one," she said.

A moment later, Ralph Tache met them out in the hall and they went inside Big Ed's office. To her surprise, Sergeant Joe Neskahi was there, waiting.

They all sat down at Big Ed's invitation. "I have good news," he said, rocking back in his chair. "The tribe has boosted the Special Investigations Unit's budget—enough to put Sergeant Neskahi on your team."

Ella was first to congratulate Neskahi, but according to Navajo customs, they didn't shake hands. There was a hearty round of welcomes from the rest of her team, then the chief looked at each one of them.

"That was the good news. Now here's the flip side. What tipped the scales in our favor on that budget request was a push from Abigail Yellowhair. All of you know she has powerful friends in Window Rock. If truth be told, almost everyone owes Abigail a favor."

"Me, too," Ella admitted grudgingly. "She helped me find Kevin and Dawn after they were forced to go into hiding that time."

Big Ed nodded. "She also got us funding for the SI team's cell phones when our radio communications were giving us fits. And now this StarTalk issue is coming to a head. Abigail, like others, wants our assurance that George Charley's death wasn't related to StarTalk in any way. Of course I couldn't give it to her at this point. Your investigation isn't complete, and I told her that. When she insisted we give the problems Benally has been having top priority, I explained that the S.I. team was undermanned as it was. Next thing I knew we got the budget increase. Then I got a call from the tribal president demanding we give anything associated with StarTalk top priority. He, like others, is afraid that unless we get things under control—immediately—StarTalk could suffer."

"We'll do our best, chief," Ella said.

"Stay active on the Charley death, but concentrate your main efforts on Benally and the incidents surrounding him. It may be that we've got a bunch of low-rent hoods out to stir up trouble. If that's the case, shut them down fast," Big Ed said.

"Understood," Ella said, then motioned for her team to follow her.

They met in Ella's office minutes later. Joe Neskahi closed the door behind them and took a seat to the side of Ella's desk.

"Joe, you spoke to the people present at the chapter house meeting after I left, but I haven't seen your report yet. I know about your conversation with the Benallys, but did you get any leads from anyone else that we can follow up?"

"*Hosteen* Nez didn't know anything specific, but news of the problems at StarTalk has already spread. Word has it that Ervin's starting to get worried. He's convinced that a traditionalist group of radicals is responsible, like with the nuclear power plant. He's afraid of them and what they may be ultimately capable of doing," Joe said.

"I thought that the traditionalists had voiced their concerns when the satellite telephone proposal first came before the council," Justine said.

"It was all vetted out. The traditionalists on the council were happy when they learned none of the sacred sites were going to be affected. Everything is *way* above ground except for the actual phone units, and they're only out when in use. You've seen how small they are," Ella replied, "not much bigger than the original cell phones. But follow up on it anyway, Joe, and see if you can get anything more."

Ella turned to Officer Tache. "Ralph, go with Joe and help out. You're with me," Ella said to Justine. "We'll interview company employees and any ex-employees. Although it seems like a long shot, we need to find out once and for all if there's any possible connection between George's death and what's happening to Ervin."

Once the two men on their team left, Justine turned to Ella. "Something else is bugging you, boss. Is it Roxanne, or this case?"

"Both." It didn't surprise her to see how well attuned Justine was to her moods. They'd known each other all their lives, and had worked together for the past ten.

"I'm still pressing for info on Roxanne," Justine said. "I asked people I trust, but what I've found out is *very* second hand. You still want to know?"

"Yeah. Fill me in on our way to StarTalk. Let's get moving."

SIX

✖ ✖ ✖

Moments later, after getting the address of the StarTalk offices, they were on the road, Justine behind the wheel.

"Tell me about Roxanne," Ella said.

"Turns out she was with the department for three and a half years, two of those working out of Window Rock. She was constantly getting in trouble because she was overly aggressive and couldn't follow orders. Then she was transferred here. She was partnered with Henry Tso and developed a crush on the guy."

Ella gave her a puzzled look. "Am I thinking of the right Henry? Short, very chunky—stubby arms and legs. He's constantly knocking things over when he comes into the station. He's married, too. Am I right?"

"That's him. And, yeah, he's married, and faithful, too, near as anyone can tell. But here's the deal. He's kind to almost anyone and, from what I hear, Roxanne took that to heart. When he requested a new partner, she stalked him—I mean seriously. She also tried to scare off Henry's wife. That's when Henry went straight through the roof. He reported her to the watch commander and filed a formal complaint. I'm not sure what happened next, but Big Ed got involved and the problem went away."

"Is that when she quit?"

"No, she didn't resign until six months later. Once Henry was out of the picture, she moved on to someone else. You'll never guess who. Ready? Ralph Tache."

Ella was having serious trouble envisioning the glum-faced officer as someone a woman would go nuts over. "Wasn't he married back then?" Ella asked.

"Separated. He ended up getting divorced at about the same time Roxanne left the force."

"Direct cause?"

Justine shrugged. "I thought you'd have a better chance of getting that information from Ralph. He's not exactly chatty, just in case you hadn't noticed," she added with a wry smile.

Ella laughed. Ralph didn't speak unless it was absolutely necessary. "I can't even begin to imagine what set her on Ralph."

"Are you kidding?" Justine sounded surprised.

Curious now, Ella looked at Justine. "What do you know that I don't?"

"Ralph has a real interesting reputation. It happened after he went out with Marlee Manuelito. She's not much for keeping a secret."

Ella knew the sergeant in booking. She was a hefty woman—not fat, but built like a linebacker.

"Marlee had it bad for Ralph, and word soon got out that he was something to see . . . you know, in the bedroom." She paused. "Haven't you noticed how long his fingers are? And you *know* what they say about a guy with big hands."

Ella made a face. "Aw, jeez! Thanks for that mental image. I could have done without it."

"You asked."

"Not about *that*, for pete's sake!"

Justine laughed. "Well, Ralph is hot these days. Lots of single gals in the department are interested in finding out for themselves, I guess."

"What about Roxanne? Is she still interested in him?"

"According to what I heard, no. When Tache didn't reciprocate, she moved on to Kevin. That's about it. But how much of this is true, I can't say."

"The more I hear about Roxanne, the less I like the woman. I have to know if my kid's in any danger from this loon. Keep digging, okay?"

"You bet."

They arrived at the compound where StarTalk was headquartered a short time later. The tall chain-link gate was open, and Justine drove through, stopping in front of the smallest of three buildings—a modern block and metal structure with large glass doors and a small sign that read, OFFICE. A large wooden sign in the xeroscaped area along the front wall displayed the StarTalk logo, a stylized version of a satellite above and between two very traditional-looking hogans.

Justine parked in front of one of the concrete barriers labeled for visitors. As they went inside the office lobby, they could hear Native American–inspired New Age music—mostly drums and flutes at the moment—coming from hidden speakers. The colors and decor were simple but tasteful, Southwestern in style with turquoise and other desert hues. Beyond the foyer was a large open room containing various-size cubicles where at least a dozen Navajo men and women were working. This work area was simply furnished, utilitarian at best.

A young Navajo woman in her late twenties looked up from the reception desk, which held a computer and multi-line phone system. "Can I help you?"

Ella flashed her badge. "I need to talk to some of the employees. How about if I start with you?"

The Navajo woman leaned back in her chair and nodded. "We were told to expect a visit from the tribal police today," she said. "I'm Lucy Yabeny. Mrs. Yellowhair asked all of us to cooperate fully with you. So how can I help?"

It shouldn't have taken Ella by surprise, but it did. It wasn't so much that they'd been expected, but that Abigail had known she'd come by today. The woman certainly didn't underestimate the scope of her own influence.

"Someone's been harassing Ervin Benally," Ella said. "You're in a good position to hear and know what's going on. Who do you think is doing that?"

"It could be just about anyone," she said in a whisper-soft voice. "Mr. Benally pushes people hard for results, not only company employees, but our vendors, suppliers, and tribal officials." Lucy looked toward the cubicles and, seeing that everyone seemed occupied with other things, continued. "He micromanages everything. He says it's only because he's got big plans for the tribe, but bullies are bullies, you know? He's even hard on his wife, Barbara."

"Is she here?" Justine asked.

Lucy nodded. "Walk down the center aisle, and turn to the left at the end. Her enclosed office is back there, on the right. The bigger office beside it with the sign on the door that says 'The Buck Stops Here' . . ."

"Is Ervin's," Justine finished for her.

"That's it," Lucy said.

"Is he there now?" Justine asked.

"Yeah, and he's in a particularly foul mood at the moment. Some problem with the bank, I gather. I could hear him shouting over the phone when I went to the lunchroom on break a little while ago."

"We already have statements on record from Ervin and Barbara, so we'll be focusing on the others," Ella said.

"Go right ahead. Supervisors and management people

are in the four cubicles closest to the Benally offices, except for our marketing director. He's got an office in the warehouse across the way. All the others here are working stiffs like me."

While Justine concentrated on the office supervisors, Ella spoke to several clerks. It soon became clear to her that despite Abigail's orders, they were afraid for their jobs. She got nowhere.

Seeing Justine still talking to the supervisors, Ella walked out back to the warehouse building. Close to the loading dock she found a smaller door with a sign that read, Toby Wallace, Marketing. A man in a western-cut jacket was just unlocking the door, so it was a good bet that Justine hadn't spoken to him yet. She walked across the gravel yard and knocked on his door.

"Come on in," he called. As she stepped into the room, Ella noted he was engaged in a conversation on his cell phone. The short, extremely round Navajo man was in his late forties as far as Ella could tell, and seemed imbued with a phenomenal amount of energy. He gestured her to take a chair and smiled at her as he put the phone down.

"I'm Toby. You're here on behalf of the tribal lumber mill, right?" he asked, then not waiting for an answer, continued. "I'm glad you came. I'm prepared to make you the deal of a lifetime. We have something to offer you that no other company in the Southwest—"

Ella held up her hand, interrupting him. "I'm afraid you have me confused with someone else." She brought out her badge and showed it to Mr. Wallace. His expression changed in the blink of an eye from hopeful to resigned. "I'd like to ask you a few questions about what's been happening to Ervin Benally," Ella added.

The man dropped down heavily into his chair. "I've heard about that, and I've got to tell you, it just doesn't make sense. Ervin's a man who deserves to be admired, not victimized, for what he's trying to do for the tribe."

From what she could tell, Toby meant every word. "You're management. Have you ever been harassed?"

"No, and that's what's crazy about all this. Logically, I'm the one who should have made enemies. It's my job to contact companies and organizations here on the Rez, and try to talk them into signing up with StarTalk. You'd think that any Navajo who's ever been stranded in his own home after a major snowstorm would be able to see the value of reliable phone service. But I come up to people all the time who just can't accept progress of any kind. Emergency services and the police department are the only ones who were open to what we had to say from day one."

"Has anyone ever threatened you?" she pressed.

"I've had arguments with a few of the traditionalists at chapter house meetings, but that's about it. Even then, all that ever amounted to was some raised voices and a dirty look or two."

"Do you make presentations at the chapter houses? I thought Ervin was doing those."

"The Navajo Nation is huge, so we have to share the load. I also do most of the follow-ups, especially with those who've given us a positive response."

"At those follow-ups, have you ever encountered any serious problems?"

"Once, yeah, but it wasn't with the public. It was with one of our former warehousemen. I had the misfortune of running into Patrick Tsosie at a meeting, not long after he'd been fired. He shouted a few obscenities at me and was escorted outside. But when I went to my car, he jumped me. He took me by surprise when he shoved me against the company car, but then I started pushing back. I'm twice his size, so I knocked him on his butt and embarrassed the hell out of him. He swore he'd be suing me, too, but I never heard from him again."

"Sue you, *too*?" Ella asked. "Who was the other person, Ervin?"

"Yeah, but it wasn't for that incident. You see, Patrick drinks way too much, so he was usually late to work, or just didn't show up at all. He also has a mouth on him. One day he made some smart-alecky comment to Abigail when she was in the warehouse and she fired him on the spot. I think he'd been drinking, because instead of leaving, he just flipped her off, then sat down on the loading dock and refused to leave. That's when Ervin came out, grabbed him in a hammerlock, and forced him off the grounds. Patrick cussed Ervin all the way out, and, last I heard, he was suing the company, hoping to get some of the money he was docked."

"Do you think he could be behind the trouble Ervin's been having?" Ella asked.

Toby didn't answer for several long moments, but Ella could see he was thinking it over and didn't interrupt. Eventually, Toby looked up. "I'll admit that he seems to be the kind who might be out for revenge, but in this case I don't buy it."

"Why not?"

"The kind of things that have been happening to Ervin require two things—timing and planning. Patrick drinks, and until the booze kicks in, he doesn't have the guts to act. And nothing he does in anger is planned. It's all spontaneous."

"But he still came after you at the chapter house."

"Not until he'd been thrown out and had stoked up his courage with that cheap fortified wine. Even then, he mostly just stumbled around and did a lot of cussing. It's not the same thing. Look at what happened to the Ervin's SUV at the chapter house. They changed the sign to StarCrock.

They also scratched up another of his company vehicles the week before and left the word *bilisaana* on it."

Ella nodded slowly, lost in thought. The word meant apple, but when used this way, it meant someone who was red on the outside and white on the inside.

"I see your reasoning," Ella said. "So if you had to take a guess . . ." She let the sentence hang.

He thought about it some more, tapping his pencil on the corner of the desk. "There's only one person I know about that Ervin flat out considers his enemy," he said, then suddenly his eyes widened. "Whoa, forget I said that."

"I can't do that, but I'll do my best to keep what you say under wraps."

"I like my job here, so I'll hold you to that." He expelled his breath in a hiss, then at last nodded. "It's just a mother-in-law thing, I'm sure, but six months ago things got really tense between Ervin and Abigail. In fact, Abigail threatened to pull out of StarTalk and take her money with her. Thing is, without her financial support, StarTalk would have gone belly-up."

"Do you know what led to that?"

"Pretty much. I sat in on most of that meeting. Abigail wanted a statewide push for StarTalk. She said that there are lots of rural New Mexican communities, especially in the mountains, that are in the same fix as we are—no reliable phone service. She wanted to expand our operations the second we got our first contract. Ervin thought we'd overextend the company and it would be a disaster. Barbara was trying to get both of them to settle down and reach some halfway compromise. Me and the other supervisors were finally asked to leave, because things were really getting intense between the executives. The doors here are pretty solid, but we all heard them yelling at each other. Everyone listened, because our jobs would have been history if Abigail pulled out."

"Unofficially, did you side with Ervin or Abigail on the issue?"

"I could see Ervin's point. It's not that I think Abigail's wrong. It's her timing I have a problem with. It might be a great idea to go statewide in a few years, but right now we have our hands full here just trying to get things off the ground. Barbara stays late almost every night doing the number crunching, and Ervin works overtime promoting StarTalk. Everyone has been working impossibly long hours. Even our receptionist seldom quits before eight at night, handling and directing calls in and out of the warehouse."

Toby's desk phone rang and he picked it up, signaling Ella to wait. After a few seconds he placed the caller on hold, and glanced back at her. "I've got to take this. It's from our factory in Mexico. They're the ones manufacturing our custom-designed phones. I've already told you everything I know. How about letting me get back to work?"

Ella nodded, started to walk out, then stopped and turned her head as he reached for the phone. "How long did Patrick work here?"

Toby placed his hand over the receiver. "I can't remember. All I know for sure is that George Charley, the man who died in that woodcutting accident yesterday, was the one who took over for him. If you need dates, ask Barbara. She oversees the personnel records and will be able to answer your question."

Ella left the warehouse office and walked back to the main building, considering this new lead and wondering just how far coincidences could stretch. The guy who'd taken over for the troublemaker was now dead—and that, while driving Ervin's flashy new pickup. Ella knew they'd be paying Patrick Tsosie a visit next.

Justine came out from one of the supervisor's offices just then. "I've spoken to the office manager and the warehouse supervisor. But there's also the marketing director, Toby Wallace. Did you get him?"

"Yes, and now I need to find out how long Patrick Tsosie worked here. Turns out George Charley was his replacement at StarTalk."

Barbara, whose office door was open, overheard Ella and called out in her high-pitched voice, "I can give you those dates, Detective Clah."

Ella walked inside Barbara's office, Justine following. Despite the title of vice president on the door, this office was no more plush than the one assigned to Toby. It had a computer, a simple desk, and two vinyl chairs.

Barbara switched computer screens then glanced at Ella. "Patrick Tsosie worked for us six weeks and three days."

"Thanks," Ella said, then in a casual tone added, "Your husband sure got lucky missing out on that wood gathering trip yesterday with George Charley."

Barbara nodded somberly. "It didn't really hit me until I got a look at the company pickup over at your impound yard. I really feel for George's poor wife."

"Were Ervin and George friends?" Ella asked. Barbara's high-pitched voice was grating, but Ella worked hard not to let it distract her.

"Ervin never met him before he came to work for us. But everyone in this company knows each other and we're not stuck on titles here," Barbara said.

"Whose idea was it to go get firewood?"

"Ervin's, I think. He loves the scent of piñon in our fireplace and he was just itching to try out that new chain saw. But they were halfway there when Ervin got a call from Toby about a shipment that came in with the wrong equipment. Ervin had to come back, but told George to go on ahead." Barbara sighed loudly. "My husband sure feels guilty about that now. Ervin thinks that maybe if he'd been there, the accident would have never happened, or at the very least, he could have given George some first aid and driven him to a clinic."

"Who else knew where Ervin was going, and that he was forced to come back early?" Ella asked.

"That's an odd question."

"Just trying to cover all the details," Ella replied. "Who knew?"

Barbara shrugged. "My mother and I knew where Ervin was going, along with everyone here that morning. Almost all of us heard when he came back, too, because of that problem with the shipment. It really ticked him off." She paused for several long moments. "Ervin works really hard. He's our show horse. He's smooth, pretty to look at, and makes a great presentation. He's got a real way with people. Our suppliers and clients all love him. That's why it's so hard for him to get away."

"Thanks," Ella said, then excused herself as Barbara went to answer her phone.

As Justine and she headed out of the building, Ella said, "Patrick Tsosie is our first solid suspect. Although Toby thinks otherwise, I know that some drunks can be incredibly clever."

"I'll get his address from Dispatch," Justine replied.

"Also, I'd like to find out how Abigail and Ervin settled that dispute on expanding company operations," Ella added, explaining what she'd learned. "Abigail has a reputation for never backing down when she wants something, so there's probably more to that story. There are a lot of ways to put pressure on someone, and I can't see her letting Ervin flat-out win."

"Abigail's hard on a lot of people, but her own life

hasn't been a picnic," Justine said quietly as they headed for the tribal SUV. "If Abigail hadn't been one major hard-ass, she wouldn't have made it."

Surprised to hear her partner defending Abigail, Ella turned to look at Justine. "What's going on? What haven't you told me?"

Justine said nothing for several long moments. When she finally spoke it was slowly, and with effort. "About five months ago, my mom and dad got themselves in a real financial bind. My sisters and I helped out, but it wasn't nearly enough."

"That was about the time your mother had to stop working?"

Justine nodded. "Her medical expenses were all met by the tribe, but fear about what would happen—whether her cancer would go into remission or not—ate Dad alive. He went a little crazy and began to gamble up at that casino on the Ute Rez. He ended up owing a chunk of money, much more than he could ever pay back. Then collectors started coming around," Justine said in a taut voice.

Justine paused for a long moment before continuing. When she finally did, her voice was resolute and controlled. "My sister Jayne went to Abigail and she loaned us the money to cover the debt. Things settled down at home after that, and Mom's health improved. Jayne and I have been paying Abigail back a little at a time, but she's refused to charge us any interest. She said that everyone gets in the hole from time to time."

To Ella, it was clear that Abigail Yellowhair had put her partner in the position of owing her a favor.

As if reading her mind, Justine nodded, slipping behind the wheel. "Yeah, I know what you're thinking. She wanted me indebted to her. But her kindness won't cut her any slack during an investigation and she knows that," Justine said firmly. "But back to what you said. I think Abigail would do whatever she thought would ultimately benefit her daughter. Blood's blood, Ella. We'd all do that."

"So what do you think happened?"

"My guess is that Barbara and Abigail reached a compromise of some sort. Abigail and she share the title of V.P., after all, though Abigail doesn't even have a formal office on site. But I'll see what I can find out using a back door. Jayne and Barbara went to school together and are friends," Justine added, switching on the ignition.

Ella nodded but didn't comment. Although she was sure Justine would never compromise her work for anyone or anything, the connection between Justine and Abigail Yellowhair bothered her.

Justine called Dispatch and received Patrick Tsosie's address. He'd been arrested before, so she was also able to get a description from records. As they started backing out of the parking space, Abigail drove through the main gate, the gleam of her luxury SUV attesting to a recent wash and wax.

Justine stopped and waited for the vehicle to pass behind them. Without even glancing in their direction, Abigail continued on, and parked in the empty slot by the main entrance. As Abigail got out of her vehicle, Justine started to back out once again.

Just then a large object came flying over the wall facing the street. Catching a fleeting glimpse of the projectile, Ella yelled to Abigail, "Duck!"

The object hit the asphalt less than three feet from Abigail's SUV and burst, splattering a thick red liquid all over the vehicle—and Abigail.

As Justine hit the brakes, Ella jumped out of their cruiser, and raced to the wall. Barbed wire was strung at the top so she couldn't climb over easily, but she was able to grab the top of the blocks and do a chin-up. A blue older-model

Chevy pickup was racing away to her left, its license plate obscured with either mud or dirt. Someone in a green shirt was sitting or crouched in the bed of the truck, obviously the individual who'd thrown the water balloon or whatever.

When she jumped back down, Justine was crouching next to what appeared to be a plastic trash bag. From the odor Ella realized the red liquid was paint.

"They were too far away for me to get much of a description," Ella said. "What have you got?"

"A paint bomb," Justine said. "Whatever happened to water balloons, or eggs?" she added, watching where she put her feet. "But it smells like latex, so it should wash off with water, providing it's not allowed to dry overnight."

Abigail stormed over to where they were, speckles of paint splattered over her carefully applied makeup and wool jacket. "Now you've seen for yourselves what we've been going through. It's just maliciousness, plain and simple, but it's getting costly. You saw who did it, so what are you still doing here? Go arrest them."

"By the time I got to the top of wall, they'd already reached the corner, too far away for a clear look," Ella answered. "All I saw was a blue Chevy pickup with a guy wearing a green shirt in the back. The license plate was obscured—deliberately, no doubt."

Ella turned to look back at the wall. "Do any of your security cameras cover the street?"

Abigail glared at her. "No. But we didn't expect to be under attack. I don't care how you do it, but take care of this problem. You understand me? I've had it with these jokers. If I have to hire my own investigators because you can't handle this, I promise you that everyone from the top down will hear about it. I have a *very* loud voice."

As Abigail spun around and went inside, Ella glanced

over at Justine. "Any chance that we can get prints off the bag?"

"I'll have to wait for it to dry and hope there's a spot that the paint didn't cover," Justine said.

Justine walked back to the unit, then returned with a cardboard box. After putting on latex gloves, she examined the torn bag carefully, then picked it up, and set it into the box. Paint dripped everywhere.

The vandalism incidents were escalating and Ella wondered what would happen when those responsible realized that their campaign wasn't working. Violence was usually the next step. But maybe that had already happened. George Charley had been driving Ervin's truck and had worked for StarTalk.

"After we talk to Patrick Tsosie, I need you to go to the impound yard and check out the Benally's Dodge pickup one more time," Ella told Justine. "See if it might have been tampered with while George was cutting wood. Also, remember the set of footprints we found just a short distance from the truck? Narrow down the list of suspects to just StarTalk employees and see what turns up. There's a lot happening beneath the surface of this company."

"All right. I'll get on that. I'll also check back with Barbara and see who took off for a few hours that day."

"Let me know the moment you have something."

"Gut feeling?" Justine asked her.

"Big-time."

SEVEN

— ✖ ✖ ✖ —

Patrick Tsosie's small crumbling gray stucco house was south of Shiprock, off the main highway, and up a dirt road that led into some low hills. Even this close to the river, the land was arid and sparsely vegetated except for some yellow galleta grass and a few hardy clusters of winter fat.

As they drove up, Ella saw an ancient American-made sedan with faded purple paint. It was parked in the inadequate shade of an equally ancient peach tree, its branches virtually naked of leaves this late in the year. Justine pulled up and Ella saw the empty sheep corral and a hogan out in the back.

Ella studied the hogan first. It looked abandoned—as if someone had lived there decades ago, then moved to the more spacious wood-frame house blessed with electricity. Perhaps the hogan now only served as a place to hold special ceremonies from time to time. That was fairly common these days. But since the family could be traditionalist, it was necessary to follow certain courtesies.

"Let's give him a chance to invite us in," Ella said. "But if he doesn't, we'll go up."

"Here comes someone," Justine said, gesturing with her lips.

Ella got out of the cruiser and saw a man who fit Patrick's description motioning her. "He's either waving or wavering, partner. Heads up."

"Yeah, noticed that," Justine said. "I hate dealing with drunks."

As they approached, Patrick took an unsteady step toward them, then fell back. Bracing himself against the wall of the house, he recaptured his balance. "Whoops. The air's kinda thick out here. Whadda ya want?"

"We need to ask you a few questions," Ella said.

" 'Bout what?" he asked, slurring his words.

Ella jammed her hands into her pockets. Like Justine, she hated questioning drunks. If he pushed her in the slightest, he'd find himself sobering up inside a jail cell. "Let's start with the job you used to have at StarTalk."

There was a flash of something in his eyes, but before she could give it any thought, he sat down on the unpainted wood plank porch and stared up at them. "Don't have much to say 'bout that place."

"Where were you yesterday, particularly at around ten-thirty a.m.?"

He looked down at his wrist, but there wasn't any watch there. His eyebrows knitted together and he stared at his feet a long time before answering. "Can't remember, lost my watch. But yesterday morning? I'm almost sure I was here."

"Do you know George Charley?" Ella pressed. Normally she wouldn't have used the deceased's name, but sometimes in police work it was necessary.

Patrick's eyes widened. "Whad's the matter wid you?" he said, trying to pronounce his words, but failing miserably. "Dontcha know he's dead?" he added in a whisper. "You'll call his *chindi*, woman."

"You're going to have a lot more than that to worry about if you don't stop wasting our time," Justine said, leaning down and getting in his face.

He moved his head back to avoid her, then had to stick out his arms to keep from falling over.

"How did you find out about George's death?" Ella pressed.

"I heard about it when I went to StarTalk late yesterday. Lucy Yabeny likes me and I thought she might be willing to help get the rest of the money they owe me. And, if not, I figured she might have a few bucks to spare, you know?"

"And she told you about him?" Ella pressed.

"Yeah. She said that everyone was really upset that he got himself all sawed in half, and that if I'd stop drinking, I might be able to get my job back. But then *she* came in."

"She, who?" Justine asked.

"Mrs. Yellowhair. Abby Crabby. That woman has too good a memory. I'd been drinking a little last time we ran into each other, and I think I made some comment about her . . . girlish figure."

"So she didn't want you back?" Justine said.

"She threatened to have me arrested on the spot for trespassing, so I hightailed it out of there. Haven't been back since. If I'd run into her daughter, Barbara, the human one, it would have been different."

Ella noticed how Patrick's speech had suddenly cleared. She wondered if maybe he played drunk when it suited him. A way to avoid responsibility . . . She focused on him. "What makes you think Barbara would have treated you any differently than her mother?"

"Barbara sits back, letting her husband take front stage, but she's the *real* power there. Everyone knows that. Ervin likes to show off, giving presentations and that kind of thing. But Barbara *works* for a living. If it wasn't for her, he'd be selling used cars in Farmington."

Ella leaned against the column on the porch, and regarded him thoughtfully. "Where does Mrs. Yellowhair fit in then?"

"She's got the cash," he answered without missing a beat. "That's what she uses to control the Benallys. Abby can't boss Ervin around, so she pressures her daughter. But it doesn't get her far, I don't think."

"How come?" Ella asked.

"Barbara lets Ervin do whatever he wants. Never argues, even when he bullies her around in front of everyone. She just takes it from him. I don't know why."

Ella held his gaze. "One last question. Why did you pretend to be drunk when we first pulled up?"

Patrick smiled at her. "It makes my life easier when people don't expect too much. Mind you, I drink more than I should. But not now. Don't have the bucks. I need a job."

Justine and Ella were on their way moments later. Justine glanced over at her. "What next?"

"We'll go back to the station. You can check out the Dodge in impound, then call it a day. I'm going to finish some paperwork and try to get home before Dawn's bedtime. I need to have a long talk with my kid. Roxanne Dixon worries me. From everything I've learned, that woman goes after whatever she wants without considering the consequences," Ella said. "I need to make sure my kid doesn't get caught up in one of her games."

"I hear you, but by notifying the school authorities, you've hopefully already taken care of that."

"Yeah, but I still worry. It goes with the territory. Wait till you become a mom someday. You'll understand then."

By the time they parked at the station, Ella noticed that they were both yawning.

"I think we should change our plans. There's nothing like the cold nighttime desert air to give us an energy boost. Why don't I help you check out the Dodge and take a look at George Charley's pickup? His wife will be needing the vehicle and nobody's had a chance to give it a once-over since it was transported from the StarTalk yard. After that we can both go home."

"Good idea. We'll need keys to get into impound, but the watch commander will have a set. I don't think the attendant will still be around this time of night and the shop is closed."

"Okay. I'll go on ahead just in case somebody is still back there, and you swing by the front desk."

Ella went to the left of the station's main building, and passed through the open gate that provided access to the rest of the yard. The impound area was past the shop, toward the rear of the property.

As Ella approached impound's six-foot-high fence, she heard a faint metallic rattling sound coming from the far end. She stopped and listened, waiting. When it sounded again, she realized instantly what it was. Someone was pushing against the fence—or trying to climb over it.

Knowing that a thief's entry into impound could compromise a case, Ella inched down the fence line, trying to see what was going on without being spotted. They'd had thieves sneak in before they'd put in the second layer of fencing and additional outside lights.

Ella worked her way down the fence, trying to see if anyone was on the impound fence or maybe on the other fence that bordered the station. That one was ten feet high and topped with a strand of barbed wire. Just about the time she started to radio for backup, she heard the creak of metal and saw someone scramble on top of one of the cars inside the fenced perimeter.

"Don't move!" she ordered, but before she'd even uttered the last syllable, the person was in the air, going over the fence.

He landed right on top of her shoulders, slamming her to the ground. Ella tried to roll away, but he was wiry and as strong as a wrestler. He pinned her to the ground, pressing his forearm to her throat.

He was wearing a ski mask and a flannel shirt that smelled like an auto shop—and he was also choking her. Ella kicked up with her knees, slamming him in the gut. He managed to stay on her and pushed down harder with his forearm. She tried to bite him then, but all she got was a mouthful of cloth.

Swinging her arms around, she hit him with both hands on the ears, then kicked up with both legs, twisting at the same time.

He grunted and fell off her.

Ella scrambled to her knees, reaching down for her handgun with her right arm. Seeing a blur to her left, she brought her arm up to block him, but she was a split second too late.

Something hard struck her on the head and bright lights flashed before her eyes. Everything started to whirl around like a carnival ride, and she fell back to the ground.

Moments later another bright light shined in her eyes. "Ella, are you okay? What happened?"

Ella blinked and turned away. "You wanna get that light out of my eyes, partner?"

"Sorry," Justine responded, moving her pocket flashlight away. "What happened, did you fall or something?"

"I got jumped, then clocked by something harder than a fist." She sat up, looking around quickly. The motion hurt her head and she held her hand up to feel the bump on her skull.

"Where'd he go? You see anyone running off?" Ella rose to her feet slowly, wobbling a bit.

Justine grabbed her arm. "Steady, boss. Maybe you shouldn't be getting up so fast. What guy are you talking about?"

"There was a man out here, at least he was as strong as a man. I heard what sounded like someone climbing the fence, then looked up and saw him standing on top of that car." She turned and pointed at the vehicle just across the impound fence.

"And he jumped right down on you?"

"Yeah. Let's check the fence line and try to see where he went. Nobody ran past you and out the main gate, did they?"

"No, I'd have seen them. You stay here and get your balance. I'll do it."

"First, let's get some more light." Ella grabbed her cell phone and called the front desk. Fifteen seconds later, the lights were turned up, illuminating the impound yard so well they could see the entire perimeter fence.

"There," Justine pointed.

Fifty feet away Ella could see that a section had been cut from the main fence, big enough for someone to crawl through. "Now we know how he got in and out of the yard." She did a slow three-sixty, and saw a metal can against the side of the impound fence, just five feet away.

"That must be what he clocked me with—that can of . . . whatever."

Justine walked over and aimed her flashlight down. "It's brake fluid. What was he doing—sneaking into a police area and clobbering an officer just to steal a can of brake fluid? That doesn't make any sense."

"No, and the brake fluid would have been kept in the shop anyway, not the impound yard. That's evidence, partner. Maybe we can lift some prints," Ella said. "We'll also need to extend our search. We'll want to check out the vehicles in impound and see why he broke in tonight. Looks like we're not going home early after all."

"Why don't you go inside and get an ice pack on that bump, and I'll get started working the scene? If you decide you want to power down some aspirins and go home, I can handle things here. I'll have plenty of help if I need it. We'll have several officers out here soon enough. Somebody's going to have to wire up that hole in the fence."

Ella reached up and touched the tender spot on her head. The swelling hadn't got any worse. "Sounds like a plan. See you in the morning."

One of the officers inside had EMT training, and he checked out her vital signs, advising her to wait a while and use an ice pack. There was no blood, only bruising, so after about a half hour, her headache better thanks to the aspirins, Ella left the station.

All throughout the drive home, Ella's thoughts remained on the investigations of the past two days. As far as the case surrounding Ervin went, she'd yet to figure out what was behind the incidents. The money trail, usually the best way to establish motive, was murky at best. She seriously doubted that any of the other phone companies in the state were behind the harassment. There was a lot more money to be made off the reservation from cell and conventional phone customers. There had to be something else at stake here.

Then there was tonight's incident. Had that been just an attempt by someone to rob a vehicle, or maybe even drive it away? Or was it just another act of vandalism like the one at the chapter house or at StarTalk, but this time in the department's own backyard? Of course that didn't explain the presence of a can of brake fluid.

Maybe by the time Justine finished working the scene they'd have at least some of the much needed answers.

A short while later Ella pulled into the driveway of their family home southwest of Shiprock. It was past seven and the outside lights were on. She could see Dawn over in the corral brushing Wind. Boots' car wasn't around, but it was past supper and Dawn didn't need a sitter when both Rose and Herman were home.

Seeing Ella, Dawn came rushing up and gave her mom a hug. "Mom, I'm so glad you're *finally* home!"

"I appreciate the welcome but what's going on?" Ella had a feeling that a brand-new headache was on its way.

Dawn sighed loudly. "It's *Shimasání*. She just doesn't understand. It's not that she's angry, but—"

"Whoa, start at the beginning," Ella said, walking inside the house with Dawn. Hearing them come in, Rose came out of the kitchen—the only room common to the two wings of the house.

"Hey, Mom," Ella greeted, grateful that her recent bump on the head hadn't left a visible sign.

"I left some supper for you in the oven, daughter. It should still be warm. My husband and I will be home tonight if you need us."

"Why don't you join us in the old living room? We haven't had a real family evening in a while."

"Not tonight, daughter. My granddaughter has things to talk to you about."

Now Ella knew for sure that there were problems brewing. Rose left, walking into the new wing she shared with Herman, as Ella stepped into the kitchen.

"You can fill me in on whatever is going on while I eat, daughter." She wasn't particularly hungry but if she didn't eat, Rose would have a million questions.

She brought a covered casserole dish full of tasty mutton stew out of the oven, then retrieved a plastic bag from the crisper that contained four pieces of golden brown fry bread.

"I won't mind if you want to share," Dawn commented, bringing two bowls and dessert plates out of the cupboard.

Ella looked at her kid and laughed.

"She ate already," came Rose's voice from the sitting room down the hall. "It's your turn."

Ella smiled. Of course Rose wouldn't have gone far, not when something was up. Two minutes later, Ella ladled some stew into the bowls.

Silently signaling her daughter to dig in, they divided up the pieces of fry bread, and enjoyed the stew, hot and delicious—filled with chunks of mutton, chopped potatoes, and green chile.

"So tell me what's going on," Ella said, feeling the invigorating effects of Rose's home-cooked meal.

"My friend Sara told me you'd be getting a letter, too, just like the one her mom got yesterday. I kinda wanted to talk to you about that."

"Are you in some kind of trouble you forgot to tell me about?"

"No, it's not like that at all. Valley Academy—over by Farmington—awards two scholarships a year. Sara got one, and her mom was told that the second one was mine." Dawn ran into the living room and came back with a letter addressed to Ella on Valley Academy stationery.

Ella opened it and verified that it was just as Dawn had said—a full scholarship, including fees, uniforms, and room and board at the academy dormitory. The last part made her stomach drop. "And how do you feel about this? Is Sara accepting?"

"Oh yeah, Mom. It's a big deal at her house. Her mom's

Anglo and she wanted Sara to go to a school off the reservation."

"But do *you* want to go?"

"They teach riding, Mom!" she said, in a tone so filled with yearning Ella had to smile. Any mom on the planet knew that sound by heart.

Ella skimmed the letter. "It says here the scholarship will be extended all through high school if you keep your grade point average at a B or better."

"That school is thirty miles away!" Rose called out, now in sight of the kitchen, having come into the hall. "And they'll require her to stay there from Monday to Friday. It's a boarding school, daughter, like the ones they used to have for Navajo children who lived way out on the reservation."

Ella had grown up a generation too late for the tribal boarding schools, and, living close to Shiprock, she would have never been forced to go anyway. But she'd heard some of the horror stories.

Ella looked back at Dawn. "Are you aware that you'd have to live at this school, not just go to classes?"

"Yeah, but, Mom, that'll make it easier to do homework and stuff. That's why they do it."

"And what if she got sick?" Rose said, coming into the kitchen.

Dawn shrugged and looked at Ella. "Then they'd take me to the doctors in Farmington, I guess. And I'd make sure they called you so you wouldn't get worried. It's not like you couldn't come and check on me, right?"

"Does that mean you want to accept, Dawn?" Ella asked, sensing that she still wasn't getting the whole story.

"You're not really considering sending your daughter to an Anglo school!" Rose said quickly.

"Mom, relax. What do you think they'll do, turn her into a blue-eyed blonde? I'm not saying yes or no to anything yet. First, I want to know what my daughter wants," Ella said.

Rose gave her a look of pure outrage. "How can you even consider this? I just don't understand either of you!" she said, and stormed back out of the kitchen.

Ella knew that her exit had been for show. She'd be willing to bet her last dime that her mother was just out of sight, still close enough to listen to every word.

"Okay, kid. What do *you* want to do?"

"I really like that they have riding lessons, and Sara's my best friend . . . but I'd miss my other friends, and home, too," she added slowly.

"You can take riding lessons here, from Boots and anyone else we can find. You've been doing that for years."

"But they have riding competitions on Saturday that really sound like a lot of fun, Mom," Dawn said, a trace of hesitancy in her voice.

"So is that a yes?" Ella pressed gently. "Or do you want to find out more about it first? There's a good and a bad side to everything in life, so think about it long and hard before you make up your mind."

"So it's up to me?"

Ella smiled. "No, I'm your parent, and I have to make the final decision. I'll have to think about this, too—long and hard."

Dawn nodded. "I thought you'd say that. What about Dad?"

"I'll be talking to him later tonight and I'll tell him about it then," Ella said. And not just about Dawn's school. She also wanted to get a better handle on Roxanne. "Daughter, are you sure you've never heard of Roxanne Dixon?"

Dawn's eyebrows knitted together as she mulled it over. "Dad used to have a girlfriend by the name of Roxie. I never knew her last name. Is that who you mean?"

"I don't know. Tell me about her."

Dawn made a face. "She was always pretending to be nice, Mom, like some girls do just before they tell on you," she said. "For a while she was coming over every weekend. I remember one time we were making cookies and she kept asking me about you."

"And what did you say?"

Dawn shrugged. "I told her what *Shimasání* always says, that one Navajo doesn't speak for another. But that didn't stop her."

"What kind of questions was she asking you?" Ella pressed.

"She wanted to know if you and Reverend Tome were dating a lot, and if you were going to be marrying him," Dawn said, then paused. "But, Mom, she was really weird. Whenever Dad came into the room, she'd stop asking about you. All she'd do then was tell me how pretty I was and stuff like that, just like we were best friends. She thought I was too stupid to know she was making it up for Dad to hear."

"Make sure that if you ever see her at school, you tell an adult immediately," Ella said.

"Okay." Dawn started to leave the room, then stopped. "Mom, I forgot to ask you. What time do you want to start out this weekend?"

It was only Thursday and Ella hadn't even begun to think about the weekend. "Say again?"

Dawn's mouth fell open and her eyes grew wide as saucers. "You didn't forget, did you?"

Ella blinked, searching her mind.

"Don't you remember our trail ride?" Dawn wailed.

"Oh . . . I just started a case," she began, then saw Dawn's shoulders slump. "If there's any way I can get away, you and

I will take off a few hours on Saturday to go riding. But we may have to get a really early start, okay?"

"That's okay. We'd have to be back home by noon anyway. I'm going on that class field trip to the water treatment plant in the afternoon, remember? But we'll have a breakfast ride and it'll be fun!"

"If you're thinking of a simple breakfast, like a snack bar, then yes," Ella said with a smile. Her daughter knew how to push better than anyone else on the planet.

"Okay, simple," Dawn said, her eyes dancing. "And we'll take apples in our saddlebags for Wind and Chieftain."

"Sounds like a plan," Ella said, her thoughts already on Kevin. She shouldn't wait any longer, it was already nine forty-five in Washington. She'd call him next.

As soon as her daughter went into her room to play on her computer, Ella picked up the phone and dialed Kevin's cell. She got him on the first ring.

"What's up?" Kevin asked, immediately picking up on the tautness of her voice.

"Several things. First, our daughter's been offered a full scholarship to Valley Academy, starting next semester."

"That's great! I went to Valley. I'm still on the board there too. Maybe that's why they took a close look at Dawn."

"Wait—you've been lobbying for this?"

"Not really, no. I assumed you and your mother wouldn't let her leave for boarding school until she got much older. But the only reason I stayed a trustee was in hopes that we could get Dawn in there someday."

"I haven't made any decision on this yet. It's one of the reasons I'm calling."

"If this scholarship just fell into her lap, it may be because they're looking to add more minority students to their enrollment. Face it, offering scholarships to minorities also generates good PR. But Valley Academy has stiff requirements. They only accept students with a three-point-five grade point average or above—so Dawn wasn't offered this just because of me—or you."

"Two scholarships were awarded—one to our daughter and one to her friend, Sara," Ella said. "But Dawn isn't sure she wants to go yet, though the horseback riding angle really appeals to her."

"Wait a second. You're not letting her make a decision like this on her own, are you? She's just a child. Graduating from Valley can open all kinds of doors for her. With the credentials that school has to offer, if Dawn keeps her grades up, she'll be able to get into any college she chooses. Ella, this is a terrific opportunity."

"I know. That's the only reason I'm seriously considering it."

"What's bothering you? Are you worried because this means she'll be going to a boarding school, or because it's going to have mostly Anglo students and it's off the Rez?" he asked.

"The first reason. I'd like to keep her closer to home because she's still very young, and I don't know if she's ready for this. Some of those kids, Anglo or not, come from very wealthy families. Snobbery crosses racial lines, and some of the privileged kids may look down on someone in my income level who would never have been able to afford the tuition. Also keep in mind that Dawn has never come face to face with racial prejudice of any kind—at least not in school. I'm not sure if she's prepared for that."

"There was some of that when I was there eons ago," he admitted after a long pause. "But it really wasn't all that bad. It was more along the lines of class snobbery than racial snobbery. From what I've heard here and there, that hasn't changed, but Dawn won't be alone. The scholarship kids will probably hang out together." He paused, then continued. "This is a golden opportunity for her, Ella, and it's practically being handed to her on a platter."

"Kev, life isn't about what you're handed. It's about what you strive for. To really succeed in life, Dawn will need to find a dream. Then she'll need the hope and courage it'll take to follow her heart and make her dream come true."

"Oh, please. To really get anywhere in this world what she'll need is *connections*. That's the only way to get ahead. Right now she dreams of being just like you. But I'd like to see her get further ahead and I'm sure you would, too."

Ella swallowed back the surge of anger that suddenly filled her. This was one of the many reasons Kevin and she hadn't made it. "I love my job, Kevin," Ella said quietly. "I dreamed of becoming a law enforcement officer for years, but that doesn't mean it's right for her. She'll have to find her own way in life. I'll support whatever decision she makes when the time comes, but you're getting way ahead of yourself."

"Valley is an important step. Don't kid yourself," Kevin added.

"I'll let you know what we end up deciding. But I won't push her. Should our daughter decide that she doesn't want to go, that'll be the end of it," Ella said flatly.

Kevin had made a good point and she knew it, but the truth was that, in her heart, she wasn't ready to let Dawn go. Yet, if it turned out that her daughter really wanted to attend Valley, she wouldn't stand in her way. Though she'd be worried about Dawn constantly, she wouldn't prevent her from following her heart.

"There's something else you and I need to talk about, Kevin." First Ella related the news about Dawn's science fair project, then she told him about Roxanne and their run-in at the school, withholding only the gossip she'd heard via Justine.

Kevin said nothing for a long time. "Thanks for not giving Roxie my cell phone number. What we had—such as it was—is completely over."

"Yet she still showed up at Dawn's school. Think hard. Could Roxanne Dixon become a threat in any way to our daughter?"

"No, I don't think so, but she may have it in for you," he said. "Here's the story. I stopped dating Roxanne about a month before I left for Washington. She'd become much too possessive, trying to keep tabs on me round the clock, and calling me constantly at work. I also found out she had a problem with alcohol. The more tense things got between us, the more she seemed to drink. Then about a week before I left, she showed up drunk at my office. I had to threaten to call the police before she finally left.

"After I came to D.C. she began sending me e-mails to our office here, two or three a day, all marked 'personal' in the subject line. I never read any of them, which is probably why she tried tricking you into giving her my home telephone number." He paused then added, "By the way, don't give her my private e-mail address either, okay?"

"No problem. By any chance do you happen to know why Roxanne left the department?" Ella asked. "Was it because of her drinking?"

"That would be my guess, but I don't know that for a fact," Kevin said. "I think she mentioned something about a supervisor who had it in for her. But it was no loss for the department, believe me. Between her drinking and psychological problems, she's far from stable."

"Okay."

"If she gives our daughter a problem, let me know," Kevin said.

"What could you possibly do from so far away?"

"Let's just say I wouldn't go through legal channels to

make my point. I'm a lawyer, so I know a piece of paper won't stop a nutcase," he said in a hard voice.

Ella didn't respond. She knew all she needed now.

"So what else is going on back home? You still dating that preacher?" he asked, attempting to sound casual, but not quite succeeding.

"Yeah, but not so much when I'm bogged down on a tough case like I am now," she answered honestly.

He laughed. "How's he like being put off?"

"I don't think he even notices. He's busy with his own church work anyway."

"Maybe that's the kind of man you need," he said after a long pause. "But you'll always come in second to his calling. You're aware of that, right?"

"We both have other responsibilities. That's why it works," Ella answered. She'd thought that she was past history as far as Kevin was concerned, but judging from the tone of his voice now, she wasn't so sure anymore.

"What about you? Dating anyone new?" she asked.

There was a pause. "There are lots of women here who find a Native American interesting, and I'm dating a few. But no one special."

Ella said nothing, wondering if maybe the real reason Kevin had left for D.C. was to get away from her. Perhaps it had been his way of moving on—physically and figuratively. Unfortunately, that had also meant that Dawn wouldn't be able to spend as much time with her father. Used to finding answers, Ella thought about the situation but, as she did, realized that some things just couldn't be fixed.

EIGHT

✖ ✖ ✖

After Ella hung up, Rose came into the kitchen and went to the stove, turning on the gas under the teakettle.

"That woman from her father's past may become a problem for your daughter. With that in mind, the last thing you should be considering is sending her away from home."

"Or maybe it's the first thing," Ella whispered. "You've got your own responsibilities these days, and Boots isn't always available to babysit at the house. The last few times, she took my daughter to her home because she had to work on her computer and finish some papers for school. A weekday boarding school would ensure that my kid's kept safe."

Rose stared at her. "How could some stranger possibly guarantee she'd be safe?"

"They have *very* good security there. The daughter of a senator goes to that school, as well as the daughters of several of the state's wealthiest businessmen. They can't afford to slop around."

Rose took a deep breath then let it out slowly. "I can stay at home more to be with your daughter," she said. "You can't, so that leaves me."

"This isn't just up to you or me, Mom. My daughter will have a say in this, too."

Rose sat down heavily across the table from her. "It's difficult to know what the right thing to do is in a case like this. All I can tell you is that my heart wants her here. I'd hoped that you would settle down with Reverend Tome and start a new life. But the more time goes by, the less I think that's ever going to happen."

"The reason things work between us, Mom, is because neither one of us makes demands the other can't meet."

Rose nodded slowly. "His God will always be there, inside, to comfort him. It was that way with your father, too. But the law won't be there for you forever. Your daughter will also grow up sooner than you realize and leave to start her own life. Then you'll wake up one day to find yourself alone and looking back at what might have been."

Ella nodded slowly, realizing the truth of what Rose had said. "That might be so, but I can't rush into a relationship just so I won't end up alone someday."

Rose sighed. "Maybe that's just as well. Right now nothing should be more important to you than your daughter. You should try to do more things with her, like this trail ride you have scheduled. Memories like those will last a lifetime."

"I'm looking forward to our trail ride, too, even though we'll have to leave really early."

"Enjoy her now. There'll come a time when she'll want to be on her own and won't want you around. When she's a teenager . . ."

Ella's phone rang, and holding up one hand, she signaled her mother to wait, and answered the call.

"Ella, I've got some very interesting news," Justine said. "I'm on my way to your house to talk about it. Is that okay with you?"

"Sure. Come on over. But don't keep me guessing. What's up?"

"After I checked the area where you got jumped, I decided to call Del, the mechanic, and have him with me while I checked the impound area vehicles. When we got around to the Dodge George Charley was driving we discovered why George ran off the road and into the brush and trees. The brakes failed and it was the only way he had to keep the truck from flying off the side of the mountain. Even if he could have avoided the chain saw accident, with no brakes and a load of firewood, he would have crashed the truck coming down the mountain."

"And the same fate would have extended to anyone riding with him, like Ervin Benally," Ella said. "Were the brakes definitely tampered with, or could it have been a mechanical problem?"

"It was no accident. Apparently, while George was distracted cutting wood, someone popped the hood and removed nearly all the fluid from the brake reservoir. There were smudges where the perp had lifted the hood up, but no prints, so he must have had gloves on. Del said the suspect probably used some kind of suction device, like a turkey baster, to empty the reservoir of fluid. There were no leaks in the brake lines or system at all—Del inspected everything and took photos with my little digital camera. He even did a pressure test. The cap to the brake fluid reservoir was in place, screwed on. No fingerprints were there either, just smudges again where the surface dust and oils were rubbed away."

"Wouldn't there have been enough fluid already in the system to allow George to slow the vehicle?" Ella asked.

"I asked Del, and he said there would have been a little braking power at first, but not nearly enough. With the weight of the truck, the firewood, a downhill road, and a panic-stricken driver bleeding like a stuck pig, George was lucky he didn't go over the edge."

"Now that can of brake fluid is starting to make sense. Was it empty or full?" Ella asked.

"Full, with the seal under the cap still in place. So you think the guy tonight was planning on topping off the brake fluid to cover up the tampering?" Justine asked.

"That would be my guess. We got lucky tonight, or we'd never have known the truth about those brakes."

Ella thought about it for a moment, then continued. "This puts a whole new spin on George Charley's death. The connection between that incident and what's happening with Ervin seems to be getting stronger. You've gotten all this down, on the record, right?" Ella added.

"Documented it all. The physical evidence is pretty cut and dried, except I didn't get anything but smudges on that can. Either way, I guess we can't release the truck back to the Benallys."

"Nope. You've done a great job, Justine, shining a whole new light on all this. And this means we've got to focus on the people at StarTalk."

Just then, Ella's phone beeped, signaling another call coming in. "Hang on, Justine, call-waiting just kicked in."

It was the station. "If you're up to it, the watch commander wants you to handle a ten–sixty-five," the operator said, giving Ella the address.

Recognizing the code for a hostage/kidnapping, Ella immediately notified Justine, who was almost at the house, and got ready to roll.

"Mom, I've gotta go. Sorry." She turned around, not seeing Dawn. She shouted, "I've got a call, daughter. I'll see you later. Love you. You too, Mom."

Rose managed a smile, and Ella heard a faint "bye" from the back of the house. Grabbing her pistol and holster from the top of the bookcase, Ella rushed out as Justine pulled up.

Justine was on the radio, getting details on the same call, as Ella slipped inside the SUV. "That address, out near Long Lake, it's George Charley's home, right?" Ella asked, fastening her seat belt.

"Yeah. According to the dispatcher, there was fighting going on in the background. Dispatch heard the sound of something crashing and a woman screaming. The caller said they were under attack, then the call ended abruptly. Dispatch tried to reach the caller again, but couldn't get through."

"Who called it in?"

"They never got a name, but it was a man."

"Maybe George Charley *was* murdered, and now someone's after his wife," Ella said. "The failed attempt to cover up the brake tampering might have forced them into action."

"But if that's the case, who phoned in for help?"

"Relatives, or maybe her neighbor, the guy whose truck was there when we dropped off Marilyn. We considered the possibility that the pair was having an affair, remember?"

Ella called the station, verified that there was more backup on the way, then glanced at the speedometer. Justine was flying south down the nearly deserted highway.

Less than three minutes later, around eight-thirty, Dispatch contacted them again. "We traced the number and it belongs to Wallace Curtis. He's the Charleys' closest neighbor."

Turning off the main highway, Justine headed west, raising clouds of dust, visible despite the darkness, in the side mirrors with the emergency lights running. Knowing the route, she made good time.

Justine slowed as she approached a junction where two secondary roads fed into the one they were traveling. Lights of any kind were few out here. That was why their unit had been equipped with a set of new, expensive headlights that had great range.

Justine had slowed to make the turn when suddenly a vehicle popped over the ridge in front of them. It came straight at them, right down the center of the road. Its high beams were blinding them as it closed in fast.

"Hang on!" Justine inched to the right, honked the horn, and hit the brakes.

Ella gripped the door handle hard, instinctively ducking down. Their SUV slipped down on the right as the passenger side tires dropped into the low drainage ditch.

"Gotta keep straight . . ." Justine mumbled, fighting to keep the vehicle from swinging to the right. The SUV fishtailed, but she managed to keep the rear end from swinging all the way around.

A mental image of them rolling flashed in Ella's mind. She managed a one word curse as the pickup rattled by, barely missing them. The glare ended, then flashed on again almost instantly.

"Oh crap, not again!" Justine yelled as a second set of headlights raced around a curve in the road and bore down on them. This time, however, the vehicle stayed to the left. As it whipped by, Ella saw it was another pickup, only this one had a wooden stock rack.

"Those idiots!" Justine yelled, easing completely back onto the road now. "You okay?" She looked over at Ella.

Ella sat back up. "Now I am. Good driving, partner." She looked in the side mirror at the fading taillights behind them. "Wish we could nail their butts for hot-rodding, but we've got other priorities right now."

While Justine drove, Ella used the unit's radio to report the two pickups racing down the mountain, but all she'd had was a brief look. Other than the relative age of each truck, the only detail she could give Dispatch was that the second one had a wooden stock rack.

They were almost at Marilyn Charley's home when Dispatch contacted them again. "Go to the Sheep Springs Clinic instead. Wallace Curtis and Marilyn Charley are there now, being treated for wounds sustained during a home invasion."

Ella looked at Justine. "We must have missed them at that last junction. Have you heard of any related crimes? I can't recall any reports of a home invasion, not in the recent past," Ella asked. "Are any of the gangs active again?"

Justine shook her head, braked quickly to a stop, then reversed directions with a three-point turn and headed back down the road. "None of the local gangs have been active for the past six months or so. The Fierce Ones have been keeping them on a tight leash," she said, referring to a vigilante group made up of traditionalists and new traditionalists. The latter group was made up of Navajos who followed the old traditional customs, but enjoyed modern amenities like satellite dishes and air-conditioning.

"I have a feeling this is tied to George Charley's death, so stay sharp," Ella said. "We haven't connected all the dots yet, and what we don't know *can* hurt us."

A short time later they arrived at the tiny clinic, located in relatively flat terrain east of the foothills. Despite the fact that it was close to ten at night, the facility was still open—a good thing considering the next medical facility was many miles away. The door was unlocked, so Ella walked directly to the front counter and pulled out her badge.

The young-looking medical technician in colorful scrub top and pants looked at Ella's ID, then gestured toward one of three small rooms behind her. "Mrs. Charley's being treated by the doctor in the room on the left. She's in serious condition from head injuries apparently sustained during a beating. An ambulance is on its way from Shiprock. She'll have to be transported to the hospital there for treatment once she's stabilized."

"And the man who came in with her?" Ella asked.

"Mr. Curtis is in better shape. He's in the center room being treated by the nurse. He asked to speak to the police as soon as you all got here, but let me look in and see if the nurse says he's ready." The tech led Ella and Justine down the hall, then motioned for them to wait outside the room. "I'll be back in a moment."

A short time later, the tech emerged. "Go on in."

Ella stepped around her and saw Wallace Curtis sitting up on the examining table. Ella brought out her ID as she entered the room.

Wallace's boyish face was badly bruised, one eye nearly swollen shut. As he stood up, he favored his right side. Ella noticed that beneath his opened and torn shirt his ribs had been taped. His skinned and bloodied knuckles told her that he'd put up a fight.

Ella introduced herself. "I understand that you're ready to make a statement."

He nodded. "I'm Wallace Curtis. I live about a mile away from Marilyn Charley's house. Marilyn and I are . . . friends. For the past day or so we both had the feeling that we were being watched. We'd assumed it was one of George's relatives. . . ." He lapsed into a long silence and stared at the tile floor.

"Did you go over and confront them?" Ella pressed at last. In most cases she wouldn't have interrupted, but it was clear Wallace wasn't a traditionalist and she needed answers as quickly as possible.

"No. Truth is, I felt sorry for them. George's death left us all in shock. Marilyn had been planning to ask George for a divorce, but after his sudden death, we put all our plans on hold. George's family deserved our respect."

"Were you two having an affair?"

He nodded. "We didn't plan it. It just happened after we met at the bank where I work." He took a deep breath then let it out slowly. "It's complicated."

"Tell me what you think led to this beating," Ella pressed.

"I don't know for sure, but I think George's relatives blamed Marilyn for his death. Maybe it was because they knew about me being in the picture. I don't know. When we realized we were being watched, I started to worry that they might do something to her. I talked her into moving in with me for a while so we could watch each other's backs."

Minutes ticked by but Wallace said nothing else. He simply stared at his hands. Ella cleared her throat and he slowly continued.

"We were right in the middle of packing up her stuff when four men drove up to the house. They arrived in two pickups, one with a wooden stock rack. At first we thought it was George's relatives, or maybe some of his friends from work. But when I saw that they were wearing hoods, I locked the front door and tried to call for help. Before I finished the call, they kicked their way in."

Realizing that the pickups were probably the same ones that had run Justine and her off the road a short while ago, Ella pressed him for more of a description. She managed to get the make and color of each, but he'd never seen the license plates.

"These men, were they wearing gloves?" Ella asked him.

He thought about it. "Three did. The one who landed a punch to my jaw was wearing leather gloves. The other two had some cheap cloth work gloves. The man who came in last and did nothing but watch wasn't wearing any gloves."

"Any idea who any of them were? Did you recognize any voices?"

"They told us they were with the Fierce Ones and that

they knew George's death hadn't been an accident. They tried to get Marilyn to confess to having killed him so she could be with me. They knew George had been drinking beer that day, too, and kept trying to get her to admit that we'd attacked him with the chain saw, knowing he would have had a hard time defending himself. At one point they even accused her of having drugged him so he'd be an even easier target."

The theory was remarkably similar to the one she'd discussed with Big Ed. What surprised her was that the Fierce Ones had picked up on it, and that they'd also found out about the beer. "When they accused her of murder, what did she say to defend herself?"

"She denied it, but the more she did that, the angrier they got. That's when they really turned on her. I managed to take down one of the guys, but before I could help Marilyn, the other two jumped me. I don't remember much after that. When I came to, the house was empty, and Marilyn was bleeding and unconscious. They'd stomped on my phone and I couldn't call for help, so I carefully moved her to my truck and came here."

"Think back. Did you notice anything that might give us a lead—a tattoo, a limp, or anything like that?"

He considered it for several long moments, then shook his head. "I don't remember anything like that, but I was too busy trying to stay alive and help Marilyn."

"What made them think that Marilyn had killed George, and how did they know George had taken liquor with him? Did they ever say how they got their information?"

"No, but I figured most of it had probably come from George's relatives. They knew about his drinking and that he and Marilyn had been having problems."

"And about your affair?"

He nodded. "At first they didn't see that as a big deal. George had been seeing a woman from Farmington, so when Marilyn and I hooked up, George's traditionalist family saw it as one way to restore the balance between them. But when George stopped seeing his friend and Marilyn kept seeing me, that changed things. Everyone sided with George. Marilyn's own relatives live very far away, so there was no one to support her but me."

Ella nodded, understanding what he was saying. But it still didn't explain how the Fierce Ones had known George had been drinking beer.

"You said that they kicked down the door?" Ella continued.

"Yeah. Go see for yourself. And if you catch them, I want to know who they are. I don't care how anyone spins it, hoods are for cowards."

"If we catch them, you'll see them in court," Ella said.

"No one's been taking the Fierce Ones seriously lately," Wallace said, gingerly touching the edge of his swollen lips. "I think they're trying hard to change that."

He'd echoed her thoughts, but Ella said nothing that would confirm or deny it. "You're pretty sure that *you* weren't their primary target?"

"Absolutely. They were focused on Marilyn."

"Are you planning to go home tonight?"

He shook his head. "The doctor advised me to spend the night. Tomorrow, I'm going to my brother's and staying with him until I heal."

"We'll want to go by your home and check it out. They might have left a message there for you."

"Beating the crap out of me wasn't enough?" Wallace shot back. "There's a key taped inside the cowbell by the front door."

After she left the room, Ella spotted Justine over by the counter, talking to the tech and the nurse. Not wanting to interrupt her, Ella went to the exit doors and waited there.

Justine joined her a few minutes later. "Marilyn regained consciousness briefly while her vital signs were being checked. She told the nurse that she thought her husband's uncle was behind what happened to her. Marilyn thinks he's got ties to the Fierce Ones."

"We'll have to check that out tomorrow." Ella then told Justine about the pickups they'd encountered.

"If only we'd known the bad guys were right in our faces, we could have rounded them up then."

"There's something else," Ella said, telling Justine how the Fierce Ones had known about the alcohol George had consumed. "And the Fierce Ones were also spouting off the *same* theory I had at the beginning—that Marilyn had found a way to increase the chances of an accident by drugging George, then taking the chain saw to him."

Justine stared at her. "Are you telling me that we have a leak in the department? But who?"

"That's a *very* good question. Big Ed will need to know about this as soon as possible. I'll call him tonight. Our next stop is securing the crime scene itself. We'll do a preliminary tonight then return in the morning. Call Neskahi and Tache and have them meet us at Marilyn Charley's house."

"What about the removal of most of the brake fluid in the truck? Only you and I know about that—and Del at the station," Justine said. "When Barbara Benally came to look at the vehicle, none of us knew about that problem."

"Obviously the Fierce Ones didn't know about that either because it didn't come up. So let's keep that info to ourselves for a while and see if it surfaces outside the PD."

They got underway after checking on Marilyn. Though badly injured and heavily sedated to help her with the pain, she was expected to make it.

Once in the cruiser, Ella took a few more aspirins, and glanced at Justine. "We need to find out which Fierce Ones were involved in what happened," Ella said. "What gets me is that they undoubtedly don't realize what a stupid move this was. By taking matters into their hands, all they've done is divert us from what we should be doing."

"It looks like they're out to recapture power on the Rez again."

"I think so, too, but no matter how they define themselves, they're nothing more than vigilantes. They need to be behind bars," Ella said.

Though it was close to eleven by now, Ella called Big Ed next. Though he was used to getting calls all hours of the night, she apologized for maybe waking up Claire, his wife.

Ella filled him in on everything, including their possible mole, and tonight's incident at the impound yard, including the brakes issue. The chief listened intently. When Ella, at long last, stopped speaking, Big Ed didn't respond right away. Ella had known Big Ed for a long time and knew that wasn't a good sign.

"No details were released publicly other than the fact that Mr. Charley died in what appeared to be an accident," he said at last, stifling a yawn at the end. "Do you recall seeing anyone, civilian or staff, nearby when we spoke in my office about George Charley's death?"

"No, but I was focused on my report," Ella answered honestly.

"What about your team? Could any of them have passed the story on?"

"I trust my team with my life," Ella said firmly. "There's *no way* they were involved. There must be another answer."

"The Fierce Ones have contacts everywhere. Even your brother was a member at one time, I recall. I trust you and him completely, so don't take that the wrong way, but do *not* overlook your own team as you search for answers," he said flatly. "One more thing. Your idea of keeping the truck brake problems under wraps is a good one. I'll talk to Del at the garage myself and remind him to keep it quiet. We might be able to use this somehow to ferret out the snitch. Too bad the weasel who clobbered you with the can of brake fluid got away. He might have led us to the others."

Ella hung up and took a deep breath as the chief's comment about Clifford replayed itself in her mind. Years ago, her brother had tried to be a voice of reason for the Fierce Ones, working among them to rein in their methods. But when his efforts had proved futile, he'd left.

"Do you know anyone currently in the Fierce Ones?" Ella asked Justine.

"No, but they don't exactly advertise their affiliation. I can nose around if you want."

"Do it," Ella said, her tone somber.

"There's more you haven't told me, isn't there?" Justine asked, reading Ella's expression.

"The chief thinks that someone in our team may have been responsible for the leak that resulted in this beating."

"*No way.*"

"My sentiments exactly, but we better find answers fast. Big Ed won't be satisfied with assurances—and neither will I."

NINE

✖ ✖ ✖

Ella and Justine arrived at the scene just as Tache set up the floodlights. It was just after midnight, but there was still a lot of work to be done before they could call it a night. Neskahi and Tache were busy taking more photographs and sifting through the mess.

Putting her gloves on, Ella went inside, noting the ruined lock on the front door. There was a footprint on the shattered door, something she knew Ralph would have already photographed.

The interior of the living room/kitchen was in shambles and looked worse with the bright moonlight filtering through the window. From what she could see the fight had been as deadly as Wallace had described. Furniture had been overturned and broken, and glass from picture frames and vases lay scattered over the floor and the oval area rug. She could also see blood splatters and an indentation in the Sheetrock wall where someone's head had been bashed in, if experience was any indication.

"I'm getting measurements from that boot print just below the front door lock," Justine said. "I'll be able to construct the shoe size soon from that."

"Good, and see if any other shoe impressions match up with those Nikes from the Charley scene. I also want you to let me know if you find any traces of blood that don't belong to either of our victims. The same goes for hair samples, tire tracks, boot tracks—the works. Pay particular attention to any prints you find, particularly on objects that might have been handled by the assailants. According to Curtis, one of the participants wasn't wearing gloves."

They'd been at the scene less than an hour when they heard the sound of approaching hoof beats. Ella stepped out into the bright moonlight and was surprised to see a teenaged girl, maybe sixteen or seventeen, sitting astride a pinto.

Ella walked over to meet her, reminding herself of the ride she'd promised Dawn this weekend. "I'm sorry, but you can't come any closer," Ella said. "This is now a crime scene."

The young girl nodded. "I know what happened."

"How?" Ella pressed instantly.

"I heard people talking at the clinic. I was there earlier with my *shizhé'é*, my grandfather," she added.

"What did you hear?"

"That Marilyn's badly hurt. They broke in here and tried to make her confess to hurting her husband. But she didn't do anything."

"What's your name?" Ella said, stepping closer. The teen slid down off the horse and stood beside it, holding the reins lightly. "I'm Carol James. I just wish I'd known what was going to happen. I saw them drive up."

"Who did you see?"

"Four guys in two old trucks, one gray, the other tan. They came up the road, and I figured they were just relatives. I didn't even think twice about it—till later."

"Did you see their faces, or notice anything in particular about the trucks?"

"Trucks are trucks to me," she said with a shrug. "The

guys . . . well, they were riding in the cab. One lit a cigarette and I saw his face for a second or two. He didn't seem that much older than me, which made me think they were nephews rather than brothers or cousins. Then the driver stopped for a few seconds right in the middle of the road and turned on the cab light. I think they were probably checking a map, but I don't really know. Just a few seconds later, a second truck joined them, pulling up beside the first one. That driver opened the door and stepped out to go talk to the others. At that point, both cab lights were on."

"And you saw them more clearly then?"

She nodded. "At least one of them had long hair, tied back," she answered. "Two of them had baseball caps, one black, the other brown, with the bills forward, like they wore them for work, not play. And one was wearing a jacket with a shearling collar. You know the kind."

Ella nodded. "What color was the jacket?"

"Blue, like in jeans. The others just had plaid shirts on, different colors, I think. Blue, red, green, like that."

"Did they call out to you?"

She shook her head. "I don't think they even knew I was there. Their trucks were rattling so much on the bumps, they couldn't have heard my horse."

"What about license plates? Did you happen to get that?"

She shook her head. "Maybe yellow, like New Mexico? I couldn't say. I was looking at the guys."

"Did any of the guys especially catch your eye?" Ella asked, playing a hunch.

She stared at the ground, then shifted from foot to foot. "The passenger in the gray truck, the second one," she said quietly. "I just thought he looked, you know, cute. He was the one with the long hair."

"What appealed to you about him?"

"I could tell he was a big guy. Even sitting, he was a lot taller than the others. His skin seemed really light, too, so maybe he was only half Navajo. But I don't know that for sure. He was just . . . interesting."

"Thanks for your help. But tell me. What are you doing out at this time of night?"

"When my parents come home late and start arguing and yelling, I usually take off. I can't sleep with all the racket and my horse Warrior's better company."

"You really shouldn't go riding by yourself this late at night," Ella said. "It isn't safe—for you or your horse."

"It's a clear night and there's lots of moonlight once your eyes adjust. We'll be fine. Warrior and I take care of each other."

Ella couldn't help but wonder if Carol's parents had a problem with alcohol. That was all too common on the reservation. Though liquor sales were banned on Navajo land, it was a short drive to the adjoining communities.

"If you remember anything else, will you call and let me know?" Ella asked, giving her a card.

"Sure."

After giving Ella her address, the young woman rode away. Ella watched her, lost in thought. It was amazing how secure some girls felt on a horse. Dawn was the same way.

A moment later Tache came out and caught her eye. "You better come in and see this," he said. "The Fierce Ones left a message."

She followed Tache down the hall into the master bedroom. Searching for evidence, one of her team had tossed back the chenille bedspread. Spray painted in red on the sheet below was the message, "We'll be back."

"They've been watching too many Arnold Schwarzenegger movies," Ella said.

Turning to Tache, Ella gave him a description of the long-haired, light-skinned man the young woman had seen. "Does he sound familiar to you?"

He thought about it for a few seconds. "I remember seeing someone who fits that description at my brother-in-law's place months ago. He's Henry Brownhat's son, Arthur. He's got long hair, light skin, and his eyes are pale—gray or hazel, I think. He hasn't lived on the Rez for long and from what I hear, he's bad news, Ella. He likes trouble. That entire family is more at home in jail than out of it."

"We need to find someone who can verify that Arthur's a member of the Fierce Ones," Ella said as Justine came to join them.

"I'm your man then," Tache said. "My brother-in-law's a member. If I push, I'm sure I can get an answer from him."

"Do you think you can get us any additional information about what happened here?" She hated the thought, but Ella suddenly wondered if Tache would turn out to be their leak.

"I'll try, but I can't promise anything. My brother-in-law doesn't trust me anymore than I do him."

Ella glanced at Justine as Tache moved away to take close-ups of the spray-painted message. "We should go pay Jimmy Levaldo a visit. He was the head of the Fierce Ones last time I heard," Ella said.

Overhearing them, Tache stopped boxing up evidence bags and glanced over. "Not anymore. And no, I didn't hear it from my brother-in-law. My sister, who knows Levaldo's neighbor, told me."

"Who's the new head?"

"According to what she said, their new leader is a younger man, a new traditionalist. His name is Delbert John."

"Get me an address from Dispatch," Ella asked him, continuing the search for prints.

A moment later, Tache handed her a piece of paper from the notepad he normally kept in his shirt pocket.

Ella looked at it. It wasn't exactly an address. It was mostly directions, which wasn't all that unusual on the Rez, where many of the dirt roads leading to the homes had no official names. "This is an area of scatter homes, right?" The term signified the nontract homes built by the Navajo Housing Authority.

"I believe so," Tache answered.

"We'll go pay him a visit tomorrow." Ella checked the time and realized it was almost two in the morning now. "I should have said later today."

"Do you want us to check out Wallace Curtis' home before we finish up?" Justine asked.

"Yeah." Ella remembered her brief talk with the battered man. Though he hadn't said so, Wallace was obviously afraid that he hadn't heard the last of the Fierce Ones, particularly now that he'd spoken to the police.

"We'll go take a look. If they broke into his place, too, we'll arrange to leave an officer posted there tonight to preserve the scene until we return in the morning," Ella said. "But we'll have to process the area outside the house before we call it quits. No one can predict the weather and we can't afford to lose evidence to Mother Nature. Unfortunately, we're all beat by now, and prone to mistakes."

"Think we should work in teams and double-check each other?"

Ella nodded, then yawned. "Good idea."

They drove to the Curtis' home and found ample evidence of a B and E. After a quick look inside to make sure there was no immediate danger, like a broken gas line or electrical device, they processed the grounds outside the residence. It was nearly three in the morning by the time they wrapped up. Justine drove Ella home first.

"Pick me up at around eight. We'll finish processing the crime scene, and then go visit Arthur Brownhat and Delbert John," Ella said, getting out of the car.

As Justine drove away, Ella stood in the bright moonlight gazing at their newly rebuilt home. Everything on the reservation was changing. Even her own family seemed to be in a state of flux these days. Yet Rose and her daughter remained at the heart of everything that gave meaning to her life. Family ties were the one thing she could always count on. That would never change. Taking comfort from that, she walked inside.

Ella woke up at around seven—and not by choice. She could hear her daughter's radio going full blast while Dawn got ready for school.

Ella opened one eye then the other and groaned. She would have traded twenty years of her life for another few hours of sleep. Oddly enough, the music from her daughter's room got even louder. Tossing the covers aside, hoping the cold air would give her some badly needed energy, Ella stood and put on her robe. As she walked to the bathroom, she felt for the bump on her head, and realized the swelling was almost gone. She'd been lucky.

Twenty minutes later, dressed and ready to begin the day, Ella joined her daughter for breakfast. As she watched Dawn fix herself some oatmeal, Ella realized just how quickly Dawn was growing up.

"Mommmmm! You're *not* listening!" Dawn cried out.

"I am. You were talking about our trail ride this weekend," Ella answered.

"We're still going, right?"

"I'm planning on it," Ella said. "But remember we'll have to get up *really* early, kiddo."

Dawn launched herself into her arms. "Great!"

Rose came in and smiled, seeing them together. "Good morning," she said, filling the teakettle with water and placing it on the stove.

"I heard what happened to the new widow," Rose commented, avoiding the use of names. Names had power, and were not to be used lightly.

Ella stared at her mom. It never ceased to amaze her how quickly word traveled on the Rez, and how well-connected Rose was. "It appears the Fierce Ones had a hand in what happened."

Rose sat down across the table from Ella, who was finishing off a piece of toast. Just then a loud car horn blew and Dawn jumped up. "Gotta go! It's Sara's mom. She's taking us to school this week."

Ella hugged her daughter and kissed her good-bye. Dawn raced out the front door, leaving it half open as usual, and Ella went over to close it. "She's a bundle of energy in the morning. I wish I could harness some of that for myself," she said, laughing.

"At her age, *you* were just like her," Rose said, then lapsed into a long silence.

After fixing herself a second cup of tea, Ella looked across the table at her mother. "What's bothering you, Mom? Are you still thinking about the possibility that Dawn may go away to school?"

"In my day, the boarding schools the Anglos set up for us were just *horrible*. This one's different, I know, but I can't imagine her really *wanting* to leave home, even for those fancy horseback riding lessons."

"Mom, I don't want her at Valley either," Ella admitted softly. "But if she thought for one second that I was against her going, it would suddenly become the one thing she wanted to do more than anything else in the world."

Rose nodded. "I know. In that way, she's just like you. You

had an independent streak like that, too. I remember your father tried to push you into going to his church, but the more he did, the more you fought it. When I tried to teach you traditionalist ways, you didn't want any part of that either."

Ella smiled, recalling how badly her mother had wanted her to become a traditionalist. Rose's methods had been subtle, but she'd felt like a piece of Turkish taffy back then, always caught between her parents. "But it's different for my kid. That's what I find puzzling. She's not in the middle of anything she has to rebel against."

"Isn't she? Her father wants her to grow up like an Anglo. Yet here at home she's been taught Navajo ways."

"But I'm more of a moderate, Mom. I'm part of the Anglo world and the Navajo."

"And that's what you want for her, too," Rose observed, a trace of regret in her voice.

"It's the path with the most options, Mom."

"We each believe that our own path is best," Rose answered with a sad smile. "Like you, your daughter will eventually make her own choices. But she loves you and, whether or not you realize it, she's already feeling much the same pressures you did."

Ella considered her mother's words. "Let's see how things play out with this scholarship thing, Mom. Truth is, I may yet say no. I don't think I'm ready to wake up and not hear her voice in the morning."

Rose smiled and nodded. "Neither am I."

Hearing a car drive up, Ella glanced out the window. "That's my partner. I better get going."

Ella took the last swallow of tea from her cup, grabbed her gun and belt from the top of the bookcase, and hurried out the door. Today she'd be facing off with the Fierce Ones.

TEN

—— ✖ ✖ ✖ ——

It was barely 8:30 A.M. when they set out. Ella glanced at Justine. "You look more awake than I feel."

"Take some coffee from my Thermos. That'll wake you up for sure."

Ella reached for the silver container. After pouring some of the thick syrupy liquid into the cup, she glanced at her partner. "Holy cow, girl. It's the consistency of motor oil."

Justine nodded. "But it works. I couldn't clear my thoughts this morning, and considering what's on our agenda, I had to find a way to do that fast. I put an extra scoop in the percolator and that's what came out," she said.

Ella took a cautious sip. It looked lethal but it didn't taste bad. "Let's go to Wallace Curtis' home first," Ella said.

"Will Arthur Brownhat be our second stop?"

Ella considered it. "There are several people I'd like to question today, including the old leader of the Fierce Ones, Jimmy Levaldo. Levaldo was replaced, so he may be more inclined to talk to us. Last time I saw him, I recall him mentioning something about a younger group coming up the ranks. But the crime scene's our first priority. After that, we'll decide who to see next."

"Tache mentioned Delbert John last night, so I ran his name before coming to pick you up. There's not much on him. He was arrested for drunk and disorderly once about fifteen years ago. That's it. He's been clean ever since. He's thirty-seven and works construction as a framer for Navajo Housing."

"Find out where he's working at the moment," Ella said.

"Already done," Justine answered. "He's at a job site less than two miles away from Wallace Curtis' place. They're building a scatter home there."

They arrived at Wallace Curtis' home a short time later. The young officer who'd been keeping watch from his unit climbed out to greet them.

"Anything we should know about?" Ella asked, joining the patrol officer on loan from the station at Window Rock.

He shook his head. "Other than rabbits and a curious skunk, it's been real quiet."

"Okay, thanks. Good job. Go home and get some sleep," Ella said, noticing how tired he was.

Ella and Justine went up to the door that they'd wired shut last night, a necessity because the latch had been destroyed after being kicked in. Judging from the boot imprint, the same perp who'd kicked down the Charleys' door had been at work here, too.

Ella unfastened the wire and they stepped inside. In broad daylight they could see the full extent of the damage. The place had been effectively trashed. Red spray paint covered the living room, ruining nearly all the furniture and defacing the walls.

Tache and Neskahi pulled up a few seconds later and joined them inside. Almost immediately Tache began taking photos while Neskahi began working the scene.

"Another message was left here," Justine said, catching a glimpse of the back of the front door. She pushed it shut with the tip of her boot so Ella could see it clearly. "Our land, our law." Justine read out loud, then pointed to the crudely painted eye below it.

Ella crouched by a small football-shaped battery-powered clock, which lay on the floor. It must have been thrown, judging from the damage, and the impact had knocked the battery out. "This clock stopped about an hour after the call to dispatch from the Charley residence. That supports what we'd already suspected—Marilyn was the primary target, and this was a follow-up. The Fierce Ones often leave that eye symbol to remind the offender that they'll be watching."

Despite the vandalism, there were no signs that anyone had been harmed here. "If anyone finds prints or something that'll help us track down those responsible, I want to know right away."

As they all processed the scene, time slipped by quickly. Noting it, Ella decided it would be better to divide their efforts. "I'm going to take the SUV and go pay Delbert John a visit."

"Are you sure you don't want me to go with you?" Justine asked. "In the past we've always had problems questioning the Fierce Ones."

"He won't pull anything at a job site. After I'm done, I'll come back here, and we'll ride together. I'd like you with me when we go question the other suspects."

Ella followed the directions Dispatch gave her to Delbert John's work site. Unfortunately, the directions were a bit vague. After wandering the back roads for about fifteen minutes, she found the tracks of several heavy trucks and those led her to a house under construction.

Ella pulled up beside three pickups, then climbed out of the department SUV. Several of the men glanced her way, and one man who'd been standing by a makeshift table inside the structure, plans in hand, came over to meet her. A radio in the background blared out country-western tunes.

"I'm the foreman, Lodis Michoby," the stocky Navajo man in the tan canvas jacket said. "Can I help you, Officer? . . ."

"Special Investigator Clah," Ella said, and pulled back her jacket to reveal her department shield. "I need to speak to a member of your crew, Delbert John. He's here today, correct?"

"Yes, he's over there, wearing the black cap," Michoby replied, pointing with his lips at two men cutting lumber with a table saw. "Is he in trouble?" the foreman added quickly.

"I just need to ask him a few questions. It won't take long."

"Good." He whistled. "DJ!"

The saw completed a cut, and both men looked at Michoby. "DJ!" Michoby repeated.

The man in the black cap, a Navajo of medium height wearing jeans, lace-up work boots, leather gloves, and a plaid long-sleeved shirt, walked toward her. His gaze was confrontational. Navajos never looked at each other in the eye. It was considered an intrusion of privacy.

Normally, Ella would have gone to meet him halfway, but in this particular case, instinct told her it would be better to wait for him to come to her. When he did, she introduced herself.

"I know who you are. What do you want?" he snapped.

"I've been told you're the new leader of the Fierce Ones," Ella said, keeping her tone deliberately flat and her voice low.

"The who?" he asked, a tiny grin touching the corners of his mouth.

"That's an old rock band. What's the problem, your ears full of sawdust?" she said, her voice hard now.

He grinned. "I think you want Jimmy Levaldo, but I've heard the Fierce Ones fell apart. They got too public for their own good."

"So what are you telling me, that you're taking the Fierce Ones underground?"

"You think too much. But if there was such an organization, their main job would be doing what the police can't, and that requires anonymity. Cops are saddled with too many *bilagáana* rules and that's why they're ineffective."

"All the Fierce Ones do is terrorize," she countered, a touch of anger clouding her words. "They act without thinking—often attacking the wrong person."

"If there was such an organization as the Fierce Ones," he repeated, "they wouldn't be afraid to use a firm hand when necessary to keep order and balance. That way everyone could walk in beauty. You can't let murderers and thieves go free just because Anglo laws have a million loopholes. Where's the justice in that?"

"There's no justice in taking the law into your own hands and striking out blindly. Everything in life is connected and actions have consequences—for the Fierce Ones, too. Those who act as both judge and jury destroy the balance they claim to want to uphold."

His eyes blazed, and his gloved fists clenched. "Justice is crying to be heard. *Our* ways are simpler and far more effective." He stopped abruptly, forced his hands to relax, then continued in an almost leisurely tone. "By 'our' ways, I meant Navajo ways. The youth gangs on the Rez are a perfect example of how Anglo thinking and laws are creating chaos here. The Fierce Ones are the only protectors the tribe can count on. They balance the scales so that the weak have recourse."

"How does beating a woman nearly to death fit in with all that fancy talk?"

"If the woman had planned for months to kill her husband, and he suddenly turns up dead, how could anyone judge her innocent?"

"Where did you get that information?"

"Get your own sources. I've told you enough."

"What you've heard is just gossip. Show me proof that she's guilty of anything."

"If you haven't found it, it's because you haven't dug deeply enough." He turned around and walked back to the table saw to join his partner.

Ella didn't have any more questions—none that he'd be likely to answer truthfully. Her next step would be to talk to Hoskie Charley, the deceased's uncle. There'd been no love lost between Marilyn and him. If the Fierce Ones hadn't received their information from a department snitch, it was likely that Hoskie, or someone in his household, had been Delbert's source.

After checking and learning that Justine needed at least another forty minutes to finish processing the Curtis scene, Ella drove directly to Hoskie's place. Remembering that he was a traditionalist, she parked, stepped outside the car, and waited. Smoke was coming from the metal chimney, so someone was home. An old pickup, the one she'd seen before, was parked by the side near the sheep pen.

Minutes ticked by but no one appeared. She continued to wait. At long last, the same elderly man she'd seen before came out to the front porch and waved at her to come inside.

He led the way into the house and immediately moved closer to the potbelly stove. "It's too cold outside today. When it's windy, the cold seeps right into these old bones," he muttered.

Ella took the seat he offered, then waited as he warmed his hands by holding them above the flat top of the cast-iron stove. A heavy kettle sat there as well, vapor steaming from the spout, adding humidity to the room. Ella knew that the extra humidity would help take some of the bite out of the cold, at least here in the Southwest where the air was very dry, especially indoors, during winter.

"Are you here because of my nephew's wife? I know she's in the hospital at Shiprock."

"Do you know why someone had her beaten up?" Ella asked, deciding to get directly to the point.

He shrugged, and stared at the stove. Small vents revealed the yellow glow of the fire inside, and it flickered constantly.

Ella didn't interrupt the silence.

"That wasn't my doing, you know," he said after a lengthy silence.

"The beating?"

He nodded. "I had nothing to do with that."

"But you know who's responsible."

He sat down on a three-legged stool, remaining close to the fire. "I didn't like her. That's no secret. She was always looking for ways for my nephew to make more money. Then she forced him to buy a life insurance policy, one of those they advertise on TV. Every month a handful of their money was going to that. I don't think she knew that he quit paying on it last year. The older he got, the more money the company wanted. He couldn't afford it, he said."

Ella knew there was no life insurance policy, and since he'd only worked at StarTalk for a short time, he hadn't even been eligible for health coverage.

"Then all of a sudden he turns up dead," he continued. "And this is after she gets herself a new man. I don't think it was an accident, you know. I just don't believe that."

"Was your nephew a heavy drinker?" she asked.

"He had a few beers now and then, but he never touched hard liquor or that cheap wine the *glonnies* around Gallup buy just to get drunk. A beer or three after work helped him relax. That's what he told me. Made it easier to take that woman of his, he said."

"Did he have any enemies that you know of?"

"I would imagine he did, most of us do, but he never said."

"Do you know Delbert John?"

He nodded slightly, then looked away.

"The Fierce Ones went after your nephew's wife. That was made very clear to me. Someone told them that she'd had something to do with his death."

"She does. I'm convinced of it," he said in a low, flat tone. "But I haven't spoken to Delbert for many, many months, if that's your question."

"Did your nephew have another woman on the side?" she asked.

"He's crawled into other beds besides his own," he said with a shrug. "His wife knew about that, but she never threw his things outside."

Ella nodded, understanding. On the Rez, the house belonged to the woman. If she'd thrown *all* his things outside, that would have been considered the equivalent of a divorce. If she didn't, the marriage continued. There were exceptions to that, of course, especially when a couple was Christian.

The interview completed for now, Ella drove back to the current crime scene. On the way, she called Neskahi and gave him the additional job of finding out if George had been cheating on his wife recently, and, if so, with whom. Jealousy worked both ways and women had been known to kill lovers who chose to remain with their wives.

By the time Ella returned to the Curtis residence, her team had wrapped things up and the van was being loaded. To her surprise, Wallace Curtis was standing with the aid of crutches near the side of the house, another man beside him.

Ella went up to them first. "I see you're feeling better," she said, looking at Wallace.

"I'm still in pain and I'll need time to heal, but I don't have to stay at the clinic anymore," Wallace said, then in a low voice desperate with uncertainty, added, "I wanted to see what they'd done to my place, so I had my brother bring me over."

"It's mostly cosmetic, paint damage, and like that," Ella said.

"Do you have any idea who attacked us and did this to our homes?" Wallace asked.

"As a matter of fact, we do."

"Good. I hope you catch them," he spat out. "We didn't deserve this—neither of us."

"Some people believe that Marilyn had something to do with George's death," Ella said, mostly to see how he'd react.

"That's ridiculous," he said immediately.

"Did you know about the life insurance policy?" Ella asked offhand.

Wallace stared at her as if she'd suddenly grown horns. "They once had policies listing each other as the beneficiary, but several months ago he decided to cancel his, so she did the same. You could verify that, probably."

Another theory shot full of holes—if Wallace was telling her the truth. . . .

"Do you know if George might have had a girlfriend—recently, I mean?"

He thought about it for a while before answering. "Marilyn told me about the affair he'd had a year or so ago. I don't know if he'd been seeing anyone recently."

Wallace turned to look at the front door as Tache and Justine came out. "Is it okay for us to go inside and get a few things?" he asked Ella.

"Yeah, we're through here," Ella said after checking with Justine.

While Justine loaded the SUV, Ella called the hospital to see if there'd been any changes in Marilyn's condition.

"Can we question Marilyn yet?" Justine asked once Ella hung up.

"No. She's still heavily sedated," Ella answered, climbing into the vehicle. "Did you find anything inside the house that might give us a quick lead?"

"The prints that didn't match Wallace or Marilyn were mostly on the spray paint cans that were tossed aside. All of those were either smudged or partials. We may have a few comparison points, but definitely not enough to make any absolute IDs," Justine said as she started the engine.

"Wallace said all but one of the perps had worn gloves. Maybe that's part of the reason. You're picking up old prints—the ones from the employees at the paint store, for example. They're mostly smudged now because people with gloves handled the items next."

"Sounds reasonable. We do have tire impressions and those boot prints to work with, but no Nikes," Justine added as they drove west toward the main highway. "You still want me to go to Arthur Brownhat's, right?"

"Yeah. Let's see if we can push him."

"Be prepared for trouble," Justine warned. "I had to arrest one of his brothers a few years back. He came at me with a knife while I was questioning Henry, his father. Bad seeds, all of them."

"So I've heard." Ella checked the small tape recorder she'd put in her shirt pocket this morning. "I think I'll turn this on, too, once we get there."

They arrived a half hour later at a neighborhood of tribal-built tract houses on the east side of Shiprock. Justine searched for the right house number, then pointed it out to Ella.

"That dog lying on the porch is huge," Justine said. "What is it, a mastiff?"

"Yeah, I think so. This is a modernist area, so we're not waiting in the car. Bring your Mace just in case Rover gets nasty."

As they approached the porch, the dog lifted his head, looked at them with drooling jowls, then lay back down. Seconds later, a man in his late fifties came to the door.

Ella pulled out her badge, identified herself, then asked to see Arthur.

"What's my boy done now?" he demanded.

"We just want to speak to him," Ella said.

"I want to know what he's done," he repeated, more firmly this time.

Ella was about to answer when a young man in his late twenties came to the door. The tall, fair-skinned, part Navajo's hair reached down past his shoulders, and was tied back with a leather band. His eyes were light hazel. He stared defiantly at Ella, then switched to Justine.

"You must be Arthur," Ella said. "We're tribal police officers. We need to know where you were between the hours of seven and ten o'clock last night."

"Right here," he said with a shrug, "watching TV with the family."

"Is there anyone who can vouch for you?"

"Me," Henry's father answered.

"Yeah, Dad and I were watching TV," Arthur said with a lethal grin. "Some cop show, I think."

Ella locked gazes with him and waited.

Seconds ticked by. Henry Brownhat glared at Ella, then mumbling something incomprehensible, walked back inside the small living room.

Arthur leaned on the doorframe. "Anything else, ladies?"

Ella noticed one of his knuckles was discolored and slightly swollen. "Marilyn Charley. Seen her recently?" Ella snapped.

"Never heard of her."

"Really? I've got a witness that places you at a crime scene."

There was a flicker of uncertainty in his eyes, but it was gone in an instant. "Man's got a right to face his accuser. Who's telling these lies?"

"You'll see the witness in court," Ella replied reaching for her cuffs.

"You arresting me? For what?"

"Come along nicely. You've got enough problems."

"Screw you!" Arthur yelled, throwing a right jab.

Ella stepped sideways and, as his fist brushed her cheek, she slipped inside the jab and countered with an uppercut into his groin.

The anger on his face turned instantly into a grimace of pain. As he doubled over, Ella spun him around, grabbing his wrists in a pinch hold while Justine cuffed him.

"Bad move, boy," Ella said. "Looks like you picked the wrong woman to hit this time."

ELEVEN
—— ✖ ✖ ✖ ——

Justine read him his rights and they placed him in the car.

"I'll be out in less than twenty-four hours and I'll have witnesses that'll swear you attacked me first," Arthur said, leaning back in the seat like it was his personal limousine.

Ella had no doubt that the punk would do as he claimed. This new generation of Fierce Ones was becoming more of a problem. They knew how to play the system.

Ella held up her audio recorder so he could see it. "I have our entire conversation on tape and you'll have other charges to face as well once you start up with the lies."

"I admit *hearing* what happened to Marilyn Charley. Everyone knows that she had something to do with her husband's death. I guess the cops are too busy arresting the innocent to look at what's right in their faces."

"If you know anything about what happened to her, we may be able to work out a deal," Ella said.

Brownhat shook his head. "Forget that cooperation bull. I wouldn't live to tell the story," he muttered. After a ten minute drive, in which Arthur kept quiet, they arrived at the station.

Justine and Ella tried to question him again, and although they kept at it for more than an hour, in the end they got nothing new. By that time, as predicted, two neighbors had showed up at the duty officer's desk to swear that they'd seen Ella and Justine attack Brownhat.

Ella was fairly certain that the elderly woman and the middle-aged construction worker who'd come in were not part of the Fierce Ones. They'd undoubtedly been coerced into making an appearance at the station. Their statements were identical except for a word or two, and shaky at times because their rehearsal time had been brief.

The sergeant who took the statements, having been warned by Ella that the Fierce Ones would be sending in people to testify against her and Justine, interviewed each witness separately. Neither had even been able to describe what Ella and Justine had been wearing. When the officer showed Ella the statements, none of it came as a surprise to her.

"The Fierce Ones aren't any better than the gangs we've got running around here," Ella told Justine, once they were back in her office.

"That audio tape you made only establishes what was said, but it does cover us somewhat."

Ella was about to reply when Big Ed buzzed the intercom and asked to see her. "Just what I needed," Ella said, glancing at Justine. "Check on the footprints to see if any are the size of those Nikes but stay at the station. After Arthur's cooled his heels in a holding cell, we'll try to question him again."

"If they haven't had to release him," Justine said. "We really won't have enough to detain him for long once he lawyers-up."

Ella strode down the hall. When she reached Big Ed's door, the chief stood. "Let's go get some coffee," he said, signaling her not to speak, then motioning for her to follow him.

Walking a step or two behind him, Ella followed Big Ed outside to the parking lot. By then, her mind was filled with questions.

Once they reached the large pine beside the rear gate, he stopped and turned to face her. "We'll talk here."

"What's going on?" she asked quickly.

"We obviously have a leak, Shorty, and I don't want to talk inside. We've got to find the snitch fast, so I've come up with a plan. We'll narrow down who's responsible by giving slightly different stories to each one of the officers who's a potential suspect. I'll make sure it's information that'll get a reaction from the Fierce Ones."

The conclusion that there was a traitor in their ranks, though not unexpected, was still hard to take. "Who do you suspect?" she asked, though she already knew the answer, at least in part.

"My office assistant, the members of your team, and the desk sergeant who was on duty when we were discussing George Charley's death. Earlier that day, I'd had him take a look at my computer. He's good with that kind of thing and I was having problems. I left him alone in my office for quite some time. He may have planted something, then taken it back out shortly thereafter."

"You had your office swept for bugs?" Ella asked.

He nodded. "I had it done by one of our own people once we'd all left so it wouldn't raise any questions. He said it was clean."

"I'd swear by my team, chief," Ella said.

"I figured you'd say that, but we've got to play this out."

Ella knew it would do her no good to argue. "So what's the plan?"

"These next few days I'll be individually asking our

suspects to give me backup while I meet with one of the Fierce Ones. I'll say it's someone I've recruited as an informant and to protect his identity, I'll be the only one who'll interact with him directly. I'll ask the officer to watch my back. That game plan will change slightly, of course, when I test out my office assistant. I'll be giving her bogus information in the form of a report to file."

Big Ed paused, getting his thoughts together and waiting for two uniformed officers to pass by on their way to their units. Finally he continued. "I've arranged to have phony New Mexico plates put on the truck my informant will be driving, and I'll make sure the officer covering my back gets at least one quick look at them. If the officer looks up the plate, Bruce Little's computer program will identify the officer accessing the data," he said, referring to Ella's friend Teeny.

"Who'll be driving the target vehicle?"

"A friend of mine from the Ute Mountain Tribe. I'll be starting the sting operation tonight. Do you care which one of your team members is tested first?"

Ella paused, then reluctantly told the chief about Tache's connection to the Fierce Ones. "He's the logical one to start with but, for the record, he's never given me any reason to distrust him."

Big Ed nodded slowly. "Let's make sure your faith in him is justified." Big Ed began walking back with her, then added, "Until we get this business all cleared up, don't discuss anything that has to remain confidential with anyone except me. And *never* inside my office, or even the building, if you can help it."

Ella nodded, lost in thought. "What do you want to do with Arthur Brownhat?"

He considered it for several moments. "You might consider letting him go and putting a tail on him. He's bound to get cocky if he thinks he got away with something, like out-witting the police."

"I see your point," Ella answered reluctantly. Envisioning the sense of satisfaction that would be mirrored on Brownhat's face made her hands ball up into fists and her knuckles itch.

"I understand the sentiment, but we'll get him," Big Ed said, accurately reading her expression.

As they walked inside the station, they passed the watch commander's desk and continued down the hall.

"Stay on your guard," Big Ed said softly, then went into his office while Ella continued to her own.

Ella returned to her desk, her thoughts on Ralph Tache. She then remembered that she'd meant to ask him about Roxanne Dixon. She hadn't seen Roxanne in the last day or so, but she couldn't ignore something that involved her kid.

Ella found Tache by the coffee machine in the hall and asked him to join her in her office. Closing the door, she gestured for him to take a seat.

Ralph said nothing and waited, looking at her curiously. Usually when he was called into her office she never bothered closing the door.

"Ralph, I need to ask you a few questions about Rox-anne Dixon."

He rolled his eyes. "Don't tell me she's back on the force?"

"No, but she's still in the area and I need to know what you know about her. I ran into her at my kid's school."

Ralph's eyebrows knitted together. "She doesn't have—" He looked up at her. "That's the point isn't it? What she was doing there? You never had any assignments with her, did you?"

Ella shook her head. "Not directly. Roxanne is playing some kind of personal game. She said she was keeping an eye on my kid for Kevin, but Kevin dumped her weeks ago and doesn't want any more contact with her. I know you two had—something—once, so I thought you could give me a heads up on the best way to deal with her."

Ralph took a deep breath. "She's bad news, Ella. Really bad news. My wife and I were already having problems when she got on the scene, but that woman had her own agenda from the start."

"You two had a relationship?"

He didn't answer right away.

"Ralph, I know I'm treading on personal ground here but, for me, it doesn't get any more personal than something that involves my little girl."

He nodded, then spoke. "We hooked up once—that's it. We'd both been drinking, one thing led to another, you know. She'd made it sound like a lark, no strings attached. But that isn't the way it played out. After that, she was always in my face, arranging 'chance' meetings, phone calls, stuff like that. Roxie was obsessed, stalking me almost. She started following me to work, on the job, then back home again. I saw her parked down the road from my home one evening and had it out with her," he said, then added, "She doesn't take rejection easily."

"What happened?"

"She told me she had photos of us in bed. I think she thought I'd fold or something. But by then, my ex and I had already decided to get a divorce—for reasons that had nothing to do with Roxanne."

"So what did you do?"

He smiled slowly. "I asked her for copies to show my poker buddies."

Ella chuckled. "Did that take care of it?"

Tache shrugged. "Guess so. I never heard from her again. But if she has photos of Kevin, a politician, that's going to be an entirely different story."

"If she'd had anything on Kevin I think she would have

played that card by now. She's trying hard to get in touch with him, and has been pressuring me to give her his new home phone number."

"As I said, she really doesn't like letting go, so be careful," Tache said somberly, then left.

Ella called Kevin next and got him before the second ring. She filled him in quickly. "I need you to be straight with me, Kevin. Is there *any* chance she took photos?"

"If she has photos, they're fakes. I never went past first base with her. There just wasn't that kind of chemistry between us, even at the beginning."

"Okay. That's good to know."

"But, Ella, there's *no* reason for her to be hanging around Dawn. If that persists, I need to know."

Ella hung up, then leaned back in her chair. She wanted to talk to Dawn away from the house, not wanting Rose to be reminded of the problem. She'd never stop worrying. Since tomorrow was Saturday, Ella made up her mind right then to make time for it during tomorrow's trail ride.

Her phone rang before she could give that idea any more thought. It was Ford. "Hello, Reverend," she said, using his title affectionately. It still surprised her that two people as different as they were actually got along so well. She only had one regret. Although it was an ever-present temptation to her, and maybe to him as well, Ford's religious beliefs forbade sex before marriage. And at the moment, marriage wasn't an option.

"Do you think you could get away for a little bit? I need to talk to you," he said.

"It sounds serious." His tone suggested it was business, not personal.

"It is. How soon can we meet?"

"How about the Totah Café in twenty minutes? I'm starving."

"Okay, then. I'll see you there."

Ella thought about their unusual relationship. They usually met in public places because his reputation had to remain above reproach. Yet she didn't mind that at all. In a way, it made things easier.

Grabbing her jacket, Ella was halfway to the door when Justine appeared. "Arthur Brownhat's about to be released."

"So quickly?"

Justine nodded. "Thought you'd like to know."

"Recruit an officer or two and have him tailed round the clock for the next twenty-four hours."

"You want to know who he associates with?"

"You bet. If we play our cards right, he'll lead us to more of the Fierce Ones."

"I'll take care of things. Are you off for the day?"

"Yeah. I need downtime. This is going to be a long working weekend for all of us."

Justine started to turn away, but then stopped. "I almost forgot. Del said that your cruiser's due for an oil change. Leave it here. He'll move it over to the shop in a while, and you'll find it back in your parking space tomorrow." She tossed Ella a set of keys. "In the meantime, take my tribal unit. I've got my own pickup outside."

"Okay. See you tomorrow."

Ella met Ford a short time later. The Reverend had picked his favorite booth at the Totah, one facing west with an unobstructed view of the mesa. Seeing her in the foyer, he stood up and waved.

Ella joined him and, already knowing the menu by heart, ordered. While she waited for her green chile enchilada, she leaned back and felt her muscles relax. "It's good to see you."

Ford gave her a taut smile. "You may not think so after I tell you why I called."

"What's going on?" She leaned forward, lowering her voice.

"I overheard something disturbing at the end of one of our youth meetings yesterday evening," he said. "A group of our teens were in the hallway talking and one of the boys mentioned that the Fierce Ones have recruited new blood. He said that it's a whole new ball game now."

"Did you recognize who said it?"

He nodded. "Jonah Talk, son of Herbert Talk."

"The man who owns the western-wear store?"

"That's him. He's not a member of our church, but his wife Lea is. Lea, who also overheard her son, told him to keep his mouth shut and dragged him outside to talk to him."

"Did you get a chance to talk to Jonah?"

"I caught him alone later while his mother was working out the details of our annual pancake breakfast. Jonah said he wasn't a member of the Fierce Ones, but assured me that someday he would be. Then he warned me not to ask any more questions. He told me that there were things no preacher should be involved with. He also mentioned that he knew you and I are friends, and suggested I tell you that the Fierce Ones weren't going to take any garbage from the police anymore. You should watch yourself."

"Maybe it's just saber rattling, or a boy trying to sound important."

"I suppose that's possible. But from what I've heard, the Fierce Ones are still embarrassed by what they consider their defeat at the hands of the police last year. What worries me the most is that their new leaders are changing their strategy. Jonah said the Fierce Ones wouldn't be holding back anymore. They plan to physically challenge any police officer who gets in their way."

"So now they're judge, jury, *and* executioner?"

He nodded. "That's my take, too, and having heard

what happened to Wallace Curtis and Marilyn Charley, it appears to be a credible threat."

"I agree," she said, suddenly very tired. As her food was served, she glanced over at his side of the table and realized he hadn't ordered anything but coffee. "Aren't you eating?"

"I'm going light this afternoon. We've got our annual pancake breakfast fund-raiser tomorrow. Why don't you come? They're always fun."

She smiled and shook her head. "I can't. I've already promised Dawn I'd take her out on a trail ride first thing. There're some things she and I have to talk about."

"It sounds serious," he said.

"It is. But let's not go over that right now, okay? I don't want to rehash things too much in my mind before Dawn and I get together."

"No problem," he said, sipping his coffee. "I've heard that the police are still asking questions about George Charley's death. Was it an accident or not?"

"I can't say for sure, not yet. There are too many unanswered questions," she added, not mentioning the news about the disabled brake system on the truck George Charley had been driving, or the intruder at the impound who'd very likely been trying to cover that up. That incident hadn't led them anywhere yet, but at least some of the suspects on the list had been ruled out.

Ella ate hungrily and Ford watched her, smiling. "I met a friend of yours today. She used to be with the tribal police. I ran into her as I was leaving church and that's when I found out that you two were good friends." Ford smiled and waved at someone across the room. "There she is now."

Ella turned her head and saw Roxanne smiling at her. Swearing under her breath, she turned to Ford. "She lied to you, Ford. She's *not* my friend and never was. Don't trust her. She's a real troublemaker." Ella stood up. "Wait for me. She and I are going to have a little talk."

Ella went to where Roxanne sat, three tables away, sat down across from her, and met her gaze directly. "Why are you following me?"

Roxanne laughed. "Following *you*? This is a restaurant. People come here to eat."

"Save it. What's going on?"

Roxanne's smile vanished in a heartbeat and she transfixed Ella with a cold glare. "The *only* thing I want from you is information. Tell me how to get hold of Kevin and I'm out of your face."

"First of all," Ella said, leaning forward, and resting her arms on the table, "I don't react well to threats. Secondly, if you have a problem with Kevin, take it up with him."

"Don't give me the little Miss Perfect routine," Roxanne said, her voice lowered to a growl. "Kevin has two weaknesses—you're one, your daughter's the other. Right now you two are the only way I've got to pressure him."

"Listen carefully, Roxanne," Ella said in a hard voice. "Stay away from my child. Consider this your final warning."

"Oh, please, like I want your skinny-assed girl? What I want is Kevin's new cell number or his home number. That's it. You want to get rid of me? Give me what I want. Otherwise, you're going to get real tired of looking at my face."

"Back off, Roxanne. If Kevin was still interested in you, he'd have called or written back by now. Deal with the rejection and walk away."

"Kevin doesn't know you—not like I do. It takes a cop to know another cop," Roxanne said, holding Ella's gaze. "By the time I'm through he'll know exactly what you're all about."

Not waiting for Ella to reply, she stood. "Be seeing you, Clah," she said, dropping some bills on the table. "Who knows? Before this is over, we may even become friends. Kevin gives us something in common."

"We have nothing in common," Ella said enunciating every syllable.

Roxanne laughed, waved at Ford, then walked out of the restaurant.

Ella returned to the booth where Ford was waiting. She could feel the excess tension thrumming all throughout her body. "She's a real winner."

"It sounds like Roxanne's got a few problems."

"More than a few. I'm glad she's out of the department. But that brings up another question. Did she ever happen to mention what she's doing for a living these days?"

Ford shrugged. "I think I heard she's gone to work for Abigail Yellowhair."

TWELVE
——— ✖ ✖ ✖ ———

Dawn rushed into Ella's room right at sunrise the following morning. "Mom, wake up! It's daytime already and we haven't even saddled the horses yet!"

Ella groaned, and reluctantly opened her eyes. "It's still early," she said checking the clock. It was barely six-thirty. "We've got time," she managed in a croak.

Dawn tugged the covers away from her. "Not if you have to go back to work later on. Hurry! And you won't be taking your phone, will you?"

"I'm taking it along only in case of a horseback-riding emergency." She'd promised her daughter this ride, and she intended to go through with it. "I'll meet you outside, and don't make too much noise, okay? You don't want to wake up your *shimasání*."

"She's up. She fixed our breakfast and already put it in the saddlebags. It's breakfast burritos, Navajo style, with eggs and sausage!"

Ella knew her mom's burritos were second to none. She wrapped them up in homemade tortillas called *naniscaadas*.

"Okay, kiddo. Start saddling up. I'll meet you in a few minutes."

Ella dressed in jeans and her riding boots, the same western-cut boots she often wore to work, then stopped by the kitchen. The saddlebags were on the counter, filled with food. "Mom, judging by the bulge in those, you made enough for the entire weekend," Ella said, smiling as she fastened the leather straps.

"Your daughter may be very thin, but she packs away two breakfast burritos to your one."

After picking up the saddlebags, Ella met Dawn outside. She saddled up quickly, attached the saddlebags, then checked her daughter's tack before they mounted. "Let's go."

They rode side by side up a long, gentle slope that circumvented the mesa to the west, the sun at their backs. Ella rode her big gelding, Chieftain, and Dawn sat tall on Wind, the pony her father had bought for her a couple of years ago.

As usual, Dawn chattered practically nonstop, ignoring the birds in the brush, the low junipers, and the occasional cottontail that darted away. Their horses, used to the wildlife, rarely spooked.

Ella listened and nodded, but her thoughts were on the one subject she'd come out here to discuss with her daughter—the danger that Roxanne posed.

"Mom, are you *listening?*"

"Yes," Ella said. "You were saying that Sara wants a miniature horse, and you want one, too. But we can't afford another animal. And it makes no sense for you to get a horse that's too small to be ridden."

"Maybe I can ask Dad."

Dawn had learned to play one parent against the other, a strategy that often put Kevin and her at odds. These days, every time Ella expressed a financial concern, her daughter would automatically bring her father into the picture. Wanting to change the subject, Ella decided to try a more emotional tactic.

"You used to spend most of your free time riding or grooming Wind, but if you're getting tired of your pony, maybe we should sell Wind before he notices you want to replace him."

"Mom, I would *never* sell Wind. Forget I said anything about miniature horses, okay?"

"Speaking of riding," Ella said, grateful to change the subject, "have you thought any more about boarding school?"

Dawn grew somber. "I'd like to go with my best friend, but I have other friends, too," she said in a whisper-thin voice, then grew silent.

Ella didn't press her. Following a trail they'd established in the past, they rode among the low hills and valleys carved by wind and water. Beyond, to the west, was a long escarpment where desert floor met the mesas and the junipers became more than low shrubs.

"Mom, I'm hungry. Can we stop and eat over there by those boulders?"

Ella laughed. "We've barely been gone fifteen minutes!"

"Yeah, but I'm *starved*, Mom. If my stomach gets any louder, Wind might think it's a mountain lion." As if on cue, Dawn's stomach growled.

"How about if we go up the arroyo instead and use the petrified sandbar as our table? We did that once last summer, remember?"

"Okay. There won't be any tumbleweeds this time of year, so we won't have to worry about the horses wanting to stop and chomp them up," Dawn replied. "Wind is such a pig sometimes," she said, holding her reins for a moment in her left hand as she patted the pony on his neck. "No offense, boy."

The pony sighed, and Ella laughed.

She led the way down into a narrow arroyo, which widened ahead into two dry streams with a small ridge of harder sandstone in the center, like a two-foot-high, miniature mesa. The horses wouldn't wander here.

Ella dismounted, removed the saddlebags from Chieftain, then looped the reins around the saddle horn so the horse wouldn't drag them around or step on them. Dawn followed suit, even removing the smaller saddlebags from Wind without help. Together they brought out the contents Rose had packed away in the saddlebags, using the flat sandbar like a countertop.

Ella had her breakfast burrito, then, while Dawn finished off her second burrito, brought out two apples. Dawn looked at her mother. "Can I give mine to Wind and yours to Chieftain?"

"Sure, go ahead." Sitting cross-legged in the sand, enjoying the cold early morning air, Ella gathered her thoughts while her daughter fed the horses.

When Dawn returned, she sat across from Ella, and looked at her mother somberly. "Am I in trouble? Did I do something wrong?"

Ella blinked, and stared at her. "Where did that come from?"

"Mom, you've been *way* too quiet all morning, and you have that look on your face. The Long Talk look, you know?"

"We do have to talk, but you haven't done anything wrong," Ella said, giving her daughter a gentle smile.

Dawn nodded, looking relieved, then waited.

"It's about Roxanne Dixon," she said. "You know her as Roxie."

"Dad's friend?"

"That's just it. She's *not* your dad's friend or girlfriend anymore. He doesn't even want to talk to her."

"What happened? Is he mad at her?"

"No. Sometimes people just find out that they're wrong for each other. Then they have to let go and make new friends. But Roxanne hasn't been able to accept that your father doesn't want to see her anymore. She's just not thinking right, and that might make her dangerous. So don't trust her. And never, ever, let her get you alone, not for any reason."

Sure she'd made her point, Ella stood up. "Come on. It's time to get going."

They retrieved the horses, got back onto their saddles, and continued up the arroyo. After another hour, Ella realized they'd wandered north toward Rock Ridge, farther than she'd intended to go, and swung back around toward the east in the general direction of home.

"Can Wind and I take the lead?" Dawn said. "I know the way back from here."

"Go ahead," Ella said, letting her pass. Chieftain didn't like taking second place, so she had to rein him in and turn his head at the last second to keep him from biting the pony's rear.

They soon reached the same arroyo they'd had their breakfast in earlier, and Dawn led them back down inside. As the wash opened up to a wide, low section, Ella caught the sound of a vehicle a few hundred yards off in the distance, judging from the sound. Since roads out here were few, she wondered if someone had managed to get lost. Ella considered riding out of the arroyo to take a look, but then the engine sounds stopped.

A trickle of unease ran up her spine, but Ella dismissed it. She had to stop being a cop at least some of the time. Exasperated, and assuring herself it was probably just somebody out for a weekend drive, she focused on what her daughter was saying. Feeling a warm spot on her neck, she reached up absently with her left hand and realized her badger fetish was warm. When that happened, danger was often close. Or maybe it was just the morning sun.

"Keep a sharp eye out for snakes," Ella said, going with the most likely threat, considering she hadn't seen any humans in the area.

"Okay."

As Dawn led them back out of the arroyo, Ella heard something moving through the brush ahead. Although Chieftain was used to the sounds of small animals, this time his head jerked up hard and he started snorting. Ella had to fight to keep him steady. Neck-reining him into a circle and then applying leg pressure, she moved him forward whether he liked it or not.

Ella concentrated on calming the horse by keeping him busy and had to take her focus away from Dawn for a moment. Then, as she completed her second tight circle, she saw Dawn had stopped Wind and was waiting quietly.

"Maybe it's a coyote, huh Mom?" Dawn asked, looking around the area cautiously.

"Maybe." Ella brought Chieftain to a stop. "He's finally settling down so I—"

Suddenly a hand snaked out of the bushes, tossing something into the air. As it hit the ground in front of Dawn's pony, smoking and sputtering, Ella realized instantly what it was. A second later, firecrackers started going off like a badly designed machine gun.

Chieftain whipped around, wanting to run, but Ella neck-reined him hard to the right, applied leg pressure, and spun him into another circle.

"Bail out!" Ella yelled to her daughter, seeing Dawn fighting Wind, too.

Wind reared up, but instead of sliding off the pony, Dawn held on, leaning forward to keep her balance. Then

Wind came down hard, spun and bucked. Dawn was tossed sideways and fell hard to the ground.

"Mom!" she yelped.

Ella was fighting hard to keep control of her own horse, and continued to spin him in a circle, struggling to keep her feet in the stirrups. If he didn't start bucking, she knew she could stay on.

The firecrackers stopped exploding on Ella's fifth or sixth spin, and finally she brought Chieftain back under control. Furious, Ella slid off her horse, hanging onto the reins, and hurried over to Dawn.

Her daughter had already scrambled up to her feet and was brushing the dust, leaves, and branches from her clothes as she looked around. Wind was nowhere in sight, but Ella could see a dust trail and hear hoof beats to her right, in the opposite direction of where the firecrackers had gone off.

"That was soooo mean! Who'd do something so dumb?" Dawn demanded, walking toward the bushes. "Julian! Is that you?"

Ella almost laughed with relief. Her daughter wasn't in tears, nor was she hurt—but she was *furious*.

"Mom, I'm going to find him and kick him where it hurts!"

"No! Stay here. That wasn't your cousin. Uncle Clifford would never have allowed him to buy fireworks, much less illegal ones. Go in that direction," she pointed with her lips, "and see if you can track Wind down. Chieftain and I will find the idiot with the firecrackers."

Ella barely had both feet in the stirrups when the excited gelding shot forward at a fast gallop. The ground was flat for fifty yards then sloped up a low hill. Ella heard a vehicle door slam somewhere up there, and urged the panting horse on with a squeeze of her legs. The road was uphill from where they'd been and, despite their breakneck pace, by the time they reached the top of the hill, a red pickup was already racing off, more than two hundred yards away.

The small pistol with the two-inch barrel tucked away in her boot was the wrong weapon to try and shoot out a tire at this range. She'd have needed a rifle and a lot of luck.

As she stared at the truck quickly fading from view, outrage and a cold determination filled her. They'd made a big mistake. Coming after her was one thing. She was a police officer and more than ready to tangle with whoever targeted her. But deliberately endangering her daughter—that was something else entirely. She'd catch the dirtbag no matter how long it took.

Ella rode back down the hill, and, by the time she returned to her daughter's side, Dawn was already back in the saddle, patting and reassuring Wind with soft praise.

"I heard the car. He got away, huh?" Dawn asked.

"Yeah, for the moment."

"I guess we'll have to go home so you can track down the dummy who did this?"

Ella nodded. "I'm so proud of how you handled yourself today! You're a terrific kid, and I want you to know that, one way or another, I'll catch whoever did this to us."

"You always do. And Mom, when you catch this clod of manure, kick him really hard in the shins for me, okay?"

"Count on it," Ella said with a tiny smile. Pushing Chieftain forward, she edged past Dawn. "I'll take the lead the rest of the way back home." Dawn didn't argue.

When Ella used her cell phone to contact the station, she learned that they were on high alert. She was patched through to Big Ed's office immediately.

"I just spoke to your mother, Ella," the chief said. "I was about to give you a call."

"Why the alert? What's going on?" Ella asked quickly.

"You first. This is just a guess, but did you call in just now because something happened to you?"

Ella recounted the events concisely and clearly. "I couldn't get the plates."

"It looks like someone's targeted the entire S.I. team, Shorty. Officer Tache had someone shoot holes in all the windows of his personal vehicle, which was parked outside his home. Officer Goodluck also reported an incident. She was at home walking toward her pickup when someone opened fire. Apparently she wasn't the target, just her vehicle. The tires and her windshield were shot out."

"There's one more team member now, remember? What about Joe Neskahi?" she asked.

"We haven't been able to make contact, so I sent an officer over to his place."

"We need to notify Agent Blalock, too," she said. "He's local, and also constantly involved with the Special Investigations team. It also wouldn't hurt if other departments in the area got a warning. It's possible that we're dealing with a sniper, or several individuals who're targeting law enforcement in general. And maybe Bruce Little. He's been involved in several cases recently."

"Good thinking," Big Ed said. "I'll take care of that."

Once finished with the chief, Ella tried to call Joe. She let his cell phone ring and ring. Cell phones lost signals and then came back on line intermittently sometimes, particularly on the reservation where there were so few cell towers.

Finally, on the eighteenth or nineteenth ring, Joe picked up and identified himself.

Ella filled him in quickly, then asked his location.

"I'm just coming back from my cousin's house near Lukachukai where I spent the night. I didn't even have phone service until a minute ago when I got on the east side of

Buffalo Pass," he said, breaking up. "Are you still there?" he asked a second or two later, the connection suddenly stronger.

"I'm here," Ella answered and, after verifying that he'd heard the update on the crisis, added, "Stay sharp."

"You've got it. Is there anything specific you want me to do next?"

"Find out where Arthur Brownhat was. Justine had him tailed so check with her for the name of the officer on that detail. Then go help the others."

Ella checked her watch. It was possible, judging from the direction she'd last seen it going in, that the perp's red truck would eventually go past either her home or her brother's. She called her mother first, and asked her to stay on the look-out and, if possible, get the plate number. "Also, Mom, if your husband's around, tell him to keep his Winchester handy, just in case," she added, keeping her voice calm.

"In case of what? Something serious has happened, hasn't it? What aren't you telling me?"

Ella gave her the highlights. "You would have been proud of the way she handled Wind, Mom," Ella said, and turned her head to see Dawn smiling broadly.

"Your daughter came into danger because of *your* job," Rose said, her voice suddenly hard.

For Dawn's sake, Ella didn't react. This wasn't a conversation she intended to have in front of her daughter. "Ask my brother to stay on the lookout for a red pickup, too," she said as if she hadn't heard her. "And tell him to watch his family."

"I know your daughter is there beside you so you can't speak freely. But if this doesn't make you think about leaving your job, I don't know what will," Rose said, then hung up.

Ella knew that learning about the incident had terrified her mother. Rose's harsh words had come from fear. But Rose had also made a very good point. It was Ella's work that had ultimately endangered Dawn. The reality of it stung, and left her stomach in knots.

"*Shimasání* must be upset," Dawn said, as if she'd heard both sides of the conversation.

"The news frightened her," Ella answered simply.

Dawn said nothing for a long time, riding Wind in silence. At long last, she answered. "*Shimasání* doesn't understand that you can't stop doing what's right just 'cause the bad guys want you to."

Momentarily at a loss for words, Ella turned her head and looked back at her daughter.

"It takes a lot to stand up to bullies," Dawn added quietly.

Ella suddenly understood that Dawn was correlating what had just happened to them with what she'd experienced at school several months back. When Dawn had defended a kid who was being picked on, the bully had turned on Dawn. Her daughter had asked the kid to walk away, but when he didn't, she'd kicked him in the groin.

The teacher, who'd seen the incident through a window but rushed up too late to intervene, had given Ella the details. Ella had been proud of her daughter's courage, and Rose had, too, though she'd mumbled a lot about the similarity between Ella and Dawn.

"*Shimasání*'s wrong, Mom. Sometimes, there isn't another way except to fight back, and you can't wait for someone else to do it for you."

Ella told Dawn once again how proud she was of her. "You've shown all the qualities I've always respected and admired."

Dawn beamed.

By the time they reached home, Rose was waiting for them by the corral. Although Herman was working on his old pickup, Ella could see his thirty-thirty lying on the running board within arm's reach.

Rose held on to Wind's reins as Dawn got off, her careful gaze checking her granddaughter for any injuries. Then she glanced at Ella, who'd replaced Chieftain's reins with a halter before tying him to a post.

"Did either you or my brother happen to spot that red truck going by?" Ella asked her.

"No, daughter, and all three of us were looking." Rose waved in the direction of Herman. "A police patrol car has already come down the road and back since you called."

She had no doubt that Big Ed had dispatched a cruiser as soon as he'd heard her story. Before she could comment, Herman, who'd closed the hood on his pickup, came over and took the horse brush from Ella's hands.

"I'll take care of this for you," he said. "You'll have business to attend to."

The look he gave told her without a doubt that one of his nephews, either Phillip or Michael Cloud, must have called and told him exactly what was happening. Ella thanked him, then, after giving her daughter a quick hug, hurried inside to change clothes.

She was on her way less than ten minutes later in the department vehicle, driving up the road leading to the spot she and Dawn had been ambushed. When her phone rang, Ella picked up the call.

"Is Dawn okay?" Justine asked quickly. "I heard about the firecrackers."

"Yeah, she's fine, but she got thrown, and I had to fight to stay on Chieftain. My kid could have broken her arm, or worse. I want those guys, partner."

"We all do. Did Big Ed tell you that they took out my tires, windshield, and the driver's side window? My pickup wasn't new, but it was new to me. I've only had it three months."

"Sorry about that, but it could have been a lot worse. At least you weren't hurt."

"Yeah, you're right," Justine answered.

"What's next on your agenda?"

"I'm at my place now taking photographs and doing a walk around. I've got one bullet hole that went through the right hand corner of my windshield and the driver's side window. It was at least a thirty caliber high velocity round. I've checked the trajectory and narrowed down where he must have been in order to make that shot. From the distance, I suspect he was using a rifle with a scope, but he still would have had to have been a fairly decent marksman. So which site do you want me to process first—the one here at my house, or the one where you and your daughter were attacked?"

"Gunfire takes priority over firecrackers, so stay where you are. I'm on my way back to the spot where they came after me and my kid. I'll get what I can there. Have you heard from Tache?"

"He's processing his own scene. He was targeted five minutes before me. I just spoke to Joe and he's on his way over to help him finish up. When they're done there, they'll join me."

"Did Joe mention anything about Arthur Brownhat's whereabouts this morning? I asked him to check on that."

"He spoke to the officer who had Arthur under surveillance and he's been home all morning working on his truck with one of his brothers."

Ella continued to where the perp had parked his red pickup. She took photos of the tire tracks and footprints, which were not the Nikes she'd hoped they were, then followed them back to the spot beside the arroyo where the firecrackers had been thrown. After locating the smoothed out marks on the earth where the perp had gotten down on his knees to stay low, she photographed them, then checked for any matches he might have used. Of course it was always possible that the perp had used a lighter.

A quick search of the bed of the arroyo revealed fragments of exploded firecrackers, and three that hadn't gone off for various reasons. Those she promptly bagged. She then circled outwards from the spot where the perp had struck, searching in a widening spiral for any other evidence that might give her a lead.

As she worked, what bothered her most was the timing of the events. There was no doubt that they were dealing with multiple assailants—at least two of them snipers. The only way Justine and Ralph could have been attacked by the same person was if the perp had traveled by helicopter—and a fast one at that.

Ella was still searching the ground, bagging a few more firecrackers that hadn't gone off and might hold prints, when she heard an approaching vehicle—a geared-down pickup, judging from the sounds. Knowing Justine was nowhere near, Ella ducked against the shallow sides of the arroyo, reaching for her holster.

THIRTEEN

——— ✖ ✖ ✖ ———

Soon the area around her grew silent. From the cloud of dust, Ella could tell that the vehicle had stopped farther down, around a curve in the arroyo.

She waited, scarcely breathing. With luck, it would turn out to be whoever had thrown the firecrackers, returning to gather up evidence he'd left behind. There was nothing she would have liked better than arresting the dirtbag who'd endangered her daughter.

"Clah, I saw your vehicle. Where you hiding?"

It was Agent Blalock's voice. Ella recognized it instantly. Taking her hand off the butt of her weapon, she called back to him. "Over here, around the curve. How did you find me?"

"Big Ed, then your family," Blalock said, coming down the hill to join her. "Big Ed filled me in, and once I got to your house, Mr. Cloud and your daughter gave me directions on which road to take."

Ella nodded, meeting the tall, broad-shouldered Anglo agent halfway. Blalock was wearing a warm-looking navy blue Bureau jacket and baseball cap, really dressed down compared to the first time she'd met him, years ago. Dwayne

Blalock had come to terms with his assignment in the Four Corners. While he wasn't really considered a friend of the tribe by most citizens, he'd gained enough respect not to be considered an enemy. That was an improvement.

As they walked to the area where she'd seen the perp, she filled him in on the details. "If my kid had been seriously hurt . . . ," she said, not finishing the thought. Remembering how her daughter had handled the experience, she smiled to herself.

"I know that grin. You're thinking of rearranging his face when you catch up to him?"

Ella laughed. "Not exactly, but that thought improves my mood, too," she said, then told him about Dawn.

He smiled. The gleam in his eyes, one brown and the other blue—hence his very unofficial Rez nickname of FB-Eyes—showed he was sincere. "She's a chip off the old block," he said, helping her complete a close survey of the surrounding area.

They found a few more fragments of firecrackers, and a wooden match, freshly used. Each was bagged and tagged, and Blalock took photos of the scene with his own camera.

After they'd gathered all the evidence they could find, Ella motioned in the direction of the road. "Let's go join Justine at the other crime scene," she said.

He fell into step beside her. "I wanted to ask you about the cases you're currently working on. Is there one in particular that might have precipitated these attacks?"

Ella told him about Ervin Benally and StarTalk, then about the vigilante efforts of the Fierce Ones. "But the Fierce Ones wouldn't have endangered my kid. They want approval from the Navajo Nation. Endangering an elementary school child with a stupid stunt like the one the perp pulled doesn't have their signature. They would have come at me directly."

"I agree with you," he said. "If I'd been on that ride with you instead of your daughter, maybe. I'm far from their favorite person. The Fierce Ones consider the Bureau, and me by extension, their enemy."

"The Fierce Ones want total control. We stand in their way so we've all become their enemies," Ella answered. "But right now they're even more dangerous than usual," she added, giving him the details about their power shake-up as she walked with him to his pickup.

Ella drove the tribal SUV to Justine's home, Blalock following, though he knew the way. Justine was standing at the end of the dirt road that led to her pitched-roof, ranch-style home, farther downhill. Parking about fifty feet away, Ella and Blalock walked over, looking at the ground, careful to avoid destroying any possible evidence.

"Is this where the shooter was positioned?" Ella asked as they came up.

Justine, who was standing beside the dirt road studying tire tracks, nodded, then adjusted the strap of her camera, pushing it farther up her shoulder. "From the trajectory of the bullet holes in the windshield, he would have had to have been in this general area, but I haven't found any footprints or casings yet, just these vehicle tracks."

Blalock looked down at the pickup that was parked in front of the house. "That your truck parked way over there?" Seeing Justine nod, he added, "to shoot from three hundred yards with any degree of accuracy takes skill. Former military's my guess, or someone who spends a lot of time on the shooting range, like a gun club member. But *where* are his footprints?" he added, mostly to himself. "And the brass? They would have been ejected."

"Don't see any," Ella answered. "Maybe he took the shots from inside his own vehicle. He undoubtedly used a rest of some kind to steady his rifle."

"If he took the shots from his vehicle, we should be able to find him. He's the newly deaf guy," Justine snapped.

"You have a point," Ella said with only a trace of a smile. She knew when her partner was seriously pissed off. "Let's look for the rounds, then. From this height, those bullets would have hit the ground somewhere down there."

After verifying that the shooter hadn't conveniently left any shell casings at the scene, they marked the area where they'd guessed the shooter had been with a small mound of rocks, and rode down to Justine's home.

"Was Emily home when this happened?" Ella asked Justine, who was riding with her. Emily Marquez, Justine's roommate, was a sergeant in the county sheriff's department.

"No. She's off on vacation, hiking and rafting somewhere in the Rockies with a tour group."

Once they arrived, they searched around the area of the pickup, but were unable to find any bullets, only two small impact spots where the low angle of the bullets had caused them to ricochet off the packed gravel driveway. Next, they lined up the bullet holes through the windows, and soon had a section of ground farther away to search for impact marks. Although they scoured the area carefully, after thirty minutes they'd still found nothing.

"The bullet might have ricocheted from here again. That means it could be hundreds of yards from here, and maybe at an angle as well. We'll need a good metal detector and remarkable luck to find anything at all," Blalock pointed out.

Before Ella could respond, her cell phone rang and she recognized Ralph Tache's voice immediately. "I've found one of the slugs," he said. "It's too deformed to be linked conclusively to any particular weapon, but the base of the bullet is intact, and I measured it. It's a jacketed hunting round from a .270 caliber rifle."

Ella conveyed the news to Blalock. "Ralph lives about fifteen miles away, and the timing of the incident here and the one at his place makes it clear they were carried out by different suspects, and with different weapons."

"Have Neskahi and Tache join me here with the metal detector," Justine said. "Maybe we *will* get lucky."

Shortly afterwards, Big Ed called and ordered Ella to the station. She glanced at Blalock. "If you can give me a ride into Shiprock, I can leave the tribal unit here for my partner. She'll need it to get to the station."

"Good thought. I need to meet with Big Ed myself."

They drove back to the station in Blalock's pickup, a tense silence stretching out between them.

"What's on your mind, Ella?" he asked at last. "Something's bugging you."

"Too many things are coming at me at once, Dwayne," she said slowly, then shook her head. "Since I don't believe in coincidences . . . ," she said, but her voice still held a trace of uncertainty.

"Go with your instincts. What's eating at you about all these incidents?"

"Let me go down the list. A guy gets killed in the wrong accident, in the wrong way—blades not brakes. My daughter gets a scholarship she didn't apply for, one that normally isn't given to a kid until she reaches middle school. Then there's this nutcase ex-cop who keeps getting in my face. And now, every member of my S.I. team gets attacked almost at the same time. Logically, I'll admit they appear to be unrelated incidents. But it's too much, too intense, and too close together."

"Follow your gut, Ella. That works better here than logic alone."

"You're right. It does. But the problem is I still can't see any firm connection between these incidents."

"How about the obvious? Complete this sentence—'All this started happening just after I . . .' what?"

"Hum. Interesting technique," she replied, the last few days running through her head as FB-Eyes drove toward Shiprock.

When they arrived at the station, Ella saw that Del had left her cruiser in her parking spot as promised. "Good thing he finished that oil change."

Blalock parked in the empty space beside Ella's tribal SUV. Spotting a small piece of paper underneath the windshield wiper flapping in the wind, Blalock burst out laughing. "Hey, Clah, someone ticketed you."

"What?" She leaned forward and, following his gaze, looked at what appeared to be a parking ticket.

"I got a ticket for using my own parking space? If that patrol officer isn't just jerking me around, he or she is dead meat," she muttered.

Ella got out of Blalock's car and strode to the SUV. As she read the note, her mood darkened even more.

"Looks like the dead meat response. Maybe it's a rookie being set up," Blalock said, accurately reading her expression.

"It's *not* a ticket," Ella said, her voice taut as a drum.

"What then?"

"It's unsigned. It reads, 'Last chance. Next time, expect a brick.'"

"I get the feeling you already know who left that message," Blalock observed. "The nutcase, right?"

Ella didn't answer right away, trying to bring her temper back into check. Nothing to excess. She could hear Rose's familiar warning echoing in her mind. She couldn't allow anger to disturb her thinking. If she did, Roxanne would win.

Ella took a deep breath. "I'm not one hundred percent certain, so I'd rather wait until I get the video from the surveillance cameras. Until recently only the doors were monitored. Now we cover the entire front lot."

Blalock followed her inside and went with her to Big Ed's office. Ella told the chief about the note right away, using clipped sentences.

"I'm coming with you to review the footage," Big Ed said.

They gathered in a small room close to the end of the hall. The sergeant in charge, Verna Poyer, looked uncertain when Ella made her request. "I'm still new to this assignment. It may take me a while to find the right one," she said. "But I'll give it my best shot."

"What happened to Sergeant Bidtah?" Ella asked. He'd run their surveillance hardware for the past four years.

"He's taken a job with another P.D.," Big Ed answered.

Ella looked at Big Ed, surprised. "He was the only one trained for this job after Teeny left us."

"I know. It's a problem. The tribe can't compete with some other departments and agencies when it comes to pay scales."

Ella had lost two from her original team to higher-paying positions elsewhere, so she was very aware of the problem. Having taken a few classes on surveillance along the way, she knew a little about the setup. Ella tried to help Sergeant Poyer now, whom she'd known from the booking desk. It took them ten minutes to locate and run the footage, which was recorded on black-and-white video.

"There," Ella said, seeing someone coming up to her vehicle and pulling out the windshield wiper. "We need to take that segment, digitize it, then run it through the computer and clean up the image."

Verna looked at the computer on the far desk. "I've done this before, and I wrote down the directions. . . ." She hurried to the desk, brought out her notepad, then following the steps, managed to do as Ella has asked.

Big Ed leaned over, taking a closer look at the screen. "What the heck is *she* doing here?" he muttered.

"I see you recognize former tribal officer Roxanne Dixon," Ella said.

"If you've been having problems with Dixon, why didn't you come to me right away?" Big Ed demanded.

"It wasn't a problem—at first. Now, it is," Ella said.

Big Ed motioned for her and Blalock to follow him back to his office.

Once they were seated behind closed doors, Big Ed gazed hard at Ella. "I want details. What exactly has transpired between you and Roxanne Dixon?"

Ella filled in the blanks she'd left out, then waited.

"Dixon is a loose cannon, Shorty," Big Ed said after a long pause. "From what you're saying, she's still obsessed with Kevin Tolino, and that makes her even more unstable. This isn't the first time she went after someone because of Tolino. I put her on suspension after she threatened Mona Todea. Not long afterwards, I asked for her badge."

Mona was Kevin's long-standing administrative assistant. She was pretty, smart, and as ambitious as Kevin. The only reason Kevin hadn't started dating her—and more—was because *she* was smart enough not to try and mix business and pleasure. "I hadn't heard about that. What happened between Roxanne and Mona?"

"Roxanne became convinced something was going on so she confronted Mona, demanding that she stay away from Kevin—hard to do since she works for Tolino. Not long after that, Mona caught Roxanne trashing her apartment. She'd broken her routine that day and had just happened to come home early. Mona recognized Roxanne's car, so she went up to a window and, using her cell phone camera, recorded what Roxanne was doing. Roxanne spotted her and tried to take away her cell phone, but Mona threw it up on the roof. Roxanne took off before the officers arrived, but we had her anyway. Besides the photos from the cell phone, Roxanne had left some of her blood behind after slicing her finger while taking a razor knife to the furniture."

"Was she prosecuted?" Ella asked.

"No. She cut a deal, and the charges were dropped, but I still fired her from the department. Could she have been the one who jumped you out back by the fence?"

"No, my attacker was shorter, stronger, and didn't fight with the skill of a woman with her training. And the motive doesn't fit at all," Ella replied. "If she'd wanted to jump me, Roxanne would have chosen a different location than the police grounds, don't you think?"

"You're right," Big Ed said.

"Kevin should have told me about this," Ella said.

"The incident happened while he was away. He may not know about it," Big Ed said.

Ella nodded. From what she knew about Mona, she liked handling her own problems, and wouldn't have necessarily involved Kevin after she'd taken care of the situation. "I'm going to have another talk with Roxanne," Ella said. "I want to know where she was when those firecrackers were tossed in front of my daughter's horse."

"Take someone with you," Big Ed said. "That's not a request—it's an order."

Ella studied Big Ed's expression, reading it accurately. "So you think she's capable of that stunt with the firecrackers?"

"She's done some crazy things, so who knows? You need someone else there with you just in case you find out she was responsible."

"All I'd do is bring her in." Damaged, perhaps, but she would have brought her in.

"I'll back up Ella," Blalock offered.

Moments later, they walked out to the parking area. Ella was very quiet, and Blalock allowed the silence to stretch out until they were well underway. "You're not going to shove her teeth down her throat, are you?"

"If you're squeamish, you might want to stay in the car while I question her."

"Not a chance," he replied. "Let *me* question her."

"Fine. I'm more interested in her answers."

"Even if she confesses, I want you to let *me* handle it," he said firmly. "Clear? I know you want this to be Roxanne's doing, if for no other reason that you could end it then. But I don't buy it. To come after you, sure, but endangering your kid? That wouldn't get her any brownie points with Kevin."

"You're right about that," Ella admitted. "The only thing that would accomplish is getting Kevin seriously pissed off. But she still may know something about the attacks on me and my team since she's been shadowing me. She may have spotted something that'll help us now. Police officers, even former ones, are observant. Or she may have heard something through one of her snitches. Officers often maintain their contacts long after they've left the department."

Blalock drove to Roxanne's last known address near downtown Shiprock. As they pulled up beside an inexpensive apartment building—a converted former church, actually—Ella saw Roxanne sitting outside at a small bistro-style table typing on a laptop computer. She was wearing a tight pair of jeans, and her feet were propped up on another chair.

Though she was determined to stay cool, Ella's muscles tensed up.

"Chill out, Clah," Blalock said, parking. "I'll do the talking."

As they walked up, Roxanne closed the top of her computer and came down the steps to meet them.

"I heard what happened to you and your girl. Is she okay?" Roxanne asked Ella immediately.

"She's fine," Ella said, wondering if Roxanne's concern was as real as it sounded, or just a new tactic.

"That was a cheap stunt. You're an officer and that makes you fair game, but your kid should be kept out of it. If you're going after whoever did this—" She paused, her eyebrows suddenly furrowing as she looked at Blalock, then back at Ella. "Why the Fed? You think *I* had something to do with that?"

"How did you find out?" Blalock asked.

"Are you kidding? By now the entire reservation knows what happened to Ella, her kid, and her team. Word travels at the speed of light here."

Although Ella knew she was right, something told her Roxanne also had a scanner that picked up police radio calls.

"Do you have an alibi? Where were you for the past three hours?" Blalock demanded.

"I was right here. It's Saturday and kids get up early. They had a game of kickball going on in the street, and they all saw me when I came out on the porch with my coffee."

"Kids come and go. How long was the game?" Blalock pressed.

"The game went from kickball to hoops at that basket over there." She pointed to a basketball net attached to a wooden pole. "They were at it for a couple of hours. After that wound down I stayed out here working on my computer. The temperature's nice outside today and I wanted to take advantage of it. Two of the moms drove by and waved."

"I'm sure you won't mind if we go talk to some of your neighbors and have them verify that," Ella said, watching her reaction. Roxanne was a hypocrite, pretending to be concerned about Dawn now, but nearly stalking her around school earlier at the science fair. Anyone who would put children in the middle when it suited her didn't deserve a lot of trust.

"Knock yourself out," Roxanne said. "And I'll even do you one better. You and I aren't buds, but you have my backup on this. Only an asshole would endanger a kid. If I hear anything, I'll pass it on. Catch this loser."

"I will," Ella growled, "even if I have to turn the entire reservation upside down."

Roxanne nodded. "See that? We're not that different, you and me."

"We're poles apart," Ella said, her voice flat and steady.

There was a flash of fury in Roxanne's eyes, but it disappeared as instantly as it had appeared. "Relax. You're upset and you want to break someone's face. I get it."

Ella started to answer, but felt Blalock nudge her. "We've got to talk to some of the neighbors," he said, reminding Ella to stay focused.

They spoke to three neighbors, two of them with children who'd been playing outside earlier, and they all verified Roxanne's alibi. At long last they walked back to Blalock's sedan. It wasn't until they got underway that Dwayne broke the silence.

"Be smart, Ella, and stop letting her manipulate you like that. Don't be your own worst enemy."

"She was right, you know. I did want to smash her face in," Ella said after a moment.

Blalock laughed. "I know!"

"Right now she's probably calling Kevin's office and leaving him a message saying that she'll be working non-stop to neutralize the threat to Dawn. That *she* knows how to get the job done. She doesn't have Kev's personal number, but Roxanne won't waste an opportunity like this, even if it's Saturday. She knows that Kevin works weekends."

"Who cares? Take it as a win. We can use any help that'll point us in the right direction."

"Having her take advantage of this only makes me want to push her face in all the more." She glanced over at Blalock and smirked. "So I'm not perfect, huh?"

FOURTEEN

✖ ✖ ✖

Ella and Blalock were on their way back to the station when her cell phone rang.

"Shorty," Big Ed said, making it unnecessary for him to identify himself, "Ervin Benally is going to hold a press conference in about ten minutes at the StarTalk warehouse. He's announcing the date of the first delivery of satellite phones destined for key public service employees—those in rescue units and a few of our patrol officers assigned to remote areas. I want you at that press conference. I've also assigned Officer Phillip Cloud to back you up there in case there's trouble."

"I'm with Agent Blalock now," Ella said. "I'll have him drop me off."

After placing the phone back in her jacket pocket, Ella filled Blalock in on the event.

"I'll go with you. I'd like to get a feel for what's going on, too," he said, turning and heading for the StarTalk offices.

Ella lapsed into a thoughtful silence, then at long last spoke. "Ervin Benally has been the primary target so far, but anyone out to get even more attention, or go for the company's jugular, might decide to switch to his mother-in-law,

Abigail Yellowhair," Ella said slowly. "The press would eat it up if anyone threatened her today. That woman has a lot of pull on the reservation."

"My only knowledge of that family comes from her late husband's ambiguous reputation. What makes Mrs. Yellowhair tick?"

"Let me give you some of her background. That'll fill in the blanks for you." Ella stopped for a moment to collect her thoughts, then continued. "Abigail came from a dirt-poor family. Her brother died from a ruptured appendix because the family couldn't get him to a doctor in time. Things were a lot different fifty years ago on the Rez, especially when it came to doctors and clinics. But like the old saying, 'what doesn't kill me will make me stronger,' Abigail persisted."

"That goes for a lot of others here on the Rez, too, I would imagine," Blalock said.

She nodded. "Abigail eventually left the Rez to attend the University of New Mexico. At night she worked at an Albuquerque restaurant to make ends meet, and that's where she met James Yellowhair, a spoiled rich kid with a law degree and more money than ambition. They got married and, as it turned out, her networking and power broker skills were instrumental in getting him elected state senator.

"After James was killed everyone expected Abigail to fade into retirement. But she came out of that even stronger, diversified their business holdings, and settled all the legal issues. Her only setback was losing her bid to replace her husband in the legislature. Now, she's throwing her considerable support behind her son-in-law's StarTalk venture."

"For her daughter Barbara's sake, you think?"

"Not exclusively, no. In my opinion, StarTalk made sound business sense to her, and she truly believes it'll be good for the tribe. She loves her daughter, mind you, but something like this would go beyond family loyalty to her.

She's always been more logical than emotional, which isn't always a bad thing."

"I think you admire her more than you'd like to admit," Blalock said.

"Admire her?" Ella glanced over at him in surprise. "I wouldn't go that far. I hate the way she gets things done—basically leaving cleat marks on the face of the opposition. She's one cold lady. On the other hand, she does finish whatever she starts, and that's worthy of some respect."

"Mixed blessing?"

"Yeah, that's a good way to describe Abigail," she answered. "I can tell you this. If she and I ever found ourselves on opposite sides, things would get messy. Neither one of us gives up easily."

They arrived at the office/warehouse a short time later and both gates were wide open. Blalock parked near the fence where overflow parking spaces had been clearly marked with white lines. Camera crews from the TV stations were there, as well as a small contingent of reporters.

As they walked around to the warehouse's lot, they saw that the big loading dock had been set up to serve as the speaker's platform. The Benallys and Abigail were seated in three chairs facing the small crowd, and Officer Cloud was to one side of the gathering, watching the crowd, not the speakers. He nodded, and Ella nodded back.

Deciding to keep watch from the other side, Ella walked forward and caught a glimpse of Ford ahead, close to a single row of occupied chairs twenty feet from the dock.

"I see that Reverend Tome is here. Let me find out what brings the clergy to this event," Ella said.

"You two are getting to be good friends, I hear," Blalock said, a hint of a smile showing through his Bureau glare.

"You might say that," Ella answered, then walked away. If Blalock was going to snicker, she didn't want to hear it.

As Ella reached Ford, he turned and smiled broadly. "I didn't expect to run into you here at the press conference. And you brought FB-Eyes. Isn't that what everyone calls Agent Blalock?"

"Yes, but not to his face. He's here on business, like I am. I was ordered to come, and Blalock offered to give the department a little more backup. Big Ed wants to make sure things go smoothly here today," she said, casually surveying the crowd for any sign of troublemakers. "What brings you here?"

"I was invited to attend. I'm sure they see clergy and missionaries as potential clients, too. Pastors sometimes have to travel long ways to visit a parishioner. And you know how unreliable cell phones can be around the Rez."

There was a scattering of applause as Ervin left his seat at the rear of the loading platform stage. He walked up to the podium, accompanied by his wife and Abigail Yellowhair, who stood at either side. He reached the lectern, where several microphones had been positioned, then finally looked up at the gathering.

"Welcome, community leaders and members of the press," he said. His voice wavered for a second, then he stooped down and looked down at a piece of paper he was holding. The paper was shaking visibly.

Having seen his confident presentation just a few days ago, Ella's first thought was that he'd been drinking. His eyes were red and he looked like he hadn't slept for a week. Allowing himself to get burnt out right before an important event seemed beyond bad judgement and not at all like Ervin Benally. Maybe he was sick.

"It's an honor . . . ," he began, then blinked, as if startled by the sound of his voice, then continued. "I want to thank you all for coming today. This . . . StarTalk is going to usher in a new era of communications for the Navajo people. The future is now," he finished, his voice dropping off almost to a mumble.

He paused, trying to stifle a yawn, and somebody in the crowd snickered. Ervin responded with a scowl, then caught himself. "Sorry. Burning the candle at both ends to get StarTalk operational has taken its toll on me. I'm sure the members of the press here today all know what it's like always being on call." He gestured with his hands, palms up, and shrugged. Unfortunately for him, he also dropped his notes. There was another chuckle from the gathering, and he reached down quickly to recover the papers.

His wife Barbara immediately bent down to help him and they nearly bumped heads. Both of them stumbled, and several people laughed out loud.

Barbara recovered first and reached over, grabbing his arm before whispering in his ear. Ervin smiled weakly, yawned widely this time, then took a step back, waving his hand toward the podium.

Barbara stepped up to the microphones. "Pardon us both. My husband is showing some of the effects of many long nights working hard to implement our dream. No sleep and too much coffee have given him a case of the shakes, as you can see. So on behalf of our StarTalk family, please let me welcome everyone today." She continued, giving an excellent presentation, with plenty of sound bites for the media as well as enough details for the press.

Ella listened to the woman, her eyes searching the crowd. Then her gaze returned to Ervin. A burly Anglo man in a brown suit with the build of a professional football player had come up on the stage. Obviously hired security, the man was now standing next to Ervin, who was clearly having a hard time keeping his eyes open.

Suddenly Ella heard a low whistle overhead, and the next instant a loud bang. Three more explosions quickly followed. The bangs must have sounded like gunshots to the crowd, and a few of the reporters crouched low while others scattered. Everyone was looking around, trying to find the source of the disturbance.

Ella, who'd grown up around a bunch of boys, recognized what sounded like souped-up bottle rockets. On the move toward what she believed to be the source of the rockets, Ella took one last glance back at the loading dock. Ervin was obviously startled and disoriented, as if waking up from a bad dream. He grabbed the arm of the security guard, pointed toward his wife, then yelled, "Get her out of here!"

The Anglo guard responded immediately, grabbing Barbara by the arm, then hauling her and Ervin quickly off the platform and into the warehouse, out of sight.

Abigail Yellowhair remained standing at the podium, alone. The bodyguard reappeared, advancing toward her. She shook her head, pointing back to the warehouse. "Take care of them, not me."

"It's just bottle rockets," someone yelled. Ella saw a reporter holding up something so his cameraman could record the image. "It's a prank."

Several people laughed and one or two others cursed. Ella stopped and looked back at the podium again.

Abigail, the epitome of confidence, stood tall behind the microphones. "It's better to be safe than sorry, so please excuse the quick exit by my business partners. There have been some threats lately, as most of you already know, and we're exercising extreme caution. But there doesn't appear to be any real danger. This is just another childish attempt by organized troublemakers, enemies of the *Diné* and StarTalk, to focus away from what's important. But StarTalk will *not* be stopped from meeting our promises to the Navajo Nation. Those who would interfere with our efforts are clearly confused and misinformed. We *can* move forward and still honor our past."

While Mrs. Yellowhair postured before the cameras and microphones, Ella continued in the direction she believed the bottle rockets had come from, just beyond the six-foot-high block wall. She couldn't recall what business operated from the adjacent property, but it was time to find out.

Ignoring Abigail's speech, Ella walked over to the wall, aware that Blalock was coming up from behind to join her. In the distance, she could also see Phillip Cloud moving toward her.

"They're illegal, bottle rockets are," Blalock said, joining her, "but they're basically harmless except during the fire season. This was meant to undermine Ervin's public image," he added in a quiet voice.

"Yeah, and it worked. The man's unraveling." Ella climbed up onto some wooden pallets stacked beside the wall, and looked over at an automotive shop surrounded by a wrecking yard full of derelict vehicles and junk.

Officer Cloud, in his tan tribal police uniform, joined her seconds later. "If you're going over, I'll go, too," he said. "There's not much we can do here. The press is in a frenzy now that they've got footage of Ervin and his wife being yanked into the building by that rent-a-cop. Mrs. Yellowhair came across as the only one in her family with the balls to stick it out."

Ella nodded slowly. Phillip had just voiced her own thoughts. But experience told her to look past the surface on anything that concerned Abigail. The fact that she'd remained behind might turn out to be far more than just a show of courage.

"You coming, Dwayne?" Ella asked, hoisting herself up onto the wall.

"I'll walk around, thank you," Blalock said, then strode quickly to StarTalk's front gate.

Ella dropped down onto the ground beside an old rental truck up on blocks. The big yard, fenced in on every side except the one facing StarTalk, was crowded with wrecked and older-model cars, most of them cannibalized. The smell of dirty oil and dust was strong, and the sound of an air hammer from an open bay of the shop startled her for a second with its machine gun rattle. Ella looked over at Phillip, who'd just come over the wall, wanting to see if he'd noticed her reaction.

He was looking back at the shop, his hand on his pistol. Glancing over at her, he grinned sheepishly. "Startled me."

"Me, too," she admitted grudgingly. "Let's find out where the rockets came from."

Several feet into the yard, Ella noticed the sun-bleached remains of an old car backseat against the wall. Two spots in the dusty fabric showed where someone had stood, probably to look over at the proceedings at StarTalk.

"Their lookout probably stood there and told them when to launch. See the footprints on the seat?" She pointed.

Phillip nodded. "If what they did was stick the rockets into the ground, and tilt them to the west, all we'll find are footprints," Phillip said. "But if I'd been launching them, I'd have used a hollow pipe, like with a bazooka. If that's the way it went down, we may get lucky and find some prints."

"Start looking," Ella said, remembering how her brother Clifford had used a short piece of aluminum pipe to aim and shoot bottle rockets when they were kids. Walking parallel to the wall, she quickly found two sets of footprints and a primitive handmade launching system. The crude but effective mechanism consisted of ten slightly scorched paper towel tubes taped to wooden stakes stuck in the ground at forty-five-degree angles, all aimed in the direction of the rally on the other side of the wall. One of the ten tubes still held a bottle rocket which had failed to go off when its fuse burned down. A closer look revealed a firecracker had been taped to the rocket to enhance the bang.

As she turned to catch Phillip's attention, she also noticed Blalock walking toward her from the wrecking yard's gate. "Guys, over here," she yelled. When they joined her, she added, "Let's bag these so we can process them for prints."

"It looks like a kid's prank," Phillip commented. "But it had to have been well thought out. Whoever it was brought their launching stuff with them."

"Kids could have easily done this, but why would they? The timing makes me think there's more to it," Ella said. "And look at the tracks. There are two sets of shoe prints, both adult-sized."

Before she could continue, three reporters, who'd obviously tailed Blalock, joined them and began taking photos of the launching system.

"Don't touch anything, please," Officer Cloud warned the reporters. "And stay back at least twenty feet."

Blalock took another look around, then motioned her to one side. "Those bottle rockets are readily available during the summer, and particularly around the Fourth of July. Pueblo fireworks stands don't always follow state or local ordinances, which might explain the illegal firecrackers. The fireworks themselves won't be much of a lead, unless the idiot left his fingerprints on the rocket that failed to launch."

"Or on the tape, or the launch tubes. We might get lucky," Ella answered. "It could also be that someone inside the garage saw whoever launched the rockets. Let's see if we can find any witnesses."

Leaving Phillip to protect the evidence, Blalock and Ella

spread out to talk to the various people, beginning with the two men working inside the auto shop. The men refused to say anything on the record, claiming that they'd been inside working and hadn't even heard the bangs of bottle rockets.

Out of possible witnesses for the moment, Ella found a camera crew willing to let them view the footage they'd shot—even burning them a DVD on the spot. She had a feeling she'd find her next lead there.

"You're looking for something specific, aren't you? What are you after?" Blalock asked her as soon as they were alone again.

"Nobody took shots of the wall itself, so we won't find photos of whoever was peering over the top. But the setup suggests that up to three people were involved. I think the one watching over the wall got a signal from someone in the crowd, then he relayed the go-ahead to the one lighting the fuses. It was undoubtedly something subtle, but I'm going to see if I can spot it on video."

They questioned as many people as they could, but got nowhere. At long last, with the press conference over, Ella and Blalock traveled back to the police station with the DVD.

As they walked in, Big Ed was in the hall, waiting. "I heard about the incident. Is it possible the Fierce Ones were responsible?"

"Using firecrackers attached to bottle rockets?" Ella shook her head. "Doubtful. That's much too amateurish for them. They use obvious force and intimidation, not noise-makers."

Taking the DVD the local reporter had given them into Big Ed's office, they studied each shot, including the incident itself and the aftermath. When they finally finished viewing the footage, Ella didn't know whether to laugh or groan, so she kept silent.

"The press will have a field day with this," Big Ed said at last. "Ervin looked as if he'd had too much to drink. His reaction was almost funny in view of what really happened."

"Not everyone blew their cool. Mrs. Yellowhair came across as one formidable lady," Blalock said.

"That she did," Ella agreed with a nod.

By the time the evening news aired, Blalock had left, but Ella was still at the station. She stepped out into the bullpen where the sergeants and shift commanders worked, and watched the broadcast. Somehow, the feed made the national news. Instead of the satellite phone system focusing positive attention on the tribe, the StarTalk incident had come across as the joke of the day.

Less than ten minutes later, Big Ed called Ella into his office. Several Navajo politicians had phoned right after the news, complaining about the lack of security the department was giving StarTalk.

"Their main concern was that the tribe had been publically embarrassed by the newscast," Big Ed continued. "And they have a point. We've got to get to the bottom of this quickly. This wasn't just a juvenile prank. It was too well timed and executed."

"I agree," Ella replied, but before she could say anything more, Abigail Yellowhair burst into the room.

"What happened today was a disgrace. This department promised to provide ample security for the press conference. What could have been a historical occasion for our tribe has been reduced to a contender for one of those funniest video programs. How could you have let this happen?" she demanded, glaring at Big Ed.

Seeing Big Ed wave Abigail to a chair, Ella stood, waiting to be excused. Suddenly Abigail turned her fury on her. "And *you* should be ashamed of yourself. My poor son-in-law has had to hire a full-time bodyguard because you've done nothing to help him. At first someone kept following him. Then he started getting threatening phone calls at all hours of the night. They won't let him sleep. Little wonder he's falling apart! He's even started drinking again."

"This is the first we've heard about these new incidents," Big Ed said. "My officers need your *complete* cooperation, Mrs. Yellowhair, and that means not withholding information."

"We told you he was being harassed," Abigail said curtly. "But we can't allow his phone to be tapped. Some of the business calls coming in are highly confidential. What you can do is catch whoever's been doing this to Ervin. For a while, every time my poor son-in-law turned around he'd see someone following him, always in a different color and model pickup. But when he'd try to chase them down, the truck would disappear. It was making him crazy. Ervin's a businessman, not a detective, and the constant harassment is wearing him down. Officer Clah and that patrolman—one of the Cloud brothers—saw for themselves at the press conference. Ervin's nothing short of a nervous wreck, and he wouldn't be that way if you people started doing your jobs!"

Big Ed stood up slowly. The gesture, coming from such a large man carried an implied threat. Abigail suddenly stopped talking, her gaze focused solely on him.

"No one waltzes in here and tells me or my people how to conduct their jobs. We work for the tribe, *not* StarTalk. Am I clear?" His voice was scarcely above a whisper, yet it reverberated with authority.

Abigail didn't answer for several seconds. When she finally did, her voice was somewhat muted. "Big Ed, this is my *family* I'm talking about, not another political cause. They deserve more from this department than they've received so far."

"We're understaffed, so we prioritize. We have a possible

homicide to solve right now and several attempts have been made on our officers. We *will* address all our cases, but this department has zero tolerance for a member of the public who tries to tell us how to do our jobs. Am I making myself clear?" Big Ed said. His voice was deceptively calm, but there was an undercurrent of steel woven through his words.

Abigail stared at the top of Big Ed's desk, lost in thought, then finally looked up and met his gaze. "I hear you, Chief Atcitty. Now hear me. It would be a big mistake to underestimate what a woman—any woman—is prepared to do for her family." The power of those words reverberated in the silence of the room as she turned and left.

FIFTEEN
✖ ✖ ✖

As Big Ed took a seat, saying nothing, Abigail's words replayed themselves in Ella's mind. As a woman and a mother, she understood exactly where Abigail was coming from on this. There was nothing Ella wouldn't have done to protect her own family.

"Abigail can get in our way and make a great deal of trouble for this department," Big Ed said at last. "Follow up on what's going on with Ervin. Even if he hasn't requested protection, we have ample reason to question him and learn more about the threats he's received."

Ella nodded. "I'll handle it."

Big Ed stood, checked the hall, and closed the door. "What's next on your agenda?" he asked, returning to his desk.

"Besides interviewing Ervin Benally, I'll continue to follow up on what happened to his Dodge pickup, the one that George Charley used to gather firewood. We don't know if that was intended to harm George, Ervin, or both of them. I also need to check on Marilyn Charley's condition." Ella deliberately kept from discussing details as Big Ed had instructed her. Until they knew where the leak was, she'd be careful.

Big Ed nodded, then added, "Keep me updated."

Ella walked back to her office. Her first call was to the hospital. She soon learned Marilyn Charley had regained consciousness and had refused any more painkillers. Ella placed the phone down and was reaching for her jacket when Justine walked in.

"I found no prints on the fireworks launchers, not even on the tape holding it all together. The wooden stakes were too rough and textured for prints, but we did manage to get a partial from the dud rocket," she said. "It didn't match anything on file."

"Anything else?"

"Footprints, a size eight, right around the launcher. Size nine and a half around the car seat. We got partial shoe patterns but they weren't from a Nike, like the ones we found at the scene of the George Charley case. I've also ruled out any Nikes at StarTalk, or at least an admission that anyone owns a pair. Several of the staff wear athletic shoes in the office, but none of that particular brand."

"Thanks."

"Do you think it was kids with those rockets, Ella? A high school prank maybe?"

"I think that's highly unlikely. What kid in today's world wouldn't want better phone service?" Ella countered. "In my opinion, this was done to rattle Ervin even more."

"So maybe the Fierce Ones hired kids to do the job," Justine said. "That way they could keep their hands clean and still create trouble."

"Not their style. They depend on everyone knowing exactly who was responsible. That's the way all vigilantes work. And why would the Fierce Ones be interested in StarTalk? I can see them going after Marilyn Charley, but who's their target at StarTalk and why?"

"We know they want fewer Anglo influences on the Navajo Nation. Maybe they see StarTalk as just another Anglo foothold," Justine countered. "The satellite phones are being manufactured elsewhere, and the satellites themselves aren't Navajo in origin either."

"All good points." Ella considered it, then shook her head. "But I still can't see it. The Fierce Ones always target Navajo people who've committed crimes, then dispense their version of justice. If Ervin's in their sights, it's because of something he did, not because of StarTalk. But maybe we're still missing something. Keep thinking about it and I will, too. Let's see if we can come up with a connection that feels more on target."

"Were you getting ready to go someplace?" Justine asked.

"Yeah, and if you're not working in the lab, I'd like you to come with me."

"Ready when you are."

"First, I want to get a copy of Arthur Brownhat's booking photo. I'll also want photos of any others we either know or suspect of being in the Fierce Ones."

"All right. I can get those for you."

After stopping by Justine's office and getting what Ella had asked for, they headed out. "We'll be paying Marilyn Charley a visit. She's conscious."

They arrived at the hospital a short time later. Ella was eager to talk to Marilyn. Her gut told her that the woman would be able to fill in some of the gaps, like maybe the identity of at least one of the men who'd beaten her. Their faces had been covered, but it was possible she'd recognized a voice or had received another kind of warning in the past. The Fierce

Ones—at least those she'd dealt with before—often put people on the line with a not-so-subtle warning before actually getting physical. Of course that had been back in the days when the group had worked more on fear and control than actual physical brutality.

After getting directions to Marilyn's room, they went down a long hallway that smelled of floor wax and antiseptic, and took the elevator upstairs. Marilyn's room was just a few doors away from the nurses' station. Ella went on ahead while Justine remained behind to question the staff.

As Ella entered the semiprivate room, she found Marilyn alone, sitting up, her head bandaged and her eyes nearly swollen shut. Seeing the mirror beside the bed, Ella knew that Marilyn was very aware of her appearance.

Ella identified herself, showing Marilyn her badge. Despite the bandages, Ella saw the fear on Marilyn's face just before she turned away.

"I've got nothing to say to the police," Marilyn said in a thick voice.

"We want to catch the men who did this to you," Ella said quietly. "But we need your help."

"I can't tell you anything," she answered, still looking away.

"Can't or won't?" Ella insisted gently.

"They said they'd come back—do worse," Marilyn answered in a barely audible whisper.

"We can protect you if you help us." Ella brought out several photos and tried to show them to Marilyn, but the woman refused to look. "You're not helping yourself, Marilyn. If we put these men in jail, they won't be able to hurt you again."

"There'll be others."

Ella remained quiet for a long time then spoke. "I know you're afraid of the Fierce Ones, and it's understandable.

But you only really have two choices—fight back, or continue to be a victim."

"I didn't say it was the Fierce Ones, and I never saw any faces. If that's why you came, you might as well leave now."

"Okay, let's skip ahead. Why did they target you? Who gave them your name?" Ella pressed.

"Maybe my husband's uncle. He probably thinks I had something to do with my husband's death. But I didn't."

"So help me get the ones who did this to you. Don't let them bully you."

"What other choice do I have? I could hide, but they'd find me again sooner or later as long as I stay on the Rez. That's why I'm leaving. It's what they wanted me to do anyway."

"You weren't the only person who was a victim of this attack and you're part of an ongoing investigation. You can't leave," Ella said.

"You can't force me to stay. You just can't do that to me."

"I'm trying to catch the ones who put you in here—the ones who invaded your home and assaulted you. Help me and I'll help you."

"I don't know anything," she said, practically screaming the words.

"Then answer some easier questions for me," Ella insisted. "Your husband was drinking the day he died. Where did he get the beer?"

"He took a six-pack from the fridge before he left that day. When he wasn't at work, he always had a beer in his hand. Was he drunk, is that why he had the accident?"

Ella didn't answer her, but continued to press her for information. "Did your husband use a chain saw often?"

"No. We don't own one. He'd always wanted one of those, but they're expensive. Did the one he was using break or something?"

"That doesn't appear to be the case." Ella answered her this time, then continued to press. "How was he around tools and machinery? Was he accident-prone?"

"No, no more than anyone else."

"Was there anything in particular bothering him lately?"

"Who knows what was going on at his work? All I can tell you is that he'd been drinking more. Maybe it was because we hadn't been getting along. We were going to split up."

"Did your assailants know you two were going to call it quits? Did they say anything to that effect?"

"Not that I recall," she said slowly, thinking back. "What they wanted was for me to admit I'd killed my husband. They just wouldn't listen to anything else."

"Who do you think did this to you?" Ella insisted. "I won't let them know it came from you."

"They'll know. I've already told you more than I should have. You can't protect me, not forever, and you've already said I can't leave the area."

Ella met Justine at the nurses' station and they left a short time later. Ella was quiet until they got into the tribal vehicle. After filling her partner in, she added, "Did you get anything from the nurses?"

"No. Apparently, Marilyn's not saying much to anyone."

"The Fierce Ones are flaunting themselves right under our noses and we can't get anything on them. This just ticks me off."

"So what's next?"

"We've got a few names, let's go rattle their cages," Ella said. "Go in the direction of George and Marilyn's home. They had a neighbor to the east if I recall right—the opposite direction of Wallace's home."

"I checked the place you're talking about. It belongs to Virgil Pete. My guess is that nobody gives him any garbage."

Ella's eyes narrowed as she tried to figure out why the name was so familiar to her. Finally she shook her head. "I recognize the name, but I can't place him."

"A lot of people believe Virgil's a skinwalker."

Ella exhaled softly, nodding. "*Now* I remember. He's in his eighties. And, no, he's not a skinwalker. I'd say he's more of a survivor. Years ago he had a problem with some of the gangs after he interrupted some punks beating up a kid. He drove his truck right at them, forcing them to scatter. They found out who he was, and after that, they kept coming after him."

"I remember hearing about that," Justine said.

"Virgil got tired of being victimized so he came up with a plan, and asked my brother for his help. He wanted to know about skinwalkers so he could pretend to be one. My brother didn't really approve, but he helped him out anyway. Once he was ready, Virgil made his move and left a few calling cards at the gang members' homes—skinwalker stuff, like bones. They actually belonged to a slaughtered cow, but the kids didn't know that. One of the kids got really sick—no connection—but it was a fortunate coincidence. Word got around that Virgil was responsible, so they left him alone after that."

"But word got around to everyone else as well. No one deals with him anymore, not unless they have to. Didn't he realize something like that could happen?" Justine asked.

"Clifford warned him about that, but Virgil said he didn't care. He just wanted to be left alone. The Christians among the *Diné* still go visit him, mostly trying to save his soul, but the bottom line is *nobody* messes with Virgil anymore. He certainly has nothing to fear from the Fierce Ones because most of them are traditionalists. So let's go see if he knows anything about what's been going on."

They arrived less than a half hour later at a square stucco home with a metal roof and a stovepipe emitting a thin wisp of gray smoke. Justine parked beside the old white pickup, not far from the front door. There were thin curtains on the two windows facing them, and Ella could see someone inside. She got out and leaned against the vehicle, letting Virgil see her. He'd recognize her, she was sure of that.

They didn't have to wait long before he came outside and waved for them to approach.

Ella and Justine joined him inside moments later. The small three-room home was warm and cozy, with the scent of tobacco in the air. The solitary end table beside the worn sofa held a big ashtray full of cigarette butts.

Virgil motioned them toward the sofa, then stepped over to get an old olive drab wool blanket out of their way, tossing it expertly onto a coat hook on the wall. "I was wondering if you'd come by. I heard what happened to my neighbors."

"We need to know if you saw anything at all that might help us catch the ones responsible."

"Sorry, I wasn't here when she got beat up. I was visiting my daughter in Albuquerque. I heard about all that after I came back and went to pick up my mail at the post office."

Ella tried to hide her disappointment, then he continued speaking.

"It's odd how things connect and come around. Barbara Yellowhair owns the company my neighbor worked for, and like my neighbor's wife, she had her wild days, too. Now she's a valued member of the tribe, like her mother."

"Tell me about Barbara," Ella asked.

"I remember when she was in college. She went around, wanting to talk to anyone who might be a skinwalker. She had a real interest in dark things like that." He paused. "But she was just a kid back then with no sense at all. Now she's a businesswoman with important things on her mind."

Intrigued by this new bit of information, Ella filed it away in her mind. "Even though you live alone, you've developed your own sources, and keep in touch with what's happening around you," Ella said, playing a hunch. "Do you know any of the newer members of the Fierce Ones?"

He shook his head. "They stay away from me, I stay away from them. It works better that way. But if you go down the road a little more and turn by the crooked piñon, my neighbor there may know more about what happened the other night."

"What makes you think that?" Justine asked.

He shrugged.

Realizing Virgil had given her all he was going to for now, Ella signaled her partner and didn't press him. They returned to the tribal car and continued down the road.

"What do you think? Should we be taking a closer look at Barbara?" Justine asked.

"Kids in college do some strange things, particularly when they first get away from home. For now, let's just file it under interesting trivia."

"So what strange things did *you* do, cuz?" Justine asked, then grinned.

"I'll never tell," Ella said.

While Justine drove, Ella got the name of Virgil's neighbor from the department. "His name is Darrell Waybenais," Ella told her partner. "I've never heard that name associated with the Fierce Ones."

"Me, neither," Justine said. "We tried to talk to him before, but we were never able to make contact with anyone there. Maybe we'll get lucky this time."

Soon they arrived at a run-down gray cinder block house.

The roof was pitched, covered with red fiberglass sheeting. There were only two aluminum-framed sliding windows, one on each side of the weathered wooden door. A gaunt-looking man in his late fifties was working outside, splitting firewood on a big pine stump. Seeing them, he put down his axe, and came over to meet them just as they stepped out of the tribal unit.

When Ella identified herself, there was no reaction in his gaze. He simply wiped the sweat and wood chips from his face with a blue handkerchief pulled from his torn shirt pocket.

"We're hoping you can tell us a bit about your neighbors, the woman in particular," Ella said, not identifying them by name since there was no need.

He thought about the question for a long time, looking pensively at his hands, gnarled and callused from hard physical labor, then finally looked up. "I heard what happened. The man and I were friends. His old truck was always giving him fits, so I gave him a ride into town a few times so he could get parts. Every now and then he and I would go get firewood together, splitting the load. We took my truck, usually, and he brought the beer. This . . . last time, he was driving his boss's truck, so I've heard."

"Going back to what happened to his wife the next day . . . ," Ella said.

"I can't help you there," he answered flatly. "That's the Fierce Ones' business and I don't mess with them. They're too dangerous, particularly these days. They used to stand for what's right, but now they just like pushing their weight around, giving people a reason to be afraid."

"Withholding evidence is a crime. Did you see anything at all that might help us, like maybe the pickups they were driving? One with a stock rack?" Ella prodded, looking down and noting he wore old leather boots.

"I was watching TV like I always do and didn't hear what happened until the next day. That's when the rumors started. Like everyone else, I've heard plenty since then," he added with a shrug.

"Tell me what you've heard. I'll keep your name out of it," Ella pressed.

"The Fierce Ones are now being run by the younger people. For the most part they're angry Navajos who actually expected the tribal council to deliver on their promises. Like me, they're fed up with the poverty they see here day in and day out." He shook his head slowly. "But they're fighting the wind . . . trying to change what can't be changed."

Ella could hear the sense of defeat in his words. From what she could see, Darrell Waybenais was just getting by. Poverty was like a vicious disease that showed no mercy and, ultimately, choked the spirit.

"Do you know the names of some of these younger members you mentioned?" Ella pressed.

He shook his head. "No names. I have my own problems just putting food on the table. But I can tell you this. Those of us who joined the Fierce Ones when they first came to be, and then left, know more than we should. Go talk to your brother. What has reached my ears has undoubtedly reached his, too."

"If your neighbors are victimized and you do nothing, who'll be left to speak up when they come for you? Somebody has got to take a stand," Ella insisted.

"I've said all I'm going to. You figure things out from here."

Ella and Justine returned to the truck. "I have a real bad feeling about all of this," Justine said.

"The Fierce Ones think of themselves as above the law, and we have to put a stop to that. Head to my brother's," Ella said. "He doesn't take crap from anyone."

Driving farther west down the road, which led past her and her mother's home south of Shiprock, Ella and Justine soon arrived at Clifford's. Noting that her brother had a patient in his medicine hogan, Ella asked Justine to park beside the house and they waited inside the SUV.

Justine studied the vehicle parked to the right side of the hogan. "I think that pickup belongs to Jimmy Levaldo. Want me to run the plate?"

Before Ella could answer, Jimmy stormed out, got into his truck, and drove away in a cloud of dust, passing by them without as much as a glance.

Clifford came out a few moments later. Seeing Ella, he waved, signaling them to come into the hogan.

Ella led the way, and Justine and she sat down on the blankets placed on the north side of the hogan, as was customary for women.

"What brings you here?" Clifford asked them in a weary voice. "It was perfect timing."

Having seen the anger on Jimmy's face, Ella quickly asked, "You all right?"

He nodded slowly. "I've been given a message to pass on to you," he said, then fell silent.

Ella waited for her brother to gather his thoughts. She could see something was eating at him. Knowing that Clifford didn't let anything get to him made this even more intriguing.

"I'm guessing that your visit is related to what I'm about to say, and you're going to know its source, having arrived when you did," he said slowly.

Ella nodded and he continued.

"The attacks on you and your team—even the one that included your daughter—*may* have been conducted by a relatively new faction within the Fierce Ones. Those men know you're actively investigating them and they might have been warning you off."

"They obviously don't know me or my team very well. If this was their doing, they're in for a surprise. They're way out of their league."

He shook his head. "I was specifically told to warn you not to underestimate them. They aren't hampered by the laws and rules you and your officers have to follow. In other words, it's not a level playing field, sister."

"Rules moderate what we can and can't do, that's true. But boundaries like those make us stronger. That's how the good guys remain the good guys. When there are no lines, you end up with things like vigilantes. The People will see what they've become soon enough, and their credibility and influence will drop to zero."

"Well said. But remember that the ones you're dealing with are only a faction within the Fierce Ones, not the whole group."

"I need names," Ella said quietly.

"I was told to pass some of the names on to you, but I'm not sure how much good this'll do. It doesn't prove anything."

"Give me the names. I'll figure out how to use the information."

Clifford began writing names down on the pad she'd handed him. Disappointment washed over her as she looked over and read Arthur Brownhat's name, then Delbert John. She knew these names already.

"This second name is their new leader," Clifford said.

Ella nodded.

He then wrote "Rudy Manus" and, pausing momentarily, glanced up at her. "I've met this man a few times, and there's a lot of anger inside him. Do you remember that huge fight about a year ago that ended up closing down Honkers, that bar just outside the reservation?"

"I heard about it," Ella said. "One guy tossed the place. Took four deputies to bring him down. That was Rudy?"

"Yes," Clifford said. "So be careful around him."

"Of course. We'll pay him a visit, and I'll keep your name out of it."

"Here's something else I think you should know," Clifford said, handing her the list. "StarTalk has enemies among the Fierce Ones. Some of the older members, like many critics within our tribe, consider a move to provide everyone with phone service a misdirection of energy and resources. But those older members, by and large, also think it's beneath them to target StarTalk. They feel it would give the business too much extra attention."

"And the younger ones?" Ella asked.

"I've been told that they insist on behaving more like a neighborhood gang than protectors of The Way. A reliable communications system would make it harder for them to exercise their brand of intimidation. If police or other help can be called easily, those they target may have enough lead time to grab that rifle from the corner, or just avoid them. Reliable phone service is the last thing they want."

"Will they target the tribal council leaders who are pro StarTalk and approved the contracts?" Ella asked.

"I don't think so. They're just not that sophisticated in their thinking. But I would expect them to put pressure on the individuals who work for StarTalk."

"It's a little late to oppose StarTalk at this point, don't you think—like shutting the barn doors after the horses have escaped?" Ella countered.

"They're hoping that StarTalk will be unable to deliver on their promises and the tribe will back off," Clifford said.

"If that happens, the Fierce Ones will gain both prestige and power. From that point on, no one who opposed them would be safe from retaliation," Ella observed somberly.

As they headed out, Justine glanced over at Ella. "You want to pay Rudy a visit?"

Ella nodded slowly, but before she could say anything, her cell phone rang. Ella recognized her mother's strained voice instantly.

"I just received a phone call from a woman who lives south of the airport, right by the highway," Rose said, her voice breaking. "The school bus . . ."

Ella's heart froze and for a moment she forgot to breathe. Her daughter had left on her field trip in a school bus. "Dawn's bus? What's going on?" Her words came out in a rush, fear winding through every syllable.

Rose sobbed and, for a moment, Ella was sure she was going to be sick. "Mom! Talk to me!" she screamed.

"There was a terrible accident and children were hurt. The woman said she spoke to a little girl with your daughter's name. She was bleeding and asked her to call us. My husband and I are going to find her."

There was a thud, and Ella could hear confused voices, then nothing. Her mom must have just set the phone down and left.

Ella hung up, but her hand remained around the phone. "Head for the airport turnoff," Ella said. There was only one route Dawn's bus traveled, the former Highway 666, and Ella knew every inch of the way. The tiny airport, just an airstrip really, was around seven miles south of the junction in downtown Shiprock. They'd be there in less than ten minutes.

"What's happening?" Justine asked quickly. "You mentioned Dawn? But today's Saturday."

In a voice that didn't sound like her own, Ella filled her

in. Then, as if she'd been standing miles away, Ella heard Justine calling Dispatch and asking for details of the accident.

When Justine hung up she gave Ella a puzzled look. "There's been no report of an accident involving a school bus—not anywhere. Dispatch even called the airport office. Nobody could see anything wrong. From their vantage point, traffic on the highway west looked normal."

"It may have just happened," Ella said, terror coiling around her and squeezing the air from her lungs.

"An officer has been sent from the station to follow the route. But Ella, it's all open country, more or less. If this is legit, somebody should have seen *something*."

Although they were racing north along the highway, sirens on and the speedometer tipping ninety, to Ella it felt as if they were standing still. Fear battled against the indefatigable hope that it was all a mistake and her daughter was fine.

A few minutes later, they could see the airport off to their right and Justine eased off on the gas. "Up ahead," Justine said. "Isn't that Dawn's school bus parked at the bus stop? And that looks like Herman's green pickup."

"Yeah, and that's one of the normal stops," Ella said, sitting bolt upright, peering ahead. "The bus looks fine to me."

Less than two minutes later, the bus passed by them, the driver waving, and they parked behind Herman's pickup. Rose was hugging Dawn as Ella rushed out of their tribal unit to join her family.

"Are you okay?" Ella asked her daughter, looking Dawn over quickly but thoroughly.

"Sure, Mom. But why is everyone so excited, and how come Grandma and you decided to pick me up, like four stops early? It was just a field trip to the water place." Dawn turned, looking back at Rose, who was almost in tears, hanging on tightly to Herman's hand. "Is it a surprise?"

Ella couldn't afford an answer. All she cared about at the moment was that her daughter was okay. Tears of relief filled her eyes, and she hugged Dawn tightly again. As she looked up at Rose, Ella realized that her mother looked as if she were about to faint. Herman had his arm around her now, giving support.

Ella took her mother's hand. "Are you okay, Mom?"

"Sure, I'm fine," she said in a weak voice.

Ella continued to hold on to her as Justine came over. "I want to find out who phoned the report in," Ella said, biting off every syllable. Her fear had now turned to cold, calculated rage. "Whoever called used our home number to contact you, right?" Ella asked, looking at Rose. "Did she give her name?"

"Yes, but I didn't recognize it, or the voice, a young woman's. If this was someone's idea of a joke, it was a very poor one."

Dawn, catching on, looked at her mom, then at her grandmother. "This wasn't a fun surprise, was it?"

Ella shook her head. "No, kid, it was not. It's an adult thing."

Dawn waved down the road at one of her friends, who was walking home now, then took her grandmother's hand. "Time to go home, *Shimasáni*?"

Ella looked at Dawn. "Go with your grandmother and stay close. I've got a call to make first, but I won't be far behind you." Ella glanced at Rose and saw her nod.

"May I have a moment, uncle?" Ella said to Herman, using a term of respect. As Rose and Dawn climbed into his pickup, he came over to join Ella.

"Be on guard when you get home, just in case this was all a diversion meant to get us out of the house for a while," Ella warned, her voice low.

"I'll handle it—me and my Winchester," Herman replied,

canting his head slightly toward the truck. His Winchester was on the gun rack behind the seat.

"Take care. I'll be home soon." Ella smiled, knowing the sturdy old man could be trusted with the lives of her family—just as when she'd placed her own life in his hands almost fifteen years ago.

As Justine and Ella walked toward their own vehicle, Ella's lips were pursed into a thin, white line. "This wasn't just a sick prank. This was terrorism—the kind guaranteed to rip out any mother's soul. One way or another, I'm going to find out who did this. Consider it a guarantee."

Ella climbed into the unit, then used the radio as Justine turned around, heading back south. Big Ed soon came on the line. "Shorty, for the time being, Michael Cloud will be watching over your home. He and his brother Phillip will take turns round the clock."

"Good. That'll be one load off my mind. Right now I'm on my way back to check my home and make sure this wasn't just a diversion to lure us away."

As Ella hung up, Justine looked over at her. "Are you sure you're okay?" Justine asked at last.

"Yeah. I'm just really pissed off, and I've got way too much adrenaline in my system." Ella grew quiet, then, after a moment, continued, her voice somber. "If *anything* had happened to my kid, I would have turned my badge in and gone after whoever was responsible." Seeing the surprised look on Justine's face, she added, "I believe in the system, but if anything had happened to my child, all the rules would have gone right out the window."

Justine said nothing for several long moments. "Don't lose it now, cuz. They wanted to rattle you. Think about it. On the Navajo Nation, family is everything. This was deliberately done to undermine you—maybe even to make you question where your loyalties really lie."

Ella looked at Justine. "I've had a million theories in the past fifteen minutes, but none that make as much sense as what you just said." She shook her head slowly. "I've been played by experts, partner."

"Somebody with children of their own, Ella. How else could they have known what it would do to you?"

"Yeah. It takes a woman to know a woman."

SIXTEEN
——— ✖ ✖ ✖ ———

They arrived at Ella's home just a few minutes behind the others. While her family waited outside, Ella searched the place from top to bottom with Justine's help, but they found nothing out of the ordinary.

While Justine answered a phone call, Ella took the time to explain as much as she could to Dawn and ask her to stay close to Rose the rest of the day. Soon thereafter, Dawn took Rose and Herman to see Wind, and Ella smiled. Dawn's cure-all was always her pony.

After assuring her family that they'd have police protection, Ella checked in with Michael via radio. He was now in position to keep watch over the house. Justine joined Ella back at the vehicle moments later and they soon were underway, traveling toward Shiprock again.

"Your mom was starting to come around by the time we left," Justine said. "I was really worried about her for a while."

"Me, too. Mom looked terrible when we arrived at the bus stop. Receiving a shock like that isn't good for anyone, but it's particularly dangerous for someone her age. If I catch the person who did this, she's going to be gumming her food for weeks." She glanced over. "Were you able to trace the number?"

"Yeah, but it didn't do much good. It came from one of those disposable phones," Justine said. "Which figures, really. They're virtually untraceable. I wonder . . ."

Ella knew Justine too well not to recognize that tone of voice. "What's up? Does it have anything to do with that phone call you took while I was talking to my family?"

"Yeah. My mom received a call telling her that my sister Jayne had been struck by a hit-and-run driver while crossing the parking lot at the Sunrise Court where she works. Supposedly, Jayne got rushed to the hospital, but Mom couldn't get anyone at the hospital to confirm it. When she called Jayne's cell phone, all she got was Jayne's voice asking her to leave a message."

"Have you called the hospital?"

"I did, right after Mom called me. They don't have a record of any hit-and-run victim, or any other patient with Jayne's name. I think it's a hoax like the one you received, but I'd still like to track Jayne down. She wasn't at the motel, but that doesn't mean anything because today she's off."

"What about Teeny?" Ella asked. "Did you think of checking at his place?"

"Why would she be there?" Justine asked, surprised.

"She's been seeing him—very seriously. Didn't you know?"

Justine blinked. "I knew they had a couple of dates, but with Jayne that usually doesn't mean much. Is it really serious?"

"From Teeny's perspective, it is," Ella answered. "At least that's what he told me a few months ago."

"Do you know Teeny's number offhand?" Justine asked.

Ella dialed it, then handed the phone to Justine. Based on Justine's side of the conversation, Jayne had answered.

Justine spoke to her sister for a few minutes, then hung up. "Jayne never was in any trouble. In fact, according to her, there's no safer place on the planet than where she is right now."

"I agree with that," Ella said, reminding Justine of the security setup at Teeny's.

"You're right. That place is on par with Fort Knox," Justine agreed. "So what do you think is going on?"

"This whole thing may be a message from the younger members of the Fierce Ones—a way of getting our attention. Or it could be their version of retribution because we're breathing down their necks. We need more facts. Check and see if our tail on Arthur Brownhat paid off."

Justine dialed a number then after a brief conversation, glanced over at her. "He hasn't gone anywhere except to get truck parts. He and his brother have been working on his truck, nothing else."

"I wonder if he made our tail."

"Anything's possible. Where to next?"

"What do you say we pay Rudy a visit?"

"I thought you'd never ask," Justine said. "I've already got his address. He and his wife live alone. Rudy's been arrested for abusing his wife several times, so watch your step around this creep. No charges were ever pressed because Martha refused to admit to the attacks."

"Better call your mother about Jayne," Ella reminded. "Just don't tell her I suggested you call Teeny, okay?"

"Gotcha," Justine said, grinning.

On the way over, they heard from Sergeant Neskahi. Joe, too, had received one of the emergency phone calls. Ella felt a new surge of anger tightening her muscles, spreading through her, and threatening to spill over. She took a deep breath. Anger solved nothing, and it destroyed her ability to think clearly.

Justine was shaking her head, grumbling loudly. "I'd love ten minutes alone with whoever made these calls. These weren't just crank calls, partner. Whoever's doing this has got some good intelligence. They not only know the people on the S.I. team, they have details. The callers even knew about Dawn's field trip."

Ella nodded. "The Fierce Ones have had years to gather information on us and plenty of reluctant sources. If they were behind this, I'm going to keep pushing them until they break, or do something really stupid we can nail them for. One way or another, we'll get the names of those responsible."

"Back at you, partner."

About a half hour later, they arrived at one of the hundreds of site-built tract homes on the reservation. There were utility poles by the dwelling so they had electricity, and Ella could see a TV set flickering just past the curtained living room window.

"With the TV going, I doubt this is traditionalist housing, despite the hogan-shaped great room. Let's just go up to the door," Ella said.

They'd just left the tribal cruiser when a large, burly man wearing a sweat-stained old gray sweatshirt and jeans came to the front door. He stood there in the doorway and watched them in silence as they approached.

Ella brought out her badge and saw an annoyed glimmer flash in his eyes. That flicker of emotion faded an instant later, giving way to a cold, emotionless stare.

"You have questions, so ask them out here," he said, stepping onto the porch and closing the door behind his back.

Ella noticed the red pickup. She hadn't had a close look at the truck that had raced from the scene after her daughter's horse had been spooked, but she'd noticed the color. Red trucks were common, so it wasn't proof of anything, but it was a coincidence she wasn't about to ignore.

"Where were you Saturday morning?" Ella asked.

He smiled slowly. "Here and there."

"This is a police inquiry, so play it straight or be charged with impeding an investigation. I'm not in the mood for any B.S.," she shot back.

"I was here, with my wife. Ask her yourself if you want." He turned and opened the door, then yelled, "Get out here." A woman appeared at the door a few seconds later. Her right eye was almost swollen shut.

"I was here with you Saturday morning, right? Was that yesterday, or the day before?" he turned and asked Ella, grinning in total insincerity.

Martha nodded wordlessly, then went back inside.

"I heard what happened to you and your kid," Rudy said. "The firecracker thing? Not my thing, risking a child like that."

Ella had the feeling he was telling the truth, but her gut told her that he was holding back, too. Maybe he'd made some of the fake emergency calls.

Ella glanced down and saw him holding what she knew to be an untraceable, disposable cell phone. He followed her gaze and then looked up at her. There was no reaction on his face.

"Why don't you let me take a look at your cell phone?" Ella said.

"What for? You trying to pin something on me?"

"I already know that you're a member of the Fierce Ones," Ella said. "Don't make things more difficult on your-self."

"You should be grateful that there are still some of us on this Rez who have the guts to do whatever has to be done. The police are too busy kissing Anglo asses to take care of our own people. For all your fancy badges and guns, you're useless—a drain on the tribe." He took a step toward her, narrowing the gap. "If you weren't wearing that badge and gun, I'd teach you some manners—like I do my wife."

Justine took a step forward, but Ella placed her hand on her shoulder, holding her back.

Moving back with great deliberation, Ella took off her holster and badge and handed them to Justine. She then pushed Rudy—hard. "Wanna give it a try with someone who knows how to hit back? Go for it," she said, her voice level. "Or are you just another gutless sissy?"

Ella wanted him to, even lowering her hands slightly, hoping he'd see an opening and take a swing. But he shook his head, turned his back on her, and walked inside the house, closing the door behind him.

Ella took back her weapon and badge from Justine. "Too bad. Breaking his nose would have given me a lot of satisfaction."

"Where to now?" Justine asked as they got underway. Before she could answer, Dispatch came through on the radio. They both listened to the accident report. A big passenger van was said to have overturned, and the details indicated that the van belonged to Ford's church.

"An ambulance has been dispatched to the scene," Dispatch said, "but SI One, you're our closest unit. Please respond."

"We're on it, Dispatch," Ella answered. SI One was their vehicle.

Ella signed off, then looked at Justine. "This may be just another hoax. This report was phoned in like the others and hasn't been verified. But step on it anyway."

They traveled at the highest speed they could risk after dark, not knowing what lay ahead. But, like it had been with Dawn's bus, there was no sign that an accident had occurred anywhere on that stretch of road. Ella checked with Dispatch again, reconfirming the location and directions.

"Reverend Campbell was notified, and indicated that he wasn't able to reach Reverend Ford on his cell phone," the dispatcher said.

Ella placed the mike down and looked at Justine. "A lot of people know that Ford and I are seeing each other. Maybe this is another way to keep me going in circles."

"But if it's just another hoax why hasn't Reverend Campbell been able to reach Ford?" Justine asked.

"He could be in a dead zone. But it still worries me, too," Ella said.

Ella then called Reverend Campbell, the other pastor at Ford's church, verifying the probable route the church bus had taken. They followed the path, a dirt road north of Narbona Pass in the southern half of the Chuskas but, despite their careful watch for tracks leading off the road, the bus was nowhere to be seen.

Although she was nearly certain that they were being set up again, she couldn't be 100 percent sure. That trace of doubt brought fear, the kind that undermined her confidence. The road was dark and narrow, winding up and down the eastern side of the mountains. There were many steep ravines that could have easily swallowed up an entire fleet of vans, or just blocked the cell phone signal.

When her cell phone rang, she picked it up. Recognizing Ford's voice instantly, she listened, scarcely breathing.

"Ella, I've got a problem and you're the only telephone number on my cell that's actually gone through and stayed connected. I think the canyon walls around here are screening out my calls."

"Where are you and what happened?" she asked quickly.

He gave her exact directions, then continued. "Before we left this morning I got a call from a man who wouldn't identify himself. I was ordered to stop seeing you because you were—and I quote—going down."

"What did you do?"

"I hung up on him, then left with my youth group to To-dacheene Lake. We had a great day. On the way back we stopped to take some photos. When we got back to the van I discovered we had two flat tires. Both valves had been removed. My cell phone wasn't getting a signal from up there, so I hiked down onto a ridge, hoping to pick up a cell tower to the east. You're still the only person I've been able to reach. Could you relay a message and have a service truck sent up to us?"

"No problem, but watch your back," she said, filling him in on what had happened with the bogus emergency calls.

Ella telephoned a local garage, then updated Dispatch while Justine listened in. Ending her call, Ella leaned back. "We popped up on the Fierce Ones' radar the moment we started trying to track down the ones who assaulted Marilyn and Wallace. So far, they've mostly run us around in circles, but I think things will get more serious once they realize we won't back off."

"Nobody wants to go up against them, particularly those who live in isolated areas. To be perfectly honest with you, I can't say I blame them," Justine said, then added, "If you weren't a police officer, would you risk standing up to them?"

"In a flash," Ella responded flatly. "I would *never* let anyone bully me. I'm just not made that way. If someone pushes me, I push back. That's the way I've always been."

"Me, too," Justine admitted with a grin.

"So with that in mind, I've got a plan. There's someone I want to go see—alone."

Though Justine had been dead set against it, Ella had dropped her off at the station and continued toward the home of the Fierce Ones' new leader, Delbert John. Officer Tache had driven by the residence, east of Shiprock and south of the

Upper Fruitland Chapter House, to check the place out. He'd reported only one vehicle parked there.

Ella's plan was to talk to Delbert *alone*. Without an audience, there was less chance that Delbert would feel inclined to posture, or that their talk would escalate into a full-blown incident. As she approached her destination, Ella called Dispatch and reported in. Less than two minutes later, Agent Blalock contacted her on the cell phone.

"I'm in the Fruitland area and overheard your radio call. Wait for me and I'll join you. If I'm with you and anything goes down, it'll be a federal crime. That'll help keep things under a tight lid."

Ella considered it, though judging from the tone of Blalock's voice, he had no intention of taking no for an answer.

"I've been following up on the Fierce Ones, Ella. Both faction leaders are being a lot more careful now. There's only one car outside of Delbert's home, but that's because they've been parking by the Chapter House and walking over. Your Officer Tache passed by a while ago and I think they spotted his vehicle. Did you send him?"

"Yeah, I did," Ella replied.

"Tache wasn't careless. They were just keeping watch."

"Are you sure they haven't made *you?*" she asked.

"Positive. I'm in a satellite TV service van, pretending to be working the 'hood."

"I'm just passing Hogback, so come back west and meet me at the Quick Stop in Fruitland," Ella said. "We'll go in using my wheels. One vehicle isn't likely to alarm them. I'll also make sure we have backup ready to roll."

Blalock joined her about ten minutes later and slipped into the passenger's side after parking the van in the small lot. "Ready when you are," he said, shutting the door.

Several minutes later Ella was across the river, driving

down a narrow gravel road east of the power plant that led into the developed neighborhood. As she turned onto the recently paved street where Delbert's home was located, an old flatbed truck stacked high with firewood started to back out of the driveway of another home, apparently unaware of their vehicle.

"Wake up!" Ella said, slowing and honking her horn.

The truck came out another ten feet, then a Navajo man looked over at them, a startled look on his face as he stared into their headlights. He braked hard, spilling firewood off the back of the truck and onto the gravel—and effectively blocking the road.

"Guy must be deaf," Blalock muttered. "Suppose we should help clear the road?"

Ella turned on her unit's emergency lights, then went to talk to the driver while Blalock checked out the spilled load.

"Must be half a cord on the ground," Blalock yelled.

As Ella came up to the driver's window, she suddenly realized the man had a knife in his hand. Instantly, she reached for her weapon, but a second man came around the front of the truck, pointing his rifle at her head. Ella froze just as Blalock spoke from somewhere behind her.

"I'm a federal agent, folks. This is a very *big* mistake."

Ella turned her head and saw Blalock with his hands up in the air. Another man was standing by the tailgate, aiming a rifle at the agent's chest.

SEVENTEEN

—— ✖ ✖ ✖ ——

I'm Special Investigator Ella Clah of the Navajo Police Department. We didn't come to make any arrests. Don't make us change our minds. Lower your weapons," she ordered.

A few seconds later Delbert John came out onto the porch of the house, standing in the porch light for only a moment before moving into the driveway. He whistled to his men, shook his head, and the men with the rifles immediately lowered their weapons. The driver lowered his knife, too, and gave Ella a toothy, lopsided grin.

"We weren't expecting anyone tonight," Delbert said, coming up to Ella, "so we took defensive measures when we saw you approaching. I've received some death threats recently. As you've already seen, I've even switched houses."

Ella reached down slowly for her handheld radio, then called and cancelled the backup. "Who issued the death threat?" she asked him.

"At first, I thought Jimmy Levaldo was behind it. He doesn't like anyone who disagrees with him, and he doesn't realize that his tactics and methods are as out of date as he is. That's why they don't work. The future of the tribe is in the hands of *our* generation—people like us who can accept change and are willing to throw out ideas that don't work." He met her gaze and added, "In the old days we survived without police departments because our people respected balance and harmony and knew how to walk in beauty. We don't need Anglo laws to tell us how to live."

"We've heard the history lesson before, so why don't you just skip ahead to this century, and get to the point, Delbert," Ella said. "Who's behind the death threat?"

"I spoke to Jimmy and he said he had nothing to do with it. At first I didn't believe him. Then I took a real close look at the facts. That's when I realized we were *all* being used. Someone out there is letting us take the heat for what *they're* doing."

"Who?" Blalock prodded.

"I'm not sure yet, but here's what I do know. Our people always clearly announce that they're part of the Fierce Ones. Or they leave a sign behind to remind those we're warning that we'll be watching them. Our symbol's an eye—and it's left someplace where it can't be missed."

Ella remembered having seen it at the Curtises' home. "I know it."

"Have you noticed that eye at any of the incidents that have recently been attributed to the Fierce Ones, like the shootings?"

She shook her head. "I assumed you'd stopped using it, or more to the point, that the newer members had," Ella said.

"When the Fierce Ones leave a warning, we want things to be crystal clear. The Fierce Ones never hide from their own actions. You can't walk in beauty that way."

"Lots of odd things have been happening today," Ella said, mentioning the calls to her S.I. people, and, finally, Ford's experience with his youth group.

"None of us—young or old—would use those tactics. There's no lesson in them. And, for the record, we don't mess with religious leaders unless they start preaching *against* Navajo traditions. I know Reverend Tome. He's an asset to the Navajo Nation. Sure, he's a Christian, but he also honors our culture and history. The records he's kept and his knowledge of Navajo life are a valuable asset to our tribe."

"Then who's making all the trouble?" Ella asked.

"That's the real question, isn't it? Someone has tried to set the tribal police against the Fierce Ones—and the Fierce Ones against each other. That's why we're now using all our people to find out who's responsible."

"It would be a lot better if you'd let law enforcement professionals handle this," Blalock said.

Delbert shook his head. "We'll get answers faster than you can, especially on our native land."

"Terror and force will get you answers meant to appease, not necessarily the truth," Ella said. "People under duress will say anything just to ease the pressure."

Without giving him a chance to argue, Ella walked back to her unit, Blalock by her side. A few seconds later, they were on their way out of the neighborhood, heading north toward the main highway.

"Were you wearing a wire?" Ella asked Blalock.

"Of course. Do you think I'd ever put myself in a situation like this without covering my butt? Everything that went down is now on the record."

"Good. I just wish we'd come out of this with some names," Ella said. "I have this feeling that all the things we've been experiencing lately are connected. There's a pattern here. If we could find it, we'd have our answers."

They were on the way back to the convenience store where Blalock had left his vehicle when Big Ed contacted Ella directly on the cell phone. After getting permission, Ella placed her chief on the speaker so FB-Eyes could hear.

"I just got a call from Barbara Benally," Big Ed said.

"Someone broke into Ervin's StarTalk office this evening after the office staff left for the day. The perp or perps set fire to his desk, computer, and chair. Your team is working the scene as we speak but, so far they've got nothing, except that the accelerant was lighter fluid."

"I'll head over there immediately," Ella said.

"I'll go with you," Blalock said as soon as Ella's conversation ended.

Ella glanced at him, nodded, then focused on the road. "Our team's working a series of crimes with one common denominator—the Benallys," Ella said in a thoughtful voice. "George Charley's death had a connection to Ervin via Ervin's truck. The harassment my team and I have been subjected to could also track back to StarTalk's problems and Ervin's. Maybe his enemies have decided to come after us because we're helping him," Ella said, then after a pause, added, "But that would also mean that Ervin's enemies are well organized and have serious manpower to draw on."

"A conspiracy theory? Where do we even begin looking?" Blalock asked.

"And that's the real question, isn't it?"

By the time they arrived at StarTalk, Barbara Benally was pacing outside the office building, waiting for them. It was nighttime but the exterior lights were all on.

Barbara hurried over to meet them as soon as they'd parked. "We got off lucky," she said. "The computer in Ervin's office didn't ignite, it melted. And though the top of his desk is charred, it didn't go up in flames. We have a sprinkler system and it quickly extinguished everything."

"Is Ervin here now?" Ella asked, thinking of questioning him first.

"No, he's been at home ever since the press conference incident," Barbara said, lowing her voice to a whisper as they walked toward the entrance to the office building. "He won't leave the house. Ervin's also lost a lot of weight and he hardly eats at all. I wanted him to go to the hospital, or at least get some kind of counseling, but he refuses. My mother suggested that maybe your brother could give him something to help calm him down, but Ervin won't hear of it. He says he'll handle it his way."

"Which is?" Ella asked.

"He's armed all the time. He won't come into a room if my mom or I are there. He even sleeps in his office at home. We conduct business either on the house intercom or by phone. He says that if they come after him, he'll be able to handle things better if I'm not around. So he's asked me to keep my distance. He fired his bodyguard, complaining that the man made him look like a fool in public. I think he's also concerned about having an armed man we don't know roaming around the house day and night. However, he wants to hire a full-time bodyguard for me." Barbara stopped right outside the door, which had been propped open.

"That sounds like an excellent idea," Ella said slowly, detecting an acrid burnt plastic smell coming from inside the building. "And not just for you, also for your mother."

"Mom makes her own decisions, in case you haven't noticed, and she already has an ex-police officer working for her part time. As for me, it's just not necessary," Barbara said, shrugging her shoulders. "Ervin's arranged for security cameras to be installed here and at home."

"That's a step in the right direction. But if you change your mind, I can recommend an extremely capable bodyguard." Ella knew that Teeny would be more than capable of doing the job.

"Are you sure you don't have any idea who might be behind all that's happened?" Ella continued. "We know more than one person is involved."

"I can't think of anyone who might go this far to strike

out at my husband, but when Ervin was trying to get the permits and the backing we needed to get StarTalk off the ground, he stepped on some toes."

"Like whose?" Blalock pressed. "Think hard."

"I . . ." She shook her head. "You'll have to talk to my husband."

Ella noted her hesitation. "But you *do* suspect someone, don't you? Ervin's in danger, Barbara. If you want us to help you, you need to help us."

"But I don't know anything for sure . . . ," she said slowly.

"We'll look into it. Give us some names, and we'll take it from there," Ella said.

Barbara took a deep breath. "Louis Etcitty," she said, at last. "My husband's complained to me about him several times."

The only Louis Etcitty she knew was a crystal gazer in his mid-sixties. She'd met him once at her brother's place. Though there were several kinds of crystal gazers, Louis was said to be able to look into a rock crystal and locate missing objects. Clifford believed in his abilities, and had once hired Louis to help him locate a jar of a very rare herb he'd needed for a Sing.

"Louis Etcitty the crystal gazer?" Ella asked, verifying it.

Barbara nodded. "He and his nephew have been dead set against StarTalk from the very beginning," Barbara said. "They've told Ervin right to his face that they're spray painting or tearing down as many posters of StarTalk as they can find. They also advise everyone they meet to oppose the project."

"Why?" Ella asked, surprised. People like Louis and his nephew, who lived southeast of Shiprock, would have benefitted greatly from a phone system that worked.

"I'm not really sure what their reasoning is on this. You'll have to talk to my husband to get the rest of the story."

As Barbara led them to Ervin's office, Ella glanced at her. "What made you come back to the office tonight?"

"I'd forgotten to bring some papers Ervin needed, so I made a quick after-dinner run to the office. That's when I found this mess."

Barbara walked past an exhaust fan Ella noticed as belonging to the S.I. team. The inside of the building was currently being illuminated by their generator-powered electric lanterns, probably because the circuits were out.

As Ella stepped through Ervin's office door, which appeared to have been kicked in, she saw Justine and Tache working.

"How did the vandal gain access to the building? Any possibility it was an inside job?" Ella asked them.

"Not likely. They didn't use a key," Justine answered. "The bathroom window was broken. But whoever slipped through wasn't skinny enough to avoid getting cut on some of the glass remaining in the frame. There was enough blood to take a sample, but that's all we've got so far. We dried out what we could around the desk and lifted prints. We'll run those against all the employees. Mrs. Benally has already given us permission to access the prints from the employee records."

"Sorry about the lighting, Ella," Tache said, looking up. "Some of the circuit breakers were tripped by the fire, and we didn't want to risk another problem until an electrician checks out the wiring."

Ella nodded, lost in thought. The scene struck her as off, somehow. While Blalock spoke to some of the warehousemen who'd been onsite, she helped her team gather evidence.

"The fire didn't spread because not enough accelerant was used," Justine said. "I got this from the trash can," she added holding up an almost full can of lighter fluid.

"The fire was also set right beneath a sprinkler, the

only one within twenty feet," Ella observed. "Had the perps wanted an out-of-control fire, they would have chosen that table stacked high with documents in the adjoining room."

"It looks like another attempt to undermine Benally," Justine answered.

"How did this get discovered?" Ella asked.

Tache turned to answer, but Barbara spoke first.

"By the time I drove up, the fire was already out, thanks to the warehouseman who heard the smoke alarm. He had a key for emergencies, and once he realized the fire was out, he went back out to turn off the sprinkler system. When I came in, I discovered this," Barbara said, waving her hand around the room.

Ella's cell phone rang and she picked it up immediately. She didn't recognize the slurred voice at the other end until Ervin Benally identified himself.

"How did you get my direct number?" Ella asked him.

"Later. Someone's sneaking around outside my home. I saw him go into the shed and then come back out. He also went into the garage. I've got a gun and if he takes one step inside this house I'm shooting him dead. You hear me?"

"Don't put yourself in danger. Lock yourself inside one of the rooms and wait for us. We're less than five minutes away. Other officers will be en route as well."

"What's going on?" Barbara asked.

"I'll explain later," Ella said.

Ella found Blalock and filled him in quickly as they hurried down the hall. "We've got to roll."

Barbara followed. "If that was Ervin who telephoned, be very careful," she called out to Ella. "These days my husband isn't thinking very clearly."

"Because he's been drinking too much? Is he having hallucinations or something like that?" Ella asked, stopping near the door.

"I think he may be, but I don't think it's just the booze anymore. Every once in a while he'll get all jumpy and tell me that he's being watched. I've gone outside to look but no one is ever around." Barbara paused, then shook her head. "But maybe I'm wrong about this. Things *are* happening. Look at his office. Go and make sure he's okay, but remember he's not himself these days."

With a quick nod, Ella hurried into the cruiser and joined Blalock, who was already inside, seat belt fastened. As she raced out of the parking lot, she called for backup, warning them to proceed with caution because the occupant may have been drinking.

"A drunk *and* a nutcase. Wonderful," Blalock muttered.

"Ervin was slurring his words, so I picked up on the drinking part when he was on the phone. But Barbara says he's been seeing things, too. That could be the booze, I suppose, but still . . ."

"I hate dealing with drunks as much as you do, Clah. If this guy is having some kind of nervous breakdown on top of that, we could all end up shot."

"Then you better make sure that vest of yours is covering whatever you *really* want to protect," Ella said, noting Blalock was adjusting the ballistic vest he wore beneath his shirt nowadays.

Ella opted for a silent approach as they drew near, hoping to catch whoever Ervin had seen—providing, of course, he hadn't been hallucinating. As she cut the engine and coasted to a stop a hundred feet up the road from the large, adobe-style home, Ella glanced over at Blalock.

"The outside lights are bright. That's good," Ella said.

"Yeah, but we better watch each other's backs."

Ella nodded. "Let me tell Ervin we're here. No sense in getting shot for our trouble."

She dialed, and Ervin picked up the phone immediately. "That you, Clah?" His voice was at a whisper.

"Yes, and Agent Blalock. We have other officers on the way, so sit tight and stay away from the doors."

"I think they're still outside. Call me when it's okay." He hung up before she could reply.

"He thinks somebody is still on the grounds, Dwayne."

"Right."

They got out together, using their respective doors to provide cover as they drew their weapons and surveyed the scene. No people or vehicles were visible from their location, but the gravel driveway led around to a garage in the back.

"Earlier Ervin said the intruder was at the rear of the property. I'm going to take a look."

"Right behind you," Blalock answered, his voice whisper thin. "Watch out for a hidden vehicle."

As they reached the back corner of the house, Ella saw that the side door leading into the detached garage farther ahead had been forced open. Inside, she could just about make out the shape of a car fender.

Ella nodded to Blalock, who came up behind her, crouching low. "Cover me while I advance to the garage," Ella whispered.

"Go for it," Blalock replied quietly.

Ella sprinted across the driveway, her gun at the ready, then took a position beside the building, right by a small red wheelbarrow. After checking out as much of the house as she could see and spotting no open windows or doors, she returned her attention to the open garage door. The room beyond was lit and she inched forward, waited for a few seconds, back pressed against the wall, then peered inside the garage. Nothing seemed out of the ordinary. A sedan, the hood popped open, occupied the half of the garage closest to her.

Ella moved in and bumped the open door slightly. Hearing a sloshing sound directly above her, she instinctively jumped back. Suddenly a glass jar came crashing down, shattering on the concrete floor and splashing liquid everywhere, including her boots and pant legs.

Ella immediately recognized the sharp, sulphuric scent of battery acid. An instant later the skin on her legs began to feel uncomfortably warm. Running out to the side of the garage, she grabbed a coiled-up garden hose. Ella turned the faucet to full blast, soaking her pant legs and boots with water. The caustic liquid had already begun to eat through the fabric of her slacks, and was leaving splotches on her leather boots.

"Battery acid?" Blalock commented, sniffing the air. "Make sure you wash off your hands and face, too, just in case."

"Hold the hose for me, Dwayne," Ella said, handing it to him. She rinsed her hands thoroughly, then cupped water in her palms and washed her face and neck.

"Oh, that's cold," she moaned.

"Better than acid burns," Blalock said, aiming the hose away for a moment. "More?"

"Naw, that's enough. Let me check out the damage." While he turned off the water, she raised up one pant leg, pockmarked with jagged holes the size of dimes and quarters where the acid had eaten through the fabric. Angry red splotches covered her shin around the boot line.

"Those idiots! They could have scarred someone for life, burned out an eye, or worse," she said in a tight voice. "This goes way beyond the prank stage."

Blalock knelt by the puddle on the floor. "We'll need a sample of this. Maybe a glass jar and a syringe?"

Hearing a vehicle pulling up, Ella looked toward the

street. From the emergency lights, she knew it was a police cruiser. Marianna Talk, one of their youngest police officers, stepped out of the squad car and hurried over. Her gaze went to Ella's soaked pant leg, the bleached-out splotches on her boots, then back up at her.

"Where do you need me?" she asked at once.

Simple and to the point, that was Marianna Talk all the way. The young Navajo woman had been on the force two years and still looked as if she'd just turned sixteen. The fact that she was barely five foot two, and that her height was enhanced by the boots she was wearing, helped create the illusion of youth. But Marianna was learning how to be tough, and her professionalism continued to grow by leaps and bounds.

"Stand guard outside this door and make sure no one wanders in," Ella said, then she stepped away and dialed Ervin's home number.

"You still okay in there?" she asked when he picked up the phone.

"What's going on?" Ervin replied.

Ella turned and looked at the house. She could see Ervin peeking out from behind a curtain, telephone receiver to his ear. "I'll be inside in a few minutes and tell you all about it. Just stay away from the windows a while longer, okay?"

He nodded, then disappeared from view.

Blalock walked up to Ella. "They won't get any prints off those pieces of glass, you know. I think the acid would have washed away any skin oils. Whoever handled that jar must have had on gloves, too—that is, unless we're dealing with complete idiots."

"They had to drain the acid from a battery with some kind of suction device, like a hydrometer. Maybe we'll find prints on the battery of that sedan, or on the hood. It's up."

"Yeah, I noticed. And I saw a big hydrometer on the workbench, still wet. But if all they touched was the rubber bulb, it'll be hard getting any latents."

"I still want my team to process the scene," she said, and called it in. "If there's something here, they'll find it."

Once the scene was secure, Ella and Blalock went up to the main house's back door and knocked. There was no answer. Ella tried again. This time she was loud enough to have been heard all the way down the dirt road.

Blalock's eyes widened slightly. "Unless he's totally deaf, he heard you. Think someone inside has a gun on him or something?"

Ella was about to reply when she heard footsteps coming toward them from the other side of the closed door.

A second later, the door was open. Ervin stood on the other side of the doorway, then cocked his head, gesturing for them to enter. "Sorry I took so long. I was on the other side of the house, checking the locks. Hurry on in. I'm not making a target out of myself by standing in the doorway."

Ella stared at him in surprise. She'd last seen Ervin up close at the Chapter House meeting. He'd seemed a little harried back then, but he'd obviously fallen to pieces since that day. His face now looked haggard and dark circles rimmed his eyes. The smell of alcohol was thick in the air, too. Ervin looked drunk and on the verge of exhaustion.

Once they were inside, Ella watched as he locked and fastened the door with one hand, his other still holding a rifle. His movements were clumsy and he had to try three times to get the safety latch in place. Once the door was secure, Ervin invited them to take a seat in the living room, and followed them stiffly. He brought the rifle with him, and set it on top of the coffee table so hard she thought the plate glass beneath would crack.

"What happened? Did you catch him?" he asked, leaning forward and sending a wave of eighty-proof breath in their direction.

"No. That's why I'm going to need you to describe the person you saw," Ella said, looking around but not seeing a bottle. As she did, Ella caught a glimpse of Blalock's disgusted expression. FB-Eyes was very aware that Ervin's judgment was impaired.

Ervin must have noticed the way they were watching him, because he abruptly sat up straight, cleared his throat, and did his best to assume normal speech. "I never got a clear look. He stayed away from the lights for the most part. All I really saw was his shadow, but he *wanted* me to see that much of him."

"What makes you think that?" Blalock asked.

"I heard what sounded like someone repeatedly kicking the side of the wheelbarrow next to the garage. That's when I peered out. The minute I did, the sound stopped but I kept looking. I caught a few glimpses of him after that, but it was never more than just a flicker of shadow and movement here and there. I kept my rifle with me and had he broken into this house, I would have shot him dead."

The conviction in his voice left no room for doubt in Ella's mind. Near as she could tell, Ervin wasn't completely wasted, but from his lack of balance and coordination, he was either flying high on something, or far from sober.

He looked at her pant leg. "How did you get wet?"

Ella told him, and he cringed visibly at the mention of the battery acid.

"That cinches it. I'm getting round-the-clock bodyguards for my wife," Ervin said.

"Why not for yourself? You seem to be the primary target," Ella said.

"I handle my own problems. When it comes to my wife, it's different. She'll get the best of the best."

"Any idea who you're going to hire?"

"I've contacted Mr. Little's company, 360 Plus."

"Bruce Little is a good man and his company is very reliable," Ella agreed with a nod.

"Consider a bodyguard for yourself as well," Blalock added. "You can't be on your guard twenty-four–seven."

Exhausted, Ervin dropped down into the leather easy chair and ran a hand through his hair. "I'm just tired of all this nonsense. I believe in StarTalk and the good it'll do, but I wouldn't have pushed for it as hard as I did if I'd known then what I know now."

"Your wife had mentioned something about having security cameras around the property, but I didn't see any outside," Ella said.

"I haven't got them installed yet," he admitted after a long pause. "Nearly all of our funds are tied up in StarTalk and I've lost two vehicles in the past week. Until the venture gets into the black we're living on loans."

"Your wife told me that Louis Etcitty has been giving you trouble," Ella said.

"That old man is making me crazy." His eyes suddenly sparked with anger. "He goes around telling people that he can look into a rock crystal and find objects that have been lost. What a scam! I'd be willing to bet he steals them first and that's how he *finds* them." He stood up on wobbly legs and began pacing again.

Ella knew better. Her brother wouldn't have used Louis' services if there wasn't more to him than that.

"Etcitty is convinced that StarTalk—actually the satellites we'll be linking up with—will interfere with his crystal gazing," Ervin continued. "He tells everyone that we'll be angering the gods and that misfortune will follow. I've also heard that he's pointing to what's been happening to me—how I'm being harassed—as just the start of trouble."

"So you're thinking he might be responsible for what's going on?" Blalock concluded.

He paused before replying. "I'd like to say yes, believe me, but I honestly don't think Etcitty could be doing *all* this," he said at last. "Tearing down posters, sure, but what happened to you outside . . . that's not his style. I also don't think he's physically up to darting around out there like the man I saw. Louis isn't that spry anymore. Not unless he's some kind of . . ." He shook his head. "Never mind."

"Now's not the time to hold back," Blalock said. "If these troubles are allowed to continue, they could end up costing you a lot more than your company."

Ervin closed his eyes for a moment and took a long, deep breath. "Okay, I don't know if you can understand this, Agent Blalock, but Investigator Clah will. I found something outside yesterday that really bothered me. I'm not a traditionalist, obviously, but, I've got to tell you, this really creeped me out."

His voice dropped to a whisper as he continued. "I went to the garage—where our washing machine and dryer are—to see if Barbara had laundered my favorite shirt. I hadn't seen it since I'd worn it to the barber's. I'd put it in the laundry because it had hair on it and wearing it made me itch. Knowing Barbara sometimes leaves clean stuff out there for days, hung up on a little rack, I decided to go take a look."

He lapsed into a tense silence. Ella didn't interrupt him, noticing the way he'd clenched his hand into a tight fist, and how his breathing had become more rapid.

"It hadn't been washed, but I only found *half* of my shirt in the basket," he said at last in a horrified whisper.

"Excuse me?" Blalock said, shooting Ella a puzzled look.

"It had some of my hair still on it, from the barber shop, remember?" he added, a touch of panic in his voice. "I mean

I don't believe in that stuff, but we all heard stories growing up."

Blalock stared at him, but getting no further explanation, looked over at Ella.

"Witchcraft, Dwayne. A skinwalker can use personal objects to make a victim so sick nothing will ever cure him," Ella said, then looked back at Ervin. "The fact that they left half of the shirt means somebody is trying to psych you out," Ella added. "You *know* that. Don't let them play you like this."

"Yeah, I know all that, but still . . ."

Ella gazed at Ervin. He was barely holding on, and shaking slightly, which may have been because of the booze. The bags under his eyes told her it had been a long time since he'd had a decent night's rest, too. All things considered, a skinwalker's curse hadn't been necessary. It was more like icing on the cake for a man who was being terrorized.

"I think what you need most is some uninterrupted sleep," Ella said. "And a lot less alcohol."

"Booze is about the only thing that helps me relax when the pressure's on. I could cut back, I guess. But it's been impossible to get any sleep the past few days. We're getting crank calls at all hours of the night, and every time I try to get some sleep during the day, a call from the office wakes me up. Besides, I need to try and stay awake during business hours. We're at a critical time in our operations."

"Get an answering machine and monitor all your calls," Ella said. "You'll have a record of everything that way—voices and times that may help us catch whoever's behind this."

"Our business has always required a personal touch, but you're right. It's time to try something different."

"What happens when Mrs. Benally answers the phone?" Blalock asked.

"Nothing. We tried that. If it's one of the troublemakers, they just hang up," Ervin replied.

"And when you answer what do they say to you?" Blalock asked.

"It's always the same voice speaking in Navajo. Loosely translated, the man says he's coming for me and my life is in his hands," Ervin answered.

"Is anything about the voice familiar to you?" Ella pressed.

"It's not anyone I know," Ervin answered.

"We need this man's calls recorded. 360 Plus will have the best monitoring equipment around. Get Mr. Little to install whatever's necessary," Ella suggested.

After Justine and her team arrived to work the crime scene, Blalock took Ella aside. "I vote we go talk to the crystal gazer tomorrow first thing."

"A crystal gazer of his standing isn't likely to be involved with skinwalkers. I think we've got two very different things going on here. But Louis Etcitty is well connected, and may know something that can help us. Let's see what he has to say."

EIGHTEEN
✖ ✖ ✖

It was shortly after seven-thirty the following morning when Ella and Blalock set out in her tribal unit to Louis Etcitty's home.

"This case gets more complicated every time we turn around," Ella said. "Justine found some footprints around Ervin's garage that appear to be from Nikes. We'll know later this morning if they're an exact match to the ones found by the Dodge. Ervin appears to be at the center of what's happening but I'm just not sure if StarTalk's the reason. Maybe this is personal."

"What about a jealous husband—or lover—out for revenge? The guy does—or did have—a promising future for an ambitious girlfriend."

Ella shook her head. "I've ruled that out. Ervin would know where it was coming from and would be more angry than terrorized."

"Okay, moving on. I've done background checks on Benally," Blalock said. "He's running a tight ship financially and he doesn't have any creditors leaning on him. I even checked with area casinos. They've never heard of him, at least as a customer or client."

"We're being skillfully manipulated, just like Ervin, but I'm not sure by whom or to what end."

They arrived at Louis Etcitty's home, about fifteen miles west of White Rock, forty-five minutes later. The country here was flat, dry, and desolate, with the closest standing water outside a stock tank more than twenty miles east at Lake Valley. An old green pickup was parked near an empty sheep pen, and smoke was coming from the chimney of the hogan-style building, which was constructed of stucco over a wood frame.

"Someone's home," she said. "But, here, we should definitely wait to be invited before we approach. If we rush it, any hope of getting his cooperation goes out the window."

Minutes ticked by. After ten minutes Blalock shifted. "Clah, maybe we should just go up to the door. He probably doesn't even know we're here."

"He knows. Around here, you can hear a vehicle coming for miles. Listen."

The only sound at all came from a slight breeze stirring up the dust. There weren't even any leaves to rattle across the hard ground.

"Okay, you're right. It's dead quiet. That means he's ignoring us. Maybe he's not even awake. Honk the horn."

"No, Dwayne, he's up. You should have learned this game by now. He's making us wait. There's a difference. Just sit tight and mellow out for a while. Questioning *Hosteen* Etcitty will go a lot easier if we show some respect."

"I don't mind long stakeouts, Clah, but . . ."

"Hush, FB-Eyes," she said with a tiny smile. "Wait." Ella glanced over a minute later, and saw Blalock grinning.

"That's the first time *you've* called me that, though I've heard it from plenty of others. I'm Anglo, not deaf," he said.

"It's just a nickname."

"Like L.A. Woman? That's yours, right?"

"Yeah, years ago when I first returned to the Rez. Now hush."

A full twenty minutes passed before Louis Etcitty came to the door and waved for them to come inside.

Ella led the way, trying to ignore Blalock's grumbling about wasted time.

Louis gave Ella a nod as she stepped into his home. "What brings you here?" he asked, waving them to sit by the fire. "Do you need me to find something for you? I helped your brother, the *hataalii*, once."

"I know and he was very grateful," Ella answered. "We came today to ask you about StarTalk, uncle. We've heard that you're responsible for spray painting their posters and, sometimes, ripping them down." Ella's gaze settled on the spray paint can behind him on the bookshelf.

He smiled slowly. "That's not me, and you can't prove it was."

"You have that can of paint," she said, pointing with her lips.

"I make little footstools, paint them in bright colors, then sell them to the tourists by the roadside."

Ella walked around the room, forcing him to follow her with his gaze. She was walking past a card table in the corner when she spotted a torn, dark brown leather band. She recognized it instantly as the same kind worn around the wrists of the Fierce Ones when they wanted to be identified.

Ella glanced back at Louis, but he didn't react. As she returned to her chair, Ella looked through to the kitchen and saw two cereal bowls and two glasses in the drain rack. "Who else lives here?" she asked.

"My nephew," he answered. "Is that against the law, too?"

"That's not against the law, but there are plenty of people who are breaking the law right now, people who don't like StarTalk. For example, did you know that skin-walker signs were left outside the home of StarTalk's found-er?" she said, then realized from his expression that she'd gone too far.

His eyes widened and a second later he stood up. "You will *not* discuss the evil ones here. Not now—not ever. Please leave. Even mentioning them can call them to you. Of all people, *you* should know better."

It had been accidental, a slip of the tongue, but it was too late to take it back now. "We need you to answer some ques-tions for us first," Ella said.

"No more talk. You have to leave," he said, his breathing ragged as he stepped back away from them. "What I pre-dicted has come true. StarTalk's founder brings evil—to himself and anyone around him. Stay away from him. If you can't because of your job, ask your brother to give you some-thing that'll protect you."

It was clear that Louis wouldn't cooperate any further, so Ella and Blalock went back to the car.

"So what do you make of that?" Ella asked.

"That guy was scared spitless, Ella. The minute you men-tioned skinwalkers he couldn't wait to get rid of us."

"That's my fault. I wasn't thinking. I was too focused on pushing him. But I want to find out more about his nephew," she said, and explained about the leather wristband. "If nothing else, maybe he's responsible for the crank calls."

"I didn't see any signs of a telephone in there," Blalock said. "But maybe the nephew carries a cell phone. We should check."

Ella nodded. "I'll call Dispatch and have the information relayed to us. In the meantime, let's stop by my brother's hogan. He may be able to fill in some gaps."

Clifford's place was on the way into town, and they ar-rived within a half hour. Judging from the old white pickup parked nearby her brother was busy with a patient. Ella leaned back, and prepared to wait.

"Time always moves at its own speed here on the reservation," Blalock said quietly. "Even now, after more than a decade, I still find the interminable waiting the hardest to take."

"Once you retire, I have a feeling you'll miss the pace of life here more than you realize," Ella said. Dwayne had spoken of early retirement many times, but he'd never actually made the move.

"These days I try not to think of retirement. When I was in my forties, I looked forward to it. I told myself I'd travel, go fishing up in Colorado, and pass the day doing all the things I never had time to do. Then, as I got older, I realized I *am* doing what I want to do. I love law enforcement, it's what keeps my heart beating. My wife discovered that many years ago, and that's why she left me."

"Do you regret the sacrifices you made to be where and what you are?"

Dwayne thought about it for a moment. "There are times I miss being married—having someone to share my life with away from the job. But the thing is, I love this job and it has always come first to me. I never minded cutting a holiday dinner short, or skipping it altogether. What I hated was having to feel guilty about it. Now I come and go as I please, and that kind of freedom grows on you," he said, then added, "What about you, Ella? Do you think you'll remarry someday?"

"I have two loves. My daughter is the center of my life, then there's police work. Obviously, both of those are round-the-clock commitments. I don't think it would be fair to bring someone else into the picture. He'd always be number three, and that's hard for anyone to live with."

"What about someone like Ford—Reverend Tome? He's dedicated his life to God so he's got his own priorities."

"There are other problems I don't think we'll ever surmount. I remember what Mom and Dad's marriage was like. They loved each other, but they were complete opposites. At times it felt like a battlefield at home, and my brother and I would always get caught in the middle." She shook her head. "I don't want to put my kid through something like that. That's not the legacy I want to hand down to my daughter."

He nodded slowly. "I hear you. We're all controlled to one extent or another by what we fear. You don't really want to stay single for the rest of your life, but you're afraid that choosing the wrong company will be even worse. Damned if you do and damned if you don't."

"Considering we're talking about a relationship with a preacher, I couldn't have said it better myself!" Ella said, laughing.

Moments later, an elderly man wearing denims, a flannel shirt, and a blue headband above his tired-looking eyes came out of Clifford's medicine hogan. He went directly to the old pickup and drove off. Soon afterwards her brother came to the curtained doorway and waved, inviting them to approach.

Once inside, Ella sat on a blanket placed on the north side of the hogan while Blalock went to the south side as was customary for an unmarried man.

"What brings you here?" Clifford asked, nodding first to Blalock, who knew not to shake hands, then to Ella.

She gave him the highlights, careful not to refer to Louis Etcitty by name or use the word skinwalkers. "Do you know if there are other crystal gazers who feel the same way—that StarTalk can hurt their abilities?"

"The crystal gazer you're talking about has complained about that many times, and believes it, but I haven't heard anyone else express any concerns."

"Is the crystal gazer a member of the Fierce Ones?" Ella asked him.

He looked at her in surprise. "I don't think so. He and I have spoken about that group in the past and he's always said that the Fierce Ones are endangering the very lifestyle they're trying to protect."

Ella thought about that statement. "He has a point. But I saw a link to the Fierce Ones at his place. Could his nephew be a member?"

He nodded slowly. "It's very possible. He's in his late thirties and, in my opinion, the man has never figured out who or what he is. In the old days, a man would prove himself by racing at dawn. It was said that Talking God and Calling God would then bless him with good fortune. Disciplines like that helped define us. But, over time, and with the influence of the outside world, a lot of our younger men, like the crystal gazer's nephew, have lost track of their real identity."

"Do you know the nephew?" Ella asked her brother.

"Not well, no, but I believe he's one of the custodians at your daughter's school. It shouldn't be very hard for you to find him."

By the time they left the hogan it was nine-thirty and the sun was high in an azure, cloudless sky. Ella glanced at Blalock. "Louis' nephew wasn't at the house when we were there. You want to pass by the school? They rent the gym out on weekend nights to local groups, so maybe he's there cleaning up."

Blalock looked at his watch, then shook his head. "I've got to make a stop by my office first. It may be Sunday morning, but I've requested an agent be sent to me to help with the workload, and I'm hoping that a decision has been made. If not, I've got to rattle the cage."

Ella nodded, aware that Blalock had been working the area alone for a long time. "How about I give you an hour, then pick you up?"

"Perfect."

Ella dropped Blalock off by the van he'd been driving, then drove straight home. Her hopes of spending a leisurely Sunday with her daughter had been placed on hold for now but, with luck, she'd still get to enjoy a little time with Dawn.

As she pulled up to their home, Ella saw that they had a guest. A luxury late-model sedan was parked near the new wing of the house—Rose and Herman's side. More curious than anything else, Ella hurried inside through the old front entrance.

The minute she stepped through the door, she caught the enticing scent of her mother's special butter cookies drifting in from the kitchen. Rose made home a place that welcomed you as warmly as a hug.

Tossing her jacket across a chair, Ella walked through the living room toward the kitchen, ready to grab some coffee and dive into the cookies. Then, as she stepped through the doorway, Ella saw Abigail Yellowhair at their breakfast table. Rose was showing her an elaborate map she'd made. Part of Rose's work for the tribe entailed finding and recording the locations of rare plants used in ceremonies and healing herbs.

Abigail looked up as Ella stopped short. At a glance, she noted Ella's acid-etched boots. Her eyebrows rose either in surprise or disapproval, but she said nothing.

Rose was another story. "What in the world happened to your boots? It looks as if you walked through fire in them," Rose said, following Abigail's gaze.

Ella sighed. Rather than discuss the case, she forced a smile. "I had a bit of a mishap with some battery acid and I haven't had a chance to buy new ones yet."

"I hear that acid was meant for my son-in-law," Abigail said softly.

"It was," Ella conceded, trying to ignore the barrage of

questions suddenly mirrored on Rose's face. Ella knew she'd be answering those later. "Your son-in-law said he's going to hire a bodyguard for his wife. It would be a good idea if he rehired one for himself, too."

"He won't hear of it, not after that press conference where he looked foolish. Now he thinks having a bodyguard makes him look like a coward. But I've been meaning to tell you. I've hired someone for myself, a former police officer named Roxanne Dixon."

Ella remembered what she'd been told. Yet as much as she would have liked to question Abigail further about Roxanne, this wasn't the right time or place.

Abigail looked back at Rose. "I would love to go out with you sometime when you go do your plant surveys. I'd like to learn more about the Plant People."

Ella knew that was an invitation Rose would never refuse.

"I'm sure we can arrange something," Rose said with an eager nod. "The trips can be long, and there's lots of walking involved, but they're also wonderfully relaxing with a little company."

It was then that Ella realized just how much her mother missed the companionship of her old friend Lena Clani. Lena had often gone with her mother on these surveys.

"Tell me when you go out again. I would enjoy going along."

Ella didn't know what had prompted Abigail's sudden interest in the Plant People, but it seemed a bit too convenient to be a coincidence.

Abigail beamed Rose a bright smile. "I better be on my way. And you should try some of these cookies, dear," she added, looking at Ella. "They're just wonderful."

"Why don't you take some with you?" Rose offered, reaching for a small plastic bag.

"No, I'll leave them here for your family to enjoy, but I'll take just one more. Thanks," Abigail said with a smile and reached for the platter.

After Abigail had left, Ella took a cookie and glanced around. "Where's my daughter? Out tending the horses?"

"Yes, and Boots is with her. She offered to come by this morning and teach your daughter how to braid the pony's mane. But just why your daughter would want to do that, I don't know."

Ella remembered the horse shows her daughter had wanted to enter and knew the answer.

Hearing a car pulling up and the sound of an ear-splitting backfire, Ella knew instantly that Lena Clani had arrived to pick up her granddaughter, Boots.

"Ask her in, Mom. You know you miss her," Ella said softly.

"My former friend and I have nothing to say to each other." Her tone left no room for argument.

"I'm going outside to talk to my daughter," Ella said, grabbing another cookie.

"Take one for her, but don't let her feed it to that pony."

Ella smiled. Dawn would sneak Wind all kinds of treats and, surprisingly enough, the pony thrived on them. Good thing that, by and large, they had good, natural, and healthy foods around.

As Ella stepped out the back door Boots hurried over to join her. "I'd like to talk to you. Do you have a minute?"

"Sure. What's up?" Ella asked.

"My grandmother's health is not good. She had a Sing done, but she refuses to go to the hospital. She's lost so much weight, too! I don't think she's going to be with us much longer," Boots said in a somber voice.

"Boots, I'm so sorry!" Ella said, meaning every word. Boots had lost her own mother just last year. "What can I do?"

"Talk to your mother. My grandmother and your mother were good friends for such a long time, and I know they still love each other. Pride's the only thing that's keeping them apart."

"The problem is that they're both convinced they were right," Ella said slowly. "But I'll see what I can do."

"Thanks," Boots answered. "I don't want my grandmother to face this illness without her best friend at her side. It'll be hard enough for her as it is."

Before she could say anything more, Dawn ran up onto the porch and gave her mother a hug. "*Shimá*, you're home!"

"Hey, sweetie." Ella handed her the cookie. "This is from your grandmother. I'll meet you inside in a minute, okay?"

As Dawn raced happily into the house, Ella walked with Boots through the covered patio area to the front, where Lena was parked. She wanted to see Lena for herself and make sure Boots wasn't overreacting. Ella wasn't sure what she'd expected but Lena's gaunt face came as a total shock. From what she could see, Lena had lost a good twenty pounds, and she'd never been a heavy woman.

Lena greeted Ella with excessive courtesy, then looked at Boots. "We have to go. It's getting late."

Boots looked back at Ella, and with pleading eyes conveyed more love and worry than Ella had thought possible. Ella's stomach tightened. There was no doubt in her mind that Lena was extremely ill.

When she returned to the kitchen, her mother was nowhere to be found. Dawn came in a second later and grabbed another cookie from the plate.

"Where's your *shimasání*?" Ella asked, taking another cookie for herself.

"She always goes to her room when her former friend comes to pick up Boots," Dawn said softly, using the same term for Lena that Rose did. "Sometimes she cries, Mom. *Shimasání's* really sad. I asked Boots to bring *Shimasání's* friend inside to visit, but she won't. Boots says they have to work out their problems by themselves."

"Boots is right. You can't make that decision for them."

"But *Shimasání* really misses her!"

"I know. Let me see what I can do." Ella said, giving her daughter an encouraging smile.

When Dawn went to play with her computer, Ella walked down the hall leading to her mother's side of the house. She found Rose in her bedroom, dusting. Rose glanced up and Ella saw that her mom had been crying.

Ella hugged her tightly. "I love you, Mom."

Rose wiped away some tears, then stepped back. "Where's your daughter? She loves those cookies and can't be trusted for long around a full plate."

"Let's go into the kitchen then. We'll keep an eye on the dish, and it'll give us a chance to talk."

"You look like you've had a very hard morning," Rose said, following her down the hall.

"Yeah, I did, but I'm okay. Right now I'm more worried about you."

Rose sat by the kitchen table and, a minute later, Herman joined them. The scent of soap and the dampness of his hair indicated he'd been in the shower.

Ella looked at her mother's husband as he took a cookie. She'd wanted to talk to her mother alone, but maybe this was better. Herman was very perceptive, and undoubtedly knew what the continued estrangement between Rose and Lena was doing to his wife.

"I saw your former friend outside, and she looks very, very sick, Mom," Ella said softly.

Rose's eyes filled with tears. "I've heard. But she and I are no longer friends. I can't help her."

"Find a way to make up with her, wife," Herman said, sitting down across from them at the table. "None of us ever have as much time as we think we do."

Rose shook her head. "I can't forgive her for endangering my own daughter," Rose said, looking at Herman. "Haven't we talked about this often enough?"

"It's true that she endangered lives," Ella said, "but when people are angry and grieving over a loved one, they make mistakes. Her daughter was brutally murdered, Mom. Fear and pain can distort even the gentlest heart."

Rose shook her head, her expression set. Ella knew that it would take more than words to heal the rift between Rose and Lena. The truth was that she'd nearly been beaten up and shot because of Lena. Despite what she'd just said, Ella knew she'd never really trust that woman again. Back then, she'd come face to face with Lena's dark side, something she'd never even known existed. Rose had, too, and that was at the heart of the rift between them.

Ella was outside watching Dawn ride her pony around the small enclosure when her cell phone rang. Ford's voice came over the speaker and Ella smiled. "It's almost ten. I thought you'd be at services," she said.

"We changed the time. We're having early morning Navajo language services these days," Ford answered. "Are you free now? I'd like to talk to you in person. It's about one of your cases."

"I'm supposed to meet with Agent Blalock shortly, but I could meet you at the Totah Café for a quick cup of coffee," she suggested knowing it was a halfway point between them.

"I'd rather keep this more private. Can you stop by my house?"

His tone alerted her. Something serious was going on.

"Sure. Let me check in with Agent Blalock first, then I'll head over to your place."

Ella called Blalock and, after finding out that he'd be tied up for another hour, said good-bye to her family and set out to Ford's place.

NINETEEN

✖ ✖ ✖

Ford lived outside the reservation in the small community of Waterflow, more of a historical location than a distinct entity nowadays. The next community down the road was Fruitland, followed by Kirtland, but there were no obvious boundaries along the river valley, an area once comprised mostly of farms and orchards.

A few years ago, Bilford Tome had opted to buy his own home. Since no one really owned land on the reservation, he'd ended up here, almost a stone's throw, literally, from the reservation borders. The Navajo language minister of The Good Shepherd Church shared his modest two bedroom home with his ninety-pound mixed-breed dog, Abednego. Ford loved the adopted stray as much as the animal loved him.

Ella knocked and Ford answered the door, Abednego at his side holding a rawhide bone in his mouth. "Come in," Ford said, motioning to her quickly.

Ella stepped into the warmth of his living room. Shrugging off her jacket, she followed the man and his dog to the kitchen. "All I've got is some decaffeinated coffee, but if you're hungry, I'll be glad to rustle up something more."

She shook her head. "Coffee's fine."

He brought two steaming mugs over to the table and took a seat. "I've heard quite a few rumors about the case you're working on—the one involving the Benallys. Although my sources are far from reliable, something has been bugging me about the stories. Late last night I finally figured out what it was. The attacks on the Benallys seem . . . unfocused," he said at last. "From what I've heard, everything has apparently been well planned but the purpose of the attacks is unclear. Then there's the attack on you and Dawn. Could someone be trying to distract you from something else that's going on?"

That was what she liked most about Ford. Their minds ran along the same lines. "That's what I've been thinking, too. We're running in all directions but still have no idea what we're really up against, or what the goals of the bad guys are. It's like dealing with the symptoms of a disease but not being able to find the cause."

"What surprised me is that they actually endangered your daughter, Ella."

Remembering the incident filled her with anger, but she pushed it back. Emotions only muddled up her thinking and that was the last thing she needed now. "That one stunt guaranteed them a bad enemy—me."

Ford nodded. "My point exactly. They struck at your *emotions*. But to what end? That's the real question."

Ella told Ford about the phone calls her team had received, then continued. "At first I thought the Fierce Ones were behind all the incidents—retribution because I went after whoever had nearly beaten Marilyn Charley to death. But now, I'm just not sure."

"The Fierce Ones go after specific targets, make it very clear why they're taking action, and leave little doubt what they expect the results to be. The attacks you and your team experienced—not unlike those directed against Ervin

Benally—are like buckshot scattering everywhere and hitting nothing in particular. Those tactics don't fit the Fierce Ones. Even the flattening of my tires on that field trip in the mountains—that wasn't like them at all."

Knowing that he'd been a cryptographer for the government, Ella wasn't surprised Ford could analyze things so clearly and effortlessly.

"What's knotting you up inside is not just that they've harassed me and your team, it's that they endangered Dawn," he added. "You're not out solely for justice now. Whether or not you admit it, deep down, you want revenge."

He was right again, but she didn't feel like admitting that out loud. No sense in giving that negative emotion even more power by voicing it.

She took a deep breath and let it out slowly. "You've reminded me of one of the old Navajo stories my mom taught me." She paused thoughtfully then continued. "When Young Man went up against Gambler, he knew he'd need to do whatever he could to break Gambler's game and shatter his confidence. That was his only chance of success." Ella stared at the coffee mug, then looked up. "Whoever it was knew how I was bound to react, and deliberately targeted my daughter to try and keep me from focusing."

"That's what I think, too," he said. "You have an enemy who's not as up front about it as the Fierce Ones."

"At one point Justine suggested that the person behind all of this might be a woman because of the apparent psychology involved. I'm beginning to think she's right. The Fierce Ones have been involved at least peripherally, but I suspect they're being manipulated, too. They're being swept up into the events to muddy the water even more."

She paused, then looked up at Ford. "You better start

watching your back. People know that we're friends. That incident with your tires could be just the beginning."

He leaned back and regarded her thoughtfully. "Start looking for a different kind of enemy—one who likes mind games. That's what you're up against."

"Agreed." Ella petted Abednego absently, aware of how quiet Ford's home always was. The silence almost resonated with a life of its own. She didn't know how he could stand it. "You're in a very public profession, but you're also a bit of a recluse. Are you aware of that, Reverend?"

He laughed out loud. "After working as a preacher all day, I need my downtime. In the quiet . . ." he started to say something, then shook his head.

"You what? Finish it," she encouraged.

"It's only in the quiet that the soul hears God," he answered. "It's part of my religious beliefs."

"When I was living in the city, a lifetime ago, I valued the silence—it was so rare. Now I look forward to the sounds of family around me. I thrive on it, in fact," Ella said, standing up. "It's time for me to get back to work. Thanks for giving me your slant on things," she said, silently acknowledging more than one meaning in her words.

"Glad I was able to help," he said, walking her to the door. "Come back soon. I miss our talks."

As Ella left and headed toward Shiprock she called Blalock. "I'm heading your way. You ready to roll?"

"I have one more thing to handle here. How about I meet you at the station at noon?"

"Done."

Ella drove through Shiprock and continued toward home, glad for a chance to spend a little more time with her kid. Before she'd given birth, she'd never really known just how deeply she could love. Nothing had ever touched her heart the way Dawn had. In her child, Ella saw glimpses of the hope and promise the future held.

After spending time around the horses with Dawn, Ella returned to the kitchen. She was reaching for the teapot when her cell phone rang. It was Justine.

"Blalock asked me to verify Franklin Etcitty's whereabouts for you. He said you'd want to question him within the next hour or so."

"That's right. Did you find him?"

"Yes. I made a few calls and found out that the school's gym was rented out to a local basketball league today. Franklin had to be there with his keys no later than eight to open up, and after the games he'll clean and lock up. The other school custodian doesn't work on Sundays."

"Good job, partner. If Blalock shows up at the station before I do, update him and tell him I'm on my way."

Ella arrived at the station twenty minutes later. Blalock was in the hallway by the vending machines, a bag of shoestring potatoes in his hand.

"Ugh, don't tell me that's lunch," Ella said.

"Trans fats are a basic food group. What did you have, Ms. Nutrition?"

Ella smiled sheepishly. "Coffee, cookies, and tea."

"Then I'll share my 'strings,'" he said.

Justine stepped out of her office holding two small plastic bowls with lids. "Here. This tastes better than those grease sticks," she said.

Ella peered inside one and discovered some corn stew. The Navajo recipe called for mutton and hard roasted corn kennels, a variety different from sweet corn but loaded with flavor. "You sure?"

"Yeah. My mom brought a big batch over to my house last night. Consider me fully carbo loaded."

Ella laughed. After a quick lunch, Blalock, Ella, and Justine left the station in Blalock's sedan. Ella shared Ford's theory with them, then continued. "I think the reverend's on the right track, but I've got no end of enemies. I don't even know where to begin."

"Let's take this one step at a time," Blalock said. "We'll start by talking to Franklin Etcitty. Maybe we'll get something if we push hard enough."

Ella nodded. "All right. Sounds like a good plan."

"Did you lift any prints off that hydrometer we found in the Benally garage?" Blalock asked Justine, who was sitting in the back seat.

"Just smudges, nothing usable. But there were traces of brake fluid on the outside of the tube, up by the bulb," Justine said.

"Could be that's the same device used to draw the brake fluid out of the reservoir of Ervin's Dodge pickup," Ella said.

"Now we have another piece of the puzzle," Blalock said.

When they arrived at Dawn's school, the parking lot around the gym was nearly full. Looking through the double doors that had been propped open, she could see people in gym shorts and t-shirts running back and forth. A game was underway.

After asking around for Franklin, they left the gym and headed to the back of the building. As they came around the corner, Ella caught a glimpse of a man crouched by the cab of an older-model pickup. A big red plastic gas container was on the ground, and a hose led from it to the gasoline tank outlet.

"I bet that's him—Franklin Atcitty," Ella said, seeing he was wearing the school custodian's green uniform shirt. "Somebody must have run out of gas."

"Out of gas, hell, Ella. The guy is siphoning gas, not adding it," Blalock replied after a beat.

Just then the custodian looked up and saw them.

"Police officers, Mr. Etcitty. We need to talk to you," Ella called out, picking up the pace and continuing toward him.

Etcitty yanked out the hose and tried to run away with the cumbersome gas container still in his hand. After a dozen yards he gave up and dropped it, gas sloshing onto the pavement, and picked up speed. He sprinted across a field of weeds toward a narrow paved road. Beyond were thick brush and the cottonwood trees of the bosque, then the river.

"Get him, Clah," Blalock said. "I'll go for the car."

Ella glanced at Justine. "Find his pickup and make sure he doesn't circle back to it."

Ella knew the area Etcitty was heading into almost by heart. When she'd gone to school here, centuries ago, the track team had trained by running along the sandy earth that lined the banks of the San Juan River. Little had changed since.

Ella paced herself as she entered the bosque, her strides long and steady. Once the brush thickened, it became harder to maintain visual contact. A short time later, she lost sight of the custodian. Ella slowed down and listened. He couldn't have run out on her. It would have taken someone in remarkable shape to cover this stretch of ground that rapidly.

Standing perfectly still, she soon heard the sounds of labored breathing coming from a thicket ahead. She also caught a whiff of gasoline fumes, the result of what he'd spilled on his clothes. "Franklin, give it up, buddy. You can't outrun me." She reached into the tall stand of basket willows and pulled him out by the collar.

"Okay, okay, jeez!" he muttered.

"You're under arrest," Ella said, reciting his rights. As she placed the cuffs on his wrists she noticed he was wearing one of the signature leather bands that identified him as a member of the Fierce Ones.

Ella was leading him down the road that paralleled the bosque when Blalock pulled up in his sedan. She helped Etcitty into the backseat, then stood by the open door, blocking any escape.

"Look, you've already made your point, so how about letting me go? It'll be more trouble and paperwork for you to book me on this little misdemeanor than it's worth," he said. "You and I both know it."

"There's more than your job and a fine at stake here. You're in a lot more trouble than you realize," Ella said.

"Over a little gas worth what, fifteen bucks?" He gave her an incredulous stare.

"You weren't just refusing to obey a police officer and resisting arrest. You were stealing from the *Diné*. The Fierce Ones won't let that go unpunished. I know for a fact that they come down hard on their own, especially when you do something that damages their integrity. When the news reaches Jimmy Levaldo or Delbert John, you're in for a major beating, or worse," Ella said. "You're going to be a lot safer in a jail cell."

Franklin said nothing for several moments. "Okay, you may have a point there. So, make me a deal. What do you need to make this go away?"

"Information. Who's making a move against StarTalk and why?"

"It's not the Fierce Ones, if that's what you're thinking."

"What about you and your uncle? I know he believes satellites can keep him from having his visions."

"He doesn't believe that, not really. So don't waste your time trying to pin this on either of us. We're not behind it."

"If your uncle's not threatened by StarTalk, then what's going on?" Ella demanded.

He paused for a long time.

"Shall we go to the station?" Ella said, reminding him.

He answered her then. "There's no love lost between my uncle and Abigail Yellowhair. Mrs. Yellowhair pressured the tribe into taking over a patch of good grazing land my father used for his sheep, so she and her son-in-law could put up that big StarTalk warehouse there. They claimed it was for the economic good of the tribe. But you know that's just bull."

"And that's Ervin Benally's fault, how?" Ella asked.

"My uncle believes that Ervin's just a front man for Abigail Yellowhair. He's working against StarTalk because he wants her to lose something she cares about—her investment—just like he lost his grazing rights. At least that's my guess," he added with a shrug.

"You need to convince him to stop defacing posters. He can say whatever he wants, that's his right. But he's got to cool it with the other stuff. Can you do that?"

"I'll try. But in exchange, you can't tell anyone I was siphoning gas. And you can't arrest me, either."

"Deal—providing you tell me one more thing. Am I being targeted by the Fierce Ones?" She brought out the key to the handcuffs, but held off unlocking them.

"You're not on our list of friends, but we're not after you. You wouldn't have to ask if we were—you'd know. But—" He suddenly stopped speaking and sat back in the seat, gazing up at the roof.

"Go on," she urged. "I want the rest of the story. Cooperate, or our deal's off." She let him see her putting the key back into her pocket.

"Okay, but you didn't get this from me. The Fierce Ones are thinking of taking credit for the things that have been happening. It's another way of letting The People think we're the ones in control."

"One last thing," Ella said. "Has your uncle been making crank calls to my people?"

He gave her an incredulous look. "You're not serious. He hasn't used a telephone since he became a crystal gazer—before I was even born."

Ella stepped back, letting Franklin climb out of the car. He walked across the road, then broke into a jog, heading directly toward the school.

"Remember that Justine went to find Etcitty's vehicle so he couldn't sneak back to it," Blalock said. "You'd better give her a call before she confronts him on school grounds."

As she climbed into Blalock's car, Ella called Justine and updated her, then slipped the phone into her shirt pocket.

"You played it well with Franklin," Blalock said, "but we just lost another lead."

As they drove around to the campus to pick up Justine, Ella reviewed things in her mind, but instead of answers, all she came up with were more questions.

"By the way, Big Ed mentioned that he was having an office problem you needed to update me on as soon as possible," Blalock said. "It came out of the blue as he was headed out the door, so I don't have any idea what he was taking about. Do you?"

Ella nodded and told Blalock about the leak Big Ed suspected was coming from inside their department. "Make sure you don't discuss anything sensitive inside the building, not until he gives us the all clear."

Blalock shook his head. "Weirder and weirder. This must really be getting under Big Ed's skin."

"Yeah, but he's handling it. He's got a plan underway to catch whoever it is. We'll know soon enough."

TWENTY
————— ✖ ✖ ✖ —————

They'd just arrived at the tribal police station when Blalock received a call on his cell phone. He'd been asking for a second agent to be assigned to the area, and from his half of the conversation, it appeared that his request was about to be honored.

"I'm scheduled for a conference call in about a half hour, so I've got to head back to my office. I'll catch up with you later," he said, not getting out of the car.

Ella walked back inside the station with Justine. Her partner went to the lab, and Ella continued to her own office, her thoughts circling around the events of that morning.

Ella sank down into her chair, but before she could even take a breath, she heard someone at the door. Glancing up, she saw Big Ed.

He came in, closed the door behind him, and took a seat. "We've carried out our sting op, but no one's checked up on the license plate. That means the leak isn't coming from one of us. Maybe it's the spouse of an officer, or someone even more removed from our direct lines of communication. Either way stay sharp, but be advised that it's *not* anyone on your team."

"Thanks for letting me know," she said.

"Do you have an update for me on Ervin Benally and what's happening with him?"

Ella told him about the incident with the battery fluid, and the hydrometer Blalock had found with traces of brake fluid on it. "The Nike footprints are also a match to the ones we found up in the mountains around the Dodge. That's no coincidence, so we can safely infer that Ervin was the intended target that day in the mountains, not George."

Big Ed nodded. "Considering everything else that's happened, it seems logical to assume Ervin *was* the intended target. But whoever did that had serious injury or death in mind, not just harassment like with these later incidents."

"The person who drained the brake fluid likely didn't know Ervin had gone back to the office early, though the tampering itself was obviously planned ahead of time. But here's what doesn't add up. Why start with attempted murder and then back off and resort to penny-ante acts like vandalism and crank calls?" Ella said.

"Maybe having the wrong guy die scared off the bad guys, at least temporarily."

Ella considered it. "Let's go back to the beginning. The wreck was supposed to look like an accident. I'm thinking that the perp was hoping nobody would pay close attention to the brakes. For all we know, the guy who removed the brake fluid was also planning to set fire to the wreck and destroy the evidence before anyone else came on the scene.

"But then the wrong guy ended up dead and the Dodge came out of it intact, so he didn't want to push his luck and try to arrange for another driving accident. The perp then changed tactics. He tried to replace the missing brake fluid before anyone noticed and at the same time decided to pressure Ervin until he cracked. Considering the guy was a nervous wreck already and liable to shoot himself or someone else, that was a brilliant strategy. Why kill Ervin when all you need to do is drive him to self-destruct?"

"But again, Shorty, to what end? Why work so hard to get rid of Ervin? What's the motive?"

"I don't know yet," Ella admitted. "I'm still working on that."

After a pause, Ella told Big Ed about the crystal gazer and what she and Blalock had learned from Franklin.

"Is the FBI going to be taking an active role in this case?"

She nodded. "StarTalk has a federal tie-in because it's linked to government initiatives from the FCC and funding from the Telecommunications Development Fund."

"Okay, then. Use whatever help they can give us," Big Ed said.

After Big Ed walked out, Tache came in. "I've been waiting to talk to you. Do you have a minute? It's important."

Ella gestured for him to take a seat. "What's on your mind?"

"I had a very strange conversation with Jesse, my brother-in-law, last night. He's the one in the Fierce Ones. Lately, he's been treating me like a long-lost friend and it was starting to creep me out. I let it slide at first, but when it was obvious that something was up, I figured I'd better start pushing for answers. Turns out that they've been getting very accurate tips concerning a few of our investigations and some of the guys thought *I* was their informant. They'd come to the conclusion that I was leaking information to them through my girlfriend, since the person who gets in touch via phone with them is a woman."

Ella considered this new information. "Do you think Jesse was involved in that incident involving Marilyn Charley and Wallace Curtis?"

"No way. A few months ago my sister cut her knee and

he fainted—I mean dead away. He can't stand the sight of blood," he said, laughing.

"And yet he's in the Fierce Ones?" Ella observed.

"He has his uses to them. The guy can't fight his way out of a paper bag, but he knows just about every Navajo in the community—where they work, what clans they belong to, and so on. And he keeps everything in his head. He's their primary source of information, a walking database."

"That's quite a skill. Under different circumstances he might have made a good law enforcement officer."

"It would have had to have been a desk job. Jesse doesn't like guns," he said.

Ella laughed. "Okay. Here's what I'd like you to do. See if you can get Jesse to tell you who *he* believes is causing trouble for Ervin."

"I've already spoken to him about that. I don't think the Fierce Ones have any idea who it could be. That bothers them as much, if not more, than it does us."

Once Tache left, Ella leaned back in her chair and looked out the window at the clear blue skies, focusing her thoughts, not her eyes. The Fierce Ones and Ervin were being manipulated. That much was clear. Ella considered all the possible suspects, mentally searching for any that were intelligent and devious enough to play successful mind games like these. One name came to mind instantly—Abigail Yellowhair.

Before she could give it any additional thought, Justine rushed into her office.

"Big Ed wants us to roll," Justine said. "Abigail Yellowhair has been attacked."

She stared at Justine for a moment. "Was she at the Benallys'?" Ella asked, trying to make some sense of it.

"No, she was at her own home. She has a huge dog, *and* a bodyguard, but the dog was locked in her greenhouse, and whoever it was clocked her bodyguard, Roxanne Dixon."

"Roxanne wouldn't have been easy to take down," Ella said. "Who made the call?"

"Dispatch said it was Dixon, so she must have managed to recover long enough to make it to a phone. But why go after Abigail now? How does she fit into this?" Justine asked.

"Good question, partner," Ella said. "This case gets more complicated with each passing minute. Let's roll."

They arrived at Mrs. Yellowhair's home a short time later. The house was relatively new, and larger than most on the reservation, but not pretentious. Two vehicles were parked side by side in front of the garage, one of them a bright yellow luxury sedan, and the other the green pickup Ella recognized as belonging to Roxanne.

They'd just come to a full stop when Roxanne came out the front door holding a bag of ice over her temple.

"About time you got here," she muttered as Ella and Justine climbed out of their tribal vehicle. "Let me give you the highlights," she added, motioning them toward the door.

"I heard a noise, then the dog barking in the greenhouse. I walked over to let him back out and that's when I got clocked from behind with some kind of sap. I never saw it coming. When I woke up I was tied to a chair in the kitchen. Mrs. Yellowhair was being roughed up in the living room by three hoods. The lady had balls, Clah. She told them she didn't respond to threats and that they were wasting their energy. They slapped her around and threw her into the wall a few times. When she finally stopped getting back up, they left, but not before spray painting a charming little message on her car—the yellow one, naturally."

"Will you be able to ID any of them?" Ella asked her.

"I can give you a general description—size, build, and approximate weight—but that's about it. They were wearing ski masks and leather gloves. And they were sweating like pigs—at least they smelled that way."

Ella followed Roxanne inside the house. Abigail was in the living room on the velvet sofa, holding a drink in her hand. Her face was bruised, one eye almost swollen shut and turning black around the edges. A small cut over her eyebrow was bleeding slightly and she was holding a damp, bloodstained dishcloth against it. The German shepherd that lay at her feet looked up as they came in, and growled, a low threatening rumble.

"Did you call an ambulance?" Ella asked Roxanne.

"No ambulance," Abigail said firmly. "I've had worse than this," she said. Seeing the questions in Ella's eyes, she shrugged. "I never back down, even when I should."

"Did you see or hear anything that might help us identify the men who did this to you?" Ella pressed, staying focused on the case.

"Their English told me that they were poorly educated Navajos; not real young, but not older than forty, probably. They ordered me to tell my son-in-law to abandon the StarTalk project. If he didn't, they said that he'd die alone—slowly and painfully. When I told them what they should do to themselves and to each other, they decided to use me as a punching bag."

Ella looked at Roxanne. "Do *you* need medical help?"

"No, but the goons who did this will if I ever catch up to them," she answered, then setting the ice bag down, gestured to the front door. "Come on, I'll show you the car. I didn't get a chance to go outside until after they were long gone since Mrs. Yellowhair had to untie me first. Considering what she'd been through, it took awhile."

Ella followed Roxanne and, as they came around to the driver's side of Abigail's car, she saw the vandal had used bright red spray paint on Mrs. Yellowhair's luxury sedan. It said, "Death to Traiters."

"They can't spell," Ella commented.

"But it still sends a clear message," Roxanne answered. "Oh, you might want to take a look at what they left *inside* the car. I haven't told Mrs. Yellowhair about that yet because she's been through enough already today."

"Tell me what?" Abigail asked.

Roxanne and Ella turned around. Neither of them had heard her coming up from behind.

Roxanne moved to her side quickly. "Mrs. Yellowhair, are you sure you should be walking around?"

Abigail stood a little straighter and glared at Roxanne. "Don't treat me like an old woman. *You're* walking around, aren't you?"

Roxanne backed away and looked at Ella, but said nothing.

Abigail glanced at Roxanne, then focused on Ella. "Since it's *your* case now, I suppose the information has to come from you. What haven't I been told?" Abigail looked at the car and read the message. "Their spelling stinks. What else is there?"

"It's what's inside the car," Ella said, leaning over to take a closer look. The window was rolled down.

There was a crudely sewn pouch on the seat. It was made of leather or skin, but didn't appear to be cowhide. There was also a brown powdery substance scattered everywhere that appeared to be ashes of some kind.

As she took a closer look, Ella realized that there were also chunks of an unidentified material mixed in with the ashes, maybe bone. Navajo witches—skinwalkers—had just cursed Abigail Yellowhair.

TWENTY-ONE
✖ ✖ ✖

Ella glanced back at Abigail just as the woman reached out and grabbed Roxanne's arm to steady herself. "This is disgusting," Abigail murmured. "That's *all* it is."

Yet, from her shaky voice Ella knew that no matter how modern Abigail was, some things were just too difficult to brush aside. Skinwalkers evoked terror in most Navajos. They represented the unknown and the uncontrollable—enemies who would break every taboo and carry out disgusting acts to get what they wanted.

"We'll be processing the scene. With luck, we'll be able to get some evidence that'll lead us to the people who did this," Ella said firmly.

"You're thinking of prints and things like that?" Abigail asked, confused. "They wore gloves inside the house. Even if they'd taken them off out here, what makes you think that these kind of people would be in your database?"

Ella noticed that Abigail had avoided using the word skinwalker. "There are many ways to follow an investigative trail," Ella said, but she knew Abigail was right. Unless the men had criminal records or had been in the military, chances were their fingerprints wouldn't be on file anywhere.

Wordlessly, Abigail turned and walked back inside.

Roxanne met Ella's gaze. "Mrs. Yellowhair doesn't have much faith in words and promises," Roxanne said.

"The knowledge needed to do something like this will narrow down the field of suspects."

"Maybe," Roxanne conceded, "but skinwalkers don't exactly announce that they're skinwalkers. They have to keep that secret if they want to survive, so they've learned to blend in."

"If you can think of anyone who's been asking questions about Abigail, let me know."

Ella noted that Justine had already started to process the scene, and Tache, who'd arrived while they were inside, was now taking photos. She considered her next step. She needed to know more, starting with what this type of curse was *intended* to do. For that she could think of only one person who might be able to help her—her brother Clifford. As a medicine man, he'd spent a lifetime countering the effects of evil. She'd go see him as soon as her work here was done.

Ella went back inside, sat down on the chair across the sofa, and looked at Abigail. "Who knows about your aversion to the type of thing that was left in your car?" Ella asked, avoiding the word skinwalker out of respect.

"This is repugnant to *any* Navajo," she said flatly.

"But why would anyone target you for something like this? You're not in control of StarTalk operations. Your son-in-law is," Ella pressed.

"You've already seen that my son-in-law isn't a strong person," Abigail answered.

"So they attacked you to pressure Ervin?" Ella asked, reading between the lines.

"Not Ervin directly," she said slowly. "It's probably just

a mother-in-law thing, but we can barely stand each other and everyone knows it. I think the ones who did this are trying to get to my daughter. They're hoping that after she sees what they've done to me, she'll put pressure on her husband to back off."

"And do you think that'll happen?" Ella asked.

"No way. Barbara is very, very tough. In a lot of ways she's even tougher than I am. People underestimate her but they shouldn't. She's a real fighter. She just has her own way of handling things. When Barbara sees what they've done to me, she'll dig her heels in, and *nothing* will make her back off. They've taken the wrong tack with our family. I guess they'll learn that soon enough."

"You should have a doctor take a look at your eye. There could be damage. That was quite a punch you took," Ella said.

Abigail shook her head. "I've got some herbs in the kitchen. They'll take away the swelling."

It was the exact answer she would have received from her mother, and that surprised her.

Seeing her reaction, Abigail started to smile, but then quickly reached up and touched her split lip. "We have something in common. My mother, like yours, was a Plant Watcher. I was, too, when I was much younger, and that's knowledge you carry for the rest of your life."

Ella found the possibility that her mother and this woman had things in common nothing short of disturbing. Even the off chance that a friendship might form between Rose and Abigail unsettled her. Although she had no *proof* that Abigail had done anything wrong, Ella couldn't bring herself to trust her. It was that simple . . . and that complicated.

Ella stood up. "With your permission, I'd like to bring my brother here and have him take a look at what was left in the car. His insights as a *hataalii* could help our investigation."

"Do you think he'll do it?"

"As a favor to me, yes, I think so."

"You might also tell him that I'd like to hire him to do a Sing. The evil that's been brought to my doorstep can't be allowed to remain. The car, of course, will be taken off the reservation and sold."

Ella nodded. Sings could cost thousands and take more than a week, but she knew money wasn't a factor for Abigail Yellowhair.

The drive to her brother's home took her a half hour. When Ella arrived, she found Clifford splitting firewood. Although he had propane heat for his home, the medicine hogan used a wood stove.

He set the heavy maul down on a stump and greeted her with a wave as she climbed out of her tribal vehicle. Seeing her expression more clearly as he drew near, his smile faded. "What's happened?"

Ella told him about the attack on Abigail and the reason she had come. "If at all possible, I'd like you to take a look at what her attackers left behind. Maybe you can see a signature or pattern in the way things were laid out. Your expertise exceeds mine when it comes to you-know-what."

There was a long silence. "All right. Give me a few minutes alone to make preparations. I'll make up some medicine pouches for you and your partners, too. You'll need the proper protection."

Ella went back to the car to wait. Things were making even less sense to her now. Why would skinwalkers have a grievance against StarTalk or Ervin Benally, and had they been the perpetrators all along? No matter how she turned things around in her mind, no answers came.

Clifford came out about fifteen minutes later and handed her one of the medicine pouches he'd prepared. "Keep it with you. It's got Talking Rock medicine," he said.

"I'm not familiar with that," she answered.

"The contents are taken from caves where an echo is present. A rite is performed and scrapings are taken from the rock wall. Mixed with certain plants, it's very powerful medicine."

"Thanks," Ella said, fastening it to her belt. "Ready to go?"

On the drive to Abigail's, Ella got a call from Justine. "We just discovered that they left some skinwalker stuff inside Mrs. Yellowhair's master bedroom, too. She hadn't been moving around more than necessary, so she didn't notice it till just a few minutes ago," Justine said in a low voice. "She's pretty upset. Are you bringing Clifford?"

"He's in the car with me now."

"Good. Things are very tense here," Justine said, then hung up.

Ella felt a trickle of unease run up her spine. She wasn't a believer in witchcraft of any sort, but she'd seen enough of skinwalkers to respect the danger they posed.

Ella told her brother what Justine had said and saw his expression darken.

"This is more serious. The car could have been driven away. The bedroom isn't safe anymore, but I can't tell you how to fix it until I see for myself," he said.

When they arrived Ella saw Abigail standing at the living room window, watching for them. By the time she'd parked, Abigail was there to meet Clifford as he stepped out of the tribal unit.

"Thank you very much for coming, *hataalii*," Abigail said. "This has been very upsetting, but I know you can restore things."

He nodded once, keeping his face expressionless. "This is bad business."

"You'll need to give us a moment," Ella told Abigail, leading her brother over to the garage driveway where Abigail's car was parked.

"You should have said something to me about how badly she'd been beaten," Clifford whispered as they walked away from Abigail. "She's a proud woman, and the last thing she needed was to see either shock or pity on my face."

"She didn't. No one outside of Mom and me can read you that well," Ella said.

While Ella handed out the medicine pouches to the other members of her S.I. team, Clifford studied the interior of the yellow sedan.

When she returned to where he stood, Clifford was ready for her. "I know what this is."

He moved back as Justine joined them, then continued. "The witch bag on the seat is made from the skins of horned toads. Inside you'll find a powder that'll look somewhat like pollen, but don't be fooled. It's ground-up corpse poison."

"Human flesh and bone mixed together?" Ella asked.

"Yes. As you've seen it was scattered to ensure that their target would be even more likely to come in contact with it."

"And if she had, then what?" Ella asked.

"It's said that her tongue would swell and become black. Her jaw would eventually lock, and she'd waste away, slowly but surely."

"So, basically, this is a death threat."

"Not the type Anglo law will recognize, but it is a *very* effective death threat against people of our tribe," he answered quietly.

"There's more of that in the bedroom," Justine said.

"Have you processed the scene?" Ella asked.

"Photos are still being taken. I wanted to finish with the car before moving inside."

"We'll get out of your way then," Ella answered.

Ella walked around the outside of the house with her brother, and Roxanne met them at the back door. "My employer is lying down on the couch in the study for now,"

Roxanne said, avoiding mentioning names out of respect to Clifford.

"Did you touch anything in the car or in the bedroom?" he asked her immediately.

"Of course not. The scene needs to be processed," Roxanne answered.

"So you don't believe in the evil this kind of magic brings?" Clifford asked.

"On a supernatural level? No," Roxanne answered. "But poison's poison, and some attack you through the skin. Even if the scene had been processed I wouldn't have touched anything in there. Mrs. Y should hire a team of Anglo maids to come in with rubber gloves and vacuums and disinfect the place. After that, I figure it'll be safe enough."

Before Roxanne had finished speaking, Abigail came up behind her. It surprised Ella how quietly the woman moved.

"I'll show you my bedroom," Abigail said, then moved slowly down the hallway.

Ella studied the floor for footprints or any other evidence as she walked, but the thick sand-colored carpet made it difficult to find anything useful.

"It's to your right," Abigail said, stopping short of going in.

Ella walked past her and took in the scene. The bed was still made, but the top had been sprinkled with corpse powder. On the pillows were pieces of yucca and what appeared to be porcupine quills. On the pillow closest to the nightstand was a small ceremonial bow.

"Those bows are usually made of human bone and the quills are ground up and shot into a victim's body," Clifford said. "I don't understand why everything was laid out like this. Maybe they just staged the scene to remind her what they could have done had they chosen to do so."

"To create even more fear . . . ," Ella said, thinking out loud.

He nodded slowly. "That's my guess, too."

"*Hataalii*, will you do the appropriate Sing for me?" Abigail asked Clifford from the doorway.

"More than one will be needed," he said, turning to speak to her. "First an Evil Way will have to be done, but preparations for that will take time. For now, I'll make a special medicine pouch for you with gall medicine." He looked around the room, then added, "To cleanse all this, I'll also have to do a special Sing from the Male Shooting Chant."

Ella heard the reluctance in Clifford's voice, and waited until Abigail and Roxanne had walked back down the hall to ask him about it. "What's bothering you?" she asked in a quiet voice.

"The prayers I'll have to do are dangerous. I'll need to confront the evil, take it into myself, and then defeat it. Any mistakes can have serious consequences for me and the intended victim."

She'd never heard her brother express hesitancy before. Although she didn't share his beliefs, she knew Clifford, and if he said there was reason to be afraid, she believed him. "Is there anything else you could do that would work?"

"Not in this case." A tense silence stretched out between them.

With effort, Ella brought her thoughts back to the investigation. "Where are the evil ones likely to meet these days? Have you heard any rumors about that?" she said.

"There's an area on the southeast side of the Hogback, close to where those big power lines pass by. About six months ago, a patient of mine was going home late one night after a long Chapter House meeting. He heard some strange chanting coming from one of the caves up against the side of the ridge and went up to take a look. Several naked men and women were sitting inside and some sticks were dancing in the middle of their circle."

Ella thought about it. In the dark, with only the moon and the firelight, the eyes could be fooled into seeing almost anything. Ella thanked her brother, then, while Clifford spoke to Abigail, helped the others process the scene.

Ella joined Justine. "I know this stuff is supposed to be corpse powder, but I want it analyzed."

"I'll take care of that and get back to you as soon as I know anything." After a pause, Justine continued. "Does this make any sense to you?" she asked, waving a hand around the room. "I mean, why would a you-know-what be opposed to better phone service?"

"It doesn't make any sense. I'll give you that. But whoever did this knew exactly what he was doing." Ella lowered her voice, then continued. "In a few minutes, providing I can talk him into it, I'll be going with my brother to check out a place where the evil ones have supposedly been gathering. He'll be able to spot details I might miss. In the meantime, I want you to take charge here and finish processing the scene."

"Will do," Justine said, then resumed work.

Seeing that Clifford was still speaking to Abigail, Ella went back outside to work the crime scene there. She'd just finished searching one quadrant when her brother came out of the house.

Ella joined him. "I know you need a ride back, but before I take you home, how about going on a small side trip with me?"

He exhaled loudly. "You want me to go with you to the place where my patient saw them."

It hadn't been a question and Ella smiled. He'd known all along she'd ask. "You'd be able to spot ritual things I'd dismiss or overlook."

Clifford considered it for a moment, then finally nodded. "All right."

Soon thereafter, Ella and Clifford were underway. The

drive took them south down the same highway Ella drove every day. Then they turned east across barren desert country crisscrossed with small arroyos and dirt tracks. The Hogback, an uplifted ridge that extended north and south for miles like the spine of some buried monster, was over six thousand feet above sea level toward the southern end.

They circled around the southern tip of the Hogback, approaching the massive electrical transmission towers that extended from the power plant farther north all the way into Arizona. Once they'd gone as far as they could by vehicle, Ella parked where Clifford instructed. They were at the low end of a narrow canyon which had its origin at the base of the massive formation.

"The cave should be up ahead, at the foot of the cliffs," he said. "Bring your medicine pouch," he added.

Ella pulled back her jacket and showed him where she'd attached it to her belt by the leather thongs. He nodded in approval.

They slid down the sandstone side of the arroyo to the bottom, then began the climb toward Hogback. They'd been in the shadow of the ridge since the beginning, but were now so close, half the sky was blocked by the naked ridge. Going around a curve in the arroyo, they saw a narrow opening below a massive layer of sandstone.

"That should be it," he said.

Ella drew her weapon, then stepped in front of her brother. It was close to dusk now, and she had no intention of letting her brother lead, unarmed. "If there's a problem, let me handle it."

Clifford glanced down at his belt, calling her attention wordlessly to the sheathed knife attached to his belt.

"I'd rather use the gun and keep our distance," she said simply. "Stay behind me."

As they slipped between a tapered crack in the ridge,

only about three feet wide at the base, Ella could see the opening widened farther ahead.

"This is an *'áńt'íí bahoogan*, a skinwalker's home," Clifford said, his voice so soft she could barely hear. "They built a fire here," he said, studying the ground and pointing ahead, "but that was weeks, maybe months ago. A lot of sand has blown in since then. You can barely make out where they sat."

"I agree. This place hasn't been used recently." She looked up at the crack in the cavern where the smoke from the fire had been able to escape and saw fine, shimmering threads. "Look at all the cobwebs up there." She pointed with a glance, not her hand. "If anyone had been here recently they would have needed a fire, and those webs would have been swept away."

As she finished speaking, Ella felt something at the tip of her boot and looked down. There was an object buried just below the sand and debris that had filtered inside the cave. Rather than reach down and feel with her hand, Ella brushed the surface with the tip of her boot. A small doll-like effigy with a turquoise bead imbedded in the area of its heart came to the surface.

"What's that?" Ella asked her brother.

"They'll torture the image of the person they want to kill," Clifford said quietly.

"This doll is very old," Ella said, bending down to take a closer look. "Something, probably moths or beetles, ate at the cloth of the dress. The fabric is rotting, too."

Ella continued looking around as did Clifford, but soon it became very clear that the place hadn't been actively used in months, if not longer. "Let's get out of here," Ella said.

He nodded. "Good idea."

As they emerged from the cave, Ella caught a flash of light coming from downhill, just inside the limit of the shadows.

Wishing she'd brought her binoculars, she squinted, trying to determine what was causing that, but it was gone as suddenly as it had appeared. Concluding that it had only been the last rays of light reflecting off something on the ground, maybe broken glass, she dismissed it from her mind.

Ella headed to the tribal unit with Clifford and they were on their way moments later. When they reached the highway, miles away from the Hogback now, Ella glanced over at Clifford. "So tell me, how does StarTalk connect with the evil ones? I can't figure out why they'd be taking an interest in this."

"Neither can I. Maybe it doesn't have anything to do with StarTalk."

Ella didn't answer. Skinwalkers *never* acted without a clear goal or target, and always focused on what they had to gain from their actions—money, land, or control over someone. What she had to do next was identify the motive behind their actions at Abigail's.

By the time she'd dropped her brother off, checked back at the crime scene, filed a report, and driven home, Dawn was in her room, getting ready for bed. Ella could hear Rose speaking to her. Curious, she moved silently down the hall and listened.

"I'm glad you've decided not to go to the Anglo school," Rose said.

"You don't like the world outside the Navajo Nation, do you, *Shimasáni*?" Dawn asked.

Rose didn't reply right away. "It's not so much a matter of like and dislike, granddaughter," she said at last. "The Anglo world has different values. Their beliefs are not at all like ours. You can see that clearly in their TV shows where the only way a person can win is to destroy their opposition. The *Diné* are taught to respect the world and others in it because all things are mutually connected. Everything that happens—whether good or bad—affects something else. That's something many in the white world have yet to learn. Here, we live in harmony and walk in beauty, protected by our sacred mountains."

"I like our sacred mountains and knowing that they're there for us. *Shimá* told me once about Bears Ears and how it was a place of protection. But I don't remember all of that story anymore," Dawn said. "I was just a child then."

Rose smiled. "Bears Ears should be a constant reminder to all of us to be careful who we trust, and the dangers of bad company."

"Could you tell me the story?" Dawn asked.

Rose took a deep breath, then in a soft, melodic voice rich with knowledge passed down through the ages, began. "Long ago, in the time of the beginning, there was a young woman who lived with her twelve brothers. The sister kept their house clean and made a good home for all of them. Then one day Coyote saw her and fell in love. He asked the young woman to marry him. Not really interested in marriage, she gave him a number of nearly impossible challenges to meet before she'd accept his proposal. She wasn't at all worried because she never thought he'd be able to complete them. But, as usual, Coyote cheated. He used magic and all kinds of tricks to accomplish the tasks.

"Though she hadn't seen that coming, the woman was bound by honor to keep her word, so she married old Trickster. As time passed, Coyote's wife slowly changed. She became more and more like Coyote, corrupted by the evil in him. She, too, started using magic and trickery to get whatever she wanted. She even learned how to change into a bear—which is how she got her name—Changing Bear Maiden. Before long, Coyote abandoned his wife and took off on more adventures on his own. The wife became bitter, and eventually began to plot against her brothers. She killed four of them before the fifth, in self-defense and faced with no other choice, killed her. After she died, her head became Bears Ears. That place is now a reminder to all that although good can overcome evil, it's often necessary to fight to restore the proper balance."

"Like *Shimá* does," Dawn murmured in a sleepy voice.

"Yes, like your *shimá*," Rose said, then after a pause, added, "It's stories like these that make us who we are. If you'd left the reservation, you might have missed out on some of the things good Navajos need to know. That's why I didn't want you to go just yet. When you're older, maybe."

There was no response, and Ella realized that Dawn had fallen asleep. Moving silently, she stepped over to the doorway, and saw her mother spreading the blanket over her sleeping daughter.

Rose held a finger to her lips, then went down the hall to wait for Ella in the kitchen.

Ella came in moments later. "I remember when you first told me that story."

"It seems like only yesterday to me. Now I was able to teach it to your daughter. Our life is good."

"Yes, Mom, it is," Ella said, and gave her a hug.

"I'm going to bed. I want to rise early and say my prayers to the dawn," Rose said.

Ella watched her go. It would probably take years for Dawn to realize how lucky they were to live here. Visitors and tourists came through, and many only saw poverty. But the *Diné* endured because they had the kind of wealth that couldn't be depleted. The Navajo tribe would continue to exist as long as there was someone to pass on the stories, and others who would listen.

TWENTY-TWO

✖ ✖ ✖

Ella went down the hallway to her room, a cup of camomile tea in her hand. She was tired, but not quite ready to go to sleep yet. As it usually was, she needed time to wind down.

Ella sat down by her small desktop computer and clicked on her e-mail. There was a letter to Dawn from Kevin, and one from an address she didn't recognize. Since the subject line read SKINWALKER, she opened it immediately.

The letter had also been addressed to Jaime Beyale of the *Navajo Times*, and a local TV station. It accused Ella of being a Navajo skinwalker and a traitor to the police department. But what caught and held her attention was the ultimatum at the bottom. Anger built so fast inside her, her face suddenly flushed with heat as she read the words.

I'm giving you a break by showing you what *could* be done, not what's already happened. There are letters missing from the addresses of the two other recipients. Be smart for once. All I need is a phone number.

There was no signature, but then again, none was needed. She knew Roxanne had sent it.

A photo below the letter showed Ella coming out of the *'áńt'íí bahoogan* she'd visited with her brother. She now knew what that flash of light she'd seen on her way out had been—the glass from the telephoto lens of a camera.

She stared at the photo, knowing that it could create all kinds of problems for her. If it was made public, rumors would undoubtedly begin circulating and be nearly impossible to stop.

Anger filled her once again. To arrest Roxanne for threatening a police office would have required her to produce concrete proof. Yet tracking down the sender's computer would be almost impossible.

Ella opened her window and took a breath of the cool desert air. Calming down a bit helped her clear her thinking. She'd make time to have a long talk with Roxanne—one on one. Roxanne was clearly unbalanced, yet some spark of decency remained in her or she wouldn't have bothered sending Ella a warning.

Ella turned off the computer and went to bed. After staring at the ceiling for a brief eternity, emotional and physical exhaustion took its toll, and she drifted off to sleep.

The following morning, by sunrise, the household was up and bustling. Ella heard her mother in the kitchen, pans rattling. Then she heard Dawn's bedroom door burst open, hitting the wall behind it, followed by her daughter's footsteps racing to the kitchen.

By the time Ella got up and dressed, Boots—Jennifer Clani—had arrived. Rose's expression was somber as Ella entered the kitchen. One look at Boots, then back at her mother, told Ella instantly that something serious had happened, probably to Rose's "former friend" Lena.

Dawn chattered away, completely oblivious to what was

happening around her as they all sat down to breakfast. "I'm going to be late coming home because I'm going to Sara's house, okay?" Dawn asked no one in particular. "She has this *great* new computer game and she's going to teach me how to play it."

Dawn didn't stop talking until breakfast was over. Once the dishes were put away, Boots checked her watch.

"If you want to arrive at school early today, we'll have to leave now," she told Dawn. Looking at Ella, she added, "They've got to take down their science projects so that the gym can be used for P.E. again."

Boots and Dawn left shortly afterwards. Breaking the long silence that had stretched out between them, Ella looked over at Rose, who was sitting across from her at the table. "I have a feeling Boots said something to you in private this morning. What's going on, Mom?"

Rose refilled her teacup. "My former friend has moved away. She's living in a hogan out on the flat land west of Blanco Trading Post. Many years ago, her aunt moved there after she was diagnosed with cancer. That way when things got bad, she could walk away from the health center and die on Mother Earth surrounded by the sagebrush. I'm afraid my former friend is there for the same reason."

Herman came into the kitchen as Rose finished speaking. "If you don't mend things between you soon, it'll be too late," he said quietly.

Rose took a deep, unsteady breath. "The hogan is a long ways from here, at least a three-hour drive. But I'm going to go see her."

"I'll go with you," Herman said. "You're too upset to make the trip alone. And once you leave the highway, the road is rough."

"I'm more than capable of going there and back by myself," she said firmly.

"Listen to your husband, Mom," Ella said gently. "This is going to be a hard journey in every imaginable way. It won't hurt to have company, even if it's just to have help changing a flat tire."

Rose considered it for several long moments longer, then at last nodded. "In that case, we'd better get ready."

As her mother left the kitchen, Ella noticed how slowly she was moving this morning. She knew without being told that Rose's joints were bothering her again. Though aging was a natural process, seeing the signs in her mother tore at her heart. Someday, Rose wouldn't be around. It was inevitable, but the thought left her aching inside, and wishing there was some way to stop the passage of time.

Unwilling to indulge those feelings, Ella stood up. The future would unfold at its own pace. Right now, she had work to do and a lot of things to accomplish before the day was done. She'd start out by going to meet with Roxanne.

Ella drove to Abigail's where she knew Roxanne would be. Though it was barely eight-thirty in the morning, as she pulled up, signs of activity were everywhere. Two white vans were parked outside, one from a janitorial service, the other a painting contractor from Farmington. Men carrying drop cloths and paint cans were going in through the front door. As she searched for a place to park she saw that the vandalized yellow sedan was gone and in its place was a dark brown rental vehicle. Roxanne's green pickup was beside it.

Ella pulled up behind Roxanne's car and blocked it. Just as she climbed out of her vehicle, Abigail came to the front door, Roxanne to her side, and waved Ella in.

"Things are moving along, as you can see," Abigail said as Ella joined her. "Do you have more questions for me?"

"Actually, I'd like to speak to your bodyguard," Ella said. There was no expression on Roxanne's face. In fact, it was so neutral, Ella knew it was taking an incredible amount of effort to keep it that way.

"In that case, I'll go make sure the Anglo painters I hired do exactly as I've asked. There seems to be some confusion about which colors go where."

As Abigail went down the hall, Roxanne's gaze stayed on Ella. "There are a lot of strangers here today and I really should be with my client. Can we talk while I work?"

"I don't think this is a conversation you'll want to have in front of Abigail," Ella warned.

"I can't even begin to imagine what's on your mind," Roxanne answered.

"Threatening a police officer is a crime. I deal with things like that quickly," Ella responded without inflection.

"If you have proof someone has threatened an officer, maybe yourself, then why don't you go arrest them?" Roxanne countered smoothly.

"I plan on it, particularly if you don't stop playing games with me."

"I *don't* play games," Roxanne answered flatly, but before she could say anything more, Abigail screamed.

Roxanne moved at lightning speed, Ella half a beat behind her. As they entered the bedroom, Roxanne and Ella saw one of the painters coming toward Abigail, holding out a small odd-looking knife in his hand.

Roxanne kicked out twice, knocking the object out of his hand, then sending the man stumbling backwards to the floor. A heartbeat later, she had her boot at his throat, pinning him down.

"Wanna do your job, officer?" Roxanne asked Ella without taking her eyes off the terrified painter.

"I didn't do nothing!" The thin, balding, brown-haired man choked and coughed as Roxanne applied just a little more pressure.

"Speak when you're spoken to," Roxanne snapped.

Ella brought out her cuffs. "Let's sort this out," she said. "Sir, would you please roll over slowly, face down? And keep your hands away from your body." Ella then gestured to Roxanne, who stepped back.

Ella handcuffed the man, then told him to get to his feet.

"What's going on? I didn't do nothing to nobody. All I did was show her the weird-looking knife I found. That's it," the man said, getting his voice back.

Abigail stared at the object, now resting on a heavy canvas drop cloth six feet away. With effort, she tore her gaze away and looked over at Roxanne. "Thank you for moving so quickly. If that had touched me . . ."

Ella took a closer look and immediately recognized the weapon. It was a crude bone knife, something skinwalkers were known to possess and use in their practices. Whether this one was really made of human bones or not remained to be determined.

"Is it a real bone knife?" Abigail whispered in Ella's ear.

"We'll find out," Ella said, pulling on two pairs of latex gloves before picking it up and easing the knife into an evidence pouch.

"Honest, I wasn't trying to stab Mrs. Yellowhair," the man protested. "I found that thing behind the dresser when I moved it to one side to spread the drop cloth all the way to the wall. I thought it was some kind of tribal artifact."

Ella nodded, then uncuffed the Anglo painter, who appeared to be telling the truth. "Okay, relax. The knife has cultural significance that would take too long to explain, so let's move on."

"Lady, you play rough," the man said, looking at Roxanne and rubbing his throat. "Gonna leave a bruise."

Roxanne's gaze drifted to Ella as she answered him. "I do whatever it takes to win."

Ella ignored her and, instead, searched the room for any other skinwalker objects. After coming up empty, Ella got ready to leave.

Abigail walked back outside with her. "Please don't tell anyone you found that here—except your brother and the tribal police, of course. Word is already spreading about what happened yesterday, and a lot of people are afraid to come by the house now. Even my own daughter kept her visit short last night. Your brother is going to do a Sing in about ten days, and a shorter ritual before then. But this is taking a terrible toll on StarTalk and my son-in-law. He found out about what happened to me and won't go outside the house without a gun now."

"I know he's been drinking, but is he also taking any kind of drugs—legal or otherwise?" Ella asked, remembering the glazed look in his eyes the last time she'd seen him.

"No drugs, just booze, as far as I know. But he's an accident waiting to happen. My daughter's not thinking right either. She's so angry after seeing what they did to me, I'm afraid she might try to find answers on her own, and put herself in even more danger." She took a slow, deep breath. "Have you made any progress at all?"

Ella considered lying, then resisted the temptation. The truth was that Abigail had been her prime suspect until she, too, had fallen victim. "I think that the incidents we've seen that appear to be random acts of violence are actually part of some larger plan. That's all I can tell you at this point."

"Good luck to you, Clah," Roxanne called out as Ella walked away to the tribal cruiser.

Less than twenty minutes later, Ella entered the station and went to the lab. Seeing Justine at the computer, she gave her a quick rundown and left the knife with her.

Ella continued down the hall and saw Tache coming out of his office.

"I'm glad you're here," Ralph said. "I needed to talk to you."

"My office then."

As soon as they were both inside, Ella shut the door. "Any leads on who's passing information to the Fierce Ones?"

He rubbed the back of his neck with one hand. "I've asked questions nicely and tried to push for them, too, but I don't think Jesse knows. He told me that the information they've been given is pretty accurate. So if it wasn't me, it has got to be someone well-connected with our team," he answered.

"Now for the interesting news," he continued. "I also pressed Jesse for any new information about the beating of Wallace Curtis and Marilyn Charley. He told me that someone impersonating one of the leaders of the Fierce Ones gave that order. The imposter knew exactly who to call and used the right recognition signals. The individuals involved— who'd already heard about the affair from one of George Charley's relatives—didn't even stop to question the move. Now the Fierce Ones are going full-out to find out who faked the orders and made those calls—and they want to know *before* we do. If they catch whoever's responsible, he's going to be nothing more than a footnote in history."

"Once they make an example of whoever betrayed them, fear of the Fierce Ones will grow. That's why they don't want us involved," Ella said. "I'll need you to talk to Jesse again. If he's as well-informed as you've said, he probably has a list of likely suspects. We now know that it would have had to have been someone who knows the members of the Fierce Ones *and* their assigned tasks."

"I'll keep working on him."

Justine came in just as Tache left. "The knife is made from deer antler, not bone. You said it was at the crime scene?"

"In the bedroom behind the dresser."

"It wasn't there when we processed the scene," Justine

said flatly. "I *always* search for anything that may have been dropped or that could have rolled beneath furniture. I used my flashlight to check under and around everything."

Ella expelled her breath in a rush. "I didn't think you would have missed it. But why would a skinwalker put it behind the dresser of all places? The purpose of a bone knife is to use it on the victim and contaminate them, if not kill them outright."

"What are you thinking, that the painter planted it there?"

"No. He was Anglo and I don't think he had any idea what that was."

"Who else could have done it?"

Ella thought about Roxanne, but that didn't seem to fit her style. She was getting her paycheck from Abigail, and appeared to be dedicated enough to the job. Maybe Abigail had planted it herself, or it could have been anyone who'd visited the woman. But, then again, to what end? The motive continued to elude her.

"I don't get any of this. What are we missing?" Justine said, just as Big Ed appeared at her door.

"You better get rolling," he said quickly. "Dispatch just sent a cruiser out to your brother's home. Two gunmen are taking shots at his family. Clifford's currently holed up in his medicine hogan with his wife and son."

Ella was on the move even before her boss had finished speaking. Justine ran, getting ahead of her. "I'm driving," she said.

Sirens wailing, they quickly passed through Shiprock, then raced south down the highway at pursuit speed. "An attack in broad daylight? And why *my* brother?" Ella asked, not expecting an answer.

"*Hataaliis* and skinwalkers are mortal enemies," Justine said, not taking her eyes off the road.

"But why get lethal now, shooting bullets at my brother's family? Why not something more ritualistic, like what we've been seeing?"

"Bullets have been used to trump rituals and magic before. Maybe they want to punish the *hataalii* by endangering those he loves," Justine answered.

Ella used the unit's radio to contact the patrol officer already approaching the scene. Marianna Talk identified herself clearly and quickly, reporting that her ETA would be less than a minute.

"We'll be right behind you, maybe four minutes," Ella said, looking over at Justine.

"Five," Justine answered, easing up on the gas as she saw an old pickup ahead in their lane, loaded down with firewood.

Every minute felt like a lifetime to Ella thinking of her brother and his family under attack. She tried to keep herself busy checking her weapon and spare magazines. At least Herman and her mom, who lived close to Clifford's, were away and not likely to be swept up in the attack.

Marianna called back to report that shots were still being fired as she approached the scene. Ella could hear the gunfire over her radio.

They raced down the dirt road by Ella and Rose's home at fifty miles an hour, leaving a cloud of dust in their wake. Thirty seconds later, Clifford and Loretta's place was within sight.

The wood-framed stucco home stood fifty yards from the medicine hogan, and halfway between the two was a low-roofed structure covering several cords of firewood. Across the dirt road, to the south, was Marianna's department vehicle. Ella could see her crouched low beside her door, using the engine block as cover. Marianna had her shotgun aimed over the hood. No perps were visible at the moment, but the direction of Marianna's aim gave Ella valuable information.

Justine pulled up a vehicle length away from the squad car, stopped at an angle to create a shallow V with the vehicles, then ducked down as Ella scrambled out the passenger side. Justine came out behind her on her knees and, shielded by the body of the car, reached back for the shotgun.

Pistol in hand, Ella crouched low beside the right front tire, out of view of the structures. Marianna, careful to stay low, glanced over at her.

"They have rifles, and fired two shots in my direction when I pulled up," she warned. "One's behind the firewood, and another shooter is more to the east, behind the boulders to our right. The last time he fired, he was near the corral, but he moves after every shot."

Ella shifted over to the front bumper, and looked at the sandstone boulders, her head low. A shot rang out from behind the stacks of wood, and she saw dust and splinters as the bullet struck the frame of the medicine hogan's entrance. The blanket that served as a door was pulled back about a foot, but she couldn't see anyone against the dark interior. Clifford had obviously extinguished his lantern—a good idea.

Ella fired two rounds at the wood pile just to keep the shooter from moving out of cover. There was not much chance of hitting him, an entire winter's supply of wood gave him plenty of protection.

Out of the corner of her eye, Ella saw Justine lying prone beside the rear tire so she could fire beneath their unit. "I've got the wood pile covered, Ella. If he comes out on either side, or moves west, I've got a clear shot."

"Tactics?" Marianna asked.

Ella looked to the east, noting that the ground sloped

away from the road on their side—the south. If she kept low, she'd have a chance to outflank both shooters from that direction. "Justine will cover the wood pile, keeping anyone from moving to our left," Ella said. "You cover the rocks. I'm going to move east down the road, and try to come up from their left. Their only escape will be retreating to the north, toward the mesa." Ella glanced back at her partner. "If the opportunity presents itself, Justine, advance to the house with cover fire from Marianna. That'll compromise the guy behind the wood pile."

Ella moved downslope, then, crouching low, ran east, using the roadbed as cover. She heard a rifle shot, then two shotgun blasts as the officers returned fire. Noting that the rifle fire had come from farther away this time, Ella suspected that the suspects were making a run for it now that Clifford had help. They would be long gone before she could outflank them. She moved upslope to take a quick look, and caught a glimpse of a rifle swinging toward her from behind a cottonwood tree beyond the rocks. Ella dove to the ground as a bullet whined overhead.

A moment later she moved downslope again, then proceeded east as before. Suddenly she heard a vehicle start up, close by. Staying low, Ella moved up toward the road again and spotted a pickup heading west up the drainage ditch on the opposite side of the road. The driver had a pistol in his left hand and was firing in the direction of the squad cars.

Ella took aim. "Police! Stop!" she shouted.

The driver looked over at her in surprise, then swung his pistol around and fired. The angle was wrong and his shot went wide to her left. Ella shot back twice, one high, one low, and the pickup suddenly lurched to its right, skidded sideways, and nearly rolled before coming to a stop.

There was a flurry of gunfire to the west, mostly coming from shotguns, and then the shooting stopped. Ella ran to the pickup, coming up from behind on the driver's side, and using the vehicle as a screen to protect herself from the shooters down the road.

Justine was across the road now as well, beside the house, but she was aiming uphill, toward the mesa. Marianna was standing beside her unit, her weapon aimed toward the pickup.

"Cover me!" Ella yelled, coming up to the pickup door from the rear. As she inched closer, the pickup door swung open. A hand fell out, a pistol along with it, followed by the driver's bloody head as he toppled sideways.

"They're running north," Justine called out.

"Cover each other as you advance, but watch out for an ambush," Ella yelled back. After taking a quick look at the crumpled body beside the pickup, she kicked the man's pistol under the pickup, then jogged to the hogan. "It's Ella. Everyone okay?" she called out.

Clifford, Loretta, and, lastly, Julian came out. "That was awesome, Aunt," Julian, Clifford's fourteen-year-old son, said. "They were coming at us from everywhere! I wanted to shoot back at them, but Dad wouldn't let me use a gun."

Clifford gripped him firmly on the shoulder. "Take your mother inside the house. Move quickly and stay away from the doors and windows."

Ella watched them. Loretta, still carrying their cordless phone, looked more frightened than Ella had ever seen her.

"What happened?" Ella asked her brother.

"They pulled up about fifteen minutes ago. I was in my medicine hogan when I heard the truck, and I went outside to invite the person in. I assumed it was a patient. Before I could do anything they jumped out and started shooting. My wife had been outside with my son, shaking out some rugs. They were closer to the hogan than the house, so they ran to join me." He paused. "Lucky I had that cordless phone with me, along with my thirty-thirty. I've been keeping both nearby after hearing about the trouble that's been going on around us. I was able to shoot back, so they never moved any closer. But I've got to tell you something. They were either terrible marksmen or they were missing on purpose."

Ella looked at him in surprise. "What makes you think that it was on purpose?"

"The shots came close, and I mean *close*, but never quite hit the mark. Bullets flew over our heads when we were running for cover, and impacted on the wood frame around the door several times. Some even hit the stove pipe sticking out of the roof. But no shots passed through the blanket and into the hogan—not even one."

Ella considered this new information, trying to make sense of it. Just then, Marianna appeared. "I think you better come look at this," she said, not elaborating.

Ella followed her. As they reached the covered wood storage area, she saw a piece of paper affixed to a pine log with a cheap pocket knife.

Ella examined the discovery, not touching anything. The knife could have easily come from any trading post or grocery store on the Rez, and the paper was loose-leaf with holes for a three-ring binder. The message was clear:

> *Ervin Benally is ours. Back off or*
> *those you love will pay.*

Ella heard her brother coming up. She didn't have to turn around to know his faint steps.

"That dead body can't stay this close to where my family lives. It has to be moved quickly," he said.

"It will, don't worry. We'll be taking the pickup and its driver away from here shortly."

"I'd also like my wife and son to leave the area now," he said. "Do you have any objections? If you want to question them, they'll be at my mother-in-law's down by Gallup."

Ella understood. To Clifford, the *chindi* was much more than simple lore, it was an irrefutable fact. Although all things could be brought under control and a return to harmony established with the proper prayers, the *chindi* was an evil best avoided.

"Okay, but have them circle around to the north to reach the highway. The shooters came from the east down the south road, right?"

He nodded, then hurried to the house.

Out of the corner of her eye, Ella caught a glimpse of Loretta as she came out to meet him. From her gestures, she knew that Loretta didn't want to go without him.

Leaving Clifford to handle his own family matters, Ella walked back to the perp's truck. The dead man was Navajo, in his early fifties. A bullet had pieced his skull behind his left ear. Ella saw the entry wound, but there was no exit wound.

Knowing the tribe's ME, who'd already been called to the scene, would handle all the medical details, Ella focused on the truck itself. After putting on two pairs of gloves, she checked the interior of the cab. There was no registration in the glove compartment, only a razor blade-type windshield scraper, two cigarettes in a pack, and a book of matches.

Justine came up a moment later. "They're long gone," she said. "There was another vehicle, but all we saw was the tailgate of what looked to be a gray or pale blue pickup. No make or model."

Marianna, who'd gone around to the rear of the truck, used her handheld to read off the deceased's license plate to Dispatch. After a moment, she got an answer. "This pickup was reported stolen a few hours ago," she told Ella.

"Let me check and see if the driver has some ID." Ella reached for the contents of the man's hip pants pockets, and then his front pockets. There was some loose change and a pack of gum. "Nothing."

As she stood up, Ella caught a glimpse of a bright-colored cloth in the storage space behind the backrest of the front seat. Reaching for it, she pulled out an almost incandescent yellow man's blazer.

Ella gazed at it for a moment. It looked familiar somehow. That's when she remembered. Flashy yellow sport coats had been the trademark of the late Senator James Yellowhair.

TWENTY-THREE
— ✘ ✘ ✘ —

When Clifford returned he stood well back, waiting. Ella went over to meet him. "I've got some disturbing news," she said, and told him about the jacket.

Clifford moved forward to take a look, and his expression changed into one of pure disgust.

"I haven't verified that the jacket is his yet, so I may be wrong, but I don't think I am," Ella added.

"Nor do I," Clifford answered. "The late senator used to wear a yellow jacket like that to almost every rally and public function."

"Lab tests can tell us if this was dug up from his grave," Ella said. "But it looks too clean for that. I'm thinking that it came from another source, like maybe a clothing bank. This man must have recognized it and made the purchase."

"Even if it wasn't dug up, it was one of the deceased's favorite pieces of clothing, and that makes it dangerous to have around. Only an evil one would attempt something like this."

"Do you know why those people are coming after you now?" Ella asked.

"They left the note for *you*, I believe," he answered. "Maybe we were only a means to an end."

"But why pick on a *hataalii* at all—someone who's clearly in the best position to defend against them? They usually go out of their way to avoid someone with your knowledge and power."

"They might have seen us checking the cave," he answered, then shrugged. "Maybe that note was partially meant for me, too—a reminder to mind my own business."

Ella didn't answer right away. Her brother hadn't known about the photo Roxanne had taken, but to think of Roxanne as a skinwalker was too much of a stretch. Yet, if Roxanne had followed them to the cave, it was possible others had, too. The area around Hogback was flat enough that anyone could keep watch at a long distance, just as Roxanne had. Unfortunately, it would have been pointless to ask her if she'd seen anyone else around. She'd never admit she'd been there.

"You're in their sights now," Ella told Clifford. "Don't lower your guard. Next time, they may shoot a lot straighter."

Clifford nodded, then added, "Everyone here needs to take part in a purification ceremony before you leave. None of you will be safe otherwise."

Ella turned and saw the crime scene van arrive, and right behind it, the M.E. They all had a lot of work to do, and this would slow things down.

"My team has the medicine bags you gave us, and, unfortunately, we can't afford to take time off for anything else right now," Ella replied.

"The bags aren't enough, not in this particular case," he answered. "And your doctor friend doesn't have any form of protection, I'm guessing. The ceremony won't take long, but it's necessary."

"I'm interested. Count me in," Marianna said from the other side of the truck.

"Me, too," Justine said, peering out from inside the cab.

Ella considered it for a moment. As police officers they were all modernists. Their need for a ceremony was more about continuity and reaffirmation. The ritual served to strengthen their beliefs that evil could be controlled—that what they did made a difference. She couldn't deny them that.

"All right. We'll do it after the scene's processed."

After the body and the truck had been taken away, Clifford called all of them to the medicine hogan, even Carolyn Roanhorse.

Repeating the prayer that Clifford intoned, and following his directions, they cast arrowheads, bits of turquoise, and white shell into the air.

When the blessing was concluded, Ella could feel its power. Confidence and new determination to do what had to be done filled each of them.

Carolyn left with the body first, and Ella and her team headed back to the station a short time later. On the way back, Ella used her cell phone to fill Blalock in on what they'd found.

"We're running in circles, Clah, but Ervin Benally is at the center of this somehow. One question keeps coming back. How much of this is a StarTalk issue, and how much a personal attack on the man?"

Before she could answer, Dispatch called them on the radio. "Shots have been fired at the Benally home. Mrs. Benally called to say that her husband took a shot at her and barely missed when she came to the door after picking up the mail."

"Any more information? Anyone injured?" Ella asked.

"No, but Mrs. Benally asked that an officer to stop by as soon as possible."

"We'll handle it, Dispatch," Ella said. "Our ETA is less than five minutes."

Ella had Justine change directions and head to the Benally home. "Step on it, partner. Somebody else might be prowling around the house."

While in transit, Ella filled Blalock in. "We'll handle this and catch up to you at the station."

"Copy that," Blalock answered.

Ella called Teeny next. "I'm going to need the footage from the cameras you set up at the Benally residence."

"No can do," Teeny answered. "Ervin cancelled the job. Once he heard what my fees were, he told me to forget it, that he'd handle his own problems. His wife wanted to go ahead and put up the cameras, but Ervin threatened to take his rifle butt to my equipment if I didn't pack it back up again." He paused then added, "Ella, the man's nuts and the booze I smelled on him didn't help matters. Watch your back around him."

"Okay, thanks for the warning."

They arrived a short time later and Barbara met them outside. "Ervin apologized for almost killing me with that idiot rifle of his," she said pointing toward the mailbox, which had entrance and exit holes running right through it. "Now he's in his study with the curtains drawn. He insists he's their target, not me, and that he has to protect himself."

"Has he been drinking again?" Justine asked, sighting along the trajectory to see where the round had gone. Fortunately there were no houses across the street, just a low hill. The bullet probably hadn't gone far.

Barbara nodded. "I hid the bottles, but he found them while I was out a while ago."

"Let me speak to Ervin. Maybe I can help," Ella said,

then turned to Justine. "Officer Goodluck, take a look around outside, but stay out of the field of fire from that window."

Justine nodded, then walked away.

Barbara waved her hand, inviting Ella into the house. "Don't get too close to the office door without telling him who you are first."

Ella announced her presence once she'd entered the hall. "Open up, Ervin, this is Ella Clah. I'd like to talk to you."

"You alone?"

"Yeah, I am," she answered. "You're safe, so relax. Another officer is outside, double-checking the grounds." She heard the door unlock, then it opened a crack.

Ervin peered out, then waved at her. "Hurry up. Don't just stand there."

His appearance shocked her. Ervin looked as if he hadn't slept in weeks. His eyes were red and almost glazed, no doubt the effects of sustained fear—and alcohol. His breath smelled of liquor and he was having problems speaking clearly. Seeing the wastebasket filled with empty bottles verified her suspicions. Worst of all, he smelled rank.

Ella looked around and spotted his thirty-thirty rifle standing beside the window, which was open about two inches. On the floor beside the baseboard was a box of cartridges. From where she was standing, the mailbox was barely visible. The branches of a purple plum tree blocked the view enough to have misled someone whose vision was impaired by alcohol.

"You need to get hold of yourself, Mr. Benally," she said in a hard, no-nonsense tone. "Shooting at shadows and the outline of your own wife? You're becoming your own worst enemy. How long have you been shut up in this room?"

"You don't get it. They want me *dead*. But they can't get me here."

"*Who* wants you dead?"

"Skinwalkers came after me."

Since Barbara hadn't mentioned this, Ella looked at him in surprise. "What makes you say that?"

"I stepped outside late last night for some fresh air. Everything was still, and I had to get out of this room, even if only for a little while. I was walking around when I saw my father-in-law's bolo tie lying out there on the ground, plain as day. I recognized it because the outer edge of the turquoise stone in its center was badly chipped. He'd never fixed it because he'd always said that it brought him good luck just as it was. My wife's family buried him with it, or maybe they gave it to charity. Whatever—but there it was, plain as day."

Ella decided to have the burial site checked, just in case. "Did you leave it where it was?"

He nodded. "Of course. I came running back here, and stayed behind my locked door. I told Barbara about it this morning, but when she went for a look, she couldn't find it. I don't think she believes me now."

Ella exhaled slowly. After what she'd seen, she wasn't ready to discount his story as just a figment of his imagination. "I believe you, Ervin, but you're in bad shape. You need to go see a doctor."

"Like a *hataalii*?"

"Maybe that, too, but I mean one of the doctors at the hospital. You're falling apart, and you have to find a way to calm down, lay off the booze, and get some rest. If you shoot an innocent bystander or start becoming a danger to the community, I'll have to lock you up. And in a cell, you'll be out of choices."

"Catch whoever's after me, *then* I'll calm down. I can't go anywhere. If I leave here, I'm a dead man."

"A doctor could give you something to help you cope

with the pressure so you can get some sleep. StarTalk means a lot to you and your family. Don't allow anyone to take it from you."

His lips narrowed, and his gaze focused on something undetermined on the wall behind her. "StarTalk . . . that's been my dream for a long time."

"Then fight for it," she said. "Get help."

"I don't want to die," he said in a barely audible whisper.

Ella's heart went out to him. He'd come up with a way to make people's lives easier here on the Rez, but he certainly hadn't planned on becoming a target. A police officer dealt with that kind of threat on a daily basis, but Ervin had no idea how to come to terms with it. Yet, unless he did, fear would destroy him.

"You think I'm just a coward, and maybe I am. But I'm not prepared to die," he said. "Is anyone?"

"You need a trustworthy bodyguard to give you a feeling of security, but keep one thing in mind. The enemy that's destroying you isn't out there somewhere. He's inside you," Ella said. "Defeat your own fears and you've won half the battle."

Leaving him to ponder that thought, she walked back outside. As she stepped out into the sun, Barbara, who'd been waiting for her, approached. "He's still not coming out?" she asked.

"He might. Give him a little more time," Ella said. "You know, I could arrest him for endangering the public with that rifle. At least he'd be safe."

"Please give him another chance. I'll talk to him and try to get the rifle, or at least the booze. We've invested everything we have into StarTalk. If anyone else sees him looking and acting like this, or he's locked up, word will get out and our credibility will be ruined. Everything we've worked for will be lost. You need to find answers quickly so we can put an end to this."

"I have a few leads that are promising," Ella said, still debating in her mind what to do with Ervin. She knew she was close to an answer, but she hadn't put all the pieces together yet in her mind.

Justine gave her a questioning look, but remained silent.

When they were back in the car, Ella glanced over at her. "I'm calling for a meeting with Blalock, Big Ed, and the rest of our team. I have an idea, but I'd like to run it past all of you first."

"It's going to be a stretch, right?" Justine asked, knowing how Ella's mind worked.

"Oh yeah, partner, and one practically guaranteed to make even more trouble for the department if we screw up."

The meeting was held in Ella's office. Big Ed was with several members of the tribal council and had told Ella to start without him.

Ella looked at Blalock and her team. "We're not making progress fast enough. We still don't even have an ID on the guy I shot during the raid on my brother's place."

"I checked with the ME and she's trying to find something that we can run a check on," Justine answered. "But he's never even had dental work done, according to Dr. Roanhorse. I ran his prints and we got zip."

"We have to make sketches of the dead man's face and post them at grocery stores and gas stations. Maybe someone will recognize him and come forward," Ella said. "Photos are out, because we'd only end up scaring people with an image of a dead man."

"The connecting thread in all this seems to be Ervin, and experience tells me to go back to one of the basics—follow the money," Blalock said. "Who has the most to gain by ruining StarTalk?

"No one—that is unless you want to count the cash Abigail would save if she stopped investing in it," Ella said. "But that brings me to the reason I called this meeting. We don't have any clear evidence against her, but I think we should take a much closer look at Abigail Yellowhair."

While she was still speaking, Big Ed had slipped into the room. "If you go after Abigail Yellowhair, you'd better have a truckload of evidence to back you up. She'll lawyer up in a heartbeat and sue us for everything she can think of."

"Abigail becomes our prime suspect if we narrow the field to someone with both the resources and malicious intelligence to keep us going in circles. She's more than capable of manipulating people, and she certainly has plenty of contacts. I'll admit that I can't see her doing all this just to save a few bucks. If she's behind it, there's something else at stake."

"Focusing our investigation only on Mrs. Yellowhair doesn't make sense," Tache said. "The kind of terror campaign we've seen takes time and effort and, right now, that woman has her hands full. She and her daughter are fighting hard to keep StarTalk up and running. In addition to that, Mrs. Yellowhair has been busy selecting the Navajo students who'll be awarded full scholarships to Valley Academy this year. She pays for those and insists on making the selections herself. I know all about this because my niece was in the running, though she didn't make the final cut."

The news hit Ella like a bolt of lightning. For a moment all she could do was stare. "Abigail's responsible for the scholarship?" Ella said dully, a very ugly picture forming in her mind.

"I thought you knew that. My niece told me that your daughter was one of the two selected to be this year's recipients."

Ella, who'd been standing, sat down heavily. "Abigail *knows* how close my mother and I are to my daughter. The possibility that Dawn might leave home has been unbelievably distracting to my family." She took a deep breath, then continued, shaking her head as she spoke. "This just reinforces it for me. Though we still don't have a clear motive, I'm betting Abigail's behind what's been happening. Giving Dawn that scholarship was just her way of trying to keep me from focusing on the case and what was happening to Ervin."

"But how does she fit in with the problems we've had with the skinwalkers or with the Fierce Ones? Are you saying she's allied herself to both of them so she can . . . what? Drive her son-in-law out of his own company?" Justine asked.

Ella thought about it for several moments, and at long last, had her answer. "Abigail wanted StarTalk to go statewide, remember? She had a big fight with her son-in-law several months ago over it and Abigail doesn't give up easily. Maybe she came up with a subtle, long-term plan to get rid of the one person standing in her way—Ervin."

"You're all forgetting one thing," Big Ed said. "Someone used her for a punching bag. How does that fit in with this theory?"

Ella was the first to break the long silence that followed. "It's possible she engineered that herself. They pull their punches but still make it look good, and suddenly she's a victim, not a suspect. There's no better alibi that than, is there?"

"You're reaching, partner," Justine said flatly. "Think about what else happened. Do you really believe she would have hired skinwalkers to put a curse on her? Even a modernist would hesitate to mess with those people. If nothing else, skinwalkers, by and large, are unstable and dangerous."

"My point exactly," Ella answered. "If she hired skin-walkers to work her over, they may have deliberately exceeded their instructions. Treachery is one of their MO's."

"Okay, I get your point," Joe said. "But why mess with skinwalkers at all, if she'd already found a way to get the Fierce Ones to do her dirty work?"

"She couldn't continue to manipulate the Fierce Ones after they found out they'd been used," Ella answered. "Ralph's informant told him that someone had used their recognition signal and given out orders. They're now determined to find out who that was. Security's super-tight for them right now."

"What makes you think Mrs. Yellowhair would be able to get those codes?" Joe asked.

"She could have bought them. We've met at least one Fierce One who was willing to bend the rules so he could make a fast buck." She looked over at Justine, then Blalock, thinking of the custodian who'd been caught siphoning gas at school.

"You're relying on inference, not evidence. You'll need a lot more than that to even bring her in for questioning," Big Ed said, just as his pager went off. He checked the digital readout, excused himself, and quickly left the room.

Ella watched him go, then looked back at the others. From their expressions, she knew that Big Ed had voiced what they were all thinking.

"I'll see what the Bureau has on Abigail Yellowhair," Blalock said, standing. "I'll be in touch."

Tache followed. "I'll make some more inquiries and find out what the Fierce Ones have uncovered about their imposter."

"Do something else for me first," Ella said. "Check out

State Senator James Yellowhair's grave site. Let me know if there's any sign of tampering."

"You mean like digging him up and stealing his jacket and bolo tie?" Justine asked.

"Exactly."

As Tache left, Sergeant Joe Neskahi stood. "Don't expect me to ask Abby out and ply her with drinks," Joe said, a solemn expression on his face. "But do you have any particular direction you want me to take on this?"

Ella smiled, remembering that Mrs. Yellowhair had flirted with Joe after the incident at the Chapter House. "Try to find out where Abigail has been going when she's not at StarTalk, and what she's been doing when she's away from the Benallys and the office. Also see if you can befriend someone in the office staff and get an unofficial look at her phone records. We don't have enough for a court order, but the person directing this operation must have a way of contacting whoever's doing the dirty work."

"I can do all that, but keeping Abigail from finding out is going to be tricky. How about if I ask about Barbara, Ervin, and some members of the office staff, too? That'll disguise our real focus," Neskahi said.

"Smart tactics. Go for it," Ella replied

Joe left, leaving Justine behind. "For what it's worth, I think you're way off the mark on this one, Ella. None of this fits Abigail. Her position and standing on the reservation are important to her, and to maintain them, she has to keep her hands clean."

"All the more reason for her to hire others to sully theirs," Ella replied.

"I know her. She's not evil," Justine said. "She's spent her entire life doing what she thinks is best for the Navajo Nation."

"She looks out for herself, too. Taking StarTalk statewide could make her a fortune."

"The tribe will get some of those proceeds."

"Just keep digging, partner."

After Justine left, Ella sat back in her chair. She didn't care if Abigail's motives were noble or not. If she was behind what was happening, she'd chosen to align herself with evil to accomplish her goals. Evil had its place in the intricate web of life that connected all things, but it was up to people like her to restore harmony by bringing it back under control.

TWENTY-FOUR

———— ✕ ✕ ✕ ————

Following a hunch, Ella decided to pay Teeny a visit next. A short time later, she arrived at the fenced-in compound, then stopped by the steel gate. A small camera was above her, to the right. She recognized Teeny's voice a moment later.

"Hey, Ella! Good to see you. I'm buzzing you in."

She soon drove up to the small metal warehouse Teeny had converted into his office and home. Of course the word *home* was open to interpretation. There wasn't much that could be considered "homey" inside. The place was wall-to-wall with computers and electronic gizmos of all shapes, sizes, and applications. The temperature was always frigid, too—something about computers running best at lower temperatures. Too bad the same couldn't be said for the person with freezing fingers at the mouse or keyboard.

Needing to warm up, Ella accepted Teeny's offer of a bowl of green chile stew. It was late afternoon and she hadn't eaten since breakfast. Teeny was an amateur chef and his skills were well known to his friends, who benefitted from his expertise in the kitchen.

Though his spicy stew, filled with chopped pork, Hatch

green chile, and chunks of potato was hot enough to make her perspire, it was delicious. Teeny always added slices of mozzarella cheese, which were soft and chewy—a special touch.

"Okay, here's the deal," she said between mouthfuls. "I need everything you can get me on Abigail Yellowhair."

He shook his head slowly. "I think I know where you're going with this. I've kept up with what's happening, but anything I could get you would be sanitized to the nth degree. If she's involved in questionable activities you won't find a paper trail. She's learned from her late husband's mistakes."

"Have you heard anything at all that might link her to skinwalkers on any level?" As Ella watched him consider her question, what surprised her most was that Teeny hadn't seem shocked or surprised by her request.

"Nothing concrete," he said at last. "But I've heard some gossip about her daughter, Barbara."

"Close enough. Tell me."

"When Barbara was in college, she was fascinated by the supernatural, the occult, and practitioners of the paranormal. Using an assumed name, she paid Virgil Pete a visit hoping to find out more about skinwalkers. Virgil recognized her, having been around at one of her father's political rallies when she was there."

"I heard about that from Virgil," Ella admitted. "But thanks anyway."

"Did he tell you about her more recent visit?"

"What? She went back?"

"Yes."

"Virgil didn't mention that."

"I'm not surprised. He, like a lot of other people on the Rez, would rather not get on that family's bad side."

"Fill me in," Ella said.

"A few months ago Barbara visited him wanting to buy some human bones. He told her he couldn't help her, so she asked him for the names of other skinwalkers she could contact. Virgil mentioned a man he'd heard people talking about because he'd been behaving strangely, a mechanic at a gas station north of Gallup, the one that closed down a while back. When Virgil realized that she wanted to hire skinwalkers, not just buy bones, he decided to try and get some cash for himself. She'd never know he wasn't legit."

"So she hired him?"

"No, he backed out of the deal when she insisted on buying the bones first. But she gave him fifty dollars not to tell anyone she'd been there. Virgil saw her to the door and noticed another person, maybe a woman, waiting behind the wheel of the car. Virgil didn't see who it was."

"Did he notice anything about the car, like its color?"

"Interestingly enough, it was one of those yellow, sporty jobs, the kind Abigail drives."

Teeny finished his bowl of stew, then, after Ella declined seconds, led the way back to the computer area.

Ella considered what she'd learned. An auto mechanic would have had the expertise to disable the brakes on Ervin's pickup, and know how to remove battery fluid with a hydrometer. "It's a good bet that Barbara and the driver of the yellow car went to the mechanic next. So now we have to find this guy. Any idea who he is or where he works these days?"

"None," Teeny answered.

"Have you heard anything relating to StarTalk lately, particularly something that might not be public knowledge yet?"

"That company interests me, so I've been keeping tabs on it. Someone from StarTalk has been contacting potential investors with future plans to go statewide. About a week ago, Jake Case called Abigail and offered to invest a sub-stantial sum. Case runs a PR firm and owns stock in nearly all the companies he represents. He's been very successful and has plenty of money to spare."

Ella didn't bother asking him where he got his informa-tion. She knew it was as good as gold, or he wouldn't have passed it on to her. "That gives Mrs. Yellowhair one heckuva motive. If she wants to expand, her only option is to get Ervin out of her way, either by getting him killed, commit-ted, or driven out of the company. Reasoning with him ob-viously didn't work."

"The likelihood that Abigail was the one who drove Bar-bara to Virgil's suggests that Barbara's also involved in this plan."

"Not necessarily. Maybe she wasn't aware of what her mother's game really was. I doubt Abigail would ever com-pletely confide in Barbara, or anyone else. But to get what she wants, Abigail wouldn't hesitate to use her daughter. She'd come up with a million plausible reasons, too," Ella replied. "Yet without evidence that connects one or both of these women to the people who are harassing Ervin, I've still got nothing. I don't even have enough for a warrant to tap their phones."

"That wouldn't do you any good, at least as far as Abi-gail goes. She wouldn't get careless," Teeny said. "So what now?"

"I've got a couple of options. First, I'm going to try and track down that mechanic. Secondly, I'm going to have Abi-gail followed. My money's still on her. She must be contact-ing her goons somehow." Ella paused, then shook her head. "No, wait a minute. Abigail's got a bodyguard and she wouldn't risk doing something like that in front of a poten-tial witness. It makes more sense to assume she already had everything in place *before* she hired protection."

"Are you talking about Roxanne Dixon?" Teeny asked. Seeing her nod, he continued. "She's not working for Abigail anymore—not as of late yesterday anyway. I ran into her at the Corner Pocket, that pool hall in Farmington. I was there with a client and she approached me looking for a job."

"Did you hire her?"

"No, I don't have anything extra at the moment."

"I wonder if Roxanne's job ended because, now that the skinwalkers did their thing at Abigail's place, Abigail has no further need for a witness."

"Maybe." Teeny glanced over automatically at one of the cameras monitoring the outside perimeter, then sat up. "Speak of the devil. Looks like Roxanne was tailing you."

"She's out there?"

"She just pulled up within sight of my camera. Since she didn't come to the gate, my guess is that she's been following you. Do you want to go have a little talk with her, or shall I?"

"How well do you know her?" Ella asked.

"She and I worked together a few times back when I was in the department. We get along okay. A few days ago she showed up here asking me to teach her a few gray area skills with computers—like how to hack into utility and other databases, phishing to get e-mail addresses, stuff like that. I didn't want to do that since I wasn't sure what she was after, so I begged off. I ended up recommending a few Web sites that specialize in data collection—for a price."

"That's bad news for me," Ella said, and told him about the e-mails, especially the one threatening to link her with skinwalkers.

He muttered an oath. "I had no idea that's what she had in mind. But don't worry. I know some ways of blocking e-mails from known sites—and I just happen to have the information we need about her particular computer. If she sticks with that machine for her e-mails, I can show you how to screen her out. She'll never know you're not picking it up, either."

"Sounds good to me."

Ella wrote down Teeny's instructions. "Got it," she said at last.

He glanced at the camera again. "So, do you want to go talk to Roxanne alone, or shall I ask her in, and we can both lean on her?"

Ella considered it for a moment. "I need information from her and you'll have a better shot if you go alone. I have to find a link between Abigail and what's happening to her son-in-law," Ella explained. "Roxanne would know everyone Abigail's met with recently. Mind you, Abigail wouldn't have hired anyone in front of Roxanne, but if there's a possible suspect among the people she's seen, Roxanne will know."

"Agreed."

"The problem is that if I go question her, I won't get very far. Roxanne wants Kevin and thinks I'm standing in her way."

Teeny burst out laughing. "She doesn't know you very well. If you'd have wanted Kevin, he wouldn't have left the reservation in the first place. You would have figured out a way to change his mind."

"You're overestimating my charms. Even if I'd been interested in Kevin, I don't think anything could have kept him from going to D.C."

"Then you would have been traveling back and forth. The real reason you're still single is because you've chosen to remain that way, Ella. The truth is, you've already given your heart—to your work, and to your daughter. There's really not much room left over."

"Hey, did you forget? I've been seeing Reverend Tome," Ella countered with a grin.

"That's only because he's safe. Ford's already given his

heart to something else, too. But the things you need and expect from a relationship may come between you eventually."

Ella knew he was talking about sex . . . or, more to the point, the lack of it. Rather than continue to discuss this, she turned their attention back to the problem at hand and gazed at the camera. "Would you talk to her? She may open up to you."

"If Roxanne knows anything, I'll get the information for you."

It was his tone that alerted her, and she gave him a worried look. "You're not going to do something that'll require legal action, are you?"

Teeny laughed. "No. She and I will have a talk, that's all. We see each other just as we are—no illusions, no pretensions. We know exactly what the other one's capable of."

The thought was frightening. Teeny was a huge man whose sheer size was a threat all on its own. That, and the arctic coldness he could project when he chose, was the reason he seldom had to carry anything through. Roxanne had met her match.

"I'll be at Blalock's," she said, then left.

As she drove out of the fenced perimeter, she spotted Roxanne's car across the road. Ella saw her duck down to avoid being seen. Then Teeny came out of the shadows behind her, having left the perimeter by some other exit. He reached into the open window and placed his hand on Roxanne's shoulder. She jumped, startled, and Ella couldn't resist a low chuckle.

Leaving them to work things out, Ella picked up her cell phone, and dialed Justine next. "Are those sketches of the man killed near my brother's place ready?" Hearing Justine reply in the affirmative, she continued. "We have to circulate those as soon as possible. We need to find out who he was and what he did for a living. If it turns out that the guy worked in a garage, we'll have a link to the incidents involving Ervin's vehicles," she said and explained.

Next she called Blalock at his new office. "I need to make an official request, Dwayne. I'm on my way over now."

"I'll be here, but I have nothing from the Bureau by way of news yet. I tried a few local contacts I've worked with in the past, but none are willing to talk to me now. I think they've either been paid off, or they're scared spitless, worried about turning Abigail Yellowhair into an enemy."

"Maybe both," Ella said.

She arrived at Blalock's a short time later. The new building was less than a quarter mile from Blalock's old office, which had been destroyed in a fire last year. Most of the offices here were still empty and the building was so quiet she could hear her own footsteps echoing on the tile floor.

Ella went directly to Blalock's office at the end of the long, dark hall. His front door was open but she still knocked on her way in. As she took a seat, she glanced over at the second desk on the opposite side of the room. It was covered with unfiled paperwork.

"When *are* you going to get yourself an office assistant?" Ella asked, as she walked in.

Blalock looked up from his computer. "I've been interviewing people off and on, but I haven't found anyone yet," he said. "Everyone around here knows that my last office was blown up, so they're not so eager to come work for me at the rates I can pay."

"They might have a point," she said with a thin smile.

"So what official business brings you here?" He pointed to the coffeepot in the corner. "Want a cup?"

Ella looked at the glass pot. She could have sworn there was a ring of something greenish black growing inside it about halfway down. "Is that sanitary?"

"Oh, the rim of scum?" Blalock shrugged. "I left the pot half empty before I went on vacation last May. When I came back, I found a really weird-looking green fungus growing on the top. I scrubbed the pot out with steel wool and got everything that would come off. What you're seeing now is just what I couldn't scrape off." He poured himself a cup. "So, you want one?"

"I'll pass," she said.

"Okay," he said, and took a seat behind his desk. "Now what's up?"

She told him what she'd learned from Bruce Little—Teeny—about StarTalk and Abigail's and Barbara's visit to Virgil Pete. "I'd like to have Abigail tailed, and Barbara, too, but the problem is that Mrs. Yellowhair knows most of the officers in my team as well as those I could pull off their patrol routes. The same goes for her daughter."

"They've both met me as well, so I guess this means you want me to import some out-of-town talent?"

"I was thinking of Lucas Payestewa. He's Hopi, but he can blend in real easily around here."

Blalock nodded slowly at the mention of the agent who'd served with him several years ago. "Good choice. It'll probably take me twenty-four hours to go through channels—that is, providing I can get him at all."

"Okay. Let me know if and when he's ready to roll. And thanks."

Ella was in her car on the way to the station when her cell phone rang. She recognized Teeny's deep baritone voice. "I've got some information for you," he said. "Though Roxanne couldn't come up with any suspects, she did give me something you may be able to use. When Abby told Roxanne that her services were no longer needed, Roxanne didn't take the news well. Before she left, she trashed Abigail's computer with a virus that screws up the operating system. She thinks

Abby will probably take it in to the Smooth Operator in Wa-terflow. That's where she bought the system. You know the place?"

Ella smiled. "Yeah, that's where I bought my new com-puter, too. Thanks for the heads up."

Smooth Operator was run by John Natani, one of Clif-ford's best friends from high school. Ella knew John from the many times he and Clifford had hung out around the house. Though Clifford had chosen the traditionalist's path, and John was a modernist through and through, the two re-mained friends.

These days, John lived off the Rez. Taking advantage of his love for computers, he'd opened his own shop. John's company had a solid reputation and many area Navajos liked doing business with him.

Ella arrived at the Kirtland-area shop less than twenty minutes later. It was mid-afternoon, and John was at a bench behind the counter, working on a computer he'd disassem-bled. Looking up when the bell above the front door jingled, he smiled broadly. "Hey, Ella, what a surprise! What brings you here?" he asked, seeing her empty-handed. "You need help carrying something in from your car?"

"Actually, no, my computer is still running great. I'm here to ask you a favor," she said. "I need to look at Abigail Yellowhair's computer—off the record—if she brought it in already, that is."

"She did, but without a search warrant, I can't let you examine any of the files I've transferred to her new hard drive," he said. Then, with a smile and a twinkle in his eye, he added, "However, if someone were to go through my re-cycle bin outside and just happened to find her old dis-carded hard drive, marked with a big black X, I'd never see it happen. I deleted the files, of course, so I've met my moral and legal responsibilities to my customer. . . ."

Before Ella could say anything, he continued. "By the way, I have this great commercial program for sale today at a real bargain. If you ever accidentally delete a hard drive, this software will restore most of the lost data. The only exception to that is when the data's been overwritten," he said. Then, as an afterthought, he added, "You should run a virus-cleaning program first, just in case one is hiding somewhere on the drive."

"A restore program sounds like just what I'm looking for," Ella replied with a smile, and reached for her wallet.

After paying John, Ella went to the two waste bins at the back of the shop. Since the trash had been emptied recently, and only one contained electronic refuse, it didn't take her long to find what she was after. With the discarded hard drive and the restore software in hand, she hurried back to the station, calling Teeny on the way.

"If you can meet me at the station, I'd appreciate it. I could use your expertise in recovering data from a faulty hard drive. I need to make sure I don't screw anything up."

"I'll see you in a bit then. I'll bring some other software with me, too, in case we need something extra."

TWENTY-FIVE
——— ✖ ✖ ✖ ———

Ella arrived at the station be-
fore Teeny did, and was heading to her office when Big Ed
met her in the hall and took her aside.

"Shorty, we're still having a problem with leaks," he said,
speaking softly. "I've ruled out the people we spoke about,
and the members of your team, but the problem hasn't gone
away."

"What makes you so sure?" Ella asked.

"I had a private meeting with two tribal leaders in my
office recently and Mary Todacheene expressed some sym-
pathy for the Fierce Ones. She said that at least they acted,
while the rest of us just talked the problem to death and
worried about what the lawyers would do.

"The next day, she went out to her corral and someone
had left her a fine-looking horse," he continued. "She thought
it was someone's idea of a bribe and called me immediately.
But I think it was a thank you, not a bribe. I thought about
suggesting she look for that eye symbol the Fierce Ones leave
as a calling card, but decided not to push it."

Ella considered it for several moments. "Chief, I'm
meeting Bruce Little here in a few minutes. When he arrives,

let's hire him to sweep the station, starting with your office, then mine. His electronic equipment is newer and much more sophisticated than anything we have."

Big Ed considered it, then nodded. "Yeah, let's do it. We're out of options. I'll put this on the books as an emergency purchase so we won't have to go through the bid process."

As Big Ed returned to his office, Ella called Teeny, and explained what they'd be needing.

"Let me return to my office and pick up some additional equipment. Expect me in half an hour."

"Just in the odd chance that there *is* a bug here someplace, sweep Big Ed's office first, then mine. Once that's done, we can discuss the hard drive and its contents."

"Got it."

Ella checked in with her team. Tache and Neskahi had been given the sketch of the dead man and were already out questioning local service stations and auto repair businesses. Returning to her desk, Ella worked on reports that had been stacking up. Before she knew it, Teeny was at her office door. "I'm going to Big Ed's office. Want to tag along?"

She nodded. "I don't know what I'm hoping—that you find a bug so we can put all these leaks behind us—or that you don't," she said softly as they hurried down the hall.

"It's better to find one, in my opinion," Teeny answered quietly. "Not knowing the source of the leak generates suspicion among officers who need to trust each other to survive."

"There's that," she admitted.

"If someone did put a bug in one of the offices since they were last swept, you'll have to figure out who had the capability and the opportunity within that block of time. Locating a bug is only the first step in plugging a leak. And brace yourself. It'll undoubtedly be someone everyone here has trusted."

"I hear you," Ella said.

When they arrived at Big Ed's office, the chief stood and, without saying a word, nodded to Teeny, signaling him to begin.

Armed with a handheld electronic device that looked like a cross between a metal detector and an charcoal lighter, Teeny walked around the office, moving the "wand" in a pattern, starting from the floor and moving up to the ceiling, one wall at a time. No one spoke as Teeny worked his way up the bookshelves, but the tension was thick in the air. The chief's fists were balled, and Ella caught herself holding her breath.

Finding nothing, Teeny moved out from the walls and began to sweep the chief's desk, again working from the floor up. When he got to the desk surface, Teeny stopped suddenly, pointing to the red light that was blinking on the device. He proceeded to move from object to object slowly, checking everything. Finally, he looked up at them and pointed to the PDA on the chief's desk.

Teeny picked it up, set it on the floor, then moved the "wand" over it. The light started blinking again. Setting the device back on the desk, Teeny took a screwdriver out of a small case in his shirt pocket, removed the battery cover, and pulled out the PDA's battery. Working in silence, he examined the compartment, then pointed to a circular device. Hidden earlier by the battery, the object was about the size and thickness of a nickel, with a tiny opening in its center. Reaching in with a tweezer-like tool, he plucked it loose from a drop of soft glue that had kept it in place. Teeny held it up to them, putting his finger to his lips, reminding them to remain silent.

"Heptane spray?" Teeny asked.

Ella hurried down to Justine's office and retrieved the small spray bottle. That would "set" any possible fingerprints, allowing them to handle the device without compromising potential evidence.

Once he'd coated it, Teeny let the heptane dry a few seconds. He then placed the device inside a small, thick-walled metal case and screwed on a thick lid. Finally he nodded. "We're okay now. We won't be overheard."

"Did it draw power from the battery?" Big Ed asked.

"No, it has its own power supply, and it's still transmitting, but the signal can't escape the shielded container. It's just an expensive paperweight now. What do you want me to do with it?"

"Leave it there for now. Tell us what it is, exactly, how it works, and then we'll have to figure out how it got in my PDA," Big Ed said.

Teeny set the case on the desk, then thought about it a moment. "This is a high tech, but not state of the art, microphone and transmitter. Around here, it probably has a range of less than five miles. Couple this with a receiver about the size of a hardback book and you can pick up any sound within its range, say this room, and automatically record it."

"Can we backtrack to the receiver?" Ella asked.

"Not really. It doesn't transmit a signal, it just listens and records. We'd have to be close enough to see it in order to pick up its power source. This was a slick op, Big Ed. Where did you get the PDA?"

"My wife Claire gave it to me for my birthday. She even had my name engraved on it. I don't carry it with me all the time though. It usually stays here on my desk."

"Where did *she* get it?" Teeny and Ella asked simultaneously. They looked at each other in surprise, and smiled.

"Great minds, and all that," Teeny muttered.

"I'm about to find out," Big Ed said. He picked up his cell phone and punched in the number. Ten seconds later, he spoke. "I need to ask you a question, hon. Where did you get the PDA you gave me for my birthday?"

There was a long pause, then Big Ed answered, "No, I

didn't break it. One of my detectives saw it and decided he'd like one for himself." He looked at them and shrugged at the white lie.

Ella chuckled softly.

After another pause, Big Ed said, "No, I don't want to give *mine* away. I like it a lot. Really. I keep it in my office instead of carrying it around because I'm worried I might lose it."

Teeny looked at Ella, started to smile, then saw the chief glaring at them. Teeny wiped the grin from his face, turned, and stared out the window.

Another two minutes passed with Big Ed doing all the listening. "Okay, that's what I needed to know. I'll explain later," he said finally. "No, it's okay, honey. Really."

After Big Ed hung up, he looked at Ella then Teeny. "It appears my wife bought it from StarTalk, via Barbara Benally."

"Ervin's wife?" Teeny asked.

"The one and only. Claire was shopping for a few things for my office and came across Barbara Benally, who was buying office supplies. Barbara was using a PDA like this one. After Claire saw it, she decided to buy one for me, so Barbara offered to get her one with her StarTalk discount. Claire told me she got a great deal and paid Barbara in advance right on the spot."

Ella studied the PDA in silence. "That would suggest that Barbara is responsible for the bug. The StarTalk offices are well within the five mile range, too. She could have been listening in from her desk."

"Yes, but it still doesn't rule out Abigail as an accomplice," Big Ed said. "Or it's also possible Barbara was manipulated by her mother and never knew about the bug at all," Big Ed suggested.

"Do you suppose all the PDAs StarTalk purchased are bugged? It could be some kind of industrial espionage," Teeny suggested.

"If it's industrial espionage, why are they passing information along to the Fierce Ones? That doesn't sound very likely," Ella countered. "I'm still leaning toward Abigail. Maybe she was afraid of how Barbara and Ervin would handle a big project like StarTalk so she had the bugs put in to keep tabs on them. When one ended up on your desk, she decided to take advantage of the situation," Ella said, then stopped and shook her head. "No, nix that thought. We're dealing with a serious leak, and my instinct tells me that this bugging wasn't accidental. It's got to be part of the overall plan to screw up Ervin."

Big Ed looked at Ella and nodded slowly. "I agree. Even my wife was manipulated."

"What we're still missing is a clear motive. If we had that I think everything else would fall into place," Ella said.

"It could be greed, distrust, jealousy, revenge, or a wife or mother-in-law thing," Big Ed said, then shrugged.

"It narrows down to the two women closest to Ervin," Ella said.

"So what's next?" Big Ed asked at last.

Ella told him about having gone Dumpster diving at Smooth Operator and the software she'd purchased.

"I've got another program that's brand new, and if what you purchased won't do it, mine certainly will," Teeny said.

"Get cracking then," Big Ed said. "Or hacking. Maybe one of Abigail's files will shed some light on all this—or rule her out."

Once their meeting ended, Teeny walked with Ella to her office. Taking the hard drive she'd salvaged, he connected it via cables to ports on his own laptop computer. Teeny was deep in concentration when Ella saw Ralph Tache come to her door.

"Do you need me, Ralph?" Seeing him nod, she stepped

out into the hall with him, not wanting to disturb Teeny. "What's up?"

"We have no hits on that dead guy yet, but we're working on it. Also the late senator's grave hasn't been disturbed," he said.

"Have you spoken to Jesse?" Ella pressed.

He nodded. "The Fierce Ones were just told by their informant that a small group of skinwalkers is behind the recent attacks on Ervin and his family."

"That did *not* come from this P.D.," Ella said flatly. Although she'd suspected that already, she hadn't discussed it with anyone in Big Ed's office, and all the vital conversations she'd had with Big Ed had been away from his desk.

"There's more. The Fierce Ones are planning to hunt down the Navajo witches. They think that the skinwalkers are behind the problems they've been having. They're armed and already on the move."

"How are they going to find the skinwalkers?"

"I don't know. It's not like a search grid would work."

"Go back to Jesse and get us more on that. We need to know exactly what they have in mind."

Tache nodded once and strode down the hall.

Going back into her office, Ella watched Teeny for a minute. He was totally focused. She wouldn't disturb him. Sitting back in her chair, she tried to sort out her own thoughts.

If she was right, and Ervin was being targeted by one of the two most prominent women in his life, he was in even more danger than any of them realized. The yellow jacket from the pickup, and the bolo tie Ervin had found outside his home could have been given to the skinwalkers by either of them. But the question still remained—which one had contacted the people that had been hired to do the dirty work, and would they be able to find that link? If no e-mails showed up in the recovered files, Ella had no idea how or where to look next.

"I've got a bunch of files restored," Teeny said. "There's some tax information, like a list of donated clothing and other miscellaneous items that had belonged to her late husband. There's also a schedule of launch dates for the different phases of StarTalk's plan. But there's one file I found particularly interesting. It looks to be a speech Barbara was writing."

"On Abigail's computer?" Ella asked.

"That's the way it appears. Come take a look."

Ella leaned over Teeny's massive shoulder. "That's the kind of speech Barbara would have to deliver if she took over for Ervin at StarTalk. I wonder if Abigail was writing it for her. . . ."

"Maybe Barbara was running what she had past her mother. We don't know if this was downloaded from elsewhere," Teeny said, turning away from the keyboard.

Ella stared at it thoughtfully. "Up to now, I've suspected Abigail Yellowhair, but maybe Barbara's been pulling our strings all along."

"It could be either . . . or both," Teeny said.

Ella tried to wrap her mind around it. "Barbara might have resented the way Ervin was running things. He got all the credit and recognition while she stayed behind doing all the paperwork and planning."

"She would have had access to everything she needed to set up her husband," Teeny answered. "And his PDA could have been bugged as well. So who's responsible—mother or daughter?" Teeny asked.

"Your guess is as good as mine," Ella said with a long sigh. "Check that file you found on the donated items, the ones that used to belong to James Yellowhair," Ella said, a new thought forming in her mind.

"Okay. What should I look for?" Teeny turned back to

the keyboard. Several keystrokes later, she saw the listing of clothing and other personal items donated to a secondhand store in Farmington, off the Rez.

"There—two yellow blazers," she said, her voice rising slightly. "And scroll down. Three turquoise and silver bolo ties valued at seventy-five dollars each," Ella said, pointing.

"Those have special meaning to you?"

She told him about the yellow blazer found in the dead man's pickup, and the bolo tie that Ervin had seen outside his home.

"So Abigail—or Barbara—could have bought those items back and used them as payment to the skinwalkers."

"I know exactly how to use this information. Thanks, Teeny." Ella walked out her door, dialing Blalock's office as she went. "I really need your help. Will you be in your office, say, in twenty minutes?"

"Yeah, come on over. Lucas is here too. Turns out he was on vacation, but decided to come back and work with us on his own time."

"Fabulous news! I'll be there shortly."

Ella sat across from Blalock and the Hopi agent, Lucas Payestewa, who'd been assigned to the reservation years ago. Lucas' hair was cut regulation short now and he seemed to have been working out. He was more muscular than Ella remembered, and had lost the baby face.

Ella filled them in, gave Lucas her phone numbers, then continued explaining her strategy. "I'd like Lucas to start by tailing Barbara Benally. She won't know you, right?"

"I never dealt with her when I was assigned to this office," the young Hopi agent replied. "And from what Agent Blalock's told me about her, I doubt she's ever given me a second look."

"Stay with her first, then switch to Abigail," Ella said.

One of the things that made Lucas an asset is that he blended in no matter where he went in the southwest. Outside the Navajo Rez he could have passed for Chicano. Here, wearing western clothes common to The People, he wouldn't even rate a passing glance.

"I checked on the way over and Barbara's working late at the StarTalk offices tonight," Ella continued. "You might be able to pick her up there once she leaves. You have that address, her home address, and the Benally residence, right?" Ella asked.

Lucas nodded.

"Good. Once you've got her in your sights, stick with her, and don't make the mistake of underestimating her."

"Ella, you said that the Fierce Ones were planning to make a move on the supposed skinwalkers," Blalock said. "What are you going to do about that and where do I fit in?"

"Tache will be meeting with his brother-in-law so we'll know more later," she said standing up. "Just be ready to roll."

"Where are you off to now?" Blalock asked.

"I'm going to go rattle a few cages," she said with a grin. "If anything comes up I'll be available."

Ella was soon driving down the highway to Ervin's. Maybe the news that they were getting closer to finding answers would help boost his courage. More importantly, it might also make Barbara nervous enough to make a mistake. Or maybe she'd pass the news on to her mother and spur Abigail into action.

Before she'd even finished the thought, Ella received a call from Dispatch. "There's an altercation in progress," the radio operator said, giving her Ervin's address. "A woman made the call, but didn't leave her name."

"I'll handle it," Ella said instantly. Switching on her sirens, she raced toward the Benally home.

TWENTY-SIX

—— ✖ ✖ ✖ ——

As Ella approached the Benally home from the south, she could see an old sedan she didn't recognize parked outside near the lights. Just as Ella pulled up beside it, a young Navajo woman in her late twenties threw open the front door and ran toward her. The woman was unarmed and frightened.

"I'm Dolores Pioche, the new housekeeper," she said, coming up to Ella's open driver's side window. "Mr. Benally saw some men trying to vandalize his new truck. When he yelled, they jumped into an old black pickup and took off. Mr. Benally raced off after them with his rifle. I couldn't stop him, he was acting crazy."

"How long ago?" Ella asked.

"Five minutes, maybe a little more."

"No vehicles passed me on my way here. Which direction did they go?"

Dolores pointed and Ella took off, racing north. The full moon was out and she could see quite well despite the late hour. A few minutes later Ella approached an unpaved road to her right. Dust illuminated by her headlights and deep furrows in the dirt told her that somebody had made a sharp, high speed turn here. The road went north for a hundred yards, then crossed a wide arroyo.

Ella followed the side road and had just driven down into the wash when she heard the rapid cracks of gunfire echoing down the steep walls of the water-carved arroyo. Coming to a stop, she saw vehicle tracks leading to her right, off the road and down the channel. A firefight was underway up ahead, and from the sounds and the number of shots several weapons were in play. Ella turned off her headlights and followed the tracks, moving slow enough to keep from smashing her mouth against the radio as she called for backup.

Seconds later, she spotted two vehicles ahead in a low spot where a second channel had eroded the arroyo floor even deeper. Stopping at an angle so the engine compartment gave her some cover, Ella slipped out of her vehicle, crouching low, and peering over the hood. Ervin's pickup was smashed against the side of the arroyo, upside down. He'd gone over the edge, apparently in a skid. The cab looked crushed and there was a mangled body dangling halfway out the shattered windshield. At this distance it looked like Ervin, and if it was, there wasn't much hope he'd still be alive.

The second vehicle, a black pickup, was motionless in the lower part of the arroyo not twenty feet away from the wreck. Just as Ella reached for her handheld radio, more gunfire erupted. Pulling out her handgun and moving over by the front bumper, she spotted a figure coming around the rear of the black pickup. He turned and fired his rifle at someone on the upper rim of the arroyo.

From her angle, and the fact that he was against the night sky, Ella couldn't see the person on the high ground. Looking back toward the black truck, she noticed a figure facedown on the ground about ten feet from Ervin's pickup. The dark spots on his light-colored shirt were probably blood. From the amount spilled he was either dead already or dying.

Ella took careful aim at the man with the rifle. "Police!" she yelled. "Drop your weapon!"

Three more shots rang out from somewhere above. The man beside the pickup door turned to look at her, then collapsed as a dark spot appeared on his upper chest.

Ella gripped her pistol, wishing she carried an automatic rifle in the car instead of the short range shotgun. There were at least three shooters up on the rim of the arroyo network firing down at the black truck. At the moment, they were in control of the situation.

Out of the corner of her eye, Ella caught the shine of chrome from another vehicle to her right in the side channel. Perhaps it belonged to the shooters who'd taken out the guy or guys in the black truck.

The shooters on the bluff had stopped firing, so Ella grabbed her department shotgun and ran toward the third vehicle, which turned out to be a white SUV. When she got close, Ella crouched down, waiting and listening.

Soon she heard running footsteps and harsh whispers. Two Navajo men came into view, both carrying rifles. One took a quick look around, tossed his rifle onto the backseat through the open window, then jumped inside the front passenger's side. The light came on. The second man, carrying his rifle with his left hand, reached for the driver's side door handle.

Ella knew she had to make her move. She jumped out from behind cover, aiming her shotgun at the two men. "Police officer! Stay where you are!"

The one by the driver's side, Delbert John, cursed in Navajo, then turned his head and yelled. "Run!"

Ella glanced to her left, and saw a third man farther up the arroyo. He disappeared almost instantly around a curve in the channel.

Ella turned her attention back to the men at the truck. The guy inside the cab—whom she recognized as Arthur Brownhat—was trapped. Delbert hadn't moved a muscle since his shout, which was the main reason he was still breathing.

"Smart man," she said, stepping closer. "Lay the rifle on the ground . . . slowly and by the barrel. And you, Arthur Brownhat, place both hands on the dashboard. Now!"

Two minutes later, both men were handcuffed to the SUV, and Ella, having unloaded the rifles and jammed them barrel first into the sand out of reach of the two, was running back to the black pickup, shotgun ready.

Even as she jumped down six feet into the lower level of the main arroyo, she didn't have much hope of finding anyone still alive. She first went to where Ervin lay, half in and half out of the windshield. His neck had been torn apart by the accident, almost decapitating him. She didn't have to check to know he was dead. The man not far from Ervin's truck was also dead. She was surprised to see that it was Darrell Waybenais, Virgil's neighbor. A hunting rifle with a scope lay in the sand beside him.

Ella checked the other figure beside the bed of the old black pickup and stared at the man's face in stunned silence. It was the twin brother of the man killed in the attack on Clifford's hogan. Only this man, though he'd been gut shot, was still alive.

Ella took his rifle by the sling and set it aside, then crouched beside him as she called an ambulance. "What happened here?" she asked, pulling out her handkerchief and pressing it against the wound just above his navel, hoping to slow down the flow of blood.

"She betrayed us," he gasped, anger fueling his words and giving him more energy than he should have had under the circumstances.

"Who?" Ella whispered harshly.

"Woman—never met her—hired us to scare Benally. Then to give cops a hard time," he said, taking a shaky breath.

"How did she hire you if you never met?" Ella asked him.

"She left notes in my truck and half the cash," he said slowly, pain making his speech difficult. "My truck's always parked across street from Pale Horse—garage in Farmington. I work there."

"How did you get the second half of the money?"

"Her notes told me which pay phones to go to. I'd wait, she'd call. She'd always hide it in a spot nearby. Woman hated Benally—called him a 'show horse.' Pretty but slow. Her words."

Ella recognized the expression. The only woman she'd ever heard using it was Barbara Benally. But then again Abigail Yellowhair could have deliberately used the term to mislead the skinwalkers. "From the voice, do you think the woman was younger or older than me?"

"Younger. Voice . . . high pitched, like junior high," he said, then taking a long, shuddering breath, fell silent. For a moment she thought he'd died, but then he took another breath.

"She wanted to drug Benally. We left her some *azuncena de Mejico* . . . to add to his whiskey. Stuff makes you crazy—if it doesn't kill you. If he died, we'd get his body. But she set us up. Got ambushed."

"Did you tamper with Ervin's truck?" Ella prodded.

"Yeah. Sucked out the brake fluid. Didn't know other guy was going to drive. Not my fault. I'm dying. Get *her*," he said, his breathing becoming even more ragged.

"Hold on. Don't give up on me," Ella said.

He coughed, then, with effort, continued. "Took pictures. Guessed which pay phone she'd pick next. Not that many in town anymore. Saw her hide the money and used cell phone camera." His breathing suddenly became shallow and his eyes closed.

"Where's the cell phone now?" Ella prodded, but he'd lost consciousness.

As the ambulance and the emergency medical team arrived, Ella moved away, giving them room to work. Meanwhile, she searched the skinwalker's black pickup. In the glove compartment she found a cell phone with five clear, sequential photos of Barbara Benally placing a paper bag into a wastebasket just outside the Quick Stop. The paper bag in the glove compartment below the camera looked identical in size to the one in the photos. If they got lucky, Barbara's fingerprints would be on it.

One problem remained. She still was short on evidence a jury would accept—just the uncorroborated word of a skinwalker and maybe traces of that herb or poison in Ervin's whiskey. Hopefully Barbara hadn't disposed of the tainted bottles yet. If the skinwalker died, she could probably use his dying declaration in court and it wouldn't be considered hearsay, but if he lived, she'd then have photos *and* his testimony.

By the time Ella returned to where she'd left the suspects handcuffed, backup had arrived, including Tache and Justine. As they began flagging evidence and working the scene, Ella questioned the suspects, who were being guarded by Sergeant Neskahi.

Ella read them their rights, then added, "Boys, you're in a lot of trouble. Your best chance is to cooperate. Being a member of the Fierce Ones isn't going to help you now."

"We were just keeping the skinwalkers from doing something profane with that Navajo's body," Arthur Brownhat said.

Ella looked at the man who'd been responsible for beating Marilyn Charley and her boyfriend nearly to death. She had no intention of letting him walk.

"The skinwalkers have been running everyone around in circles. They even made calls to our people, giving orders, and pretending to be us," Brownhat added quickly.

"Who are the men back there? Did you recognize them?" Ella asked him.

"All we know is that they're skinwalkers," he answered flatly.

Ella looked at the other suspect, Delbert John. "How did you know they'd be here?"

"We got a call from our informant," he said. "She told us that the skinwalkers would be here setting a trap for . . . the man who died first," he said, refusing to name the dead. "She's always come through for us, and I knew we could trust her information."

There was something about his tone of voice that tipped her off. "*You* know who she is, don't you?"

He looked away and said nothing.

"Give yourself a break. I already have an idea of who we're dealing with. She's a big businesswoman now, on her way to becoming a millionaire. Do you honestly think she'd protect *you* if the chips were down?"

Delbert exhaled softly and finally answered. "I can't prove it, but I'm pretty sure it was Barbara Benally. She's always known I was in the Fierce Ones. She tried to disguise her voice, but she and I have been friends since high school."

"You told her?" Ella asked.

"She visits me sometimes, and I think she probably overheard me on the phone once or twice."

"Any chance she might have learned the codes you use to notify your people?" Ella pressed.

He hesitated, then nodded. "It's possible."

Satisfied, Ella turned the suspects over to the patrolman. Barbara was going down. "Book them."

TWENTY-SEVEN
——— ✗ ✗ ✗ ———

Twenty minutes later, they were on route to make the arrest. Ella had called a judge, and search warrants were being prepared.

"Barbara left work and drove home to wait for word on her husband, according to Agent Payestewa," Justine said. "Abigail is there as well."

"Hopefully, they won't be aware of what went down yet. That's the only way this'll work. We need to catch Barbara cold, before she has a chance to destroy any evidence," Ella said.

"Once she finds out Ervin's dead, she'll get rid of everything that'll link her to the crimes," Justine agreed. "So how do you want to handle this?"

"We'll be over at her house soon, but until we actually have the warrant in hand all we'll do is deliver the news that Ervin was killed in a vehicle accident. Nothing more—nothing less. She doesn't need to know that until the body's extracted from the wreck and the M.E. has a look, we won't know if he took bullet hits from the rounds that penetrated his vehicle, died in the crash, or was poisoned. Once Officer

Talk arrives to serve the warrants, we'll arrest Barbara and search everywhere for that receiver. Just make sure she doesn't have a chance to use her PDA."

"Do you think it'll have some of the numbers needed to contact the Fierce Ones?"

Ella nodded, then waved to Lucas Payestewa, who was parked, watching the Benally home from down the street. Barbara's vehicle and Abigail's sedan were side by side in the driveway, and, as they came to a stop, Barbara came out the front door, accompanied by Abigail.

Ella walked over, meeting the anxious-looking Barbara halfway up the sidewalk.

"Ervin, is he okay?" Barbara asked quickly. "My new housekeeper called and said he'd gone after some men who were messing with his truck. I came home as soon as I heard."

"I'm sorry, Mrs. Benally. His pickup crashed into an arroyo," Ella said.

Barbara's expression of shock looked almost genuine. Her mouth fell open, and her body sagged. "Then he's dead? No, it can't be. Not Ervin."

Abigail rushed up and put her hand around Barbara's waist, holding her tightly. "It's all right, daughter. I'm here. Come back into your home and sit down."

Justine slipped around them, reaching the front door first to keep watch as they went inside. Ella followed close behind Barbara and her mother as they made their way slowly into the living room. Abigail's expression was grim, but she'd shed no tears. Barbara sat still on the couch, cupping her hands over her nose and mouth, a gesture that reminded Ella of a shy young Navajo child attempting to hide her emotions. Overall, it was a good performance, but not good enough.

Abigail sat down beside Barbara and glanced across to

the doorway to the kitchen. The young housekeeper was standing there, her eyes wide with horror.

"Mrs. Benally just lost her husband, woman. Bring her something to drink. Anything will do," Abigail snapped.

Then Abigail faced Ella, who, along with Justine, had remained standing. "If you'd have caught the people harassing him, this wouldn't have happened."

Out of the corner of her eye, Ella noticed a squad car pulling up outside. It was Marianna with the search warrants. "You might want to hold off on the blame game a few more minutes, Mrs. Yellowhair. We're here to make an arrest." She nodded to Justine who was already bringing out her handcuffs.

"Barbara Benally, you're under arrest for conspiracy in the murder-for-hire death of your husband," Justine said, stepping forward.

"What?" Barbara and Abigail yelled almost simultaneously. Barbara jumped up from the couch, and Justine grabbed her by the arm just in case she was planning on making a run for the open door.

"Turn around, and place your hands behind your back, please," Justine said, her tone making it clear it wasn't a suggestion.

"Read Mrs. Benally her rights, Officer Goodluck. And, Mrs. Yellowhair, please remain seated until we have the opportunity to ask you a few questions."

Marianna Talk came in holding a folder in her hand. "Here they are, Investigator Clah."

"Good. We now have search warrants. And you know exactly what we're looking for, don't you Barbara?" Ella added, "We're particularly interested in *azuncena de Mejico*."

"That's a variety of belladonna found along the Mexican border. Why would you think there's any here?" Abigail asked, looking at Ella for an explanation. "What *is* going on?"

"I want my lawyer," Barbara said in a cold, emotionless voice. "I know my rights."

As she was led out, Barbara's gaze met Ella's and for one brief moment, Ella saw unbridled hatred reflected there.

When Ella glanced back at Abigail, the older woman's face held no emotion. A sudden chill touched Ella's spine, but she pushed the feeling aside. She had work to do.

The next afternoon Ella poked her head into Big Ed's office. He looked up, then waved her toward a chair. "So what's the update?" he asked as soon as she was seated.

"The surviving skinwalker's name is Sonnie Yazzie, and he's in the hospital," Ella said. "Looks like he's going to make it. His testimony and the photos he took of Barbara making a payoff should seal the case against her, even if the tests for belladonna don't come back positive. Of course, finding the receiver for the listening device under the seat of her car with her fingerprints all over it didn't hurt. Neither did all those incriminating numbers and Navajo code words on her PDA. Brownhat and Delbert John, too, have also offered to implicate Barbara in exchange for reduced charges. Barbara has just spent the first of many nights in jail."

"You know that Abigail's going to fight us tooth and nail on this," Big Ed said. "The lawyer she's hired will do everything in her power to discredit the witnesses and the physical evidence. So watch yourself, Shorty. Abigail's got powerful friends."

"And total control of StarTalk now, too."

"Have you found anything linking Abigail to what was going on?" Big Ed asked.

"No, and Barbara's keeping quiet. If her mom was a partner in all this, she's not saying."

"All right. You've worked hard, so take the rest of the day off. You've earned it."

Ella arrived at her home a short time later and saw Abigail's rental sedan parked out front. Her stomach in knots, Ella hurried inside. She wasn't sure what she'd expected, but seeing Abigail chatting amicably with Rose in the kitchen had been the furthest from her mind.

Seeing Ella, Abigail stood and looked back at Rose, a satisfied expression on her face. "The grant allowing you to continue your plant work was extended. I made sure of that. Don't give it another thought. Our children will thank us someday for the preservation work."

Abigail then turned to look back at Ella. "Our own future is never as important to us as that of our children. Don't you agree?"

There was no hiding the malice in Abigail's confrontational stare, even when her bruised lips widened into a shaky grin. Abigail then turned her head and smiled innocently at Rose. "I guess you and I will be seeing a lot more of each other."

Abigail waved good-bye and walked toward the door past Ella, nodding slightly as she went by. Though she'd only given Ella a passing glance, Ella had felt her rage as clearly as if it had been a living, palpable presence.

Standing at the window, Ella watched Abigail climb into her car and drive away. Once she was gone, Ella stepped over to the table and studied the little plant in front of Rose. "Gift?"

"Yes, and I have to admit I'm very relieved to know she didn't blame you for having to arrest her daughter. I think she may have suspected what was going on for some time." Rose looked at Ella and shook her head sadly. "Arranging for the death of your mate is such a . . . black widow thing to do."

"Spiders like spinning elaborate webs, Mom. Ask a bug." Turning her attention to the plant, she added, "What kind of plant is this?"

It's *tsinyaachéch'il*, what we call oak under a tree. Depending on how it's used it can either heal or make you extremely sick."

Abigail's message was suddenly crystal clear. Her association with Rose had been a way of reminding Ella that everyone had weaknesses and Ella's were right in this house.

"I need to drive over to my friend's home to take care of her plants," Rose said, standing up. "They've suffered while she's been away. Boots is helpless with native plants."

By the time Ella realized that Rose hadn't referred to Lena as her "former friend" her mother had left the kitchen. Ella was still sipping coffee, wondering what she'd missed, when Herman came in.

"Have you seen my glasses?" he asked.

"No, but I'll help you look. In the meantime, why don't you tell me what's happened between Mom and her friend?" she asked. "It sounded to me like things were back to normal between them."

"No, not back to normal, but better. I wish I knew the details, but I don't. She spoke to her friend alone, and she never mentioned anything about her visit when I drove her back," he said, searching through the pens and papers beside the phone for his glasses. "All she told me is that we'd be taking care of her friend's plants every afternoon until she came back and could do it herself."

Ella found Herman's glasses behind the coffeepot and handed them to him. "Here you go."

"Thanks," he said, then hurried out of the kitchen.

Ella walked back into the living room and saw the new piñon lamp resting on the end table. Herman had done a magnificent job. The twisted grains and knots of the wood had been stained and finished to perfection, and the simple white shade with a turquoise trim added a slash of color.

Maybe, she thought, Herman could make a cane or walking stick for Carolyn. He was a real craftsman when it came to woodworking. If he agreed, the whole family could go looking for suitable materials this weekend and make it a picnic as well.

Ella looked out the window and waved at her daughter, who was outside teaching her pony a new trick. To the young, hope was never ending, Ella realized. To adults, it came harder. Her own life was about the hope that harmony could always be restored, despite the long odds against it sometimes. For others, like Abigail Yellowhair, hope of revenge was all they had, and was what kept them going.

Hope, in all its forms, was permanently woven into the fabric of life on the Rez. It gave the *Diné* courage and was at the heart of all who walked in beauty.

Ella went out to join her daughter, and gave her a hug. "It's a fine day. Let's go for a ride."